A SONG OF SORROW

ISLES OF BRIGHT AND SHADOW
BOOK ONE

I0593278

C. E. PAGE

First Published in 2023 in Australia by Enchanted Castle Press

ISBN: 978-0-6 452 845-0-8

 A catalogue record for this work is available from the National Library of Australia

Cover by: Joolz & Jarling – Julie Nicholls & Uwe Jarling
Map by: Fictive Designs
Formatting by: Enchanted Castle Press
Edited by: Creating Ink – Anna Bishop

Author website: www.cepageauthor.com

A SONG OF SORROW

ISLES OF BRIGHT AND SHADOW
BOOK ONE

C. E. PAGE

ENCHANTED CASTLE
— PRESS —

SPOILER WARNING

The events of this book take place approximately five years after the events of the *Sovereigns of Bright and Shadow* trilogy. Whilst it is not necessary to read that trilogy before this book it is advisable to do so if you wish to avoid spoilers.

CONTENT WARNING

Please be aware that this novel is intended for a mature audience; as such, there may be some situations or scenes that readers may find confronting. It contains sexual violence (off-page but heavily implied), mild violence, and coarse language.

Reader discretion is advised.

FARIDEAN ISLES

ARMADA

DUMURA

(THE ISLE OF SPLENDOUR)

WATCH
TOWER

REEF

WEEPER'S COVE

RUINED
FORT

SPIRE

SPLADE'S WATCH

For the dreamers and the misfits.
Don't ever stop embracing the parts of you that others deem too
loud, too weird, and too different.

CHAPTER ONE

DEANA

Shadows pooled in dark swathes beneath the trees, the last vestiges of night clinging to the world as the promise of dawn began to paint the landscape in muted tones of blueish grey. A golden line appeared across the horizon, throwing splashes of apricot and lilac against the fluffy clouds that dotted the sky, and Deana picked up her pace as she pushed through the tangled brush. This was an annual ritual, one she would normally undertake with her older brother, Kai. He'd hurry her along, giving her a frustrated smile when her clothes became tangled in the grasping vines that covered the tallest trees. Those vines strangled even the mightiest host, stealing its life until nothing was left except an intricate woven tower. It was a parasitic relationship birthed by the random placement of an errant seed. Deana often felt like one of those creeper-shrouded trees; the way people would stare at her with pity when they heard the undulating notes of her song. Even if she could pretend to be normal, her song would reveal the truth. She was the tree, her song the vines—telling all who could hear magic that her soul belonged to Grandmother Ocean.

She rested her hand against one of the smooth, grey trunks. The song of the forest reverberated through the wood, taking her deep beneath the rich loam. Above her, a large, purple parrot let out a shrieking call before taking wing. Not much farther. She increased her pace, thin branches and vines whipping at her as she broke into a run.

Her lungs burned as she burst from the trees and stumbled to her knees beside the pool. She lifted her head, expecting to see Kai sitting on the flat boulder by the water's edge, ready to chide her for being too slow.

Sorrow settled heavily in her stomach, and she swallowed a hollow breath before taking a seat on the stone and leaning over the pristine water to study the dull silver fish resting there in the shallows. Their fins shifted gently, keeping them in place as the scales that were starting to slough away glittered against the sand. Soon the scales would cover the bottom of the pool in a sparkling carpet as the fish revealed the technicolour coats they would wear for the duration of their mating season.

As the sun got higher, bathing the pool in warm light, the fish went into a frenzy. Colours flashed through the cloud of discarded scales—blue, green, red, and on to every colour of the spectrum—before it finished as abruptly as it had begun, with the bulk of the fish darting towards the rush of water that would lead them back to the ocean.

Deana drew her knees to her chest and rested her chin on them. "There were more red fish again this year," she whispered. "Blood on the water."

If Kai were here, he'd tell her she was being dramatic, like he had two years before. She'd begged him to listen, but he'd just ruffled her hair and gone off with that wide grin of his. Savita said that Grandmother Ocean had taken Kai because he was too beautiful, but Deana knew better.

Kai had sacrificed himself to buy her more time.

She toyed with the braided leather that hung around her neck, retrieving the stone attached to it from under her shirt and thumbing the hole at its centre before pressing it to her lips. "You should have just let her have me."

When his death was still fresh, she had come to this pool and pelted the stone into its centre. But throwing it away wouldn't end her curse, and it wouldn't bring Kai back. It had made her feel better in the moment though, at least until the guilt had clawed its way onto her shoulder, and she'd spent the afternoon searching the bottom of the pool with her magic to retrieve the stone.

"You were all I had left." Tears stung as they caught in the corner of her eyes, but they wouldn't fall. They never fell—not since those early days when his death had still been raw. She sniffed and tucked her loose curls behind her ears. Enough dwelling on what couldn't be changed.

"I've been to Beldaren since we last spoke." Her attempt at a lighter tone was marred by the thickness of her voice. "It is such a strange place. The magic there is delicate, like it has been shattered and put back together. And the songs ..." She drew a slow breath. "... so many songs that are unlike anything I had heard before. I went with Indi. Chief Soma sent her and Amara to meet the young prince. Henry. His song is strange—it's like Nazali's or Samir's, but it also stirs with the deep wisdom of a seer ... And his mother's song is stranger still; it shifts and bends and is almost as deep and cold as the fathoms. It was woven together with the song of her heart mate so intricately that I almost couldn't tell where one finished and the other started. Like the old stories of souls colliding and forming an unbreakable bond. And then there was this man ..." Her fingers tightened on the stone. "He had hair whiter than the purest sand and his song was cold and deep— almost as deep as Henry's mother's, but at times hollow, like an echo bouncing back from a great distance. It called to my song the way Grandmother Ocean—" A parrot squawked sending a jolt through her.

The sun was higher than she was expecting it to be. "Oh, no. Sorry, Kai, I have to go," she called over her shoulder as she pushed to her feet and ran into the forest.

Leilani would have her head for sure this time. Vines and branches left their stinging marks on her skin once more as she raced through the trees. Bark scraped her palms as she stumbled and righted herself against one of the towering trunks before charging off again.

She broke from the forest into her mother's overgrown garden, her legs quivering and her breathing hard. But she couldn't slow—not yet. She darted between the beds, only stopping when she reached the back door of her house. There she allowed herself a moment to gather her calm before placing her palm against the doorframe and sending her song out to brush against the songs of her ancestors in greeting. They flooded over her in a brief cacophony of sound and magic that soothed the edges of her soul before pulling away like a wave dragging flotsam along the shore. Releasing a breath, she grabbed the orange sash that marked her as a member of Chief Soma's staff and tied it over her saffron-coloured uniform. One last pause to place her hand against the doorframe once more and bid her family goodbye for the day, and then she charged out into the village, dodging around people in her mad rush to reach Chief Soma's palace.

"There you are, Deana," Savita said as Deana slid into place beside her. The other woman reached out and plucked a leaf from Deana's curls before smoothing her own glossy, black hair with a frown. "Is that new?" Savita's obsidian gaze dropped to the stone hanging around Deana's neck. As her fingers inched towards it, Deana tucked it away beneath her shirt.

"No, it's just a silly old thing Kai gave me." She swallowed over her brother's name, and Savita's brow furrowed.

Deana smoothed her skirts and adjusted her bangles, ready to change the subject. "Did Leilani notice?"

"Did I notice you were late again?" The woman's voice was thick with ire, and Deana turned what she hoped was an apologetic glance towards her. "See to your tasks," Leilani said as she waved the others away. Settling her deep brown gaze on Deana, Leilani's mouth twisted as though she wasn't sure exactly what to do with the young woman before her. "Deana—"

"I'm sorry, Leilani. I know I promised it wouldn't happen again, but—"

"What was it this time? A beached dolphin? A dog tangled in the fishermen's nets? Collecting feathers along the east beach?"

Deana licked her lip and looked at her feet. "It was the brightfish moult."

Leilani let out a slow breath as a ripple of pity went through her song. "We all miss Kai"—her voice thickened on his name—"but you are too old to be shirking your duties to run off and watch a bunch of fish."

"I know, but—"

"I don't want the excuses, Deana!" Leilani let out a frustrated noise. "I promised Kai I would watch out for you, but this is your last chance. If you fail me today then you will have to find work elsewhere, and we both know there aren't many people in this village who will work with you, given the nature of your song and your connection to Grandmother Ocean."

Deana pressed her lips together.

"I know it's hard. Believe me, I do. But there are plenty of others who don't understand, which is why you need to keep your head down. Now, off you go. Savita is waiting for you in the guest quarters. The delegation from Beldaren is arriving today."

"What about Indira?"

"She is spending the morning with the queen. You will resume your normal duties once the guest quarters are prepared."

Deana nodded and turned to leave.

"Dee ... I—"

"I won't be late again. I promise." She said before hurrying towards the guest quarters. She didn't need to turn back to see the pity in Leilani's eyes; she could hear it in her song.

Normally, Deana and Savita took care of Princess Indira, who was a gorgeous girl of six years. Her hair was a black-brown mass of tight coils and her eyes a warm golden colour that matched the brightness of her song. Grandmother Ocean wouldn't dare touch a girl like Indira because she belonged to the sun.

"You are really off with the sand sprites today," Savita chided her.

"Sorry."

"What did Leilani say?"

Deana pushed open the shutters and let the late morning breeze into the room. "The usual. Stop letting childish whims rule my life and try harder to fit in." She added insect-repellent oil to the night lamp.

"She does care, you know? And Grandmother Ocean didn't just take your brother, she took Leilani's heart mate. That's why she's so lenient with you. If it were any of the rest of us, we would have been tossed out on our backsides long ago," Savita said as she collected the pile of dust she had swept up and tossed it out the window. "Did Leilani happen to tell you who we are preparing the room for?" she asked as she studied Deana through her long, thick lashes.

"No, but I am sure you are going to."

"Apparently it is a couple of Beldaren mages who have come to meet with the Guild of Singers. I wonder if they will look like King

Leith. He was very handsome."

"He's nearly twice your age."

"That doesn't mean I can't admire him. That warden commander wasn't too bad either. I can't remember his name—the one with the long, dark hair and amber eyes."

"Emil," Deana said automatically. She had paid attention to the ones that the Beldarens called wardens. Their songs were like those of the silencers, thick and thrumming as though they could quickly drown out every other sound.

"Deana!" Indira came running into the room and threw herself onto the bed.

"I just made that," Savita complained.

The princess blinked up at her with a wide smile. Her hair was a dark, tangled halo around her face, her golden eyes sparkling. "I'm just so excited!" A folded piece of parchment was crushed in her hand. "Prince Henry wrote to me. He promised he would and look." She brandished the letter. "Read it for me, please." She presented it to Deana, snatching it back when Savita made a grab for it. "No, I want Dee to do it."

"Of course you do. Go on then, Deana. I want to hear what the little prince has to say to our darling girl."

Deana took the letter from Indira. Henry's song twisted across the back of her mind; its eerie, melancholic notes left a chill against her fingers.

"Henry is my heart mate," Indira said brightly.

Savita laughed. "We'll see how you feel about that in a few more years. Arranged marriages very rarely result in a heart mate bond."

It wasn't an arranged marriage, not yet, anyway. Though if it were, Deana was sure that the trade negotiations between Beldaren and the isles would go much more smoothly.

She unfolded the letter and started reading. "Dear Indi, I hope you don't mind me calling you that. Father said I should address you as Princess Indira, but it doesn't sound quite as pretty as Indi."

"The little prince has charm—I'll give him that," Savita said, but Indira shooshed her.

"Garret showed me how to carve one of those chimes I was telling you about. It turned out a little lopsided, but Molly still loved it. I will make one for you once I have had a little more practice. Do you have a favourite colour?

I was right about Mother having a baby. That is why she sent Bran and Niall to help your brother instead of coming herself. I wish she had been able to come; she wouldn't let me go with Bran even though Niall would be there too—"

"I remember meeting Niall, but who's Bran?" Savita asked.

"He's a soul-singer like Henry. In Beldaren they call them nec-ory-mancers. No. Necki-mances. Oh, what was the word?" Indira sat up and rubbed the middle of her forehead as she squinted.

"Necromancer, perhaps?" a voice said from the door.

They all turned, and Savita made an appreciative noise that sounded almost like a purr. Deana couldn't have uttered a sound even if she wanted to. It was the man from the Beldaren market—the one she had told Kai about earlier. His white hair was a wild tangle of thick waves, and his eyes the dark blue of the deepest water. But it wasn't just his eyes that had halted her breath. His song was as fathomless as his stare, twisting and alluring—the kind of music that led sailors to their deaths.

"Bran!" Indira said and launched herself off the bed towards the stranger.

Deana caught her arm as she darted past, pulling her up short.

"What's the matter, Dee?" The girl stared up at her, but something Deana couldn't explain had shifted in her stomach. The same heaviness that had settled there the morning of the day Grandmother Ocean took Kai.

After the number of red fish in the moult, the dragging fingers of dread conjured by Bran's song were more than she could take. She chewed her lip, her desire to escape warring with a deep-seated need to be polite. Fear won out, and she tugged Indi towards the door. "We are late for your lesson."

Indi dug her heels in as though she might protest, but then her golden gaze widened as it met Deana's, and she let herself be led from the room.

Once they were a short distance along the hallway, the princess pulled away from her. "That was rude, Dee. Why didn't you want to talk to Bran? He's really nice."

"I'm sure he is. But if I don't get you to your lesson, Leilani will be angry, and if I make her angry again then she won't let me take care of you anymore."

"But you're my favourite ... Mama can just tell Leilani she's not allowed to send you away."

She was touched by the sincerity in the princess's voice. Few people could put up with Deana's *strangeness* for too long. Kai was the only one who had truly understood her, or maybe he'd just loved her regardless of her idiosyncrasies because that was what big brothers did. "Maybe. Leilani can be pretty stubborn though."

"No one is more stubborn than Mama."

Deana laughed. "Come on. Let's get your lesson done, then I will finish reading the letter from Henry."

As she shooed the girl down the hall, the sound of Savita's laughter reached her and she shook her head. Darkness was coming, and somehow Bran was caught up in it. Kai hadn't listened to her when she warned him. He had insisted everything would be okay, but then Grandmother Ocean had taken him. Deana wouldn't make the same mistake.

"What are you doing here?" Indira's older brother, Samir, asked as they entered the room that functioned as a schoolhouse for the children of the village leaders. He was looking gaunt, and there was an ashen tone to his normally warm brown skin. His song was rent with a discordant screeching that set her teeth on edge and built pressure behind her eyes. Something was very wrong with the boy, but then that was why Chief Soma had sent Idir all the way to the Beldaren for help.

"Ah, I remember you," an older man said. He had pale skin and long, dark brown hair shot through with grey. His eyes were a very pretty shade of violet, the same colour and shape as Henry's mother's. Deana had only met him briefly during her stay in Beldaren, but she would recognise him anywhere based on those eyes alone—Niall. "Deana and Princess Indira, if I am not mistaken." The smile he gave them was warm.

"Oh, please just call me Indi."

Niall chuckled. "As you wish."

"I didn't realise you had a lesson planned this morning. I thought Niall and Bran could use this time to meet Samir," Idir said. He was leaning by the window, his dark eyes narrowing as they studied Deana. His song nudged against her, and she increased the volume of her own song to drown him out. He frowned but said nothing.

"I would hate to interrupt Indi's lesson. I am sure we can find somewhere else to get acquainted with Samir," Niall offered, though the look he gave Deana was calculating, and his song as it brushed against hers was very similar to Idir's. Could his song invade the mind of another and twist them to his will the way Idir's could? She gave a tentative push back against the Beldaren mage's song, and a small smile touched his lips.

"Could we go for a walk along the beach?" Samir asked hopefully.

"No," Deana answered, not quite able to keep the panic from her voice.

Idir's gaze narrowed as it snapped to her, but she turned her attention to Samir. "I didn't mean—I ..." She studied her fingers before looking up. "There were more red fish in the moult this morning."

Indira gasped and covered her mouth with both hands. Samir's shoulders slumped, and Idir shook his head.

"More red fish?" Niall asked.

"The brightfish moult," Idir replied wearily. "You know the colours have no significance, Deana. It's just superstition and old wives' tales."

"It's not. Kai—"

"Enough," Idir snapped, his song overcoming her for a moment and compelling her to silence.

Deana drew a slow breath as her song struggled under the weight of Idir's. "Come on, Indi. We can skip your lesson for today." She dipped her head in Niall's direction and backed towards the door. "A pleasure to meet you again, Niall."

Indira flicked a look from Idir to Deana and then followed her.

"Why didn't you tell me about the fish, Dee?" she asked once they were a short distance down the hall.

"Idir's right. It's just a silly superstition."

The princess shook her head. "Idir's wrong. Do you think something bad will happen to Samir?"

"I don't know. But Niall and Bran are here to help him." She didn't have the heart to mention the dread she had felt when Bran's song brushed hers, or that she agreed that Idir was wrong about the red fish. Instead, she forced a smile and grabbed hold of the girl's hand. "Let's go find Savita and head to the market. I'll read the rest of Henry's letter on the way."

A bright smile broke across Indira's face, and she tugged Deana eagerly down the hall.

CHAPTER TWO

BRAN

The view from the deck of the ship was beautiful. White sand stretched in a sensuous curve, creating a long beach fringed by lush, green vegetation. Flanking the beach was a smooth patch of cleared ground on which the shapes of people were moving about. And beyond that, a run of huts on stilts with thatched rooves led back to the edge of the jungle that shrouded the mountain at the centre of the isle. Near the top of the mountain, a section had been cleared, and something there glinted in the sunlight, but the glare made it impossible to tell what it might be.

Nea had told him the isles would be unlike anything he had ever seen. She had almost seemed sad that she would not be coming along, but she didn't want to risk the journey in her current state, which was understandable. Garret probably would have objected anyway, not that Nea would listen to him. But ever since they had defeated Leon, he had been rather protective of her. Bran couldn't blame him; Nea had died to defeat the Usurper, and it was sheer luck that the plan to make her a deathwalker had worked. He traced his fingers along the indigo crescent that still marked his wrist. Nea's magic was gone from it now, but Donnic had told him the mark would never go away. Like the silver scars of corruption that stained the skin of those who had been inflicted. The tattoo was not the only *scar* he bore—housing even that tiny piece of Nea's keen had changed his own magic irrevocably. He hadn't explored what that meant—he wasn't entirely sure he wanted to.

"Beautiful, isn't it?" Niall asked as he joined Bran at the rail. "It feels like it has been an eon since I last set foot on the isles." He closed his eyes and tilted his head back as he inhaled.

"It's certainly like nothing I have ever seen before, but I thought that about Osmar too."

"Oh, we love the isles," Pippa said as she sidled in beside Bran, her arm brushing against his.

"The Farideans really know how to party," her twin, Kiki, slid up next to Niall.

Physically, the women were identical, almost down to the last freckle. They had chestnut hair and golden skin that hinted at a combination of Beldaren and Osmarian heritage. Their blue eyes seemed to always be sparkling with some sort of mischief, but their keens could not have been more different. Pippa's was the warm flicker of fire magic, and she had a temper to match. But Kiki's was playful, like a flow of water bubbling over the stones of a stream.

"Oi!" Rufus called down the deck. "Stop gawking at the scenery and get your arses into the boat."

"Oh, Rufus, don't get your drawers in a tangle," Pippa said as she pushed away from the rail and sauntered towards the boatswain.

"Pippa, leave poor Rufus alone," Wren said as she emerged from her captain's cabin. The bulk of her rust-coloured ringlets were secured beneath a turquoise scarf.

The crew of the Queen was one big, found family, much like Bran's back home in Beldaren. He had been left outside Hartswood as an infant and, despite necromancers keeping thorough records on their bloodlines, no one knew where he had come from. He had wondered if he was like Harvey; the result of someone like Ambrose trying to create a more powerful type of mage. But more likely, he was just one of those freak occurrences where a necromancer popped up in a bloodline that had been dormant for several generations. He would have liked to know why his parents chose to leave him, but he couldn't say his life had been terrible. Nea and Niall had welcomed him into their little family without a second thought. He also had Margot, Emil, and Nonna, and during the events of the fight against the Usurper, his family had widened to include Garret, Molly, Harvey, Janey, Declan, and Zephyr. Not to mention the next generation that was starting to emerge. Family, it seemed, didn't always mean blood.

"Come on, Bran," Kiki said, gripping his elbow and guiding him towards the boat. "If you're worried your legs won't handle the transition back to solid ground, fear not. Pippa and I will be more than happy to carry you."

"I think I can manage well enough on my own."

Kiki gave him a roguish grin but said nothing else as they reached Rufus and Pippa.

When they stepped out of the boat and onto the shore, Wren pulled Bran aside. "I have other business in the isles, but we'll be back within the month. If you need the Queen before then—" She held out a small snail shell. Magic twisted over it as she placed it in Bran's hand. "It will summon the Queen to your location. Now, off you go." She waved him towards Niall, who was waiting beside Idir, the man Chief Soma had sent to Beldaren to seek their aid.

Bran wasn't sure what to make of the large islander with his coal-dark eyes and carefully chosen words. He had been friendly enough, but something tickled the hairs at the back of Bran's neck when his keen-sense brushed against the edges of Idir's.

Idir led Bran and Niall through the centre of the village towards the palace that clung to the cliffs rising from the western end of the beach.

A woman with deep brown eyes and thick dark curls was waiting for them at the foot of the stairs at the entrance to the structure. She dipped her head in greeting, a warm smile widening across her lips. "Welcome to Lethata, pride of the Faridean Isles. I am Leilani, head of the house staff here in Chief Soma's home. If there is anything you need, please don't hesitate to ask. We have prepared rooms for you in the guest wing. I can show you to them if you would like."

Niall unshouldered his pack and handed it to Bran. "I believe Idir and I have some business with Chief Soma, but if you could show Bran to the rooms?"

"What about Samir?" Bran asked as he took Niall's bag.

"Once we have seen to our business, I will introduce you to him. Leilani will give you directions to the schoolroom."

"Bran, is it?" Leilani asked as she turned to study him. She wasn't much older than he was, perhaps twenty-five at the most, but her eyes seemed to hold a deep, world-weary sorrow. Her keen was hard to place, smooth and warm, much like Margot's healing magic, but there was something else attached to it. A seed of something, like a burr stuck to cloth.

Niall's finger jabbed against Bran's ribs.

"Sorry. Yes, it's Bran."

A warm smile spread across Leilani's lips. "Come." She headed along the hall and waved for Bran to follow.

Leilani led him into the west wing of the palace. "We've set Niall up in here." She indicated a door to their right, and Bran stepped inside to deposit Niall's things on the bed.

When he emerged again, Leilani was studying the next door with a frown, her keen stirring in a warm cloud around her as raised voices drifted to them.

"It sounds like Savita and Deana aren't quite finished with your room," she said with a similar long-suffering look to the one that Nonna wore at times. "You're just in there. The schoolroom where Samir will be waiting for you can be reached by taking this hall to the end and then turning left and following the covered walkway. It's the second door on the right. I need to be getting back to my queen, but if you need anything, the house staff can be recognised by the orange sashes." She tugged at the swathe of orange silk that was wrapped intricately over the saffron top that covered her chest and the upper half of her torso, leaving a slice of dark skin bare at her waist.

"So, just look for someone wearing yellow and orange?"

She gave a short shake of her head that turned into a nod. "All staff wear the sash, but Queen Amara and Princess Indira's handmaidens are dressed in yellow, Chief Soma's personal aides green, and general house staff blue. Anyone will be more than happy to help you, though." With that, she indicated his door with an open palm then turned on her heel and headed back the way they had come.

As Bran reached the door, he heard his name.

"He's a soul-singer like Henry." Princess Indira's voice carried into the hall. Henry was quite besotted with the girl which, given the bent of negotiations between Leith and Chief Soma, was probably a good thing. "In Beldaren they call them nec-ory-mancers. No. Necki-mances. Oh, what was the word?"

"Necromancer, perhaps?" Bran said as he stepped into the doorway.

Two women were in the room with the princess. The taller woman had a long, black braid that hung to her hips. Her yellow uniform left more of her torso bare than Leilani's did, and her skirts swirled around her legs as she straightened and made a soft

16

noise. Her eyes were so dark a brown that they almost appeared black.

The second woman Bran had seen once before, in the upper market in New Brenna. She had been watching him and Henry but then disappeared into the crowd. Her dark hair was loose over her shoulders, with braids of various sizes adorned with beads and ribbons scattered through the thick curls. But her eyes caught his attention. They were a vivid sea foam green. Her full mouth pulled in at one corner as she studied him, her keen swelling out like a wave crashing on the shore but then dragging back again as though it might drown him. He'd never felt a keen quite like it, and he'd encountered more than his share of unique mages.

"Bran!" Indira's exclamation broke through his thoughts, and he turned to her as she vaulted off the bed and started towards him.

The green-eyed woman caught her arm and drew her back. There was something akin to fear in those strange eyes—no, not necessarily fear, but definitely wariness.

"What's the matter, Dee?" The princess twisted to study the woman's face.

"We are late for your lesson." There was an almost panicked tightness to the woman's tone, and without sparing Bran another glance, she pulled Indira after her.

Indira planted her feet. Her golden gaze flicked from Bran's face to the woman's. Then her posture softened, and she gave a minute nod before allowing herself to be led towards the door.

Bran moved farther into the room to get out of the way as they brushed past him and into the hall.

"It's nice to meet you, Bran." The taller woman's voice drew his attention.

She was still standing beside the bed, her dark eyes unreadable as she studied him. After a few moments, a small smile quirked the corners of her mouth. She brushed her hip-length braid over her shoulder. "I'm Savita." The bangles around her wrist jingled as she held her hand out. "I hope Deana hasn't soured your opinion of our beautiful island. She's used to getting away with rudeness, given her *peculiarities*."

Peculiarities? The way she said the word seemed to imply it was more than Deana's strange keen. "What do you—" he started to ask, but Savita's gaze flicked to her fingers still waiting in the air between them, and a small pout chased the smile from her lips.

Bran shook the thought away and stepped towards her to take hold of her offered hand. "I'm not offended." He was curious, however, almost insanely so. He had come to help Niall study Samir's keen, but Deana's was an anomaly as well, one that intrigued him more than the prospect of another necromancer's. Back home, necromancers with unique abilities nearly outnumbered those who presented as typical, but he'd never encountered a mage like Deana before. Though Dara, one of the crew members from the Azure Queen, had an uncanniness about her as well. Was Deana a dream-singer like Dara? He didn't think so. Their keens felt too different.

"Am I boring you?" Savita's laugh broke through his thoughts.

"No. Sorry, I was lost in thought. You have my full attention now."

Her eyes still shone with mirth, but the corner of her mouth pulled in. "I was just saying that you've arrived in time to join us for the annual celebration in honour of Grandfather Moon, and if you would like, I can give you a tour of the village."

"I need to find Niall and Idir, but perhaps I will take you up on that offer later."

A wide smile returned as she dipped her head. "I won't keep you any longer then but come find me when you are ready."

He gave her a nod and placed his things on the bed before heading out to find Niall.

As he rounded the corner onto the covered walkway, he nearly collided with another body. Its owner gave a startled yelp and dodged to the side. One of her hands gripped the balustrade and the other held tight to the much smaller hand of the princess. Her bright eyes met his for several heartbeats before she dropped her gaze and a small smile worked across her mouth. It was an expression Nea often wore on those days her mind was heavy with the memories of the purge; polite, but joyless.

"Hello again," he said as he stepped back to give them some space.

Indira smiled widely. "Deana decided to cancel my lesson for the day, and we are going to the village; would you like to come?"

"Indi—"

"I can't right now. Niall and Idir are waiting for me, but thank you for the offer."

Deana's shoulders lowered as though the tension was leaving her body. Was it just him? Or was it the peculiarity that Savita had mentioned?

"You'll be able to help Samir, won't you?" Indira asked as she shook her hand free of Deana's. "It's my fault he's the way he is." The princess's bright keen swirled between them for a moment.

Deana's features softened, and she cupped the girl's face as she bent to look into her eyes. "Indi, you know that's not true. It's not your—"

"But it is! I should have listened to you. Then Samir wouldn't have gotten hurt and Kai—" Indira slapped her hands over her mouth at Deana's sharp intake of breath.

"Kai made a choice," Deana whispered tightly.

"You were right about the fish, and he ignored you. Just like Idir did today."

Deana licked her lip, then knelt and gripped the girl's shoulders. "Kai was in the wrong place at the right time. He wasn't there to save you or Samir. Neither of you was the soul the shrouded ones were seeking that night ..."

They seemed to have forgotten about Bran, but as he went to back away, the boards creaked, and Deana's uncanny gaze snapped to him. There was a sheen of unshed tears in her eyes, and her mouth pulled tight. Bran wanted to ask who the shrouded ones were, but he doubted that she would tell him. He got the distinct impression that he had heard more than she had intended him to. But it was worth asking Idir. If these shrouded ones were responsible for the change to Samir's keen, then there might be a clue as to how to help the boy.

"We should go find Savita," Deana said as she dragged Indira around the corner.

Bran blinked and rubbed his forehead before turning to continue along the walkway.

"Wait." Indira ran up to him and pulled him to a stop as she caught his hand. "Dee is scared because there were more red fish this morning. She said she agreed with Idir that it didn't mean anything, but she just says things like that because the other grownups don't listen to her. Kai didn't, and the shrouded ones took him. She said they were after her, but they are the ones that infected Samir and ruined his song." She spoke so fast that it was almost hard to follow. Then she spun on her heels and rushed away again as Deana called for her.

He shook his head and blew out a breath as he continued in the direction of the schoolroom.

When he entered the modest-sized room, he found Niall sitting cross-legged on the floor with a boy several years older than Indira. The boy had the same dark skin as most of the other Farideans Bran had encountered, but his hair was a deep charcoal grey, almost the same stormy shade as Nea's. His attention swivelled to Bran. There was a distinct gauntness to his features, and the heaviness around his eyes reminded Bran of the look those afflicted with corruption had often worn. But corruption had seemed to disappear when they defeated the Usurper.

He let his keen-sense examine the boy and met the soothing cool of necromancy, but something else clung to the boy's keen. A thick taint spread out from his core like rot. Bran shared a look with Niall. '*Corruption?*' He thought when he felt the cloying touch of the other mage's keen.

Niall shook his head, and his voice entered Bran's mind. '*It bears a resemblance to it, though.*'

"Hello, Samir. I'm—"

"Bran," the boy said. "I know." He frowned, and his keen brushed over Bran, causing a shudder to rush down Bran's spine. "You're the reason Dee was acting stranger than normal."

"Stranger than normal?"

Samir shrugged. "She's *different*. Like her mind doesn't work the same way everyone else's does ..." He glanced out the window. "I didn't understand it until I became different too," he whispered before turning to Bran again. "Now that I've heard your song, I know why she was worried."

"We are not here to discuss Deana's peculiarities," Idir said.

There was that word again. Bran studied Idir. There was something about the shape of his eyes and the curve of the mouth that was similar to Savita's. Was she his daughter perhaps?

"What do you mean, until you became different? Your sister mentioned that the shrouded ones took someone called Kai and ruined your song."

Idir's nostrils flared, and Samir's gaze dropped to the floor. "The shrouded ones are a myth."

Even the wildest of myths held a grain of truth. That fact, and the importance of stories, had been ingrained in Bran by Nonna and the spirits of the Hartswood grove. Not only that, but he had also experienced enough myths and legends come to life in his time to be wary.

"Kai was Deana's older brother. He was involved in an unfortunate incident that coincided with the beginning of the change in Samir's song," Idir explained.

"An incident?" Niall asked.

"He gave his life to save both Samir and Indira from drowning."

Niall made a soft noise and rubbed his fingers along his lower lip. "There is a chance that the trauma of such an incident might have altered Samir's keen. But it is a very slight chance, and given that his keen seems tainted rather than permanently altered, I would be inclined to think that there is some kind of magical influence at work here."

"Indira also mentioned something about red fish," Bran said.

Idir gave a long-suffering groan. "There is an old wives' tale about the brightfish moult. If there are more red fish than any other colour it is an omen of misfortune and, in some cases, death. But it is just a story. The colours of the fish have no significance."

"Deana didn't seem to think so," Niall said softly. "Tell me about her keen—her song. Is the way it presents why she is considered different? Why her presence seems to be suffered rather than accepted?"

Idir's mouth tightened. "You are here to help Samir, not some scatterbrained slip of a girl who had the misfortune to be born during the wrong phase of the moon."

"So, you believe that the moon phase at one's birth has some bearing, but not stories about prophetic fish or these shrouded ones?" Niall seemed to bite down on a smile, but he couldn't quite keep the lilt of amusement out of his voice.

"No. I do not. But most people in the village do, and they will tell you Deana belongs to Grandmother Ocean; her eyes mark her as such, as does her song."

"Her song? I will admit it feels like nothing I have encountered before, but it doesn't feel malignant." Niall ran his teeth along his lower lip.

"Deana's song *is* dangerous, especially for someone who follows her whims and puts too much faith in stories." Idir's tone suggested this was a discussion he had had one too many times before. He drew a breath and shook his head. "Deana dances to the beat of her own drum—she always has—and people mostly ignored her out of respect for her parents and then Kai. But they are all gone now, and the only reason she hasn't been cast out is a promise that I made to her father."

"And Indi loves her," Samir said, and one corner of Idir's mouth twitched.

"Yes, there's that too. Deana does have a way with the princess that none of the other handmaidens seem to possess."

"And it was after this incident with Kai and the near-drowning that you first noticed the change in Samir's song?" Niall asked.

Idir gave a nod.

"And yet it didn't seem to alter Indira's song at all? Why was her brother affected and not the princess?"

"Deana says it's because Indi belongs to the sun," Samir replied.

"She belongs to the sun?" Bran asked.

Samir nodded. "Her song is bright and clear, and everywhere she goes she makes people feel"—he frowned like he was searching for a word then gave a little shrug—"better."

"Like a healer?"

Both Idir and Samir shook their heads.

"What sort of mage is she then? A mind mage?" Niall asked Idir.

"The princess was born without magic."

"She's not keen-less though," Bran said.

"I believe in Beldaren you call it keen-touched. She has a gift, but it has never emerged completely, and it is not a true form of magic." There was something in Idir's tone, an edge that suggested he was getting annoyed with the deviation from discussing Samir.

Bran flicked a look at Niall, who was studying the other mind mage with a blank expression. That wasn't good. Niall was always animated—there was usually a twist to his mouth or a glint in his eye that indicated the path his thoughts were taking. Bran could count on one hand the times Niall had worn this same expressionless stare, and none of them had ended well.

"How did you discover the exact nature of the change to Samir's necromancy?" Bran asked, and Idir's attention shifted to him.

"Nazali was the first to note the change during one of her lessons," Idir replied.

"And Nazali is?"

"The head soul-singer from the Guild of Singers," Samir answered. "She comes down from the pavilion to teach me how to use my song."

"Then we should meet with her and discuss her theories about the change. There is no point in covering ground that she has already explored," Niall said as he pushed himself to his feet. "And I believe I would like to hear her thoughts on the shrouded ones."

Idir grunted. "She will tell you the same thing I did."

One of Niall's brows twitched upward. Idir was hiding something about the shrouded ones.

"Regardless, there is very little we can do for Samir until we understand the nature of his song both before and after the incident. If Nazali is his mentor, then she is the best person to speak with regarding both."

"Very well. I shall summon her," Idir said before stepping out into the hall.

Niall followed him, but Samir caught Bran's hand, pulling him to a stop and flicking a cautious look at the door before giving a small nod.

"If you want to know the truth about the shrouded ones, you should talk to Dee. But make sure Idir isn't around when you do." His tone was tight and the look in his eyes brought a sudden dryness to Bran's mouth.

"You think Idir is lying about them being a myth?"

"I know he is. I saw them, and Dee did too. But when I told him, he said it was just our imagination playing tricks on us." He shook his head and removed the leather cuff from his wrist. "If they are not real, why did he tell me to hide this?"

Bumps of what looked like pink coral dotted the skin of his wrist. The flesh around the lumps was darker and appeared almost necrotic in places.

Samir met Bran's eye squarely and gave a nod before replacing the cuff. "Talk to Dee. She knows the truth, and she can tell you more about the shrouded ones than anyone else, even Nazali." He left the room.

Bran ran a hand through his hair and blew out a breath. *Talk to Deana? Sounds simple enough.* Except he'd gotten the distinct impression that talking to him was the last thing she wanted to do.

A cool breeze broke through the muggy heat of the night and ruffled Bran's hair as he leant against the windowsill of his room. He'd tried to find Deana all afternoon, to ask her about the shrouded ones, but whenever she'd glanced his way, her eyes had been filled with a haunted wariness and she had promptly disappeared.

He plucked the silver rose pendant out from under his shirt and examined it in the moonlight. It was a spirit anchor. The one that had allowed them to save Nea's life during the fight with the

Usurper. A tiny piece of her keen still clung to it, and she had enchanted it so that he could use it to contact her if he needed to. She had told him it was for use in cases of emergency, but maybe she knew something about shrouded ones. Even if she didn't, he could really use her input right now.

With a sigh, he let his keen run over the rose and it shimmered lilac for a second. Cold pooled behind his navel and the source in the room tightened before a seam of light appeared in the air and sprung open to reveal a shimmering purple oval. The miasma of the portal cleared, and Nea appeared on the other side.

"Bran, are you alright?" Concern shone in her violet gaze as she studied him.

"Yes. I'm fine." He rubbed a hand over his forehead. "It's just ... Things are weird here. It's almost like they're hiding something, and there is this girl—I think you might have met her. She was with the Faridean delegation; she's one of Princess Indira's handmaidens. Deana."

"Ah, so it's girl trouble?" Declan joined Nea on the other side of the portal, his wolfish grin firmly in place.

"Declan," Garret's voice reprimanded.

"Am I interrupting something? We can talk later," Bran said.

"It's fine. Declan just dropped in to see Garret," Nea pushed Declan away from the portal before making a shooing motion. "Have you met Samir yet?"

"Yes, and he said that creatures called the shrouded ones are responsible for the change in his keen, but Idir is adamant they are not real. Apparently, Deana knows something about the incident, but she won't talk to anyone about it. Not that I blame her, the way some of the others treat her."

Nea tapped her fingers against her lower lip. "I've heard of the shrouded ones before, but where?" She moved to the bookshelf behind her desk and muttered to herself as she studied the tomes there. "Of course." She let out a laugh and pulled a very beaten-up book from the shelf. Moving back to the portal, she said, "Catch," as she lobbed the book through.

Bran studied the cover. "Capernibald's Bestiary?"

"There is a chapter on creatures of the Faridean Isles and shrouded ones are mentioned, only briefly mind you, but it might be a good starting point. I would suggest talking to Samir and Deana about what really happened as well."

"Samir already shared everything he was willing to, and Deana is doing her absolute best to avoid me."

"She's avoiding you?"

He let out a breath. "I don't know why, but Samir said I scared her. I've hardly said more than a few words to her, but I have to agree with him. She gets this look in her eyes ... It's"—he let out a small laugh—"almost unsettling."

"From memory, she is particularly sensitive to the keen of others. Perhaps there is something about your keen that bothers her. I know she tended to avoid Garret and I at first while she was here with the Faridean delegation. And your keen was altered when you housed a piece of my soul. Does she show the same aversion to Father?"

"Not that I have noticed."

"Maybe he can talk to her then." She frowned. "I can't keep the portal open much longer, but Bran, please be careful. If Idir and the others are harbouring secrets or only revealing half-truths, things could turn dangerous very quickly. If anything happens and you can't get back to the Queen, use the anchor straight away and we'll get you and Father out of there."

"I'll be careful. And thanks." He lifted the book and gave her a smile.

Declan started to say something, but Nea gave Bran a wave and the portal snapped shut.

Bran flopped back on the bed and stared at the ceiling. Things here were definitely not what they seemed. A stone had lodged deep in the pit of his stomach. He hadn't felt this way since those days before they'd defeated the Usurper. Something just as big was coming—he was sure of it.

The sand shifted beneath his bare feet as he wandered along the shoreline. Every so often a slightly larger wave would wash in and splash up his legs, dampening the cuffs of his pants which he had rolled up to just beneath his knees. He had always liked this time of day when the world was silent and new. He glanced towards the horizon where a line of red was starting to bloom, announcing the imminent emergence of the sun.

He paused and studied the beach, noting the dark shape sitting on the rocks ahead. She was hunched over, her chin resting on her knees, but the ebb and flow of her keen was unmistakable.

"You're up early," he said as he approached.

She twisted to face him, curiosity giving way to caution as her bright gaze shifted from the top of his head to his toes and then back up to his face. She said nothing, but her entire body tensed as though she might flee, and guilt stirred in his stomach.

"Sorry to disturb you, but I needed to ask you a few questions about what happened with Samir, and you seemed to be avoiding me."

She stood at his words and folded her arms. "There is nothing I could tell you that Idir doesn't already know, and I believe he has sent for Nazali. She can fill in the gaps that Idir can't."

"Samir believes otherwise. He told me to ask you about the shroud—"

"Don't say it." She cast a panicked glance along the shoreline.

"They aren't real and—"

"Did Idir tell you to say that?" Samir had implied that was the case, but Bran wanted her to confirm it.

She hopped off the rock and shook her head. "I can't tell you about them. Please don't ask me again." She hurried past him.

So, they did exist? But why lie about it? "Deana, wait."

She stopped but didn't turn to face him.

"I'm sorry. I just want to help Samir and to do that I need the truth of what happened that night."

A quiver ran through her, but she kept her back to him. "I can't help you. I'm sorry." She broke into a run.

Bran rubbed the back of his neck as she disappeared into the village, and then with a sigh he marched after her.

He met Niall and Samir in the corridor that led to the schoolroom a short while later.

"Enjoy your walk?" Niall asked.

"Until I ran into Deana."

"Did she talk to you?" Samir asked.

Bran shook his head. "I just don't understand why everyone is so adamant that the shrouded ones don't exist. Deana *knows* they are real, and she stared me straight in the eye and lied about it. But she was terrified—almost as though if she admitted they were real, something bad would happen."

"They did steal her brother and ruin my song," Samir said. "And Idir—wait, do you hear that?" Samir's gaze tracked along the hall to the schoolroom door.

Bran couldn't hear anything, but he could feel a wild keen surging from that direction. It was like an angry swell churning against a jagged shore and beneath it was the sweet compulsion of mind magic. He shared a look with Niall, and they hurried to the door.

But Samir reached it first and threw it open. "What are you

29

doing to Dee?" Samir demanded, and Idir's attention snapped to him.

Deana was backed against the far wall, her eyes shut tight and her chin pressed to her hands, which gripped the front of her shirt.

"Stop it. You're hurting her." Despite his young age, there was a deep authority in Samir's tone.

The pressure of Idir's keen dropped, and Deana's surged again as she drew a rasping breath.

"Deana ..." Niall said softly, and her attention snapped to him as he lifted a hand in her direction. "Are you alright?"

She let out a sob and went barrelling between Bran and Niall.

"She's fine," Idir said calmly. "We were just having a little talk."

"You drowned her with your song and invaded her mind," Samir's hands clenched by his sides.

Idir sighed. "I did nothing of the sort. I was just making sure—"

"A person's mind belongs to them alone! You had no right to sift through her thoughts. She would have told you what you wanted to know." The rage coming off Samir was almost palpable.

Niall cleared his throat and settled a calculating stare on Idir.

"I realise how what you just witnessed looks, but I would never do anything to hurt Deana. Now, if you'll excuse me, I have business with Chief Soma today. However, Nazali will be here sometime this morning to help you with Samir."

Samir glared at him as he left and shook his head.

"Should someone check on Deana?" Bran asked.

"It won't help. And if she didn't want to talk to you before, she certainly won't now," Samir answered.

Niall studied the boy for a few moments. "Do you mind answering a question about the night Deana's brother died and your song was altered?"

Samir shrugged and gave a small nod.

"Did Idir enter your mind? Or perhaps Deana's?"

Samir's mouth tightened, and his cheek puckered as though he was biting the inside of it. Then he let out a rush of breath and gave another nod, this one firmer than the last. "He entered mine and he told me the shrouded ones weren't real. That it was just our imagination playing tricks on us." He shook his head and looked at his feet, but there was a fire in his gaze when he lifted it again. "But I know what I saw and so does Dee."

CHAPTER THREE

◯DEANA

The gentle lapping of the tide against the rocks soothed the rawness left in the wake of Idir's invasion into her mind. It had been a hard night, memories both real and imagined pervading her dreams and twisting them into the same nightmares that had plagued her in the weeks after Kai's death. Those nights the shrouded ones had stalked her across a solemn landscape of drowned earth, all the while their song beckoning her down into the bloodstained deep.

An errant spray of water misted over her, chilling her skin and driving away the creeping sensation of the nightmares. She shifted back on her perch and let her gaze wander the horizon.

"I can't do it anymore, Kai," she whispered, her breath catching in her throat as tears edged along her lash line. "I'm not brave enough. I'm not—" She bit down on her words as the melancholy lilt of Bran's song reached her.

A glance back in the direction of the village told her he was walking steadily towards her. She stood and brushed her palms on her thighs before pressing the backs of her hands to her eyes to dispel the unshed tears before he reached her.

"Sorry. I didn't mean to disturb you ... again." He rubbed a hand over the back of his neck as he spoke. "But I just—"

"I told you yesterday there is nothing more I can tell you about Samir." She hopped off the rocks and stood in front of him.

"I know ... I wasn't going to ask you about that." His tone seemed sincere and there were no signs of deceit in his eyes. "I wanted to make sure you were alright after yesterday. Idir—"

"It was nothing. I'm fine ... really."

His mouth twisted as though he didn't believe her.

"Thank you for your concern, but I really need to be going. The festival of Grandfather Moon is tonight, and I have to help Leilani with the preparations," she said as she backed away from him.

"Deana, wait. Don't let me chase you away from what is obviously a morning ritual for you. I'll go ... I shouldn't have disturbed you. I'm sorry."

She studied the ocean and then let her attention shift slowly back to Bran. "It's alright. I am done now anyway."

He frowned but said nothing else, and she turned on her heel, wobbling slightly as the sand shifted beneath her feet, then she walked away as fast as she could without breaking into a run.

"Dee? Were you listening?"

Deana studied Indira's fingers as they rested against her wrist. "I'm sorry, Indi."

"Perhaps you should ask Leilani for the rest of the day off. You've been more scatterbrained than normal today," Savita said as she placed a crate of decorations on the table.

"I just didn't sleep very well last night. I can focus." Between the nightmares and the encounter with Bran earlier that morning, her thoughts had been a turbulent mess.

Savita's mouth pulled in at one corner as she started sorting through the box. "You haven't been able to focus for the last few days."

"Nazali arrived yesterday. Do you think she came to help Niall and Bran?" Indira asked.

"She couldn't work out what was wrong with Samir before, so I doubt her input will be beneficial. Soul-singers are almost as vague as Deana." Savita's playful tone didn't soften the barbs of her words. "I don't know why Father bothered to go all the way to Beldaren just to get another one; it's not like their soul-singers are all that different from ours. But at least Bran is nice to look at."

"Savita, will you please escort the princess back to the palace? Queen Amara has requested she return to her quarters to begin preparations for tonight," Leilani said as she crossed the square to join them.

Indira pouted over her shoulder as Savita led her away.

"Are you alright, Deana? You've been frowning all morning."

"I'm fine. The air just feels tight today, and I didn't sleep much last night."

Leilani's mouth twisted from side to side as she studied the decorated square around them. "It looks like you are almost done here; if you want to take the rest of the day—"

Deana shook her head. "I can manage."

"Niall said that he wanted to talk with you about the night Kai died." Leilani wobbled over the words, as though her heart couldn't bear hearing them out loud. It was a pain Deana understood well; she, too, could barely stand the weight of Kai's name on her tongue, even now, two years since he had been taken. "He said you've been avoiding both him and Bran ... If there is something you know about that night that can help Samir—"

"There is nothing I haven't already told Idir, Chief Soma, or Nazali." Deana's tone was tighter than she meant it to be, but she'd been over the events of that night more times than she could count and every time they told her that what she had seen wasn't real. That the trauma of losing her brother had altered her memory. Had created monsters that didn't exist outside of children's stories.

"Maybe hearing the story firsthand from you will help Niall and Bran though."

Deana shook her head. Niall's song was too much like Idir's. Even though he had been nothing but nice to her, she couldn't trust him not to abuse his power and force his song into her mind to take the answers she wasn't willing to give. And Bran. Every time his song brushed against hers, the feeling of it dragged her back to those days before the shrouded ones had come and taken Kai. There was darkness tangled in his destiny, and she wanted no part of that. "I'm tired of no one believing me," she whispered.

Leilani squeezed her shoulder gently. "I do believe you, Deana."

She studied Leilani's gaze and found only sincerity there. "Then why didn't you tell Idir?"

"Because Kai didn't trust him, and neither do I." Her fingers lifted from Deana's shoulder. "You should talk to Niall. I think you'll find he *will* believe you. Now, come on. Let's get the rest of these decorations up so we can go and get ready for tonight."

What did Leilani mean she didn't trust Idir? Was he somehow responsible for what had happened to Samir? He couldn't be associated with the shrouded ones; his song wasn't tainted by Grandmother Ocean.

A thousand questions rolled across her mind as she went through the motions of helping Leilani finish decorating the square for the festival to honour Grandfather Moon. They continued to snap at her heels as she wandered towards her hut.

Most of the palace staff lived in quarters within the palace itself or in the huts just beyond it. But Deana preferred her parents' old dwelling, which was situated at the very edge of the village. It marked the beginning of the climb to the Singers' Pavilion, the complex at the top of the mountain that housed the Guild of Singers.

As she entered the hut, she touched her fingers to her lips and then the doorframe. The wood was velvety smooth after decades of her ancestors completing the same ritual. Beneath the grain of the wood memories stirred, the caress of multiple songs at the edge of her mind. She could pick the newer ones out from the others, the deep vibrating thrum of Kai, the soft whisper of her mother, and the playful staccato of her father. Soon their songs would fade and become one with the rest of their ancestors.

She moved to the scarred table and closed her eyes as she ran her fingertips across it. After her parents' death, she had lain across the tabletop committing the scent of her mother's herb craft to memory. The whole hut was still imbued with the familiar smells of herbs, oils, and fats—the tools of her mother's trade. They were stale now, fading with each passing season the same way the magic clinging to the doorframe was.

She pulled the stone charm from beneath her shirt and thumbed the hole at its centre. The magic of it tickled the tips of her fingers and settled in her core. It was the magic of secrets, soft and alluring with the potential to unearth great darkness.

After a few moments of finding her centre and mentally preparing herself for the evening to come, she opened her eyes and moved to her mother's old clothing chest. She ran her hands over the carved top before lifting it open and digging into the silken folds within. What she was looking for was at the bottom of the chest. It had been her favourite of her mother's festival outfits. A pair of pants, the navy blue of deep water with turquoise waves embroidered on them and a gossamer overskirt, the silver-white of moonlight on the sand. The top was the same turquoise as the embroidery, overlayed with the skirt fabric. That same translucent fabric formed loose sleeves that buttoned at the wrist.

Once dressed, she tucked the stone charm beneath the top of the shirt and secured a turquoise and sapphire necklace around her throat. The teardrop-shaped stones fanned out over her collarbone and shone in the afternoon light.

Just as she was finishing her hair, an eerie song brought a chill to her core. A knock sounded against the door a heartbeat later, and she glanced its way as she cleared her throat. "Who is it?"

She didn't need to ask. She recognised Bran from his song, but what was he doing here?

"It's Bran. I'm sorry ..." He made a sound that could have been a short laugh. "I didn't want to disturb you again when you've made it clear that you would rather be left alone, but Leilani said you might be ready to talk about what happened to Samir. Do you mind if I come in?"

If she welcomed him in, she was welcoming the darkness that clung to him into her home. But her mother's voice was ringing in the back of her mind, urging her to be polite. And Leilani was right; even if he and Niall didn't believe her, they might be able to help Samir if they knew the whole story. Or at least the part that had led to the change in Samir's song. With a steadying breath, she moved and opened the door. Bran was already halfway down the stairs. He glanced back over his shoulder, his deep-water eyes widening. Had he expected her to ignore him?

"You want to know what happened to Samir," she stated.

"Only if you are willing to share. You don't have to, and if you're worried Niall is going to use his keen to force you, then don't. He would never enter someone's mind without their permission." Bran's behaviour over the last few days suggested he did not approve of people like Idir abusing their gifts; the twist of his mouth now confirmed it.

She had managed to keep Idir out of her head yesterday, but just barely. After the incident with the shrouded ones, he had flayed her mind apart, scouring it and making her relive every detail. He insisted that her version of the night wasn't real, that she had somehow fabricated the story in such a way that even his song would be fooled.

"Would you like me to go?" Bran moved down another step.

Yes. She would like nothing more at that moment. "No, I will tell you the events of that night ... if you think it will help. Do you know what the shrouded ones are?"

"Not really. Some kind of reanimation would be my best guess. But I only have a few stories from the other villagers to go off, and most people seem to believe they are nothing more than a story made up to scare children into behaving. The only other reference to them is a very scant paragraph in a book written by a scholar who most people considered a reclusive crackpot."

Perhaps she and this scholar had a bit in common. She fought the smile that tugged at the corner of her mouth at that thought. "They are the handmaidens of Grandmother Ocean. They can appear as beautiful women whose songs lead the careless to the deep, or as they did on the night they stole my brother and infected Samir." She clenched her fists, digging her nails into her palms to cut through the sorrow. "Half-decayed corpses, shrouded in seaweed and adorned with coral. That is how they come when Grandmother Ocean sends them to collect that which is hers." Her song swirled out of her control for a moment, and she drew a breath to calm it. "If they are denied their prey then they spread disease and decay. That is why they infected Samir."

Bran licked his lip and moved up two steps so his face was level with hers. "Who was their target that night?" The question was flat, as though he knew the answer and was just waiting for her to confirm it.

"Kai wouldn't let them take me and he made sure they couldn't find me again."

"How?"

She touched her hand to her chest, fingering the lump of the stone through the fabric of her shirt. It was the one thing she had managed to keep from Idir, even as he'd torn her mind to ribbons searching for answers. "I—I don't know." The lie cut her to the core even though Bran was a stranger and she owed him nothing, especially not her trust. She never lied. Not directly. But Kai had been clear—*no one* was to know the true significance of the stone.

"Niall said I might find you here," Savita announced as she neared the bottom of the stairs. She was wearing a skirt that seemed constructed from strips of silk in varying shades of pink. It clung low to her hips and twirled about her legs like the arms of an anemone. Her top was sleeveless and stopped just below her bust. Thin chains of gold and glittering pink stones hung across her midsection from their anchor points along the hem. "Running late as usual, Deana? Surely you don't want our guest to miss the beginning of the festival?"

Deana wouldn't care if she missed the entire festival— pretending she wasn't an outcast was exhausting at times. "Savita is right. You shouldn't miss it."

Bran turned to face Savita.

"Well?" she asked and did a little twirl.

"Ah ... you look lovely," he said as he joined her at the foot of the stairs.

Savita smiled up at him and looped her arm through his. "Come on." She tugged him towards the village square with enough enthusiasm to make him stumble.

He glanced over his shoulder, a question in his eyes, but then Savita said something that drew his attention back to her and they disappeared into the crowd.

Deana shook her head. If Savita could feel the darkness woven into his song, then she wouldn't be so quick to entangle herself with him. Or maybe she would; she had always been entranced by beautiful things despite the danger they might possess.

When Deana reached the square, Indira came running over to her in a flash of scarlet and gold.

"Wow! Dee, you look so pretty!"

"Thank you. You look lovely as well."

Indira did a twirl like Savita had done for Bran. "Did you know red is Henry's favourite colour? Do you think he'd like my dress if he were here?"

"I think he would."

"Oh, it's starting." Indira grabbed Deana's hand and dragged her towards the edge of the platform on which Chief Soma and Queen Amara were standing. They each held an unlit parchment lantern.

Beside them stood Nazali. Her grey hair was secured in countless tiny braids, the beads of shell and bone adorning the ends rattling against each other as she moved. She was wearing a blood-red dress, the skin around her eyes covered in a smear of white paste.

Turning to Chief Soma, she lifted the bowl-shaped shell she was carrying towards him. Her song built to a cold dirge that spoke of death as purple light flickered over the bowl. Chief Soma dipped his fingers into the white paste and dragged them down his face, stopping just above his lip. He then turned to Amara and ran his thumb from her hairline to the tip of her nose, leaving a pale line.

Amara's song lifted to join Nazali's. Warm and crackling, it drove the chill of death from Deana's bones. Twin flames burst to life within the lanterns and after a moment they started to drift towards the sky.

Another coil of song reached Deana and she scanned the crowd. It was a lilting lament that spoke of loneliness and loss, and beneath it came an all-pervading vibration of dread. She glanced over the shoreline behind the podium. White water glittered in the last light of the sun. A figure was standing by the rocks at the far end of the beach. A woman. Dressed in the yellowed tone of aged bone, seaweed tangled in her hair and coral embedded in her skin. She lifted one skeletal hand—

"Deana!" Savita snapped her fingers in front of Deana's nose, and she stumbled backwards.

"Where's Indi?" A fist closed around Deana's lungs and the weight of the stone charm burned against her skin.

"She's over there with Niall and Amara." Savita pointed. "What were you looking at?" She turned and scanned the beach.

Deana followed her line of sight, but the shrouded one was gone. Had it just been a trick of the light? The stone was supposed to prevent them from hearing her song and finding her, but what if the magic on it was fading or what if they had discovered a way around it?

"Are you alright?" Bran had joined them, his brow furrowed as he studied her face. He lifted his hand as though he would touch her. "You're safe. It's okay."

She shied away from him, bumping into Leilani.

"Dee?" Leilani's eyes searched hers.

"I'm fine," she managed around the lump that was thickening in her throat. "Just a little overwhelmed." She spun until she found an opening and darted away, her fingers closing tight around the stone.

It couldn't have been real. Kai had made sure they wouldn't come for her again. Dread settled heavy in her stomach. Why was her song trying to drag her towards the ocean?

CHAPTER FOUR

BRAN

The source tightened, bringing a sensation Bran had not felt for several years to the edge of his mind; a heavy cold, like he was being dragged down into thick mud. He swallowed and scanned the crowd.

Savita was beside him, her arm linked through his. The warmth of her body was not enough to drive away the chill that had gripped him. On her other side, Idir was watching something—Deana. Her shoulders were hunched, one hand curled against the centre of her chest as she stared past the podium where Chief Soma and Queen Amara stood. Her keen was surging around her, but that wasn't what he could feel. He followed the line of her wide-eyed stare. Something was moving along the shore. A woman. No, there was something otherworldly about it, but it was too corporeal to be a spirit. It lifted a skeletal hand. Coral studded its death-pallid skin and seaweed had all but replaced its hair; the yellowed rags clinging to its decaying form fluttered in the breeze. Was it a shrouded one?

He searched the crowd again. No other mages present seemed to have noticed it, except Nazali and Samir. Samir was staring at the creature transfixed. He took a step forward, but Nazali caught his shoulder. She lifted her other hand and a spike of cold magic jarred along Bran's spine. The creature paused. Turning its attention towards Nazali, it opened its mouth as though letting out a silent scream before it disappeared.

Bran turned to Savita, but she had moved from his side to Deana's.

"Where's Indi?" Deana asked, her chest heaving as though she was struggling to draw enough breath.

"She's over there with Niall and Amara. What were you looking at?"

"Are you alright?" Bran asked as he reached them.

Deana's eyes met his. Her mouth worked like she was swallowing, and the hand pressed against her chest trembled. She was spiralling into a full-blown panic. He'd seen Nea enter a similar state before. He slowly lifted his hand towards her. "You're safe. It's okay."

She flinched as though struck and backed into Leilani.

Annoyance crossed the woman's features as her eyes met Bran's, but she dropped her attention to Deana and worry chased the ire away. "Dee?" she asked softly.

"I'm fine," Deana choked out. "Just a little overwhelmed." Her voice broke on the last word as she whirled around and fled.

Bran and Leilani shared a look.

"I'll go after her," Leilani said.

Savita's mouth twisted, and she shook her head as she watched Leilani run after Deana. "Always so dramatic," she muttered. Then her dark gaze met Bran's and a warm smile broke across her lips. "Don't worry about Deana. She gets easily overwhelmed by large gatherings. Leilani will talk her down and then send her to bed." Sliding her hand around his elbow, she tugged him towards the beach. "Come on. They are about to light the pyre."

Bran shook her off as they reached the edge of the sand. "I just need to speak to Nazali. I'll catch you up in a little while."

Savita closed her fingers around his wrist, holding him back as she looked over her shoulder at her father. He glanced at Bran, and then his gaze dropped to his daughter's and he gave a small nod. When Savita turned to face Bran again, she was pouting. She traced a finger down his chest and a thin coil of magic smoothed across the back of his neck. "I am sure whatever you need to discuss with Nazali can wait until tomorrow," she almost whispered.

Bran shook his head. Not to disagree with her but to try to shift the fuzziness that had settled. His lips felt strangely numb, and he licked them. The world spun around him in flashes of colour and light. Notes of song and snatches of conversation drifted past, and he couldn't remember what he had been about to do. Savita drew closer, her dark eyes shining in a way that set a tightening at his core, but it had nothing to do with desire. Her breath brushed over his lower lip as her fingers laced into his hair. A warning stirred in the depths of his mind, but it was brushed aside by the seductive melody of a song that silenced all his inhibitions and set his entire body a flame. Her mouth met his and the skin on the inside of his wrist burned with cold. The warning sounded again, sending a discordant note through the song and bringing a surge of clarity through the fog.

He pulled away from her, gently gripping her arms and taking a step back.

The cool night air rushed into the space between them, scattering the last notes of the song. A few people sat sleepily around the dying embers of the pyre. The sky above was the deep black of midnight, studded with glittering stars and the bloated circle of a full moon.

Savita was frowning as she studied him.

"What did you do to me?" he asked. He had thought she was keen-less, given that his keen-sense hadn't noticed anything about her. Now that he was aware of it, he didn't know why he hadn't felt it before—the cloying sweetness of mind magic.

"I thought you wanted—"

"No." His tone was sharp, and her frown deepened. "I mean, not like this. Not without—"

A scream tore through the stillness of the night.

The inside of Bran's wrist burned with cold again, and he rolled his sleeve back. Nea's magic was radiating out of the crescent moon mark in a soft violet glow. No, it wasn't Nea's magic. It was his own—the part that had been tainted by hers and changed.

"What is that?" Savita's eyes widened. "I thought it was just a tattoo."

Bran closed his fingers over the mark and didn't answer her as another scream sounded and a shadowed figure came rushing towards them. He pulled Savita out of the way as the moonlight highlighted the figure, revealing it to be the shrouded one from earlier. It had a small form slung over its shoulder.

"She's got Samir!" Deana yelled as she came charging across the sand, only to be tackled by another dark shape. She rolled beneath her attacker, kicking and struggling. Her keen built until it drowned everything out and the ocean beside them roared into a massive wave that blocked the moonlight. An arm of water slammed down on Deana and her attacker, cutting a deep furrow into the beach as it receded and collapsed into the surface of the ocean with an arcing splash.

Deana got to her feet; her attacker forgotten as she charged after the shrouded one again.

"Get help," Bran said to Savita as he ran after Deana.

He understood now why the shrouded one felt so familiar. It was some kind of wraith, and as such, it should be vulnerable to necromancy. He channelled his keen and focused on the fleeing creature. Violet light shrouded its body and it jerked to a stop, nearly losing its grip on the boy.

It turned and hissed in his direction. The sand beneath him shifted and his stomach swooped towards his throat as he plummeted several feet before the sand closed around his middle.

Deana's keen surged again, and she gestured in a sweeping motion. The ocean rose in a wall and surrounded the shrouded one. It hissed at her, and then the thick numbness of a warden's suppression dropped on them, and the wall of water collapsed.

"No!" Deana made a lunge to go after the shrouded one again, but someone grabbed her and drew her up short.

"Don't worry, pet. You'll get to join your brother real soon." The attacker pinned her arms to her sides as she kicked and thrashed in his grip.

Bran finally broke free of the sand and tackled the attacker. The three of them rolled across the beach in a tangle of limbs, but Deana gained her feet first. As her keen surged again, Bran drew a deep breath and held it.

Cold water slammed against him, rolling him towards the embers of the dying pyre—the revellers had scattered when the fight started. Coals hissed and steamed as the water rushed over them before dragging them towards the ocean.

Deana was facing the hooded attacker, something squeezed tight in her fingers. A shout sounded and the pounding of feet reached them as several people charged down the beach, mage lights bobbing ahead of them.

The attacker let out a snarl and then took off.

"Leave him," Idir's voice commanded as Deana moved to pursue the hooded man.

She froze and stuffed whatever she was holding into her shirt before turning to face Idir, her eyes downcast.

"What happened?" he ordered.

"They took Samir. We have to go after them," Deana said as she flicked a look at Idir and the men who surrounded him.

"Who took Samir?" Idir asked.

Deana opened her mouth but then snapped it shut again, her gaze dropping once more to her feet.

"A shrouded one. At least that is what I think it was," Bran replied. "It felt like a very complex reanimation."

Idir gave an indignant snort. "The shrouded ones are a myth."

"I tried to stop them, but they had a silencer with them," Deana said.

Silencer? Did she mean the warden? That would make sense, given that Faridean mages experienced magic as sound more so than a feeling.

Idir studied the torn-up beach and then their wet forms, his mouth tightening. "You used your song." The steel beneath his tone made Bran straighten.

"I had no choice," Deana murmured. "They—"

"You know how dangerous your song is." Idir's voice was like ice.

"I ... they ..." Deana drew a series of shallow breaths.

"Shouldn't you be going after them instead of reprimanding Deana for trying to stop them from taking Samir?" Bran asked. It took a great effort to keep his tone level.

Idir glanced at him, his gaze flicking briefly to the wrist that was marked by the oathbond tattoo. He then nodded to the men on either side of him and pointed in the direction the attackers had fled. "The pair of you get back to the palace. I want a full report of what happened and spare me the wild stories."

Deana made a tiny noise but dipped her head to Idir and then hurried away.

Bran met Idir's eye. The mind mage's dark gaze narrowed and

he jutted his chin towards the palace before starting after his men without sparing Bran another look. Bran watched him for a few moments before turning and leaving the beach.

The palace was a bustle of activity, house members and servants rushing about. Most of them appeared rumpled as though they had been pulled from bed. Several, like Savita, were still in their finery from the festival. She was sitting with a blanket wrapped around her shoulders and a steaming mug in her hands. When she spotted Bran, she placed the cup aside and stood. Her keen had left a residue of sticky fingers on the back of his mind, and he had taken several involuntary steps toward her before he caught himself.

"Where is Niall?" he asked, and a servant pointed to the hallway that led to the schoolroom.

Sure enough, Niall was there with Nazali, who looked almost frail in her thin nightdress. They both glanced towards the door when Bran entered.

"What happened at the beach?" Niall asked at the same time Bran said,

"Did you know Savita was a mind mage like her father?"

"Get her hooks in you, did she?" Nazali asked, her eyes shining with mild amusement.

"I don't know what she did to me. One minute I was looking for you, the next it's after midnight and a shrouded one is kidnapping Samir."

"You saw it?" Niall asked.

Bran nodded. "I saw it during the ceremony as well. Deana did too, and ..." He settled his gaze on Nazali. Would she deny they were real like Idir had?

"There was a shrouded one present during the ceremony. They often show their faces when we connect with Grandmother Ocean or her consort."

"Deana said that you didn't believe her when she told you the shrouded ones were responsible for what happened to Samir's song. She said you agreed with Idir that they are not real and she must have gotten confused."

The corner of Nazali's mouth twisted. "I did that to protect her."

"How is trying to convince someone they are crazy to the point of seeing things protecting them? You didn't protect her; you made her an outcast."

Nazali shook her head. "Deana has always been an outcast. People turn a blind eye to her out of respect for her parents, but they will never accept her. As far as most of them are concerned, she was born cursed. And the tragedy that has permeated her entire life is proof enough for them."

"This *curse*," Niall started. "Several people have mentioned that she belongs to Grandmother Ocean, but they have not elaborated on what that means ... The only explanation I could get from Idir was that her song is different and dangerous."

"Saying she belongs to Grandmother Ocean is a very simple way to put it. But it is the essence of the curse. Sometimes people are born who have been touched by Grandmother Ocean. Their song is louder than that of other singers. And you can see the Grandmother's claim in the colour of their eyes."

"Stronger magic is not necessarily a curse though. It can certainly be dangerous, especially when left untempered, but when nurtured with the right precautions and treated with respect it can be a boon."

Nazali nodded. "In most cases I would agree with you. However, Deana's song—the magic she is capable of—" Nazali drew a long breath and rubbed her fingers along her forehead. "She has the power to command the entire ocean. If she chose to, she could drown cities or sink entire islands. The last time a mage like Deana walked the isles that is exactly what she did."

"Surely that would necessitate a thorough cultivation of her keen," Niall said.

"Precautions *were* taken when she was younger to limit the potential danger, but a song like hers is better silenced completely. That way it cannot be exploited."

"Her keen *was* impressive," Bran said. "I've seen Kiki play with the waves, but her keen has limitations. When Deana used her magic to fight off the attackers, it was something else. She caused more damage than a king tide and didn't even break a sweat. But I can't see why silencing someone's keen would *ever* be the best course of action." He shot a look at Niall, who pressed his lips together.

"Fear can be—"

"She used her song tonight?" Nazali asked, cutting Niall off.

"She didn't really have a choice."

"Did you see the faces of any of the other attackers that weren't the shrouded one?"

"No, they were hooded. One knew Deana though. He told her she would join her brother soon."

"How did Idir react to Deana using her keen?" Niall asked.

"He was furious."

Niall and Nazali shared a look. That infuriating look that elders often shared when they were holding back what could be important information in the hope it would all just go away. But holding back hadn't stopped Evard and then Leon from dragging the world to the edge of destruction, and it wouldn't help now. He opened his mouth to tell them exactly that when a scream tore through the building.

"Not again," Niall said, reaching the door in several long strides.

"No," Nazali's tone was heavy. "That was Deana."

CHAPTER FIVE

DEANA

A guard grabbed Deana the moment she entered the palace. Stony faced, he dragged her to a familiar room in the cliff-side wing of the palace.

"You are to wait here until Idir gets back," the guard ordered as he closed the door, leaving Deana alone.

The space was small, barely three strides by four strides, with a single window that looked out to the ocean. But the window didn't provide an escape route, just a long drop to a hopefully quick death against the jagged rocks below. Deana had spent a fair amount of time in this room over the past few years; the days immediately after the shrouded ones had come and taken Kai, she had barely left it.

Was that to be the case now? Even if they found Samir, Idir would want to question her about the attack, and Bran, too, most likely. He had admitted to seeing the shrouded one. Surely Idir couldn't let that slide. She drew a breath and paced from the window to the door and then back again. It was surprising that she hadn't worn a channel in the floor over those days she had spent locked in here.

After a while, Idir finally entered. His mouth was drawn tight and there was a sternness in his gaze that sent her thoughts reeling back to the time after Kai's death.

"Shouldn't you be out looking for Samir?" she asked.

"The guards are scouring the shoreline and the forest, but I fear the boy is already lost to us."

Sorrow thickened her throat, and she swallowed.

"I need you to tell me everything that occurred on that beach tonight. Everything you saw ... or *thought* you saw." He leant against the door and folded his arms.

"I—"

"The *truth,* Deana. Every. Last. Detail." His song pushed against hers, and her hands started shaking. "It will be a lot less painful if you just let me in. You know that."

She licked her lips as she tried to organise her thoughts. There were things she didn't want him to see—to know. She needed to hold those secrets tight and give him everything else he wanted.

"Let. Me. In." Each word was punctuated by a push of his song.

Closing her eyes, she lowered her mental walls just enough for his song to surge into her mind. It dragged against hers, pulling her beneath the waves of her own memories as though it would drown her. Her whole being trembled, lungs screaming for air, but no matter how hard she fought she couldn't break free from that cruel undertow. Then pain sliced through her temples, and she fell to the floor. Images of the day flashed across her mind at sickening speed, but they slowed as they reached the ceremony when she had seen the shrouded one on the beach. They picked up speed again until—

Moonlight danced over the rock pool. Deana hugged her knees tighter to her chest as the song of the ocean pulled against her. It wanted her to use her magic, to enter the waves and drift down to the deep. To give her soul to Grandmother Ocean. Her song was a piece—

She fought against Idir, pushing him from her mind.

"Deana," he warned.

Her breath was coming in rapid gasps, but it was not enough to fill her lungs and spots were dancing across her vision. Idir's song increased until it drowned out even the rush of her own blood in her ears.

She was wandering back to her house when she heard the first scream and then saw the shrouded one fleeing the palace with Samir slung over her shoulder. The creature stopped and studied Deana; her skeletal arm lifted. Flesh twisted over the bone as the hand transformed. The rest of her form changed along with it; she had been beautiful when she was living. She moved closer to Deana, and time seemed to stand still. Then she tilted her hand as though she would cup Deana's cheek, but Deana's fingers gripped the—

"No!" Deana pulled herself to her feet and shied away from Idir.

"What is it you don't want me to see? Why did the shrouded one spare you?"

Deana's eyes widened. "You know they're real," she whispered.

"Of course, I know they are real," Idir growled.

"Then why—" She didn't get to finish as his song crashed against hers, dragging her back under.

The sensation of rolling head over tail washed over her as his song surged through her mind, bashing against the wall that held all her secrets. She couldn't let him wear it down. Her teeth sunk into her lip, the pain and taste of blood strengthening her resolve, and she managed to free herself from his hold again.

The stone was burning against her chest. Instinctively, she reached for it, but Idir tracked the movement and pounced. He slammed her against the wall by the window with one broad forearm as he tore her fingers away from the neckline of her shirt with his free hand. His eyes widened as they studied the stone gripped in her fingers.

"That little bastard sold his soul for divine protection." He looked like he might laugh but instead he reached for the stone.

The moment his fingers brushed it, he let out a yell, tearing his hand away as though he had been burned. One half of his face decayed before her eyes, gaunt, coral-studded skin replacing the soft, deep-brown flesh.

Deana couldn't hold back her scream. Thrashing free of his grasp she rushed for the door, but it was locked tight. She pounded her fists against the wood. "Let me out. Please?" Her voice caught in a rasp at the back of her throat as she hammered against the door once more before turning.

Idir had recovered. He edged towards her.

There was no way to escape. Her gaze landed on the window, and she took a hesitant step towards it.

"You won't survive that fall—just ask your brother."

What had he just said? The shrouded ones had taken Kai. She'd seen—

Idir lunged. She dodged around him and grabbed the windowsill.

Sucking in a breath, she vaulted out into the night. She was weightless for the space of two heartbeats then the air rushed around her as she sped towards the rocks below. Fear had stolen the sound of the world, twisting everything into a void of white silence. She found the tread of her own song in the static and latched onto it, fanning her fingers out to the ocean and then closing them and pulling her fist towards her. A funnel of water lifted from the waves, spiralling into a reaching arm that sparkled in the moonlight. The second it touched her it enveloped her, slowing her fall and cradling her as it carried her downwards.

Her lungs tightened as another wave of sorrow and fear rippled through her song. She desperately tried to focus on holding the melody, but it faltered and the waterspout collapsed, pulling her beneath the waves. A current grabbed her, dragging her out into the deeper water. She kicked to the surface, drawing in a burning breath. Her song built again, and she used it to force the current in the opposite direction. It shunted her towards the shore once more and when she reached the shallows, she let it go, digging her feet into the sand to keep her position as it dragged back out.

Once the current had fully righted itself, she waded to the beach and collapsed onto the sand. She couldn't stay here. Idir would have seen her save herself and it wouldn't be long before he came looking for her. After pulling her aching body up, she took several stumbling steps before breaking into a run. She didn't know where she would go, but she had to get out of the village.

Hurrying into her house, she spared only a moment to brush her fingers against the doorframe before she grabbed a bag and started throwing various items into it. She turned to leave, only to come face to face with Savita.

"What are you doing, Deana?" she asked sweetly.

"Nothing." She hid her bag behind her back.

"It doesn't look like nothing. It looks like you're running away."

Deana swallowed. In her panic she had let her guard down and the cloying notes of Savita's song had slid around her as effectively as the silken coils of a python.

"Why don't we just sit down?"

"I don't want to sit down," she replied, but her body jerked towards a chair.

"I am sure you'll feel much better once we've had a little chat," Savita purred.

Deana's knees shook as she fought against Savita's song. "No. I don't want to have a little chat. I want you to leave!" The second the last word left Deana's lips, the air in the room tightened, and Savita's eyes widened as her song lost its grip on Deana.

A flurry of wind and mind-numbing sound started in the room, and Savita jerked towards the door.

"What are you doing to me?" she hissed.

"I'm not doing anything." But her ancestors were—generations of magic soaked into the very foundations of the house—there was no more powerful protection charm in the world.

Savita gripped the doorframe as the wind in the room increased. With an enraged screech, she was dragged outside and tossed unceremoniously down the stairs.

Deana didn't wait to see if Savita got up. She slammed the door and bolted out the back.

Her mother's garden was blanketed in shadows, but Deana could navigate it with her eyes closed. She hurried between the overgrown beds, careful to avoid the plants that tumbled over the sides. The tree line was her target. If she could reach it, she would be hidden. Savita certainly didn't know the forest like Deana did, and by the time anyone from the palace caught her trail, she would be long gone. She wasn't sure where she was going; at this stage, she was simply running on instinct.

Staying was not an option. Not only did Idir know about the stone, but he was one of them. The shrouded ones. The myths had always said they were female, but Deana had seen his true face with her own eyes.

Footsteps sounded behind her, followed by a thump and a muffled curse. She picked up pace, pushing through the dense undergrowth and trying to control her breathing. If she let her panic overtake her and left a clear trail, she might as well have just laid down in the centre of the village and waited for Idir to find her.

Dawn was colouring the world as Deana stumbled. She bit back her cry of pain as her already grazed knees took the brunt of the fall. Her entire body was exhausted, but she couldn't stop now even though she was certain she wasn't being followed. She needed to get off the island; if she stayed, Idir would find her.

Fighting the urge to just lay down in the loam and let sleep claim her, she pushed herself to her feet and leant against a tree as she brushed the detritus from her knees and palms before starting forward again.

The trees were beginning to thin. If she hadn't gotten herself turned around in the dark forest, then she would emerge onto a small beach with a dilapidated fishing hut. Kai had shown it to her several years ago. He'd said it belonged to a widow who had lost his heart mate during a storm. No one else came here because they thought it was haunted. But Deana loved the song of this beach despite its melancholic nature.

Sure enough, she broke from the tree line onto a small crescent of white sand. The waters of the cove were glistening with the first rays of sunlight. The hut was mostly unchanged. Perhaps the roof looked a little more sunken and the deck was missing a few more boards. She nearly stumbled again, this time from relief and not fatigue, but caught herself and hurried across the sand to the side of the hut before carefully climbing onto the deck. She and Kai had stashed a canoe inside last time they had been here. It was perfect for exploring the bay, but now it would have to serve as her means of escaping the island.

Over the last few hours, she had formulated a plan. She would head for Armada, the floating city. Kai had always said that if you wanted to hide then Armada should be the first place you went. It was technically part of the isles and yet it had its own culture. Much like the fabled island of Quel'sapar. She had often wondered if Quel'sapar had been inspired by Armada or if it was the other way around. The only problem was she had never been to the floating city. She knew, though, if she set a course to the east, she would eventually crash into it. Once she reached Armada, she would hide there or maybe find someone willing to take her away from the isles. She didn't have much she could pay with, but her mother's turquoise and sapphire necklace was still around her neck. Perhaps it could buy her passage to Osmar.

Her limbs trembled as she started to push the canoe outside, and she paused, rubbing a hand across her brow as she studied the tree line. *Would it be safe to stop here and rest?* Reaching Armada would rely heavily on the use of her song, and her reserves were running extremely low. She shook her head. There was a chance others would think to look for her here. She could get herself to one of the smaller islands and rest there before moving on. Nodding, she gave the canoe another shove and it scraped out the hole in the wall.

By the time she got the canoe into the water, she was covered in sweat. It combined with the tackiness left on her clothes and skin from her dowsing in the ocean last night. Not to mention the grime from her dash through the jungle. She would have loved to have a quick wash, but the sound of branches crunching snapped her to attention.

"There!" Came a shout as several men emerged from the trees.

She vaulted into the canoe and drew her song to the surface. Hopefully none of them were silencers. The ocean surged beneath her boat, and she was thrown back as it rocketed forward.

The men had rushed into the shallows as though they would give chase, but she was moving too fast. She released a sigh and gripped the sides of the boat as their forms became smaller and the canoe raced out into the open water. Now she just had to maintain her focus and hope she could find a place to rest before her song gave out and the ocean devoured her.

CHAPTER SIX

BRAN

Bran started for the door, but Nazali caught his arm.

"Idir is questioning her about what happened with Samir. You need to stay out of his way."

"People don't scream like that when they are being *questioned*." He pulled his arm free and darted out into the hall.

He didn't know which way to go, but then he heard an enraged roar and rushed towards it. As he raced around a corner into a hall he had never been down before, a door to his right was wrenched open and a furious Idir appeared on the threshold.

"What did you do to her?" The words were out before Bran could stop them.

The fury in Idir's face shifted into a cool indifference as he studied Bran then flicked a look over his shoulder at the room behind him. "She jumped. I couldn't stop her," he said without even the barest hint of emotion.

Bran dodged around him into the room. The space was empty of furniture and there was only one door and window. He rushed to the window, gripping the sill as he studied the sickening drop to the jagged rocks below. No one would survive a fall like that, but it was hard to tell if any of the pooling shadows were actually a body lying broken against the rocks.

What had Idir done? Had his line of questioning driven Deana to jump, or had he simply thrown her out the window when she refused to give him the answers he wanted?

A hand on his shoulder made him tighten his grip on the windowsill.

"What happened on the beach?" Idir asked him slowly.

"Nothing that we didn't tell you already," Bran said, keeping his voice level as he shrugged the hand from his shoulder and casually stepped away from the window.

"So, you stand by the story that a shrouded one took Samir?" There was a note in Idir's voice that Bran couldn't quite place.

"It was a wraith of some description. Whether or not it was a shrouded one I don't know, but Deana certainly thought it was." He edged towards the door.

"Well ... Deana would know." The corner of Idir's mouth twitched.

Was that an admission that the shrouded ones were real?

The cloying fingers of mind magic brushed the edges of Bran's thoughts. The moment he tried to pull away, Idir's keen surged forward, the weight of it burrowing into his mind drove him to his knees. He gripped his skull and tried to bring his mental walls up, but he couldn't stop the onslaught. His keen fluctuated erratically as Idir tore through his memories before he zeroed in on one in particular ...

Nea's keen ran like ice through his veins, melding with his own until it was nearly impossible to distinguish where one keen stopped and the other started. He looked down at his wrist. The bloodied skin was now marked with a dark-purple crescent moon.

With a grunt, he pushed back against Idir, but it was futile. Then a familiar sensation reached the edge of his keen-sense and Idir was driven out of his mind as the heavy numbness of suppression rolled over them.

Bran opened his eyes to a pair of booted feet. The large, auburn-haired warden who owned them had Idir pinned to the wall. Beside the two men was the glimmering miasma of a portal. Bran blinked. The rose pendant was digging into the palm of his hand—in his panic he must have used it to call to Nea.

The door slammed open, and Bran sat up as Niall and Nazali came rushing in.

Nazali stared open-mouthed at the portal and stepped toward it with her hand lifted. "How?" she whispered as the portal snapped shut.

"This is unnecessary." Idir shifted in Garret's grip, but the warden didn't release him.

"I am sure Garret would not have left Beldaren without good cause," Niall said.

"Nea gave me this before we left, so I could contact her if I needed anything." Bran showed Niall the spirit anchor. "When Idir attacked me, I reached for it on impulse."

"I didn't attack him. I was making sure he wasn't withholding details about Samir's disappearance."

"It seemed to me like you were torturing him from inside his own mind," Garret said, a hint of a growl in his tone.

"Where's Deana?" Nazali asked softly, and Bran's gaze flicked to the window.

"Idir—"

"She jumped before I could stop her."

Bran bit down on the inside of his cheek.

Nazali rushed to the window and leant out of it. When she turned back to the room, there was a dark look in her eyes. "What did you do to her?" she asked coldly.

"I did nothing. She was raving about the shrouded ones and

then she threw herself from the window."

The old necromancer held up her hand and the air around her instantly cooled. The warm crackle of Garret's brightling keen rose in response. It brushed alongside Bran's magic in an inquisitive, almost hungry, flurry. Nazali closed her eyes and the world stilled. Bran let his own keen out and it followed the path of Nazali's magic before merging with it just as the re-enactment started. Hazy shadows appeared in the room. They flickered with streaks of violet magic until they solidified.

Idir stood over Deana as she writhed on the floor, her hands clamped tightly over her ears. Suddenly, she stood.

Re-enactments had no sound, but it was clear she had shouted 'no'.

As Idir said something to her, she backed away from him, eyes wide. He advanced again, and she squeezed her eyes shut as her knees buckled. Her hand reached beneath the neckline of her shirt, and Idir lunged, slamming her against the wall and wrenching her hand away from her chest. She had a seer stone clutched tightly in her palm. When Idir reached for it, he recoiled as though stung and one side of his face transformed. Deana screamed and broke from his hold to rush towards the door. She pulled against the handle and pounded her palm against the wood. Her wide, panicked gaze fell on Idir as she spun around to face the room once more. Then he said something that sent a tremor through her body before making another lunge for her. She dodged around him and vaulted out the window—

Bran followed the re-enactment to the window.

Deana's body twisted through the air, and she threw her hands out. A massive swell rose from the surface of the ocean, forming into a reaching arm and—

The re-enactment ended. Nazali slumped beside him, her fingers against her chest as she drew a series of ragged breaths.

"You're one of them," Bran said, turning to Idir. "You're a shrouded one."

Idir let out a snort of laughter. "No, I am not one of those bottom feeders. I have much more autonomy than that." He twisted, and Garret lost his grip.

Before any of them could stop him, he charged between Bran and Nazali, grabbing the old necromancer and dragging her out the window. Nazali let out a scream as her body plummeted and smashed against the rocks below. The ocean rose to meet Idir as it had done Deana. It cushioned his fall and deposited him neatly beside the rocks.

"We have to get out of here," Bran said. "Garret, you need to get Niall home now. I am sure Idir will blame us for Nazali's death and possibly Samir's disappearance as well."

"Fleeing will only confirm our guilt. We need to speak with Chief Soma," Niall argued.

Bran shook his head. "I know what running will look like, but Idir has the power here. With Deana and now Nazali gone, there is no one to confirm our side of the story. And Idir can plant any ideas he wants in Soma's mind."

"Bran's right. Idir has shown that he has no qualms about killing to get what he wants. Nea would never forgive me if I didn't take you home now. You too, Bran. It did not escape my notice that you intend to stay, but I can't allow it."

"I have to find Deana. There is something big at work here, and I think she might have an idea of what it is."

Garret studied Nazali's broken body far below, "Deana wouldn't have survived that fall."

"She used her keen. I think the ocean saved her. I need to find her before Idir does."

Niall let out a long breath. "Bran is right. There is much more to that girl than meets the eye. I believe you will find an ally in

Leilani or even Queen Amara. I would avoid Chief Soma for now and get out of this village as fast as you can." He turned to Garret. "I would like to collect my things before we depart." Niall's keen stirred.

Garret gave a nod and lifted his hand. A glittering oval of purple light opened in front of him. They stepped through into Niall's room and the old mind mage moved to gather his belongings.

"Thank you for the rescue. I imagine Idir would have killed me once he was done tearing information out of my head," Bran said to Garret.

"You're welcome. Be careful, Bran. The sorts of secrets and machinations that appear to be at play here are exactly the sort that the Usurper exploited to free himself from the Between. You could very well be dealing with a similar problem." He clapped Bran on the shoulder. "Do you want me to send you anywhere before we go?"

"No, I'll just gather my things and get out of the village. Wren gave me one of the summoning shells for the Queen, so I will find a secluded spot and use it."

"Ready," Niall said.

"Alright." Garret lifted his palm and another portal appeared.

Niall studied the shimmering oval with a sigh then turned to Bran. "Now, please try not to get yourself killed. Nea will never forgive me for letting you stay if you do." He pulled Bran into a rough hug and then gave him a fatherly smile before nodding to Garret and stepping into the portal.

"Bran, you know where to find us if you need us," Garret said and pointed at the silver rose still hanging outside Bran's shirt.

"I know. Tell Nea not to worry too much. I can't promise I'll stay safe, but I'll try."

Garret laughed and clapped him on the shoulder again. "Good luck. I have a feeling you're going to need it." The warden then disappeared into the portal, and several moments later it snapped shut.

Bran drew a breath and crossed the room to the door; he pressed his ear against the wood. There were no sounds in the hall. He opened the door a crack and peeked out, then he made a quick dash into his own room. After throwing everything into his bag, he crept back out into the hallway and to the door at the end that led to the covered walkway. He wasn't sure where he should go, but he wanted to check Deana's house first. It might hold clues on where to find her.

Sticking to the shadows, he edged from building to building until he reached the short incline to Deana's house. A dark lump was slumped at the foot of the stairs and his pulse quickened. Had Idir reached her first? He rushed forward, but it was Savita. She was still breathing but there was a nasty gash above her eye and a thick bruise forming along the side of her face. Someone moved inside the house, and Bran hurried up the stairs.

"Stop," Leilani cautioned as he went to step over the threshold. "You need to introduce yourself to the house. Deana set off the protection charm before she fled."

"Introduce myself to the house? How?" The lock-stone outside Hartswood required blood.

"Touch your palm to the doorway and let it hear your song. The ancestors will then decide if you may enter or not."

Bran placed his hand against the doorframe where the wood was worn so smooth it felt like velvet under his palm. He let his keen out. A small piece broke away and burrowed into the wood, then the whole house seemed to give a shudder.

"Well, Deana doesn't seem to like you, but her ancestors sure do," Leilani said a little breathlessly. "You can come in now."

"Is it some kind of ward?" he asked as he stepped inside.

The green mage light bobbing around Leilani's head cast

shadows across the floor, highlighting the overturned chairs and other debris. It looked like a storm had raged through the house.

"It's not a ward as such. It's ..." She placed the instrument she was holding, a kind of lute maybe, on the table and ran her fingers over the strings. "I don't know how to describe it really. It's ancestral magic. Old and almost forgotten, we go about the time-honoured rituals because our parents did and their parents before them. That gives the charm its power."

He could understand that part. Hartswood existed within its own enchanted bubble. The ancestors were so powerful there that even the weather was affected to a degree. "Is that what happened to Savita? She tried to enter without honouring the tradition?" If someone tried to enter Hartswood without performing the ritual at the lock-stone, the ancestors would simply not reveal the true path to the estate.

Leilani shook her head. "Before Deana triggered the protection charm, you would have been able to come and go as you pleased. It's complicated magic. Savita must have done something to make Deana activate it."

Bran examined the room before settling his gaze on Leilani once more. "Idir is a shrouded one and he killed Nazali."

Her hand went to her mouth. "It can't be. He wouldn't have been able to hide it from everyone for so long."

"He's a very gifted mind mage. I am sure erasing someone's memory if they found out would be child's play for him." It was clear he wouldn't find answers to where Deana had gone here, and he needed to keep moving. Idir would be looking for him. "Do you know where Deana might have gone?"

"Armada," she said, retrieving a journal from a small cabinet at the side of the room. "Kai told me that if anything were to happen, I should take her to Armada. I should have taken her there after Kai ..." The name had a certain weight to it, like the way Nea said

Kalhanna, as though she needed to steady her own resolve before it could pass her lips. "Died. But I didn't think Idir—there was no way I could have known he would—he was." She gripped the journal so tight her knuckles paled. "Here." She held it out to him. "If you find Deana, give her this and tell her to find Elijah. He can help her."

"You don't want to come with me?" he asked.

She gave both the journal and her head a small shake. "I need to stay here with Indira and Amara. If Idir is as you say, I want to be here to protect them and, if it comes to it, help them escape."

Bran licked his lip and took the journal. "And how exactly does one get to Armada?"

"Follow me."

Leilani led him through the dark village. They moved slowly from shadow to shadow until they reached a hut at the edge of the beach. She climbed the stairs and knocked quietly, then as the door opened said, "Sorry to wake you, but I need a favour."

The woman inside opened the door wider and waved them in.

"Bran, this is my sister, Malani. Mal, this is Bran. He needs to get to Armada."

The woman in question was tall and slender, her skin several shades darker than Leilani's and her eyes a bright whisky-brown. But there were similarities in the lines of their faces, and when Malani's mouth split into a welcoming grin those resemblances only deepened. "Run afoul of Idir have you, Whitecap?"

"How?"

"It might be the middle of the night, but news travels fast in this village. So, did you push poor old Nazali out that window?"

"No. That was Idir. If you thought I had murdered your highest-ranking soul-singer, why did you welcome me into your home?"

She shrugged. "Curiosity. Also, I don't believe you did it. But Idir? Now that I can believe."

"Mal, we don't have a lot of time."

"Always in such a hurry, little Lei-Lei."

"If Idir catches us—"

"He's too busy searching for Deana, and he's already been by here tonight. He thought she might have come to me looking for passage off the island. Actually, you only just missed him."

"We should move while we still have the cover of night," Bran said. "It will only be harder once the whole village is awake."

Malani grabbed a bag and threw some things into it. "Come on then, before the pair of you birth those kittens in the middle of my kitchen."

"I'm not coming. I have to get back to the palace," Leilani said as she made for the door.

"You be careful, little Lei-Lei." Malani gave her sister a hug and then turned to Bran. "Alright, Whitecap. Let's go rouse the crew."

CHAPTER SEVEN

AGNES

Armada had been Agnes' home for as long as she could remember. It might be called the floating city, but it wasn't technically floating in that it drifted about the ocean completely untethered. It was anchored to a small hunk of land that really couldn't be called an island. In fact, the construction of the city was rather fascinating once you got past the surface view of it being a bunch of wrecked ships clinging to a pathetic slice of rock in the middle of the boundless deep blue sea. The ships had been cobbled together over time to form a semblance of a raft that shifted with the tide. A necessary construction feature given the island sometimes completely disappeared under the ocean. That's how the first ship, The Whore's Mongrel, ended up marooned. Her captain, Lord Ferdinand, of some place that no longer existed, had thought he had met his doom, but another ship—The Grey Spaniel, captained by a merchant prince whose name Agnes could never remember—came to Lord Ferdinand's aid only to find himself likewise wrecked. And on it went until more than a dozen ships had fallen victim or been *salvaged*.

Now Armada was home to not degenerates and pirates as such—

most of those preferred Quel'sapar—but society's rejects. Those who didn't fit in for whatever reason ... or didn't want to. Those who were hiding because they knew something they shouldn't, like Agnes' father.

Agnes let out a breath as she leant over the balcony and admired the view. This time of morning had always been her favourite. When the purple-grey of twilight gave way to a line of gold on the horizon and splashes of apricot and rose were thrown across the sky like a child had run amok in a room full of paint pots. The rolling swell that lapped gently against the edges of Armada reflected the colours in shards like a rippling field of broken glass. Watching the display was almost enough to stir her keen and she inhaled slowly, quelling the rising urge before the telltale tingle started in her fingers. After giving herself another few moments to admire the view, she moved away from the balcony and headed down to the section of the city known as the underbelly.

Here on the tide-slick rocks beneath the bulk of the city it was always gloomy. But the crabs liked it—probably because farther around towards the other side of the city was where Kent dumped the bodies of those who he took offence to. A convenient disposal system and an easy meal of waterlogged flesh for the scavengers. The crabs were what Agnes was here for; she and her father set traps for the large crustaceans. Most people on Armada did. The cargo ships were not always frequent and space in their holds was at a high premium, one which the wealthier citizens of Armada tended to monopolise. But the ocean would always provide, not just food but other resources too, which was why scavenging was such a big part of life on Armada. One man's trash and all that.

As Agnes moved to check the first crab pot, a scraping sound followed by a bump caught her attention.

She followed the sound, climbing carefully over the slippery rocks until she found its source. An abandoned canoe. That was certainly something you didn't see every day, at least this far out in the ocean. The islanders used these small vessels, but they never took them outside the safety of their shallows. How did this one get here?

Edging closer, she adjusted her satchel so it sat against the back of her hips and had less chance of dragging through the water. There was a lump in the bottom of the canoe. At first it looked like a pile of old cloth, but one dark shape stuck out that looked an awful lot like a leg and another that—

"Yeah, that's a hand." Agnes had seen plenty of dead bodies before. It was just one of those things that came with living in a place like Armada. This one looked and—she gave a tentative sniff—smelled fresh. That was almost a relief. It would make looking for salvageable items a little less gruesome. She didn't enjoy salvaging, not the way some of the others did, but it was a necessary part of life in the floating city.

The fingers attached to the hand twitched, and the pile of cloth let out a long groan as a young woman around Agnes' age sat up.

"How in the Bright's name?" As Agnes spoke, the girl's attention snapped to her.

She had the brightest teal-coloured eyes Agnes had ever seen. The islanders referred to it as touched by Grandmother Ocean and, depending on other factors surrounding the birth of the person, it was either a blessing or a curse. To Agnes, however, the contrast of the bright eyes against the girl's warm brown skin and the dark curls that hung around her face was simply beautiful.

"Hello. I'm Agnes," she said.

"Where am I?" the girl asked. Her voice was raspy, and her lips, on closer inspection, cracked and dry.

How long had she been in this canoe? Depending on which island she'd come from, it could have been days. The girl's mouth twisted as Agnes studied her. "Oh, sorry. You're at Armada. Or more technically, underneath it."

Was that relief that dropped the girl's shoulders or something else?

"What's your name?"

The girl's attention seemed fixated on Agnes' hair, which wasn't really a surprise. Red wasn't exactly a common colour on the islands, but even other Beldarens, at least her father said they were originally from Beldaren, often stared. After all, it wasn't a lovely deep red but a bright, almost glowing, copper. Apparently, she got it from her mother—her freckles, too—but Agnes had never met her. She had died when Agnes was just a baby.

"So ..." She shifted, suddenly uncomfortable under the girl's scrutiny.

"Deana," the girl said after a few moments.

"Well, Deana, are you hungry? My dad should have breakfast ready by the time we climb back up. You're welcome to join us."

Deana's brow furrowed and something flashed behind her eyes. "You don't have to ... I can just find my own way."

Was this girl not used to people with manners?

"Ah," Agnes said with a nod.

If she had to guess, she would say that on the island Deana was from she was considered one of those cursed by Grandmother Ocean, not blessed. The waterlogged canoe made a little more sense now. So, was Deana running away or had she been driven out? And how had she managed to survive the journey in that tiny excuse for a boat?

"Come on. My father and I don't turn away those who need help, and we don't believe in curses."

The furrow in Deana's brow deepened.

"You could stay here if you'd rather, but the other scavengers won't be so friendly."

That got her moving. She stood and the canoe gave a wobble, nearly tipping her out onto the rocks.

"Take it easy. It's slick as an eel's stomach out here, and watch the barnacles—they slice you to ribbons before you realise they've done it. Do you mind helping me check the crab pots before we head up?"

Deana shook her head.

"Come on then. It won't take long."

"Dad?" Agnes called as she led Deana into the berth she and her father occupied. "Crab pots were light today. I've already taken Nari's share to her."

Silence greeted her. That was strange.

"Wait here," she said to Deana, then headed along the hall to her father's study.

She knocked once. "Dad?"

The door pulled open so suddenly that she had to bite back a gasp. "Dad, you scared—" She bit down on her words and backed up. "Kent, I didn't realise you were here."

Kent was as close to a ruler as Armada had. He wasn't exactly what you would expect—thin and wiry and much younger than his predecessor. His dark hair was twisted into a series of thin dreadlocks that reached the tips of his shoulder blades. He wasn't an islander. Agnes wasn't sure where he was from. She couldn't really make sense of the lines of his face or the olive tone of his skin. He looked like some combination of Osmarian and Islander but with a little Beldaren thrown in for good measure. A true mongrel if ever there was one, with the personality to match.

"Agnes." He almost purred her name, and she fought the urge to snort. Kent really did like to play up the whole charismatic overlord persona. "I was actually looking for you," Kent continued as he closed the distance and touched a finger to her chin. "I have a commission for your particular skills."

She turned her face away from him and pressed back against the wall. "I think you're in the wrong berth. The girls you're looking for are down the other end of the row."

"Very funny. You are lucky that you and your father are so useful. Otherwise that tongue of yours would make you shark bait."

"Kent, leave the girl be," a voice Agnes hadn't heard in a while said.

"I'm serious about that commission. Come and see me later," Kent said softly before taking a step back. "Your business is concluded then I take it?" he said louder as he turned to face the man who had spoken.

He was as tall as Kent but a little thicker set. The sides of his head were shaved to reveal a tattoo in the shape of crashing waves. A heavy gold earring hung from one of his ears, and his lips were split into a wide, easygoing smile. His features were some combination of Osmarian and Faridean, his skin a deep bronze and his eyes a warm brown. He tilted his head as he studied Agnes, and she shifted her feet as a ticklish feeling made the hairs on the back of her neck stand on end.

"Hello, Agnes." His voice had a smooth, deep timbre that sent a quiver down to her knees.

"Varlan?" Agnes hadn't seen him in a good two—maybe three—years, but when her mind drifted to that time, some parts were foggy and others almost completely blank. "What are you doing here?"

His mouth quirked and he thrust his thumb over his shoulder to indicate the door to her father's study. "I have a job for Elijah."

"Are you done here or not?" Kent asked, snark evident in his tone. He seemed to begrudgingly respect Varlan, which Agnes had always found a little odd; Kent didn't respect anyone. He categorised people into those who were useful and those who were not worth his time.

"I'm done for now," Varlan replied, dragging his attention away from Agnes to settle it on Kent.

"Good, let's leave." Kent moved to go but then turned around. "Please don't keep me waiting, Agnes. I would hate to have to make an example of you and your father."

She puffed her cheeks out as she watched the two men disappear into the kitchen and then rushed into her father's study. "Dad? Are you alright? Did Kent and—"

"Slow down, Agnes. I'm fine. Varlan just needs a map, and Kent was a perfect gentleman. He always is when Varlan is around." He chuckled but sobered quickly. "You shouldn't delay seeing Kent about that commission." He stood behind his desk. "Now, what were you saying about the crab pots?"

Crab pots? Shit. She'd left Deana on her own in the kitchen. Varlan and Kent would have seen her on their way out for sure. She spun around and raced back into the other room. There was no sign of Deana. The bag of crabs was on the table where Agnes had dumped it. One of the large, green crustaceans had navigated its way free and was edging across the tabletop.

"What's the matter?" her father asked her, his hand landing on her shoulder and giving it a squeeze.

"I met someone and she—" A sneeze sounded from the direction of the door. "Deana?"

The cupboard tucked in the corner opened and Deana crawled out. "I heard them coming and I—" Her teal gaze locked onto Agnes's father and her brow furrowed.

An unsteady feeling rocked across Agnes as though she were standing in a small boat on a choppy ocean, but it passed quickly.

"Something happened to Kai then? You have my sincere condolences; he was a good lad."

Hang on. Who was Kai? How did her father know Deana? *What in the stars is going on today?*

"You knew my brother?" Deana's lip quivered.

Agnes' father nodded. "Did you bring his journal?"

"Journal?" Deana shook her head. "I don't know anything about a journal."

"You are here to see me, aren't you? Kai told you to come find me if anything happened to him?"

"I don't think she is, Dad. I found her washed up in the underbelly when I was checking the traps," Agnes said, moving to make a pot of tea.

"I thought that I might find help on Armada, but I didn't have any names, and Kai never mentioned a journal."

Agnes' father shooed the crab onto the floor and dropped into his usual seat at the table. "Without the journal, I can't—Varlan." He snapped his fingers. "It's not a coincidence he showed up today. Agnes, get my parchment and quill, please. Deana, I need to know everything that happened the night you fled. Every last detail you can remember."

Deana chewed her lip and hugged her arms around herself. "I'm not—"

"I know it might be hard to relive, but it's very important."

Agnes studied Deana. "Could it wait, Dad? She's been through a lot and look at her. She needs a good meal and a warm bed. She can stay here, right?"

Her father blinked. "Of course, she can stay here. And you're right, it can wait. Sorry, Deana, I just get carried away sometimes."

"It's a family trait, unfortunately," Agnes said brightly. "We haven't got much, but I'll fix you some breakfast and then show you to my room. You can rest there while I go up and see what sort of commission Kent wants."

"Commission?" Deana asked, but her gaze was on the crab that was making a break for the shadows in the corner of the room.

"I'm a tinkerer. I build things. The best one on Armada actually, on account of my tiny hands and big brain. The hands make it easier to get into tight places and complete the delicate tasks and the brain helps with the calculations and inspiration."

"The keen helps too," her father said, and at Deana's confused look, added, "Her magic. She's what we call a creationist. Her knack lays with building things, though she has an affinity for metal specifically."

"Oh, that explains her song then," Deana whispered, and Agnes' father laughed.

"I'm told it's not the prettiest of sounds to you islanders."

Deana shook her head. "It's unique, more like tapping and drumming, very little melody, but it has a distinct rhythm. I wouldn't say it's not pretty; all songs are beautiful." Something darkened her eyes. "Most songs," she added so quietly Agnes nearly had to read her lips to catch it.

Once she had Deana settled, Agnes grabbed the bag containing her sketching materials and headed out of the berth. Her father had returned to his study to work on whatever map Varlan had commissioned. Maps were her father's gift, so much so that he could draw them in his sleep, and he often did. He was a sleepwalker, and Agnes worried that one night he'd wander right off the side of Armada. But he didn't seem to leave the house. In fact, it wasn't so much sleepwalking as it was sleep-cartography. Still, she made sure to lock the berth door every night just in case.

She hummed to herself as she walked along the catwalk towards the stairs that would lead her to the market level. There were other ways to reach the upper levels, but she enjoyed going through the market, especially on days when the cargo ships came in. She had seen the sails of Malani's ship on the horizon earlier when she and Deana had been checking the crab pots. Malani always brought the most interesting cargo. She probably hadn't had a chance to unload it yet, but a quick wander through the stalls wouldn't hurt.

As she crossed the open space, the vendors called out to her, but it was Gethyn whom she stopped in to see. The old Osmarian tented his long, gnarled fingers as she ducked under the purple awning of his stall.

"Out of ink already? Or just wasting Kent's time?" he asked with an almost feline grin.

"Oh, you know, a little of both," she replied as she reached for one of the bottles of ink on the top shelf.

Gethyn stood from his chair and retrieved the bottle for her. "It is a dangerous game to play. One day he will decide your disrespect has outweighed your usefulness."

She shrugged and took the bottle from him. "I respect him. Knowing what he is capable of, I would be a fool not to. But I refuse to be intimidated by him."

"He would not make that distinction." He moved to his counter again and pulled out a tray from beneath it. A beautiful collection of wooden quills lay on the green velvet cloth. "These just arrived from Osmar."

Agnes stroked her finger along one of the thin wooden rods, stopping as she reached its pointed tip. It was a deep red piece of mahogany and seemed to zing against her skin. "You know I can't afford the likes of these."

"How about a trade?"

She curled her fingers back from the tray. "I doubt I have anything you would want."

"Not yet, but you will." He leant closer and lowered his voice. "I want to know what Kent is up to. You fill me in on what he asks of you today and you can have your pick of these."

"I don't know. If he found out that I told you ..."

Gethyn shrugged and slid the tray back beneath his counter. "I am certainly not going to tell him. But I will leave it up to you." He held his hand out for payment of the ink.

"Why do you want to know what he is up to?" she asked as she dropped a few coins into his palm.

He tucked the coins away and settled into his chair. "Because this time I believe he is planning something that could destroy everything we have here, and if that is the case, I can't just sit back and let it happen."

"I'll think about it," she said as she backed out of the stall.

"That is all I can ask."

Very little could dampen Agnes' mood, but Gethyn's request had settled a lump deep in her stomach that refused to shift as she crossed the market to the stairs that led to Kent's berth. The guards posted at the bottom stepped together to block her path.

"He's expecting me."

One of them snapped his fingers and pointed to her bag. "You know the rules."

Fighting the urge to roll her eyes, she handed the bag to him.

He rifled through it with no concern for the items inside; the bag still had stains from the time one of the guards had managed to smash one of her inkpots. After a few moments, he thrust it back at her.

"Satisfied?"

"With the bag, yeah." He nodded to the other guard, who took a step towards her. "Arms out."

"Oh, for the love of Bright." But she complied, spreading both her arms and her legs.

The guard gave her a rough patting down then nodded to the other one before they both stepped back to let her pass.

Agnes took the stairs two at a time and was slightly out of breath when she finally reached what the locals referred to as the crow's nest—Kent's berth and the city's guard tower all in one. She made her way along the wide catwalk that encircled the entire level. Ignoring the smaller rooms that broke off the walkway, she headed straight for the spacious chamber that Kent used as a mockery of a throne room. As though he was king and not just the self-appointed leader of a bunch of riffraff living in the middle of the ocean.

"Agnes, so nice of you to finally join us." He waved his hand and several of the people in the room left until only Kent, Varlan, and herself were present. "If you would give us a moment, Varlan."

The man in question studied Kent and then Agnes, his mouth tucking in at one side before he gave a nod and exited the room.

"Finally," Kent said and flopped into his throne-like chair. He didn't sit in it like a proper king, but rather he lounged with one leg tossed over the side and the other in front, booted toes pointing towards her as he rested an arm over his cocked knee and his chin on the knuckles of the other hand. "What do you think makes a great ruler? The kind that people will remember generations after his death?"

"History likes the heroes, I guess. They're the ones who get all the stories told about them."

He drummed his fingers against his chin. "Do you think I am hero material?"

"I don't know, and unless there is a great cataclysm looming, we're not exactly going to find out."

A laugh rumbled from him, and he sat up straighter. "So generous to give me a chance in this hypothetical scenario. But what if it wasn't hypothetical, and what if instead of being the hero, I wanted to be the villain?"

She swallowed. "You certainly have the melodramatic personality for it. But I don't see how I can help—"

He silenced her with a lifted hand. "Get your drawing things out." He indicated the small table and chair set off to the side from his throne.

She sat and pulled her journal, inkpot, and pen from her bag. Then checking the nib of the pen with the pad of her thumb she settled her gaze on Kent again.

"I am finding Armada constrictive of late, and an old acquaintance has come to me with a most alluring proposition. I can have complete rule of the isles if I assist him in his endeavours to find the unfindable."

"Does this acquaintance have anything to do with Varlan's return to Armada?" Agnes asked. A tingle had started in her fingertips as Kent spoke.

"Varlan?" He let out a laugh. "No. He is simply one piece of the puzzle, much like you are."

"You know if you or this acquaintance are looking for something, my father—"

"I don't need a map, my precious little tinkerer. I need a war machine the like of which has never been seen before."

The tingle intensified, and she clenched her fist a few times to dispel it.

"A monstrous machine, a leviathan like those found in the old legends—"

She didn't hear what he said next as a savage twist pulled through her navel and an idea burst to life in the back of her mind. Then her fingers were moving of their own accord, tracing lines and calculations across the page. Her vision went blank as her fingers worked and she was dragged into the trance that accompanied her magic.

A while later, she had ten pages of rough sketches and a lump of dread at the back of her throat.

"Marvellous," Kent said as his hand fell on her shoulder, and he leant forward to examine her work. "That will do for today."

She gathered her things, but as she moved to slide her journal away, he snatched it from her fingers.

"I'll hold on to that." He waved her towards the door. "Oh, and Agnes, this little project is just between us. I would hate to lose a cartographer as skilled as your father."

CHAPTER EIGHT

BRAN

The seabirds swooping overhead filled the air with mournful shrieking as Malani's cargo ship pulled up to what looked like a city constructed from the wrecked carcasses of dozens of seafaring vessels. Cargo carriers and warships had been shackled to longboats and caravels and all manner of boat that Bran couldn't name. It was nearly impossible to distinguish where one ship ended and another began.

"It's magnificent, isn't it?" Malani asked. "A true feat of engineering and more than a little magic."

She was right about the magic. There was a distinct thrum of energy in the air. It wasn't as prominent as it was at Hartswood or magically scarred places like Kalhanna, but it was an undercurrent tugging at the very edge of his keen-sense. Almost like the city was a living thing with a heartbeat. "It's certainly unlike anything I have seen before. Do you know where Elijah might be?"

"He's not the easiest man to find if he doesn't want to be found. You're better off keeping an eye out for his daughter. She stands out like a freshly moulted brightfish."

"Does this daughter have a name?"

"Agnes. Look for the fire-bright hair."

Bran nodded and headed for the gangplank. "Do you think Deana made it here?"

Malani shrugged. "I know most people think she's cursed, but there is something far greater than you or I watching out for her. Chances are if reaching Armada was her goal, she made it. But really, she could be anywhere from here to Osmar."

"Right." He stepped onto the dock.

"If you do find her, Whitecap, send her back here. I may have a contact that can get her somewhere Idir and his undead minions can't reach her." With that, she turned and barked an order at her crew.

Wide walkways connected the different ships to each other. He followed one which seemed to be a main thoroughfare. It led through the outer ring of ships and opened out into a vast room. Stairs branched off at various intervals around the edges of the space, and what looked like a market had been set up in the middle. Natural light was unable to reach this level, so the whole area was lit with strange, glowing lanterns. Each lantern was an intricate cage of filigree metal with a small ball of light at its centre. Were they permanent mage lights? They certainly looked magical in origin, but they didn't feel quite right. Almost as though they were a living entity—or at least an animated one. Like the magic used to animate golems. As he reached toward the closest light, a flash of vibrant copper caught his eye and he half-turned.

At the foot of one of the sets of stairs on the other side of the market, a young woman with vivid, sunset-orange hair was getting patted down by a guard. Seemingly satisfied with his inspection, he and his comrade stepped back to let her pass. She pranced up several steps then threw them a scowl and a rude gesture over her shoulder before continuing.

A quick glance told him it was the only guarded staircase, but there were other armed men, all wearing similar leather armour, dotted about the market. Why the need for so many? He'd have to ask Malani about it when he returned to her ship. Right now, he needed to find somewhere he could watch that staircase for when the woman came back down. Agnes, Malani had said her name was. Across the way was a space that looked like some kind of tavern; the few tables scattered in front of the scarlet and teal tent would provide a good view of the stairs.

He started across the market again when the touch of cloying fingers on the back of his neck drew him up short. Not another mind mage. After Savita and Idir, he'd had his fill of mind mages for a while. He glanced over his shoulder; the feeling was coming from a man standing at the foot of the stairs between the guards. His features were not quite Faridean and yet not quite Osmarian either. The sides of his head were shaved, and he wore an assortment of golden rings around his fingers. Catching Bran's eye, he gave a tiny nod and then strode towards him.

"I recognise your keen," he said by way of greeting. "Except, and no offence meant, it came in a much prettier package last time I felt it."

He had to be referring to the influence of Nea's keen on Bran's. "Some offence taken. I might not be as pretty as Nea, but I don't think I'm that hard on the eyes."

The man stared at him for a moment then let out a laugh and clapped him on the back. "I'm not generally a fan of necromancers, but you I like. Varlan." He held out a hand.

"Bran," he said as he shook the offered hand. "So, how do you know Nea?"

"I double-crossed her and then let her borrow my keen to send a ship through a portal and save both our arses. You?"

"She's family."

"That explains the keen."

It didn't really. Bran and Nea weren't related by blood, but he wasn't going to tell a complete stranger the real reason his keen felt similar to Nea's.

"Were you looking for someone just now?"

Bran shook his head. "It's my first time on Armada, so I'm just learning the lay of the land, so to speak."

Varlan nodded slowly. "Are you here for any particular business?"

"No, I caught a ride on a cargo ship, and this was one of the stops." Not a complete lie. He had arrived on a cargo ship, after all.

"Well, be careful who you trust around here. It's not as seedy as Quel'sapar, but folks here have their own agendas and most would be happy to sell their own mothers if it came to it."

"Present company included?"

Varlan gave a deep, rumbling laugh. "I'm too terrified of my mother to sell her. Do you want to join me for a drink? I'll give you a little history of Armada in exchange for some insight into how Nea managed to fix the barrier."

Bran glanced towards the stairs Agnes had disappeared up. "Sure, why not."

"Excellent." Varlan led him towards the tavern. "Can you create portals like Nea?"

Maybe. He did suspect that he had picked up a few traits of Nea's keen. "No."

"That's a shame. I might have had a job for you if you could."

"I'm not looking for work."

Varlan shrugged and settled himself at a table by the door. "The offer stands if you ever do figure out how to make portals."

Bran lost track of time while he and Varlan sat chatting. It wasn't like when Savita had entered his mind to keep him distracted; Varlan was reasonably good company, even if he was a pirate or at least a thief. Despite the distraction, he kept an eye on the guarded staircase, hoping to catch Agnes on her way back. But a good hour or two had passed and there had been no sign of her.

"Well, thank you for the company, but I have business to attend to," Varlan said as he stood. "Tell Nea I said hello. And let her know I have a job for her if she has changed her mind about using portals for morally questionable activities." He gave a nod, then strode across the market and disappeared up the guarded stairs.

Bran spotted a flash of copper hair rounding a corner. Agnes. He hurried after her, darting between two women and calling a quick apology over his shoulder.

Agnes came to an intersection and turned left. Bran moved to follow her, but a large guy carrying a crate blocked his path. They did a back-and-forth dance before Bran pressed himself against the wall and let the man pass. Once the man was out of the way, Bran continued along the corridor he had last seen Agnes disappear into. It led to a set of stairs heading to the lower level. There was no sight of her, but this must have been the way she had gone. He rushed down the stairs and, as he turned to follow the corridor, found himself shoved against a wall with the tip of something sharp pressed against the side of his throat.

"Why are you following me?" She had dark, mahogany eyes, and freckles covered her pale skin like stars across a night sky. Her keen was like Donnic the tattooist's: bright, almost playful, and whispering of creative potential. But unlike Donnic's, which brought the smell of ink to the edges of his senses, hers was thrumming with the promise of new life and the tangy scent of metal.

"I was told you could help me find Elijah."

"You need a map then?"

"No. I don't need a map." He wasn't sure what else to tell her. Would Deana and Kai's names mean anything to her? "A friend sent me."

"Dad doesn't have any *friends*," she said softly, almost to herself, and she pressed the tip of her weapon harder into his neck. "Who are you?"

After Kieran had taken Nora and Henry from Hartswood, Bran had asked Garret to teach him how to fight. And whilst he wasn't the best swordsman, he now knew enough to hold his own. He certainly could have gotten away from Agnes if he'd wanted to, but he needed to earn her trust. "I'm Bran. Leilani sent me."

She shook her head. "Never heard of her."

"What about Kai? Or Deana?"

Her mouth twitched when he said Deana. She studied his face a few heartbeats longer and then let go of his shirt and pulled the weapon away from his throat. It turned out to be a pen. "I'll humour you, but if my father doesn't want to speak with you, I'm throwing you out."

"That's fair."

She led him along the corridor and then across a narrower catwalk to an emerald-coloured door. "Wait here a minute." She disappeared into the dwelling and snapped the door shut.

Bran rested his hands against the rail that flanked the walkway. It was a flimsy barrier between himself and the drop to the next level. The whole city had been constructed from the wreckage of ships and other debris that had been salvaged from the sea. Varlan had implied that the salvage was sometimes more of a violent acquisition than an actual salvage though. These catwalks and the staircases that branched off them were the roads that connected each section to the next. It made the city a twisting warren of dark spaces and bolt holes where those seeking obscurity could hide.

The door opened, and Agnes stuck her head out. "Alright, you can come in." She stepped back to let him enter what looked like a small kitchen. "You have a smudge of ink on your neck."

Ink from her pen. He rubbed at the mark as he took in the small space. A man who had similar eyes to Agnes but dark hair shot with grey was standing across from him, his arms folded over his chest. There were tattoos beneath his rolled-up sleeves, and Bran wondered if any of them were Donnic's work. They didn't seem to ripple with magic, but that didn't mean Donnic hadn't done them. The man's keen was much like his daughter's, which was surprising. Creationists were rare. Two living under one roof was something Bran had never heard of. But there was something else—a familiar keen that felt like it was dragging Bran into the depths of the ocean. Deana. She wasn't in the room, but she had been, and not long ago.

"You must be Elijah. I'm Bran. Leilani sent me." He held his hand out.

Elijah studied his hand before giving it a shake. "Do you have Kai's journal?"

Straight to the point then. Bran fished the journal out of the folds of his coat and passed it to Elijah.

The older man ran his fingertips gently over the cover before fanning the edges of the pages with his thumb and then tapping the spine against the centre of his palm as a shadow crossed his face.

"Dad?" Agnes asked as she flicked a look between her father and Bran.

"He was a good lad; do you know what happened to him?" His russet eyes met Bran's.

"Not really. There was an incident with Chief Soma's children and some ..." He ran his index finger along his lip. Did Elijah and Agnes know about the shrouded ones? Did they believe they were more than a myth?

"Some what?" Agnes leant against the counter nestled along the wall.

"Shrouded ones."

Elijah's eyes narrowed and the corner of his mouth tucked in, but Agnes made a *pfft* sound that dissolved into a small laugh.

"Good one. Someone sold you a great story by the sound of it. Everyone knows that shrouded ones are just a myth." Her mood sobered as she glanced towards her father. "They *are* a myth"—her attention moved back to Bran—"right?"

"All stories ring with a grain of truth," Bran whispered. Then louder he said, "They are very much real and Chief Soma's advisor, Idir, is one of them."

"Idir? Deana said he—" Agnes slapped her hands over her mouth.

"I already knew she was here or has been. I can feel her keen. Look, I only came because Leilani asked me to, but I should be getting back to the docks. Just keep Deana safe. I don't know if Idir will look for her here, but whatever business he has with her is certainly not finished. I'll be on Malani's ship. She said she has a contact who might be able to hide Deana from Idir." He turned towards the door.

"Don't worry about Deana—we'll take care of her. But I'll tell her about Malani's offer," Elijah said.

Bran gave him a nod and then left the berth; he'd gone several paces along the catwalk when the door behind him clicked open and then shut again.

"Wait," Agnes said as she caught his arm. "I'm sorry I threatened to stab you with my pen—it's been one of those days. Look, this Idir, Deana seems terrified of him. Do you think whatever he has planned might be ..." She twisted her fingers together before her eyes lifted and her gaze bored right into his in a fashion that reminded him of Nea. "... big? Like *death and destruction and bringing the entirety of the isles under his heel* big?"

He rubbed his hands over his face as he whispered, "Shadow's teeth, I hope not."

"What was that?"

"Possibly. But whatever it is, it seems to centre around Deana. So keeping her safe is top priority."

Agnes nodded, but there was a distant look in her eyes, and she clenched and unclenched her hands several times before giving them a small shake. "Right, well, thank you. Umm, I've got to go and ..." She pointed over her shoulder with her thumb. "Bye." She spun and hurried into the berth, leaving him once more alone on the catwalk.

He shook his head and blew out a breath before heading the way he hoped would lead him to the docks.

Several corridors and one wrong turn later, he reached the place where Agnes had cornered him and the set of stairs that would lead him to the market level. The distant sounds of the market echoed down the staircase, and he had taken several strides towards them when a pair of hands grabbed him and yanked him into an alcove. His back collided with a wall of muscle and leather as he was thrust away from his assailant.

"Well, now, what have we here?" a voice said in his ear before something heavy smashed against the side of his head. His knees buckled, and the brute behind him caught him as the floor swooped upwards and his vision blurred to black.

CHAPTER NINE

DEANA

Deana waited until the door clicked shut before she emerged into the kitchen. Elijah gave her a nod and then disappeared to his study with the journal Bran had given him. Agnes had muttered something about needing to apologise to Bran before rushing off and leaving Deana alone. Something moved under the table, and she leant forward to investigate.

The large, green crab that had escaped earlier was hunkered down between the legs of one of the chairs. Its beady eyes swivelled this way and that before it scuttled towards the door, which opened to reveal a flustered-looking Agnes.

"Oh, go on then. I didn't really want to eat you anyway," she said to the crab and shooed it out the door. "Right. That's taken care of. Are you hungry?" she asked Deana.

"Not really. Did Bran say anything else about Idir?"

Agnes blinked slowly and ran her tongue along the seam of her lips before meeting Deanna's gaze once more. Her eyes were a deep red-brown that almost felt as though you could fall into them. "No, he didn't. Not that I really gave him much of a chance." She cocked her head. "Why didn't you want to talk to him yourself? He doesn't seem like a bad sort; he actually seems quite friendly."

Deana had seen enough of his interactions to know that he was both friendly and kind. The latter being a trait she hadn't experienced much; in fact, he had been kinder to her than she had been to him. But his song still spoke of death, destruction, and something dark attached to his destiny, and she couldn't get entangled in that. Not when her own song held so much despair. But then destiny seemed to keep throwing them together, as if somehow they were both part of the larger puzzle. Perhaps she should—

"Deana?" Agnes asked, drawing Deana's attention to her. She was sitting on the bench, braiding her hair. It was such a beautiful shade of orange, the same colour the sun sometimes painted the clouds in the late afternoon. "Why didn't you tell me about the shrouded ones?"

Deana stilled, but inside her heart was beating a wild tattoo against her ribs. "I don't ... It's—Idir ... It's complicated." She drew a long, steadying breath and closed her eyes. "No one believed me before. Except—" She swallowed and opened her eyes again. "Except Kai."

"Bran believes you. He said Idir was one of them," Agnes said gently.

Deana gripped the edge of the table. "He saw one back on Lethata, but I don't know how he knows Idir is one. I didn't know until the night I fled." She rubbed her fingers along her brow; her mind still felt raw, the edges fragile and tattered as though they had been torn and stitched roughly back together. "Maybe I *should* go and talk to him."

"Now you want to talk to him?"

She didn't *want* to talk to him, but she needed to know how he knew about Idir. "No, but I think I should."

"I think he was heading to the market. I can take you, but we need to get you a change of clothes first." Agnes hopped off the counter and beckoned Deana to follow her along the hall to her room.

It was the same room Deana had slept in earlier. Every available surface was taken up by the most curious contraptions Deana had ever seen. She couldn't make sense of how most of them worked, but they responded to Agnes' song, some lighting up with a magical glow and others activating as she neared. One was a mechanical cat, built from plates of what looked like iron with little studs of a rose-gold metal that made Deana's fingers numb. Robrillium, Agnes had called it. The cat was the only thing that still worked when Agnes wasn't in the room. Not that it did much other than occasionally pacing back and forth across the top of the trunk at the foot of Agnes' bed before curling up again.

Agnes picked the cat up and placed it on the floor. "I don't think anything of mine will fit you, given that you're a good bit curvier than me. But I have some of my mother's things that might." She pulled a bundle out of the trunk and ran her thumbs over the fabric. "Here."

"Are you sure? I can just make do—"

"I'm sure." She pushed the bundle into Deana's hands and then scooped up the cat again. "I'll give you a minute."

Once Agnes had left, Deana laid the clothes on the bed and inspected them. A pair of dark pants and a wheaten shirt. There was also a green tunic with a strange white bird holding a sprig of a plant she didn't recognise in its beak embroidered on the left side of the chest. It looked almost like a uniform of some kind. Deana had seen mages in Beldaren wearing similar outfits, though she didn't recall seeing any of them dressed in green. Grey, blue, red, and purple, but definitely no green. Agnes' song clung to the clothes like it did everything else in the room, but beneath that was a faded melody very similar to Leilani's. Had Agnes' mother been a healer?

"Are you decent yet?"

"Not quite." Deana hurried to strip and then pull the new clothes on, but she left the tunic on the bed. "Okay," she said as she tucked the protection stone under the neck of the shirt.

Agnes opened the door and then studied her for a few moments. "You didn't like the tunic?"

"It's not that. Beldaren mages wear tunics like these as a kind of uniform."

"I didn't even think of that." Agnes traced her fingers over the embroidery before dumping the mechanical cat on the bed and then rifling through the trunk again. "Here." This time she held out a bright blue tunic. Unlike the first, this one didn't have sleeves and there was a row of darker blue lacing up the sides as though it could be let out or taken in to adjust the fit.

Once Deana had fastened the bone buttons, Agnes tweaked the lacing on each side so the tunic fit comfortably. She then held out a pair of boots like the ones she wore herself. "At least our feet are the same size."

Deana slid the boots on, then braided her hair into two thick plaits and fastened the ends with a pair of blue ribbons before giving Agnes a nod.

Agnes led her through the corridors and catwalks to the market. After the dark catwalks, the open space with its collection of brightly coloured stalls, vibrant sounds, and layered smells was an assault on Deana's senses. So many songs crammed into one space; it was a mind-numbing cacophony, and picking a single song from the rest was almost impossible.

"Where do you think he might have gone?" Deana asked.

"I'm hoping he's down on Malani's ship. Come on." Agnes slipped between two stalls. One sold an assortment of dried fish and fruits, and the other expertly carved fishhooks, lures, and traps. The stall holders seemed to be having an argument with each other about something and paid Deana and Agnes no mind as they passed.

Deana bumped into Agnes' back as she stopped. She followed the other woman's line of sight to a stall across the way. It had a purple awning that hung slightly lower on one side. The stallholder, an older man with a slender build and light bronze-toned skin, nodded his head before ducking inside.

Agnes studied the purple stall for a few short moments before she turned and crashed into Deana. "Sorry. Come on. The docks are this way."

Deana glanced at the purple stall again before following Agnes.

Malani's cargo ship wasn't the only one tethered at the dock. A second ship with sleek lines and a siren figurehead was berthed a little farther down. Deana swallowed the lump that formed in her throat as she studied the figurehead. It resembled the shrouded ones when they wore their more alluring faces. She took a step back and a pair of large hands caught her shoulders.

"Whoa, easy there," a deep voice said as the man released his grip on her.

She turned and rocked back another step. He was one of the biggest men she had ever seen—tall and broad-shouldered with a thick beard and a tangled mess of dark hair. Her eyes locked onto the nasty scar that split his face from the corner of his left brow to the middle of his right cheek. The beard parted into a wide smile as Deana studied him.

"Gendry, my love, stop scaring the locals," a woman's voice called.

The voice belonged to a short, very curvy woman with hair as bright as Agnes'. She was leaning against a stack of crates beside Malani. Her song came with a howl of wind and the deep rumble of thunder, but it was the young girl standing beside her who commanded Deana's full attention. Her song was deep-rooted but subtle, and it brought the heaviness of sleep to the edges of Deana's eyelids. When she turned to smile at Deana, her eyes were the crystal green of still water over white sand. Deana started to back away, and Gendry caught her arm again.

"Keep jumping about like that and you'll end up taking an involuntary dip. I can assure you the water is not at all pleasant today."

"Deana?" Malani strode towards her. "Are you alright?"

She fought the urge to retreat. Malani had always been kind, but the concern in her warm brown eyes was overwhelming. Kai and her parents were the only ones who had ever looked at her like that. "Yes," she managed. And she followed it up with, "I'm okay."

"Leilani will be pleased then. Did Bran find you?" She scanned the dock as though looking for him.

"I haven't seen him, but he gave Kai's journal to Agnes' father."

As Deana mentioned the other girl's name, Malani's gaze flicked to her, and a wide smile broke across her lips. "Been taking care of my girl Deana have you, Sparky?"

Agnes' nose scrunched at the nickname, but that was just Malani. She'd never had a nickname for Deana though. She didn't even call her Dee like Leilani, Samir, and Indira did. Always just Deana.

"Since I found her washed up in the underbelly this morning, yes," Agnes said. "So, you haven't seen Bran since you docked?"

Malani shook her head. "He went out looking for your father and hasn't returned."

"I saw him in the tavern chatting with Varlan," Gendry said. "But they both disappeared before I could join them."

"Well, he can't be too far away," the red-haired woman said as she and the girl joined them.

The girl looked to be ten or eleven. Her pale eyes shimmered as she studied Deana. "Why are you so sad?"

"Sad?"

"Your song. It's ... broken ... Only sad people have broken songs."

"Would you duck onto the ship and fetch Rufus for me please, Dara?"

Dara tilted her head as her song brushed Deana's again, but she smiled at the red-haired woman and then skipped away towards the ship with the siren figurehead.

"I'm Wren, by the way," the redhead held out her hand.

"Deana." The moment her fingers touched Wren's, a spark jumped across her skin and she couldn't bite back her hiss of shock.

"Sorry about that. It happens sometimes when my keen meets another. Your keen is rather intriguing, actually."

Deana withdrew her hand and ran her fingers down one of her braids. "My song has been touched by Grandmother Ocean." Cursed, more like, but these people didn't need to know that.

Dara returned with a tall, hook-nosed man in tow and a pair of women who looked identical to each other. One of the women had a bright, crackling song and the other the soft, playful lap of ripples upon a shore. They both smiled brightly at Deana and then Agnes.

"Hello, I'm Pippa, and this is—"

"Kiki. Would you look at that gorgeous hair?" the second twin said as she circled Agnes. "I've never seen anyone with brighter hair than Wren."

"Ah, hello. I'm Agnes, and this is Deana."

"Your keens are—"

"Stars above, give the girls some space, the pair of you," Wren reprimanded, but there was a lightness beneath her tone. "I believe

I sent for Rufus and not half the ship."

"You did. But when Dara mentioned that Bran might be missing," Pippa said.

"We knew we had to help look for him. It would be a tragedy for the world to lose something so pretty," Kiki finished.

Gendry let out a low, rumbling chuckle. "I am sure Bran would appreciate your *concern*."

"Don't encourage them, my love. Bran is not missing. He's probably just caught up with Varlan somewhere. That man can be the worst of distractions when he puts his mind to it."

"If you weren't worried, why did you send for Rufus?" the twins asked as one.

"Because—"

"She's a mother hen who fusses after everyone, and she won't be content until she has confirmed that the lad is fine," the man who had arrived with the twins, Rufus, said with a half-grin.

"I promised Nea I would watch out for him, and from what Malani has told me, he could be in a lot of trouble with Idir. If Idir followed him here—"

"He didn't follow you, did he?" Deana asked Malani, wincing at the panic that tightened her voice.

"I don't think so. The only other ship that has docked since we arrived was the Queen." She indicated Wren's ship with an open palm.

"We should check the market again; he can't have gotten far." Agnes tucked her fingers around Deana's elbow and gave her a tug towards the stairs that led to the upper levels.

"We'll come with you," the twins said, falling into step on either side of them.

What felt like hours later, they wandered back to Malani's ship having found no sign of Bran despite asking everyone they had encountered and searching the market twice. Pippa had even braved the brothel despite Kiki's insistence that Bran wasn't the type. No one had seen Bran since he had been in the tavern with Varlan. Agnes had even tried the guards who blocked the stairway leading up to the crow's nest, but they apparently hadn't seen Bran and refused to let her up to speak with either Varlan or Kent.

"No luck?" Malani asked as Agnes propped herself on a stack of crates.

"Kent has him," Agnes groaned.

"The guards didn't say that," Deana said, rubbing her arms and scouring the shadows. The longer they had searched, the more she'd felt like she was being watched.

"Not directly." Agnes scrunched her nose.

"Why would Kent need a soul-singer?" Malani asked.

"He's a necromancer?" Agnes nearly toppled off the crates.

The mages all looked at her like she had grown a second head.

"Of course, he's a necromancer. Even if the white hair wasn't a giveaway, you had to have recognised his keen," Pippa said.

"You are a mage yourself, right? I mean, you feel like our friend Donnic, so we just assumed," Kiki added.

"Of course, I'm a mage. I just ..." She picked at her cuticles. "... didn't notice his keen."

"You didn't notice? Bran's keen is stronger than the average necromancer. The only other mages I have met with stronger keen are Nea and Garret, and they are both divine-blooded, so they don't count," Pippa said.

"There's a silent spot in her song," Dara said. "It's like it skips several beats before starting again."

Deana focused on Agnes' song, and the girl was right. She had just assumed the pause in the song was part of the rhythm, but it wasn't. It was like those notes had been deliberately silenced.

"You know what I have told you about reading people without their permission, Dara," Wren reprimanded gently.

Agnes slid off the crates. "If Kent does have Bran, then it's likely he won't return him before morning. We should get back and see if Dad is done with your brother's journal. Unless you want to stay here," she said the last to Deana.

"I'll come with you, but we should check back here in the morning in case Bran shows up overnight." She still wasn't convinced that Idir or shrouded ones hadn't somehow managed to take him. If that journal he had given to Elijah was important, then she was certain that Idir would stop at nothing to get it. Or what if Savita had come? She could burrow into your mind before you realised she was doing it.

Dread settled heavy in Deana's stomach as they said their goodnights and she followed Agnes to her berth. She didn't know why she was so concerned for Bran now when she had wanted nothing to do with him and his tainted song before today. But something had shifted when she had hidden away and listened as he spoke with Elijah and Agnes earlier. It was almost like her song had recognised something in his that was the same. Kai probably would have called it a realisation of a shared destiny, and that thought terrified her.

CHAPTER TEN

AGNES

Agnes slid from her bed and carefully stepped around Deana's sleeping form. A thin slant of light shone under the door to her father's study, but the subtle rumble of his snores told her he had once again fallen asleep at his desk. She probably should wake him and send him to bed, but instead she crept into the kitchen and grabbed her hooded capelet from behind the door.

The lighting in the common areas had dimmed to a deep blue that mimicked moonlight, as it did every evening. It had been her first commission for Kent's predecessor, Olen. She had been barely eleven when he discovered her talent for creating wondrous things that blurred the lines between science and magic. It had been an accident. She had overheard him discussing the issues with lighting the city, particularly since most of the areas inside never saw actual daylight. As he'd spoken Agnes had slipped into the trance that accompanied her magic; ideas had torn across her mind at lightning speed while her hands itched and burned. When she had come out of it, her fingers were black with coal dust, the ground before her covered in a series of crude drawings. Olen had been crouched beside her inspecting the sketches, then he'd turned to her with a shrewd smile she would never forget. Over the years he had commissioned her to make many improvements to Armada, but his focus had always been on taking care of the people who found themselves here because they had nowhere else to go.

When Olen died and Kent took over, things changed. Kent seemed content to boost the seedy element that had wound its way into the lower levels. He wasn't focused on improving the lives of the general populace but more on his own gain. This new commission, his first in a good while, had her conflicted. When she entered the trance, she had no control over what her fingers produced and little memory of it until she had a chance to go over her notes and diagrams. The process happened in stages, and the more complex the project the more refinement it would need. Kent's commission was the most challenging she had ever faced. It came to her mind as a monstrous machine that spewed fire and death. Plates of metal, covering its sinuous form, riveted in a way that allowed movement but protected the delicate internal mechanisms. It would need a heart. Like her mechanical cat, only bigger and much more powerful.

The telltale tingle started in her fingertips. She stopped and leant against the wall, focusing on her breathing to clear the thoughts before she spiralled into a trace. The problem with this gift was that once the kernel of the idea had been planted, it would consume her until she had completed the project. The harder she fought it, the more insistent it would become until she lost autonomy completely.

Once she had found her centre, she started off again, staying at the edge of the shadows.

"I was starting to think you wouldn't come," Gethyn said as she slipped into the empty berth where he was waiting.

A small orb of amber light bobbed around his head. Mage light had always fascinated Agnes. Her own was a soft bronze with ribbons of black and gold twisting through it. But mages didn't get to choose the colour of their light—it was a visible cue to the magic they wielded. Fire mages like Gethyn always had warm, yellow-orange light, water mages a soft blue, and healers green.

"You were right about Kent being up to something," she said as she moved to the only table in the room and sat on the edge of it.

Gethyn folded his arms and leant his hip against a bench across from her. "Do you think the necromancer's disappearance has something to do with his plans?"

She shook her head. There was no way a necromancer fit into Kent's plan, but then—her fingers started to tingle, and she clenched her fist before releasing it and giving it a shake. The automatons she had created all needed her to be nearby to work, except for the cat. It had a basic set of functions it would perform without the need to feed off her magic. The shard of crystal that served as its heart made it something between a golem and an automaton. But Kent didn't know about the cat and how it was powered when Agnes wasn't around. Did he assume that his war machine would need a more permanent power source? Of course, that would make it—

The edges of her vision started to dim and her shoulders shook as the trance threatened to take her. She bit down hard on her lip and squeezed her eyes shut as she drew a deep breath in. *One, two, three, four* ... She released it as she reached six and the tingling stopped.

Gethyn traced his fingers along his chin as he studied her. "He wants you to build something of a considerable magnitude then?"

She ran a hand through her hair. "He wants a war machine, one that will cripple the isles."

"And you think he would stop at the isles?"

"I'd like to think so, but—" She shook her head. "I think once he has a taste of power, he'll turn his attention to bigger targets."

"I always knew you were a smart girl."

"Why are you so concerned with what Kent is up to?"

"Because I happen to live in the isles, and I like the simple life I have for myself here. If Kent were to make a lunge for power, then that life would be threatened." He pushed off the wall and crossed the room to stand in front of her. "Thank you for keeping me informed. And don't worry. You have my word that Kent will never find out what we have discussed here. I do not wish to go the way of my dear brother." He placed something on the table beside her and headed for the door. "I would appreciate you keeping me in the loop about any developments in Kent's plan." He left, and his light went with him.

Agnes summoned a light of her own. The bronze orb bobbed merrily beside her as she picked up the pen Gethyn had given her. It was slender and smooth, carved in a way that made it look like two pieces of dark mahogany twisted together. It throbbed against her fingertips like the crystal that powered her cat.

The next morning, Agnes stifled a yawn as she made a pot of tea. Neither Deana nor her father had seemed to notice her absence during the night, or if they had, they didn't ask any questions. She had hidden the new quill away in the pen roll at the bottom of her bag. It had felt strangely heavy in her fingers as she wandered the dark catwalks back to the berth.

A knock sounded on the door, and she crossed to open it.

Malani was on the other side. "Good morning, Sparky. You look like you barely slept," she said almost too brightly as she stepped across the threshold.

Between sneaking out to meet with Gethyn and the dreams that had plagued her through the wee hours of the morning, Agnes didn't feel like she'd slept at all. Fingers of dread were still crawling across her shoulders in the wake of those dreams. "It was a bit of a rough night. Would you like some tea? I have some Faridean black in the pot."

"No thanks. I just dropped by to let you know Bran didn't return last night and I saw Savita this morning."

"Savita?"

"Idir's daughter. She didn't see me, but she was asking about Deana. Wren and I both believe it would be in Deana's best interest to move to the Azure Queen. I'd say she could come and stay with me, but I need to be getting back to Lethata, and there are more mages on Wren's ship."

"More mages? To protect Deana, you mean? She's in a lot of trouble, isn't she?"

Malani nodded, the movement making the beads and shells attached to her braids jingle. "I don't know the whole story, but Chief Soma's son, Samir, was taken. Bran said it was the shrouded ones and that Idir had something to do with it. I wouldn't be surprised—Idir's always been a snake in the reeds."

"But why does he want Deana? Do you think she knows Idir had something to do with the kidnapping?"

"The shrouded ones want me because I belong to Grandmother Ocean," Deana said as she emerged from the hallway. "And Idir is one of them."

"Idir can't be a shrouded one—they are always female," Malani said.

"I thought so too, but I saw his true face."

"Is that why Idir killed Nazali? Because she found out the truth?" Malani asked.

Deana's eyes widened and her hand went to her mouth. "Nazali's dead?"

"I thought you knew ... I'm sorry." Malani frowned.

A small sound escaped Deana as she sagged against the wall. The sensation of being on a rocking boat rolled over Agnes.

After drawing a deep breath, Deana straightened again. "Did ... did Bran return last night?" she asked Malani.

"No, I am starting to think Agnes is right. Kent has him, but I haven't the slightest idea why."

Agnes knew why. Or at least she suspected it, and her dreams had seemed to confirm it. "Kent is expecting me again this morning. I'll keep an eye out for any clues while I am there," she said as she poured Deana a cup of tea and set it on the table. "Are you sure you don't want one, Malani?"

"Oh, why not?" Malani pulled a chair out and settled herself into it. To Deana, she said, "Wren and I were thinking it might be better for you to stay on the Azure Queen."

Deana ran her fingers along the braided leather cord that disappeared below the neckline of her shirt. Something heavy hung from it, but Agnes hadn't seen what it was, and Deana didn't seem to want to share, so she didn't pry. She knew better than most that people were entitled to their secrets.

"I like it here with Agnes and Elijah."

"I know, but I saw Savita this morning."

"Savita's here?" Deana's fingers shook as she gripped her cup.

"Yes, and she was asking questions about you." Malani took the cup Agnes offered her. "Which is why it is better for you to be surrounded by mages. And if you are on the Queen, then Wren can get you away quickly if the need arises. The Azure Queen is one of the fastest vessels on the ocean."

"I agree with Malani. Dad and I can't really protect you if anyone comes looking here, and after everything I learned yesterday, I think you need all the protection you can get," Agnes said before taking a sip of her own tea.

Deana stared into her cup as though it held all the answers of the known realms.

"Good morning," Agnes' father said as he entered the kitchen. "It's not often you grace us with your presence, Malani."

"Cargo routes rarely change, so I have very little need for maps."

"True enough," he said as Agnes passed him his cup and he sat down at the table with Deana and Malani.

Agnes propped herself on the end of the bench and cradled her own cup in her hands.

"We do have chairs you know, Agnes?" he said with a grin as he blew on his tea. "You didn't tell me what Kent wanted yesterday."

She took a big sip of her tea, her eyes watering at the heat of it. But it bought her time to organise her thoughts and figure out exactly what she was going to tell her father. "He forbade me from telling anyone until it's ready."

"He forbade you? Agnes, if he has asked for something—"

"It's nothing like that," she said almost too fast. "But you know what Kent is like."

Her father twisted his mouth as he studied her. "Just be careful."

"I always am," she said and took another large sip of her tea.

"Are you finished with my brother's journal?" Deana asked.

"He's written part of it in a code that I can't decipher," Agnes' father replied. "There has to be a key somewhere. Did Kai ever mention anything?"

Deana stiffened at the mention of her brother's name. "No, I didn't even know he kept a journal." She touched her fingers to the hidden pendant.

"That's a shame, but I'll keep working on it. Do you think anyone else knows about the journal?"

"I don't know. Leilani might know something because she gave it to Bran. Maybe she would be the one to ask about a key," Deana said.

"I doubt Leilani knows. I think the only person who could have told you anything about it was Kai." Malani finished her tea and stood. "Do you want to come back to the docks with me now, Deana?"

Deana nodded. "I'll just get my things."

"Where are you going?" Elijah asked.

"I'm just taking Deana down to Wren's ship. Idir's daughter has been sniffing around for her—she already knows Deana is here. Even if no one told her outright, she would have plucked the information straight from their heads," Malani said.

He nodded. "Good. She'll be safer on the Queen."

"I should be getting up to Kent's berth, but I'll drop by the docks when I am done." Agnes hopped off the bench and grabbed her satchel from the hook on the wall before holding the door open for Deana and Malani.

Kent was the only person present when she arrived in his mock throne room after the routine patting down by the guards. Her journal was already laid out on the table, and he indicated she take a seat with an open palm as he lounged across his giant chair.

"I hear you were looking for a necromancer yesterday."

Agnes blinked. She hadn't expected him to just come out and discuss Bran without a bit of careful prompting. "A friend of mine was looking for him, actually. He came in on her ship and she's worried something might have happened to him."

"My men say he was sniffing around the market, looking for you. Curious that immediately after our little chat yesterday he should show up. Especially as my acquaintance has recently had a run-in with this particular necromancer."

"I don't know why he would have been looking for me."

"Not you perhaps, but maybe someone close to you."

Did he know about Deana? The acquaintance had to be Idir.

"Perhaps he just needed a map." Kent's tone was light, but there was something pointed in the look he was giving her.

"Perhaps." She forced a smile and then dug out her ink and pen —not the new mahogany one Gethyn had given her. "Shall we begin?"

Kent rubbed his fingers along his lip as she studied her. "In a hurry today, are you?"

"I'd rather get this over and done with as soon as possible."

The door opened, drawing Kent's attention. "I said no interruptions," he growled at the guard who entered.

The guard blinked at him, his mouth going slack as a young woman stepped out from behind him.

"Terribly sorry, but I insisted."

Her dark skin contrasted against the turquoise outfit she wore. It was a common outfit on the isles—a top that was cropped at the waist and a skirt that swished around her knees. Her long, dark hair hung in a sleek sheet over her shoulders, reaching to her hips, and her eyes appeared almost obsidian as they slid over Agnes.

"You see, your little friend here has something I want and I'm not in the business of waiting."

Agnes suddenly felt lightheaded. She pressed her fingers to her forehead and swallowed—

"That will be enough of that." Varlan brushed by the woman as he entered and gave her a wide grin as she scowled. "Oh, you are good. But sorry, sweetheart, I'm better."

The woman let out a growl and pressed her fingers to her temples. "Get out."

"You can dish it, but you can't take it? Is that how it goes?"

"How dare—" Her words ended in a sharp gasp, and she gripped the doorframe as she gave a faltering step back.

"Varlan," Kent cautioned.

Varlan gave Agnes a wink. "Don't try it again, sweetheart, or next time I'll turn your mind inside out and own all those pretty secrets," he said to the woman. His tone was honey over steel.

"What is your name?" Kent asked.

"Savita."

Agnes bit down on her gasp. The girl Malani had mentioned was looking for Deana. A mind mage. Was Varlan a mind mage too? That would explain the little altercation. Not having a properly working keen-sense was a challenge at times.

"Ah, so nice to be able to put a face to the name. I take it your father sent you."

She nodded. "And he will not be pleased to hear your lackey threatened me."

"I am not *pleased* that you barged into a private meeting with my dear Agnes. Whatever dispute you have with her can wait until my business is concluded. Varlan, if you would be so kind as to escort Savita to a guestroom."

"It would be my pleasure." He took hold of Savita's arm and guided her out the door, pausing briefly to shoot a look back at Kent, who gave a tiny nod.

"Now, where were we? My war machine. Did you have any great epiphanies overnight? Or has the news of my acquisition of a necromancer given you a new *perspective?*"

The tingle started at her fingertips but this time she didn't fight it. Her vision went blank as she picked up her pen. Waves crashed across her mind, a colossal metallic serpent coiling through them.

CHAPTER ELEVEN

BRAN

His arms ached and he wiggled his fingers to dispel the numbness that had settled there. Slowly he opened his eyes and then blinked to try to shift the grittiness. How long had he been chained up? The artificial light made it impossible to tell. A headache was throbbing from his temples to the back of his head where the thugs had hit him to knock him out. He had thought at first it was a simple mugging, but then they'd dragged him down here and locked him away.

Someone stopped in front of his cell, and he lifted his head. He didn't recognise either of the men on the opposite side of the bars, but they wore the same leather cuirass as all of Kent's other guards.

"I'm going to take those chains off now. Don't try anything or you'll be back in them before you can blink," one of them said as he opened the cell door and stepped inside.

The guard unlocked the shackles, and Bran fell to the floor; he wouldn't have been able to do anything even if he wanted to. The ache in his arms was replaced with a wild rush of hot and cold prickles that made his arms feel much heavier than they should.

He propped himself against the wall and rubbed his wrists as the guard exited the cell once more.

"Here." The second guard placed a tray containing a hunk of bread and a mug of water just inside the door. "Kent will summon you for a little chat later. If he finds you agreeable, you might get yourself moved to a more comfortable cage." With that, both guards left.

They hadn't bothered to bind his magic. Necromancers weren't a threat, after all—unless they were like Nea, but she was one of a kind, given her divine blood. Tearing into the bread, he studied the tattoo on the inside of his wrist. Housing Nea's keen had changed his own. He knew that much. Maybe it was time he stopped avoiding it and embraced whatever his new abilities were. Portals weren't a pleasant way to travel. However, they could be useful ... But what if it wasn't her ability to create portals. What if it was her ability to kill by separating a soul directly from the body? He wasn't sure he wanted that part of her keen.

If he had the spirit anchor, he could have contacted her, and she would have been able to get him out of here or send Garret like she had when Idir was attacking him. But he had left it with his things on Malani's ship, so he was well and truly on his own. He tossed a piece of the bread from one hand to the other. When Nea or Garret created a portal, the source seemed to bristle before splitting open. It was a more focused feeling than just bringing up the barrier, the magical wall that stopped the known realms from colliding with each other. He leant forward and glanced down the hallway to see if anyone was around. His keen-sense hadn't picked up on any other mages or wardens, but you could never be too careful. Satisfied he was alone, he closed his eyes and focused on his breathing. Pulling up the barrier was second nature, but that wasn't what he was trying to do. He needed to invoke the feeling of the barrier and then somehow puncture it to create the portal.

The source prickled, and he rolled his shoulders. He lifted a hand and opened his eyes, focusing on the air just beyond his fingers. "Come on now," he whispered, and the source that brushed against his palm grew hot. "Easy does it." His fingers shook and a flicker of lilac twisted over them. The air shimmered and then a small seam of violet light appeared. It sprung open into an oval of glittering miasma barely big enough to stick his hand through before it snapped shut again.

He'd done it. He'd created a portal. A very small and extremely unstable one, but it was still a portal. He ran a hand over his hair. The effort of creating the portal had brought a sheen of sweat to his skin and increased the throbbing in his skull. Given time to practice, he could probably at least double the size of the portal and stabilise it. A person might not be able to pass through it, but maybe it could have other uses.

He finished the bread and then downed the mug of water before laying his head back against the wall. If he was going to practice creating portals, he was going to need his rest.

Sometime later, he couldn't tell how long, another pair of guards appeared outside his cell.

"Hands against the wall," one of them said as they both entered.

Bran complied, and the one who had spoken strode forward and grabbed his wrists, pulling them behind his back and securing them there with a length of rope. "Come on." He gave Bran a shove towards the door where his partner was waiting.

They led him up several staircases and ramps to the top level of the city. Afternoon sunlight washed the walls in a golden glow, making the space almost unbearably warm. The guards nudged him along to a door near the middle of the catwalk.

The room on the other side of the door was a large, mostly open space. A small table and chair sat just to the side of a larger carved chair that resembled a throne. Papers and a single journal cluttered the tabletop. A hand at Bran's back guided him to stand directly in front of the throne, and he fought the urge to turn around as deliberate footsteps sounded behind him.

Movement at the table caught his attention, and he turned his head just enough to get a look at the man the footsteps belonged to. His dark hair was secured in dreadlocks that reached to the middle of his shoulders. His skin had the smooth olive tone of an Osmarian, but there was something about the curve of his nose and the shape of his mouth that made him look somehow both Beldaren and Faridean at the same time. This must be Kent—the one Varlan had said had proclaimed himself ruler of Armada.

"Agnes is quite a treasure," Kent said as he lifted one of the sketches to study it. "But her skills will only take my project so far and I find myself in need of someone with a certain ability. I don't know if you have noticed that mages of your ilk are in short supply here on Armada."

"Mages of my ilk?"

"Don't play coy with me," Kent said sharply. "My project will require a power source, one that allows it a certain amount of autonomy whilst also keeping it subservient."

Bran bit the inside of his cheek. Was this man trying to create some kind of golem? "I doubt I can help you with this project."

Kent chuckled. "Either you are stupid or being deliberately obtuse, and I think it's the latter. But I assume the prospect I am presenting you with is a gruesome one so I would repay you for your assistance most handsomely."

"I've seen your generosity already." Bran nodded to his bound wrists and rolled his shoulders.

"An oversight on behalf of my men. I can't let you free to roam

Armada, of course, but I can provide you with quarters far more comfortable than the dungeon."

"And if I refuse to help you?"

"Well, that would be unfortunate."

The tip of what felt like a sword pressed against Bran's back.

"You have several choices. Either you agree to help me, or she will force you to." He lifted a hand towards a door behind the throne and Savita stepped out. The cloying sensation of her keen roved across the nape of his neck and he threw his mental walls up.

"And the third option? You said I have *several*."

Kent gave a short laugh. "The third option is I toss you back into the dungeon and have my men beat you into submission. If that should fail to work, then this lovely little treasure will burrow her way into your mind and make you her puppet."

"So, there is no option where I just walk out of here and you find another necromancer?"

"No." As Kent said it, the sword at Bran's back gave a little twist.

"I guess I will take option one then."

Savita's eyes darkened. "You should just let me—"

"Loyalty earned is far better than loyalty forced, and there will be plenty of time for me to earn his loyalty. And if that should fail, you will still get your chance." He turned his attention back to Bran. "I think you will find I can be quite agreeable." He nodded to the man behind Bran.

The guard guided Bran out of the mock throne room and along the catwalk to another room at the very end of the row. He pushed Bran inside and then untied the rope at his wrists. "You made the right choice. It's going to be much easier breaking you out of here than the dungeon."

"Who are you?"

The man grinned, and Bran became aware of the warm

numbness of a warden's suppression radiating from him. "Just a friend of a friend. Keep your head low, do as Kent asks, and avoid Savita. We'll get you out of here as soon as we can." He left, locking the door behind him.

A friend of a friend? Bran studied the room. The space was definitely more comfortable than the dungeons. It had a small table and chair to one side and a bed. But it was still a cell; the heavy door and barred window were evidence of that.

With a sigh, he lay on the bed and stared at the ceiling.

Do as Kent asked? At least Kent hadn't asked him to reanimate anyone, but animations like golems were just as bad. He would still need to take someone's life force and shackle it into a constructed form. There were other options, of course; he could use a spirit from the Between, one that had never been human. But Kent wanted a golem that would be subservient, and golems powered by non-human spirits were often unstable. And regardless, Bran wasn't fond of the idea of forcing *any* spirit into the body of a golem. Necromancers who started down that road found it to be a slippery slope to losing their humanity.

CHAPTER TWELVE

DEANA

Deana sat on the deck of Wren's ship. The twins, Kiki and Pippa, were a short distance away playing a game with Rufus, one that involved a handful of dice and lots of shouting. She drew a breath and pressed her head against the side rail of the ship.

"Are you alright, lass?" Gendry asked as he settled beside her.

"Yes." She wasn't sure it was entirely true.

"You've been staring at that piece of goosefruit for a good while, which would suggest that something is bothering you. Of course, it could just be that you don't like goosefruit, and then I would say, get off my ship." He gave her a cheeky smile.

"It's not your ship though," Dara said as she joined them. "It's Wren's."

Gendry ruffled the girl's hair and tucked her under his arm for a hug. "I know who won't be joining my side when I stage a mutiny."

"You wouldn't dare." Dara blinked up at him as he released her.

"No, you're right about that." His gaze wandered down the ship to where Wren and Malani were discussing something with a large map spread out between them.

"I do like goosefruit, and I am alright. I'm just worried," Deana said.

"About Bran?" Dara asked and her song swelled against Deana's.

"No, Agnes. She snuck out last night, and this morning she seemed different. Almost like she was afraid of something." You learned how to read people when you spent most of your life as an outsider, never sure of another person's motives.

"Why don't you ask her?"

Deana rolled the fruit around in her fingers. "I don't want to force her to talk about it if she doesn't want to, but what if it has something to do with Bran?" She bit down on her lip; she hadn't intended to voice that particular concern.

Gendry fixed her with a calculating look.

"If Bran has been captured, I don't know why he doesn't just make a portal and get himself out of there," Dara said before Gendry could speak.

"Can Bran make portals? I've never heard of a singer who could do that."

"The only mages I know who can are Nea and Garret. Bran's just a necromancer, as far as I know, and they can't make portals," Gendry said.

"But his song is more like Nea's now," Dara argued.

Gendry scratched underneath his chin. "I haven't the foggiest idea when it comes to magic. Everything I know about it is secondhand."

Deana let her song brush against Gendry's. Every living thing had a song, even those things not touched by magic. Gendry's song was deep and steady, building to a playful rhythm before backing off again. It didn't speak of magic, but it spoke of a deep connection to those he loved. The stormy sounds of Wren's song were twisted through the edges of it in such a way that even if she hadn't seen them together, she would know they were heart mates.

Could other people share songs like heart mates did? If Bran's song had changed as Dara was implying, had it somehow become woven with Nea's? When she had met Nea and Garret, their songs had been almost confronting, and it was impossible to tell where one song ended and the other began, almost like they shared a single song. But that made some sense, given they were heart mates. Why would Nea's song have altered Bran's? How had it?

"Can I borrow you for a moment, my love?" Wren called, and Gendry was on his feet in the blink of an eye.

"Of course, lass." He gave Deana a smile and ruffled Dara's hair again before marching along the deck to join Wren and Malani.

Sensing eyes on her, she turned back to Dara.

The girl's head tilted, and her mouth twisted at one corner. "I can't quite figure your song out. I think I understand it, and then it changes, shifting like the tides."

"It's probably because I belong to Grandmother Ocean."

"I don't know much about Grandmother Ocean. Is she like the Bright Mother?" Dara folded her hands in her lap and settled her pale gaze on Deana.

It was hard to imagine a girl who had also been touched by the goddess of the seas not knowing about her. "The Bright Mother is a Beldaren and Osmarian goddess, isn't she?"

"She's one-half of the Sovereigns. She and her consort, the Shadow Man, are the source from which everything comes."

Were they two different names for the same deity? Was the Shadow Man just another face of Grandfather Moon? "She is similar in that she birthed the islands and all in them, but she can be cruel, too. She doesn't do it out of spite but simply because you cannot have the calm without the storm. The light without the dark."

"That is what your song is like!" Dara leapt to her feet and clapped her hands. "The calm and the storm, but the pattern is not predictable. Sometimes one lasts longer than the other. Bran's song has the same rolling pattern. It fluctuates from his necromancy into the part that has been changed by Nea's song." Her expression went blank, and a shudder passed through her. "Songs aren't meant to exist in a state of flux like that. The magic you possess was never meant to walk the realm of men. That's why *she* stalks you." With another shudder, her knees buckled, and she slumped towards the deck.

Deana caught her before her head hit the floor. "Wren!" she yelled, and the captain came running. "I don't know what happened. She just slipped into some kind of trance and then passed out."

"We should have warned you. It can be frightening when she does it, but she's fine. It's just one of the quirks of her keen." Wren took the girl from Deana's arms and passed her to Gendry. "She'll sleep it off and then wake up with something profound and infuriatingly confusing to say."

As Gendry carried Dara away, guilt settled deep in Deana's stomach. If they hadn't been talking about Grandmother Ocean, would Dara have slipped into that vision or whatever it was and lost consciousness?

"Did she say anything right before she collapsed?" Wren asked as Malani joined them.

"Only that there were similarities in my song and Bran's, and that my magic was never supposed to walk in the realm of men. That's why Grandmother Ocean wants me."

"Well, none of that is exactly new information," Malani said as she shifted her braids over her shoulder before holding her hand out.

Deana took the offered hand, and Malani pulled her to her feet.

"I shouldn't stay here; bad things always happen when I'm around."

"Nonsense," Malani scoffed.

"You had nothing to do with what happened with Dara. She'll be fine. I promise," Wren said.

"Deana." Agnes came running onto the deck. She held one finger up as she doubled over and took several deep breaths. "I saw Savita."

"Where?" Deana cast a panicked glance along the dock.

"In the crow's nest. She pretty much confirmed that Kent is working with Idir, and it gets worse—I know why Kent would want Bran." Her fingers shook as she pulled a crumpled piece of paper from her sleeve. She smoothed it out and handed it to Deana.

It was a sketch of a giant serpentine monster made of what appeared to be metal plates. Behind it was a village that looked eerily like her home, the houses smashed and charred, the palace clinging to the rise above the town completely destroyed.

"What is this?" she asked, her voice barely above a whisper.

"It's Kent's commission. I didn't understand how I would power it until I realised Kent *had* captured Bran."

Wren made a noise, and Deana flicked a look at her.

"He means to create a golem, and for that he needs a necromancer to shackle a spirit into it."

"How can you help him build this when you know what he means to do with it?" Deana asked, her voice trembling. Despite Agnes' friendliness, Deana really didn't know her or what she was capable of.

"I have to complete it. I can't fight the idea once it takes hold, and even if I could, Kent will hurt Dad if I don't help him." Agnes pressed her face into her hands.

Malani slid her arm around Agnes' shoulders. "It's alright,

Sparky. We'll figure it out. Perhaps there's a way we can include a weakness that Kent doesn't know about. A way to cripple it and make it easier to take down."

"Or maybe we can rescue Bran and then Kent won't have the necromancer he needs to animate it," Wren said.

"Kent will just find another necromancer." Agnes sniffed.

"What do you mean you can't fight an idea once it takes over?" Deana asked.

"It's just the way my keen works. The more I fight an idea after it has been planted, the harder my keen fights back until it just shuts everything down and forces my body into the trance. Once that happens, I have no control over what I do." She worried her lip. "Normally, it doesn't matter, but Kent knows how to exploit my keen for his own gain. He knew exactly how to plant the seed of this idea, so it engaged my magic in a way that makes it impossible for me to fight." She snatched the drawing from Deana's hand and studied it. "There is one silver lining which may buy us time. Kent wants the golem to be somewhat autonomous. That's why he needed a necromancer to shackle a soul to it. Only without a heartstone, there's nothing to house the soul and the magic won't work. And the kind of heartstone required to power something of this magnitude will be extremely hard to find without a—Dad!" She tossed Malani's arm from her shoulders and bolted along the deck.

"Agnes, wait." Deana ran after her.

"No, Deana, you should stay here," Malani caught her arm, pulling her up short.

Deana shook free of the other woman's hold. "I have to go with her, if something has happened to Elijah ..."

"Gendry, go with them," Wren said.

"Come on then." Gendry kissed Wren's temple and then waved Deana after him.

When they reached the berth, the door was hanging from its hinges. The kitchen was a mess. Chairs were overturned and shards of broken crockery littered the floor. The table that normally stood in the centre of the room was on its side and several cupboard doors hung open. Agnes was nowhere in sight, and neither was Elijah.

Deana started along the hall, pausing when she heard a sob from Elijah's study.

This room hadn't fared any better than the kitchen. Ink dripped from the side of the desk creating a dark puddle on the floor. Ruined papers and books torn from the shelves were scattered all over the place.

Agnes was sitting on her heels in the middle of the room.

Deana took a step towards her, but her toe bumped something and she bent to examine it. A few notes of an alluring song clung to the object. She reached for it but drew her fingers back at the last second. It was a piece of pink coral. Not just any coral—it was the kind that grew from the skin of the shrouded ones.

She pressed her hand over her mouth as she studied the scene with fresh eyes. Pieces of seaweed were littered among the books and papers; a purple shell and more pieces of coral were on the desk, along with drops and splashes of green-black and red that were not ink.

"I'm so sorry, Agnes," Deana said.

"He always told me this could happen."

"It looks like both this room and the kitchen were searched. Do you think they took anything?" Gendry asked from the doorway.

"I can't tell."

"Have you checked the other rooms?" Deana asked.

Agnes shook her head. "He's all I have, Dee," she whispered.

The shortening of her name struck a cord deep inside. "I'll go check." She blinked and backed away. "Don't touch any of the coral or shells," she said before continuing along the hall to Elijah's room. Like the kitchen and the study, it had also been ransacked—the bed covers torn and Elijah's personal items scattered and broken. She hadn't been in this room before so there was no way to know if anything was missing.

Agnes' room had also been overturned, the delicate contraptions smashed, and the trunk at the foot of her bed upended.

"What were they searching for?" Deana asked as she sat on the edge of the bed and took in the destruction.

A sob caught her attention, and she turned to the door.

Agnes was leaning against the frame, her face extremely pale as she studied the room. She fell to her knees amidst her belongings and scooped up a crushed machine. It whirred and made a grating sound as it tried to respond to the proximity of her magic. "Why would someone do this? What could we possibly have that they would want?" she asked.

"I'm so sorry, Agnes. I don't know what else to say, but—" Something thumped under the bed, drawing both of their attention.

Agnes lifted the blanket and peered underneath, only to drag out the mangled body of her mechanical cat. She let out another sob, and Deana's eyes grew hot in response, her heart aching all the way to her throat.

Agnes and Elijah didn't deserve this. She should have kept running instead of staying here and bringing her curse down upon them. "Agnes ..." she said softly, and the other woman looked up. Tears had settled along her lashes, and several had already fallen, leaving tracks down her cheeks.

Deana carefully took the cat from her; one leg had been torn clean off and its head was caved in on one side, the ear a crushed mess. A small glimmer of light was visible through a crack in the metal plates that formed its chest, a twisting song emanating from whatever was causing the glow. She placed the cat gently aside and slid her arms around Agnes, pulling her close and resting her chin on her shoulder as Agnes finally let her grief out in a torrent of sobs that shook her whole body.

"It's going to be alright," Deana said thickly as she stroked Agnes' back.

After a while, Agnes pulled away with a sniff and rubbed her hands over her face. "Thank you," she whispered as though she didn't trust her own voice. She gave another sniff and looked down at the cat.

Its head was pressed hard to the side of the overturned trunk, its legs working like it was pushing itself against it. Agnes picked it up and placed it on the bed along with a few other objects she had gathered from the debris of clothes and personal items that littered the floor. The cat refused to stay put, though. It shifted forward until it dropped off the side of the bed with a *thunk* and then proceeded to shunt against the side of the trunk once more.

"Is there something in there?" Deana asked.

Agnes shook her head. "Its programming is probably damaged." She picked the cat up again and shifted it to the side while she pushed the trunk upright.

It was empty, but there was a strange song just at the edge of Deana's hearing. It was so soft that the sounds of both Agnes' magic and Deana's own had almost drowned it out. The cat worked its way over and bumped the trunk and the song surged loud enough for Deana to catch hold of it.

"I don't think the trunk is empty, Agnes. I can hear something." Deana leant forward to peer into the trunk. The boards across the bottom appeared loose and she shifted one with her finger. The sleepy song that was radiating out intensified, and she slid her fingers along the broken board, careful on the sharp edges, and pulled to free whatever was stuck beneath it. When she touched the bundle of grey cloth hidden there, the entire world grew silent and numbness smoothed up her arm. She lifted it out and unwrapped the cloth, letting it fall to the floor as she studied the large green stone sitting on her palm. It was housed in a cage of rose-gold filigree as though the metal had been used to fuse the broken pieces of stone back together. The song radiating from it was louder now and the tempo had changed as though it were waking up. "I have a feeling that this might be what they were looking for."

Agnes made a noise. Her deep red-brown gaze widened and she rocked back as though trying to put as much distance between her and the stone as she could.

Deana hastily covered the stone, the grey cloth silencing its song. "Do you know what it is?"

"No—I don't know—maybe." Agnes pressed the heels of her palms to her forehead and squeezed her eyes shut.

Gendry cleared his throat, drawing their attention to where he stood just outside the door of the room. He had Kai's journal in one hand and what looked like Elijah's satchel in the other. "We shouldn't linger here. Let's get back to the Queen and keep that thing hidden." He gestured to the hidden stone with the corner of Kai's journal.

Agnes grabbed her father's satchel from Gendry and stuffed the cat and its severed leg into it, then she took the journal and tucked it inside, along with several other items from her room. She held it open while Deana placed the wrapped stone inside before Gendry herded them back to the Queen.

CHAPTER THIRTEEN

AGNES

Agnes was hiding in the hold of the Azure Queen, the broken mechanical cat laid out on a makeshift table in front of her. She didn't know why she had bothered bringing the cat. It wasn't like she could fix it. Or could she? She examined the dented body and severed leg. How it was still functioning despite the magic that powered it leaching out she didn't know. Her fingers tingled. Fixing the cat was better than trying to figure out why the mysterious stone had been hidden in the bottom of her trunk. She was certain she had never seen it before, but at the back of her mind something akin to a blooming headache niggled.

The stone was important, and somehow it was tied into Kent's plans for his war machine, the way the trance had tried to take her when Deana revealed it was indication enough of that. But how did it fit in? It wasn't a heartstone, and even if it were, it was certainly not big enough to power a golem the likes of what Kent wanted. She slammed her hands against the table to dispel the tingling that thoughts of Kent's war machine had brought on.

Her gaze fell on the cat once more. Fixing it would be a good distraction for her magic. "Focus on the cat," she whispered and fished her tool roll out of her bag. It was one of the things she had salvaged from the berth. *Salvaged.* As though the home she had known her entire life was just another wreck to be gutted and repurposed.

Her fingers trembled as she traced them over each tool. They were special, one-of-a-kind items she had designed herself and created with the aid of a metalsmith her father knew.

There had been splatters of blood at the berth as though her father had put up a fight. Had he survived? Had they dragged him off and thrown him in some dungeon somewhere in the bowels of Armada? Had it been Kent or someone else from her father's past? Deana said the broken pieces of coral and shell scattered about the berth had come from the shrouded ones.

She sniffed and dashed at the wetness on her cheeks as a knock sounded on the wall.

"Do you want to talk about it, Sparky?" Malani asked.

"There's nothing to talk about."

"Agnes," Malani said softly, and Agnes turned to meet her gaze. "Someone kidnapped your father and tore your home apart, and an arrogant arsehole with a superiority complex is forcing you to build a war machine. I understand if you don't want to talk about it, but if it were me, I would appreciate the shoulder to cry on."

"I'm not crying." She rubbed her eyes. "I just have a headache; it's been a long day."

Malani laughed and sat on one of the crates. "I'm not surprised about the headache. Deana mentioned that there was evidence of shrouded ones in the berth."

"There were little pieces of coral, shell, and seaweed. Deana told me not to touch any of it."

"It is said that if you touch the cursed coral it will burrow under your skin and you'll become one of them. I don't know if that's true, but I'd rather not take my chances. I don't fancy the *sea flora growing out of my rotting flesh* look."

"Surely someone would have noticed them moving about the city if they look as gruesome as Deana says," Agnes folded her arms.

Malani shrugged. "Maybe, but they can appear as beautiful women who lead sailors to their deaths, and if whoever kidnapped your father works for Kent then it would be easy enough for him to move them through Armada unnoticed."

Agnes chewed her lip.

"You said that Kent would need a heartstone to power the war machine right before you ran off, panicking about your father. Is that the stone Deana found at the berth?"

Agnes shook her head. "I don't know what that stone is. I thought if Kent needed to find a heartstone all he had to do was force Dad to draw him a map to one. That's why I ran to the berth. But I was too late." She hated how vulnerable this whole situation made her feel, like Kent was proving just how much he could influence her life. Even if she could fight the urge Kent's request for a war machine had activated in her magic, she couldn't refuse him because his threats were not empty. Both she and her father were not beyond his reach as long as they stayed on Armada.

"Agnes?" Dara called as she came down the stairs into the hold. "Wren wants to see you up on deck. Varlan has ..." Her eyes, which were several shades lighter than Deana's, zeroed in on the cat. She lifted her hand and lightly touched one of its crushed ears. "Its song is fading, and it doesn't want it to end. It was a good cat. It did what it was told." Her eyes were shining as they met Agnes'. "You can fix it, can't you?"

"I don't know." Her fingers tingled and she rubbed them together. Her magic seemed certain the cat could be fixed. "The heartstone that powers it is only a shard and it doesn't contain a spirit, just a piece of my magic. If the shard is too damaged to hold the magical charge, then there's nothing I can do."

"That's sad," Dara stroked the metal cheek of the cat.

"We should go and see what Wren wants," Malani said, placing a hand on Dara's shoulder and guiding her towards the stairs.

Agnes followed them up to the deck.

Gendry and Varlan were leaning against the side rail, both staring out at the ocean as they conversed quietly. Wren and Deana stood a short distance away with the twins. The rest of the crew was scattered about, seemingly focused on their own business. The air, however, felt tight, as though something was about to happen that would change everything.

As Agnes approached, Varlan turned to her and gave her a nod.

"Does Kent have my father?" she blurted out.

"I don't know for certain, but if it was Kent then he wasn't working alone."

"Who then?" Agnes already suspected the answer, but she needed to hear it all the same.

"If Kent is working with someone then without a doubt it is Idir," Varlan said, and Deana gasped.

"What could Dad possibly possess that Idir wants? If he wanted a map, Dad would have just drawn one for him. Unless it was something else entirely ... like the green stone?"

One of Varlan's brows rose. "Neither Idir nor Kent know I had that. No, I believe Idir had his minions ransack your home to find Kai's journal."

"Why would he want Kai's journal?" Deana asked, her voice tight.

Varlan studied her, and his features softened. "Because they believe the journal contains instructions on how to raise the Isle of Splendour."

"Dumura is just a myth though," Malani said.

"Bran said all stories ring with a grain of truth," Agnes bit her lip. "But why the Isle of Splendour?"

"It is rumoured to be the resting place of Grandmother Ocean, and those who can restore it to its glory can wake her and take her powers for their own. Except once they do all the gods will wake and the isles will be consumed by the forces of chaos," Varlan replied.

"Is that why Kent wants the war machine? To protect himself once Idir raises the Isle?"

Varlan gave a small nod. "I imagine Kent expects Idir to double-cross him, but right now Idir needs Kent, so that won't happen for a while. Or maybe Kent plans on double-crossing Idir. He's stupid enough to try it, but Idir isn't exactly human anymore."

"Why are you telling us this?" Deana asked. "Don't you work for Kent and, therefore, Idir?"

Varlan grunted, "I don't work for Kent; I've been trying to figure out what he and Idir are up to for the last few years. When I realised that Idir was sniffing around the old myths about Grandmother Ocean and Dumura, I removed the keystone from the equation. Even if he manages to raise the isle, he won't be able to reach the tomb that holds the goddess without it. If it has been removed from its hiding place, though, it will be calling to him like a beacon."

"Why exactly did you hide it in my trunk?" Agnes asked.

Varlan's mouth dropped open, and he gave a small laugh as he shook his head. "Well, now, that was clever. I wonder if that was your idea or Kai's. I didn't know what you had done with it, only that you and Kai hid it somewhere, and then you created that little guardian golem as a kind of compass that would lead you to it again when the time came. You still owe me for that heartstone, by the way."

She did what? She shook her head. "I have no idea what you are talking about. I never met Kai, and I certainly don't remember conspiring with him to hide the ... whatever that thing is." But something was niggling in the back of her mind; the headache and the feeling that she did know even if she couldn't remember.

"Of course you don't." He let out a heavy sigh. "I wiped both your and Kai's minds once the task was complete—Elijah's, too, for the little bit he knew about everything. Here, I'll show you." He held up a hand and beckoned her forward. "I need to touch you," he warned as though he expected her to hit him when he did.

"Go ahead," she said, and the moment his fingertips touched her brow the whole world tilted.

Her father was pacing across the berth kitchen. Varlan sat at the table, a steaming mug between his hands and a bundle of grey cloth on the table in front of him. Another man was leaning against the far wall. He had brown skin and warm brown eyes, and there was something about the curve of his jaw or the shape of those eyes that reminded her of Deana. Another Agnes was sitting on the end of the bench, her hands folded neatly in her lap as she watched the three men.

"How?" Agnes asked, patting herself down.

"It's a memory," Varlan said beside her, and she flicked a look from him to the other version of himself seated at the table. "Just watch," he pressed a finger to his lips.

"I can draw you a map to someplace Idir can never find," her father said.

"I thought of that already, but—"

"Why don't we just destroy it?" the other Agnes asked, cutting Varlan off.

"I don't think it can be destroyed, at least not by any tool of this world. It was constructed in the Between."

Her father stopped his pacing and rubbed his hands over his face. "I don't know how you expect us to be able to help you. Kent —"

"Doesn't know we have it. At the moment, no one knows—except Vince. And he's locked himself away in Quel'sapar. I'm just asking Agnes to construct a container to shield it. Once she's done, Kai will hide it, and I'll alter the memories of all three of you so no one will know you had any part in it, even if they try to read your minds."

The other Agnes lent forward, rubbing her fingers together. Agnes could tell by the way she held her mouth and shifted her hips that she had started to feel the tingle of her magic. Even if her father threw Varlan and Kai out, that past version of herself would have no choice but to complete Varlan's request.

"And what of your mind? What if Idir decides to go sorting through it? He'll know we helped you and come straight to us."

"I'd like to see him try," Varlan muttered.

The Varlan standing beside Agnes laughed under his breath. "I was a cocky son of a bitch, wasn't I?" He whispered to Agnes before muttering a quick, "Sorry, Mother."

"No, Varlan. I know I owe you, but I will not have you dragging Agnes into this," her father said as he slammed his hands on the table, drawing Agnes' attention back to the memory.

"It's too late," the other Agnes slid from the bench. "My keen has already been triggered."

The bottom fell out of Agnes' stomach as the memory shifted and she was jostled into Varlan. He steadied her and then pointed to the scene that had replaced the last one. The other Agnes was sitting at the kitchen table, a collection of metal plates and other parts scattered in front of her. She muttered to herself as she worked, her eyes oddly blank as she ran her fingers over her tool roll and selected one of the delicate instruments. Is this what she looked like when the trance took over?

The door opened and the Agnes from the past looked up, her eyes no longer staring blankly.

"Catch," the past Varlan appeared at the doorway and lobbed something at her.

She lunged forward and caught the object before holding it up to the light. It was a small shard of amethyst. Something swirled in its depths. "Is this real?" her past-self asked reverently.

"It's just a piece of one. It's the best I could do."

"It will work fine," past Agnes set the stone into the piece she had been working on. A bronze glow rolled over her fingers and the blank look returned as her hands became a blur. The parts on the table lifted into the air—bronze, black, and gold magic twisting over them—they locked together and the glare from the magic grew so bright Agnes had to shield her eyes.

After a short while, the magic dimmed, and the construct lowered to the table. Past Agnes lifted her head and took a step back, her eyes shining brightly as the cat stood. "We have our guardian."

"Thank you for helping me, Agnes. I know Elijah doesn't approve."

"It's not like I had a choice. Once the magic gets focused on an idea, I just have to hold on and see it through. But I've never created a real golem before. I didn't know it was possible without a necromancer to provide a spirit." Past Agnes scooped the cat up. "I'll just be a minute, then you can wipe my mind." She disappeared down the hall and moments later returned without the cat. "Alright."

The Varlan from the past stepped forward and brushed her hair behind her ear. "It's probably better if you lie down for this. Once I take the memories, you will lose consciousness for a little while." He rested his hands on her shoulders and met her eyes. "And are you certain you agree to this? In order to avoid discovering where you and Kai hid the keystone myself, I will have to blindly wipe the time from when you left to hide it to this moment. The rest of the memories I can alter more carefully, but you still won't remember anything from the last few months."

"I'll lose everything?"

"Everything," he confirmed with a nod.

Past Agnes' gaze dropped to her feet, but then she lifted her head, her eyes oddly bright and her mouth a determined line. "Come on. Best to get it over with before I have a chance to change my mind." She took hold of his hand and tugged him towards her room.

"We've seen all we need to," the Varlan beside her said, grabbing her hand as she started to follow the past version of herself.

The world lurched and she found herself once more on the deck of the Queen. She stumbled as the boards beneath her feet seemed to buck and roll.

Varlan caught her arm and held her steady. "I should have warned you it can be a bit disorientating." He waited while another wave of dizziness rocked over her then released his grip on her.

"The cat was a real golem. I just thought it was my magic powering it, that the stone wasn't a real heartstone. But you—how did you find it?"

He held up a finger. "That is a long story and one we really don't have time for."

"How do we know whatever you just showed Agnes is real? You could have planted anything you wanted inside her mind," Malani said, her arms folded as she studied Varlan.

Agnes shook her head. "It was real. I can't explain it, but I *know* it was." She had the impression that Varlan had hidden some details from her but what he had showed her was real. She could feel that at her core.

Malani studied Varlan for a few moments then gave a nod. "If you trust him, Sparky, then I will as well."

"So did you just come here to tell us that you believe Idir took Elijah?" Deana asked.

Varlan's gaze flicked to Agnes. "No. I came to tell you we need to break Bran out and then get away from Armada as quickly as we can."

"I can't leave," Agnes said. "Kent triggered my keen. Until I finish his war machine, I will be a slave to it. And even if that wasn't the case, I won't leave Dad behind."

"What if you still built the war machine but didn't do it for Kent?" Malani asked. "We can rescue both Bran and Elijah then get our arses out of here. You can build the machine once we get somewhere Kent and Idir can't reach us."

"Idir is a shrouded one. There is nowhere in the isles that he won't be able to find us," Deana said.

"Nowhere in the isles ..." Wren repeated. "What if we left the isles?"

"Where would we go?" Agnes asked.

"Osmar or Quel'sapar are options," Varlan offered.

"I was thinking of somewhere that is far from the ocean and nearly impossible to find unless you have been shown how to reach it," Wren said.

"And where exactly is that?" Varlan asked.

"Hartswood."

"Hartswood?" Both Deana and Agnes asked.

Wren nodded. "It's where Bran is from."

"Could we block your keen with a pair of bind-shackles, Agnes?" Gendry asked. "If your keen was blocked then the compulsion to build Kent's war machine wouldn't be there."

"And where are we going to get a pair of bind-shackles, my love?" Wren asked. "Though maybe you have a point. I know mind mages can place blocks on keen," she added with a look in Varlan's direction. "What if you isolated the compulsion to build Kent's machine and blocked it?"

"No." Varlan, Agnes, and Deana all said together.

"Okay." Wren lifted her hands in defence.

Agnes didn't like the idea of placing any kind of block on her keen. It was bad enough that she had been born without proper keen-sense.

"Isolating a part of person's keen is extremely difficult and there is a great deal that can go wrong. I could end up doing permanent damage to both Agnes' keen and mind," Varlan explained.

"Is wiping memories any different?" Wren settled her hands on her hips and stared him down.

"It is completely different. Taking a memory or even altering one is simple and straightforward as it does not directly affect the keen of a mage. When you start messing around with keen you are walking the line between mind magic and necromancy. Very few mind mages are capable of successfully isolating a single part of a mage's keen in that fashion. It would be better for Agnes to build the machine and include some kind of vulnerability, a vital weakness or an easy way to shut it down."

As he spoke, Agnes' fingers started to tingle. She could include a weakness—a flaw somewhere in the structure that Kent wouldn't be aware of. She rubbed her hands together, and a small smile quirked the corner of Varlan's mouth. It was clear from the memory he'd shown her that he knew how to trigger her keen, but what was his intention here? Why help her undermine Kent's plans?

"Regardless of what we decide, we are going to need a plan," Wren said.

"Kent doesn't have a heartstone for Bran to shackle a soul to. Even if I build the bulk of the war machine, I can't finish it until he finds a suitable stone. We can leave Bran where he is for now and use the time to find out where Idir took Dad."

"What about Savita? She's still sniffing around," Deana said.

"Which is why you are staying hidden," Agnes said.

"You should follow your own advice." Varlan folded his arms and levelled his whisky-coloured gaze on her. "If Savita turns up again while you're at the crow's nest and I'm not there, she will have full access to your thoughts. Without kee—"

"I don't think she'll try that again." Did Varlan know about her keen-sense? Just how much time had they spent together in the past? How many memories had he altered?

"There might be a way to protect your mind from her," Wren said.

"The surest way is to stay here and not go anywhere near the crow's nest," Varlan said, his tongue probing the inside of his cheek as he folded his arms across his chest.

"That's not an option." Agnes said before turning to Wren and asking, "How?"

"Nea had a small disc of robrillium with runes carved on it. Niall made it to see if he could block a specific keen and use it as a protection charm of sorts; apparently he was successful."

As Wren spoke, a ticklish prickle started in Agnes' fingertips.

"And where would we find such a charm? It's not like one will just fall into our laps out here in the middle of the ocean," Varlan gestured towards the waves lapping gently at the side of the ship.

"I think I can make one," Agnes said before spinning on her heel and running into the hold.

She retrieved a small piece of robrillium from her tool roll. The rose-gold metal vibrated against her skin, tugging at the back of her mind. Robrillium was most commonly used to block magic, specifically the magic of an individual mage through the use of bind-shackles. But it was also highly conductive to magic and could be programmed for a variety of other uses. It was, however, volatile to work with, and prolonged exposure to the ore it was mined from caused a wasting condition called Keldar's syndrome, which meant very few mages ever really experimented with it.

How exactly would one program it to form a shield of sorts? She rubbed the piece she held between her forefinger and thumb. Wren had said there were runes on the piece she had seen. Rune magic was beyond complex, and she wasn't sure she could recreate it. But maybe she didn't have to ... Maybe if she gave her magic enough cues it could create exactly what she needed. She needed to see these runes for herself. Perhaps Wren could remember them enough to draw them for her.

She grabbed her journal and a pen and turned to head back to the deck only to slam into a solid form behind her.

Varlan gripped her shoulders as she stumbled, and then he took a step back as he released her. Her ink pot had slipped from her fingers and smashed against the floor at their feet, splashing its contents across their boots and the boards of the hold. Agnes tucked her journal under her arm and bent to collect the shards of the pot.

"Agnes," Varlan said softly as he crouched to help her. "You have to know this charm idea is madness. If Savita gets inside your mind, she could—"

"My magic doesn't think it's madness." She met his gaze squarely, and he let out a sigh before the corner of his mouth quirked and he shook his head.

"What do you need?"

She rocked back on her heels. "I need to know what those runes looked like."

"May I?" He gestured towards her journal and held his hand out.

They both stood, and she placed the journal on his open palm before balancing the pen on top. She then set the broken ink pot on the edge of the crate she had been using as a table and folded her arms.

Varlan flipped slowly through the journal until he came to a blank page. He dipped the pen into the small pool of ink left in the broken pot and began drawing.

His work was neat, the lines crisp and clear as he drew three runes. "I doubt the runes themselves will be enough. You'll need—"

"A mind mage to charge it and set the magic," she whispered as she stared at the marks. "How do you know what the runes look like?"

He shrugged. "You pick up a lot of random knowledge in my line of work." With a slow nod, he passed the journal back to her. "You know it is still highly likely that this charm won't actually protect your mind from Savita?"

She chewed her lip and held up the piece of robrillium as a fizzing sound dulled her thoughts. "I trust my magic, Varlan. And if history is anything to go by, you do too." Then the trance washed over her, sending her mind blank.

When her senses came back to her, she had a smooth disc of robrillium between her fingers. The face was marked with an eight-pointed star.

"Well?" Varlan asked, drawing her attention to him.

He was standing across from her, palms resting on the top of her makeshift table. The shards of the inkpot were gone but the ends of his fingers were still stained. There was something in his warm, brown gaze—a question?

Her stomach gave a small swoop as a prickling sensation raised the hairs on her arms and neck, telling her she had experienced a moment just like this before. She blinked at him as the sensation dulled once more. "I think it worked."

"Do you want to test it?"

"One moment." She retrieved a piece of leather thread from her tool roll and looped it through the hole in the top of the charm, then she secured it around her neck and gave him a nod.

His eyes met hers again and there was something in his gaze that stirred a feeling deep in the back of her mind. Like the echo of a dream, or maybe it was a memory. After several heartbeats, his gaze broke from hers.

"Well?" she asked, mirroring his question from before.

"You did it." He gave her an off-kilter grin. "It should keep Savita out of your mind. Leave it on and keep it hidden." He paused and drew a long breath, a contemplative frown chasing his mirth away. "I had best be getting back before Kent gets suspicious, but I will find out what I can about Elijah. Please be careful, Agnes. Even if Savita can't enter your mind, you shouldn't underestimate her." Then he left the hold and the space seemed suddenly empty.

Her gaze dropped to study the pieces of the mechanical cat and she placed her hands delicately on the curve of its body. It was a real golem. Never in a million years could she have thought herself capable of creating a true golem. It changed everything. She swallowed and pushed down the thoughts of what it meant for Kent's war machine, instead shifting her mind to mending the cat. Not only would she do whatever she could to fix it—she would make it better. If only she had a bigger heartstone.

CHAPTER FOURTEEN

VARLAN

"Where have you been?" Kent asked as Varlan entered the main room of the crow's nest.

"I went to see Elijah," Varlan said, keeping his voice level and casting a look around the space before letting his gaze fall back on Kent.

"Elijah?" Kent sat forward in his throne-like chair and rested his elbows on his knees.

"Yes. So, you can imagine how surprised I was to find both he and his daughter missing and their berth ransacked."

Kent stiffened at that news; did he not know about the kidnapping? "Agnes is missing?"

Of course, he wasn't concerned for Elijah. No matter how useful the cartographer was, he would never be as valuable as his daughter in Kent's eyes. Especially now she had been tasked with building Kent a war machine with which he could claim the entire isles if he so desired.

"She is safe." As safe as she could be while she insisted on staying on Armada. If Varlan had his way, he would have thrown her over his shoulder and dragged her off to Hartswood as Wren had suggested.

"Are you certain she will remain that way? Perhaps she should stay in one of the rooms here."

"You can always suggest that to her when she comes by tomorrow morning to work on your commission," Varlan said as he walked to the small desk that Kent had brought in for Agnes. Her journal and sketches were gone but her keen still clung to the surface of the table. "So, you know nothing of Elijah's disappearance? I thought perhaps you had him brought up here to ensure Agnes' cooperation."

A strange expression touched Kent's features before he gave a minute shake of his head. "There has been no need to threaten Elijah. Agnes may not have been completely willing to work with me, but she has been compliant thus far. I would not have made a move on her father until she showed outright defiance."

"Who then?"

"You seem awfully concerned about Elijah." Kent's eyes narrowed.

"He was completing a map for me, and his disappearance is inconvenient." He fought the urge to twist his mouth at the words. Over the years of dealing with people like Kent and Vince, he had gotten rather good at playing their games. But he had never grown to enjoy them. He also needed to keep Kent in the dark about his feelings for Agnes. Feelings she no longer returned; if only he had been able to wipe his own mind. Those carefully guarded looks she kept giving him were affecting him more than he had expected.

"Perhaps you should ask Savita about the disappearance."

Ah, yes, Idir's darling little snake-in-the-grass daughter. He let his keen-sense brush over Kent for a moment. There were no signs of Savita's keen on him, but her magic was subtle, and he wouldn't put it past Idir to use Savita to control Kent. Especially if he learned that Kent had intentions to double-cross him once they found the Isle of Splendour. Did Idir know about the war machine? Surely, Savita would have told him if she herself knew.

"Where is Savita now? You do realise that Idir sent her here to spy on you."

"She's probably off pouting somewhere." Kent waved his hand through the air in a dismissive gesture. "She is disappointed that I will not let her near the necromancer, and she is also very annoyed at that stunt you pulled earlier."

"So, you would have been happy for her to pluck the details of your secret project out of Agnes' mind and deliver them to Idir?"

"No. And thank you for preventing her from doing so." Kent gave him a calculating look. "Though I do wonder if it was your loyalty to me that made you step in or something else entirely."

Several years ago, when he had gone to Elijah and Agnes for help to hide the keystone, he had been careful that no one knew or even suspected that he was working with them. He had certainly kept his dealings with Agnes under wraps. To anyone at the time it would have simply looked like he was catching up with Elijah. They were, after all, old associates. Not even Elijah had known just how close Varlan and Agnes had become; at least, not until just before Varlan had altered his memory of those months.

"If Idir finds out about your plans to double-cross him, that also implicates me, and I don't want that particular target on my back. It's bad enough that I lost his precious keystone."

Kent leant back in his chair, seemingly placated. "Any luck tracking it down again?"

"No, that is why I came to Elijah; I was hoping he could draw me a map. But now he's missing I am back to following tenuous rumours and gossiping fishwives."

"Do you think Vince reclaimed it?"

Varlan twisted his mouth as though he were considering it. "Perhaps. Though if he has, he isn't letting on and I have people watching him just in case."

Kent nodded. "You know, you're not the only one who Elijah's disappearance inconveniences? Both Agnes and the necromancer are clear that I will need to find a certain type of heartstone for my project. And normal heartstones are hard enough to come by ..."

Varlan licked his lips. "So perhaps we need to focus on finding Elijah, as that move seems to be in both our best interests."

"Perhaps." Kent nodded slowly and when he met Varlan's gaze again, there was something there that unsettled him. "Of course, once I have a map, I will need someone with a particular set of skills to seek out the heartstone and bring it to me."

"Of course," Varlan said with a nod of his own. "So where do we start?"

Once night fell and the general populace of Armada turned to their beds, the artificial lighting that had been Agnes' first commission shifted from the bright mimicry of daylight to a soft blue that left pooling shadows in the corners of the common areas. Those shadows were old friends to Varlan. He slipped through them like a ghost, footfalls silent from years of honing his skills as a thief.

Agnes seemed to have no idea she was being followed, but then again, she had managed to lose Kent's guard before they had left the market square. Varlan wasn't so easy to shake, and he wasn't an amateur who made stupid mistakes that alerted her to his presence.

She paused at the end of a corridor, and he slunk deeper into the shadows. Where was she going? As far as he knew, this section of Armada had been empty for a while. When she started forward again, he kept his distance. The farther she went along this particular corridor, the fewer places he had to hide.

Eventually she slipped inside one of the abandoned berths. She had to be meeting someone, but who?

He settled back out of sight to wait for her to re-emerge, but after what felt like an hour, it was the merchant Gethyn who appeared as the door to the berth opened. He glanced both ways along the corridor then hurried away. What was Agnes up to? If Kent found out she was meeting someone like Gethyn late at night he'd lose his shit entirely.

Varlan shifted against the wall. What was taking her so long? Was there another exit to the berth? Had Gethyn done something to her? He straightened ready to march over and investigate the berth when she stepped out of the doorway. She did the same check of the corridor that Gethyn had then headed away in the opposite direction. Varlan rubbed a hand over his face and hurried back to the market level. Unless she decided to risk taking the underbelly at high tide, she would need to cross the market to reach the Queen.

When she emerged from the corridor that led to the berth she shared with her father, he stepped out of the shadows into her path.

"A little late to be running about the city, isn't it?" he asked softly.

Her eyes, which looked black in the blue gloom of the artificial lighting, widened. "I could say the same thing to you," she whispered and cast a glance over the silent market.

"True, but Kent wouldn't consider it quite the same act of betrayal if I was the one he caught meeting with questionable acquaintances in abandoned berths."

She took a step back from him. "I made sure no one was following me."

"I wouldn't be a very good thief if I didn't know a thing or two about keeping hidden and trailing a mark."

"Are you going to tell Kent?"

"Of course not, but you need to be more careful. Why are you meeting with Gethyn anyway?"

She licked her lips. "He wanted to know what Kent was up to and now he wants to help me sabotage the war machine. We all have the same goal."

That was debatable. Gethyn suspected Kent was responsible for his brother's death. His quarrel with the current leader of the floating city was personal. For him, Agnes was just a convenient tool to get the revenge he wanted.

Footsteps sounded across the market, and he grabbed Agnes' arm, dragging her into a shadowed alcove. He touched a finger to his lips as they waited, bodies pressed close in the dark. A soft-fingered magic reached the edge of his keen-sense, and he fought the urge to swear. If Savita found him here with Agnes, she would definitely tell Kent. Varlan wasn't sure how he could brush that off easily as he had before. And what would it mean for Agnes herself?

"Stay here," he whispered, and moved out of the alcove.

Making sure to put a little unsteadiness into his step, he strode into the market square as though returning from a late night of drinking. "Does Kent know you're sneaking about his city so late at night?" he drawled.

Her gaze narrowed and her keen burrowed against his.

"You sure you want to try that again, sweetheart?" He cocked an eyebrow. "Didn't work so well for you the first time, did it?"

"Where have you been?" she asked.

"That's really none of your business, is it?"

Her lip curled. "I'm sure Kent would be equally as curious to know why you're out so late."

"Nice try, sweetheart." He chuckled.

"Stop calling me that!" She stamped her foot.

"Would you prefer princess?" He swayed to keep up the drunken charade.

"I don't have time for this."

"Well don't let me keep you from your clandestine affairs." He gave her a mock bow then sauntered towards the stairs to the crow's nest. He paused when he reached them and glanced out of the corner of his eye. Savita strode straight past the alcove where Agnes was hiding and disappeared into a dark corridor.

Varlan let out a breath and headed back to the place he had left Agnes. He half expected her to be gone by the time he reached it, but she was leaning against the wall with her arms folded.

"Why does it feel like we've been in this situation before?"

"We might have once or twice."

"Once or *twice*? Just how many of my memories did you take?"

A good few months' worth. He sighed and said, "Only as many as I had to, to keep you and your father safe."

Her gaze dropped to the floor at the mention of her father. "Did Kent know anything about his disappearance?"

He wanted to touch his fingers to her chin and draw her eyes back to his, but he kept his arms at his sides. "No. Or at least, he didn't *seem* to know, but he blamed Idir. And he wants to rescue him. Though I am not sure rescue is the right word given he'll just be tossing him into the glorified cell next to Bran."

"Let me guess—the only reason he wants to get Dad back from Idir is because he wants a map to a heartstone that will be suitable for his commission."

"Exactly ... I'm sorry, Agnes. I should have told Elijah to get you out of here several years ago, but I had no idea when all of this was going to come to a head."

She shrugged. "I am sure Idir and Kent would have still found us, and it's not like you were personally invested in our safety but rather in keeping the keystone hidden."

He shook his head. Sure that was how it had started, but he couldn't tell her the truth now. And besides, it was better this way. The less she knew about what had really transpired between them the harder it would be for Kent to use that to his advantage. "You should be getting back to the Queen. I'll let you know as soon as I learn anything about your father's whereabouts."

She stepped out of the alcove and turned towards the corridor that led down to the dock.

"And, Agnes."

The look she threw back over her shoulder halted his breath for a moment. He swallowed and said, "Be careful who you trust. Nearly everyone in this city has an ulterior motive."

"Oh, I know. I was raised in this city, remember?" she waved his concern away and disappeared into the darkness.

Varlan rubbed a hand over his face before heading back to the crow's nest. He had one last bit of business to complete before he could fall into bed and get a couple of hours of sleep.

The guard posted outside Bran's door was keen-less, which made it easy to slip inside his mind and deliver the suggestion of sleep. Varlan's keen had barely settled over him when he rubbed his hand over his face and stifled a yawn. A moment later his eyes slid shut and he mumbled something incoherent before sliding into a heap on the floor. Varlan stepped over him and took out his lockpicks.

When he entered the room, Bran was sitting on the bed, a violet mage light bobbing above him.

"Come to break me out, have you?" he asked as he ran a hand through his snow-white hair.

"Not just yet. I wanted to check in and see how you were going."

"I'm bored out of my wits but otherwise fine. Are Deana and Agnes okay? I overheard the guards saying Elijah was kidnapped."

"Idir got to him, by the looks of it, but I'm not convinced that Kent isn't also involved. And Deana is fine for now. However, Savita is sniffing around, and it won't be long before she finds her." He took up the chair by the desk.

"What does Idir want with her?"

"He needs her magic to raise a sunken isle and reach the temple of Grandmother Ocean."

"And Agnes? I know she was here this morning, but that was before I found out about Elijah."

Agnes was walking a very risky line, but how could he phrase it without sounding too concerned for her? "As long as Agnes keeps dancing to Kent's tune, she will be alright. She's too useful for Kent to get rid of."

Bran nodded slowly, his deep blue eyes narrowing as he studied Varlan. "And what is your stake in all of this? Are you hoping Idir and Kent will knock each other off then you can sweep in and take over?"

"That's not my style. I'm just content to take care of my own arse and steal things from time to time. Speaking of which, I am sure you are aware that Kent lacks a heartstone for the golem he is having Agnes construct. You wouldn't happen to know where I might find one?"

"No offence, but even if I did, I wouldn't tell you."

Varlan chuckled softly. "Yeah, I probably wouldn't tell me either. But if we don't find a heartstone, I fear that Kent is going to resort to more drastic measures. Do you think Nea would help?"

"Maybe ... She could certainly point us in the right direction. But without a spirit-glass or access to my things, I have no way of contacting her. I have a silver rose that links our keens, but I left it on Malani's ship."

"I can fetch it. You haven't figured out how to create portals yet, have you? It might save us a whole heap of trouble if you have."

Bran snorted. "Do you think if I had figured it out, I'd still be sitting here waiting for Kent to get all his ducks in a row?"

"Probably not." Varlan stood and moved to the door. "I promise I'm working on a plan to get you out of here, but I need to make sure doing so doesn't endanger Agnes. I'll try to keep you informed of what's going on. If I can't drop by myself, I'll send word with Wes. He's the only member of Kent's guard who can be trusted, so if you need to get in touch with me let him know."

Bran nodded. "Alright."

Varlan stepped out into the hall and relocked the door. The guard was still asleep, but he stirred as Varlan stepped past him and melted into the shadows. This business between Kent and Idir was going to prove a huge mess. Normally Varlan would just wash his hands of it and disappear over the horizon, but this time he didn't have that luxury. This time, the one person he had ever cared about more than himself was caught in the middle of it.

CHAPTER FIFTEEN

DEANA

The Azure Queen was silent save for the gentle lap of water rippling along her hull and the soft snoring coming from the other side of the hold. Deana felt like she had barely slept. It could have been that she was in a strange place with so many other people or the excitement of the past few days. Perhaps it was some combination of the two. Or maybe it was her dreams, which had been a landscape of churning, grey water. A glow beneath the surface beckoning her deep into the fathoms where the shrouded ones waited with open arms to welcome her home. The song of the keystone had permeated those dreams in such a manner that the echo of it still rang across the back of her mind an hour after waking.

She had checked the stone when she first woke, but it had still been tightly wrapped in the grey cloth that silenced its song. The wrapping was somehow imbued with the power of the silencers and completely blocked the stone's song, which Varlan had said would be a beacon for Idir. Varlan's explanation for why Idir wanted the stone had left a writhing mass in Deana's stomach, one that stole her appetite and increased the sour taste of dread at the back of her tongue.

Rubbing her hands over her face, she sat up and dropped her legs over the side of the bunk. She studied the crew members of the Queen who took up nearly every other bunk in the room. Agnes' bed was empty; had she left sometime during the night? She had seemed on edge after their talk with Varlan. He had apparently shown her a memory, but what if he had done something else to her? Planted some compulsion in her mind? His song was very similar to Idir's and as far as they knew he was working with Kent, who was also working with Idir. Could Varlan really be trusted? Gendry seemed to trust him, or at least enjoy his company. The pair of them had spent a long time yesterday quietly chatting. But Wren seemed more guarded around him, and as far as Deana could tell, the captain was a fairly good judge of character.

Careful not to wake the others, she crept to the stairs. As she emerged onto the deck, her feet faltered, and she tipped her head back to study the expanse of brooding sky. It was hard to tell if the sun had risen yet or not; the dark clouds above gave the world a soft, greyish tone that reminded Deana of her dream. She swallowed and moved to the side of the ship, leaning forward to examine the charcoal water. Something dark moved beneath the waves and she leant farther forward to try to see it clearer—

A hand grabbed her shoulder and pulled her backwards, another clamping over her mouth to muffle her scream. The scent of decay and brackish water brought a wave of burning bile up her throat.

She thrashed in her attacker's hold and drove her elbow into their sternum. They let out a grunt and dropped her. She dove away from them, rolling across the deck and pushing herself onto her hands and knees.

It was a man. Or it had been once. Orange and red coral studded the skin of his face and seaweed was woven through his ragged clothes and hair. His once full lips pulled back to reveal blackened teeth as he inhaled slowly.

She reached for the protection charm, and his head tilted.

"There's no need for that." He held one hand out, the withered fingers curled as though holding something. "A message," he prompted when she made no move to take whatever it was.

The door to the captain's quarters slammed open and Gendry came charging out with Wren close behind him, her song roaring across Deana's mind.

Her attacker let out a hiss, and she scuttled backwards as he made a lunge towards her, but he simply deposited whatever he had been holding at her feet before diving over the side of the ship.

Wren rushed after him, her rust-coloured hair flicking forward as she caught the side rail and let out a curse.

Gendry crouched in front of Deana and reached for the item the man had dropped. It was a black spiral shell; a ripple of aqua-coloured magic twisted over its surface.

"Don't touch it!" Deana warned, and he snapped his hand back.

The song coming from the shell was burrowing under her skin, setting barbs into her mind that urged her to pick it up. The stone burned against her chest, and she pulled it from her shirt with a gasp. Everything grew too loud as the rest of the crew emerged from the hold and gathered around.

Dara pushed through them, her pale gaze meeting Deana's. "The song won't end until you pick it up," the girl said as she squeezed her eyes shut and pressed her hands over her ears.

Deana lifted her hand towards the shell, and threads of black-laced-aqua magic reached for her fingers. The song grew louder, tearing through every corner of her soul until it was the only sound she could hear, the only thing she could feel, see, taste, and smell. It was barbed and acrid, permeating her being. She had to

make it stop. She had to—

The shell shattered under her fingers. Shards of black obsidian burrowed under her skin as images flashed across her mind too fast for her to make sense of. Her temples throbbed and the light from the seer stone grew blinding as its song rose and tangled around the music of the shell. Heat inflamed every inch of her, destroying the barbs that had set themselves under her skin. With a strangled gasp, everything grew silent, and darkness claimed her as her cheek met the cool boards of the deck.

Soft sand slipped under her feet as she ran along the beach with a loud squeal of laughter. Kai was chasing her with a tangled clump of seaweed in his hands. She led him into the shallows, her song singing along her veins as the water rose in a wall around her.

"No magic, Deana. That's cheating." Kai laughed as his own song built around her and the sand beneath her shifted, breaking her concentration. She lost her grip on the waves and they splashed around her, soaking her from head to toe.

When she looked up, Kai was older; the light was gone from his eyes and his lifeless skin was dotted with coral—

Deana sat bolt upright. She didn't recognise the room, but the soft notes of a healing song clung to everything around her. Movement at the corner of her eye caught her attention and she met Agnes' worried stare.

"Nari," Agnes called. "She's awake."

An old woman who Deana vaguely recognised entered the room and the healing song grew louder. She almost looked like an older version of Malani with her dark brown skin and grey dreadlocks, but the eyes that settled on Deana were a clear sky-blue.

"How are you feeling?" Nari asked.

Like she'd been half drowned. "Sore and tired." She lifted her hand, noting the thin scars that marked her fingers.

"I managed to get all the shards out. You were lucky you had that protection charm, or you would likely be resting against Grandmother Ocean's breast right now." She held up a corked glass bottle and rattled the shards of black shell within. "The magic is gone but there should be enough residue left behind to distil its purpose."

"The shrouded one said it was a message," Deana said, rubbing her forehead.

"Did you *see* anything when you touched the shell?" Nari asked.

"I don't know. It all happened too fast to make sense of."

Nari let out a long breath as she studied Deana. "You may find that this message comes to you over the next few days. But be careful—it may not have been a message at all."

"Do you think it was some kind of trap?" Agnes asked.

"It is a possibility, but until I work out exactly what magic was used to create the shell, I won't know for sure."

Agnes worried her bottom lip between her teeth before asking, "Is it safe to take her back to the Queen."

"As safe as if she were to stay here ... safer perhaps, given the amount of keen-folk on that ship. I will study these shards then come find you when I have some answers." She placed the jar down next to another one that contained several lumps of pinkish coral. The largest was the size of Deana's thumb.

"Is that shrouded-one coral? Why do you have that?"

Nari picked up the jar and gave it a little shake. "For the same reason I have the shards I took from your hand. To gain an understanding of the magic that imbues them and perhaps figure out a way to combat it."

Was this woman insane? Why would she take such a risk?

"Come on, Deana. I'll walk you to the Queen before I go up and see Kent," Agnes said as she stood.

"You're going back there today?" Deana asked as she studied Agnes.

The dark circles beneath the other woman's eyes stood out against her pale skin. Her hair was coming undone from the twin braids as though she hadn't brushed it since the day before.

"I don't have a choice." She ushered Deana towards the door. "Thank you, Nari."

Nari waved her hand. "Any time, my dear. Be careful with Kent. He's more slippery than eel in a barrel of oil." She followed them to the threshold. "I'll be in touch if I learn anything from the shell, but if you figure out what the message might have been, please come back and see me." She placed a hand on each of their arms and her song rose around them, bringing with it a wave of energy that rolled through Deana's body and left her skin tingling.

They were almost back to the Queen when Agnes pulled Deana behind a stack of crates.

"What—" Deana bit down on her question as Agnes pressed a finger to her lips.

Agnes leant forward and glanced around the edge of the crates. Deana tried to follow her line of sight, but it was impossible without moving from her hiding place. After a few moments, Agnes waved for her to follow but she didn't head towards the Queen. Instead, she hurried along a shadowy corridor and then opened a hatch and darted down a short, slanted ladder.

The hallways in this section of the city were all dark, the berths silent as though the area had been abandoned. Agnes navigated it like she had been here a hundred times before and when Deana stumbled, she reached back and took hold of her hand, her song picking up tempo as a bronze light burst to life beside them. Ribbons of black and gold twisted through Agnes' mage light, and Deana almost wanted to reach out and touch it. It was one of the most beautiful lights she had ever seen.

"We're almost there," Agnes said as she gave Deana's hand a tug and led her farther along the dark corridor, the light casting long shadows in either direction that ducked and weaved as they ran.

They finally emerged onto the slick rocks of the underbelly where Deana's canoe had washed ashore. Agnes kept hold of her hand but extinguished the light and slowed her pace to navigate the treacherous ground. When the belly of the Queen came into view, Agnes stopped as though listening then gave a satisfied nod and led Deana to a set of seaweed-encrusted stairs.

As they stumbled onto the dock at the top of the stairs, Agnes finally let go of Deana's hand.

"Are you going to tell me what that was about?" Deana asked.

"The guards were watching the other corridor—there was no way we could have gotten around them without being seen," Agnes said and gave Deana a nudge towards the Queen. "Go. I have to get up to the crow's nest, but I'll see you tonight."

Deana drew a long breath before she wandered over to the gangplank that led up to the Queen. As she stepped onto the deck, the twins swamped her in a hug, and she tried not to stiffen. She wasn't used to people who weren't Indi or her family embracing her, but the women pulled back with genuine smiles on their faces.

"How are you feeling?" Pippa asked.

"You had us terribly worried," Kiki added.

"I feel fine. Nari healed me."

"Did Nari say what that shell was? Was it really a message?" Kiki asked.

"She's didn't know for certain, but she is going to study the shards to see what she can learn." Deana wasn't sure what the healer would be able to learn from the shards or why she seemed to be so interested in studying things associated with the shrouded ones. If even the tiniest fragment of that coral got under her skin, she'd be dead before she learned any of its secrets, her body turned into a shrouded one and her soul shackled to an eternity of service to Grandmother Ocean.

The twins both nodded. "Are you hungry?" they asked.

"Yes. Starving, actually." The burst of energy Nari had given her was starting to wane and in its wake was a hunger that left her head swimming.

Pippa chuckled and Kiki looped her arm through Deana's and said, "Come on then. Let's get you fed."

CHAPTER SIXTEEN

AGNES

"You're late," Kent said as she entered the crow's nest.

"I had an emergency," she said before dropping into the chair at the desk. Her journal and sketches were already laid out.

"I have been lenient with you, but it has come to my attention that you may be wilfully delaying this commission and conspiring with others against me. If I get any indication that these rumours are true, I will not hesitate to punish you. Is that clear?"

She shuffled the sketches and picked up her pen.

"Agnes?" There was a touch of venom under his tone and a sharpness in his gaze as she met it. "Is. That. Clear?"

The temptation to defy him stirred but she bit back her retort and instead gave him a single nod.

"Good." He smiled and settled himself into his throne. "Now, you are not leaving here again until those plans are complete. So get to work."

She shuffled through her sketches again. Normally by now the tingling would have started and she would be slipping into the trance, but something was wrong.

"I said begin," Kent growled in warning.

Drawing a deep breath, she closed her eyes and reached for the kernel of magic at her centre. It stirred but refused to lift completely to the surface.

"What are you waiting for!" Kent slammed his hands on the desk in front of her.

Startled, she leapt from her chair. It teetered then crashed to the floor. "I don't know what's wrong, but I can't access my magic."

He scratched the underside of his chin and shook his head. "You are playing a very dangerous game, but I have ways of making you do exactly what I want—Savita," he called towards the door.

Savita entered. She was dressed in a vivid scarlet today, her dark hair hanging free down her back.

"Now, Agnes, either you get started or Savita will enter your mind and force you to. Varlan isn't going to step in and save you today. So, which will it be?"

Agnes shook her head. "I can't force the trance to take me. That's not how my keen works."

Savita's obsidian eyes met Agnes' and her brow furrowed before she shot a look at Kent. "I cannot get inside her mind. Something is blocking me." Those dark eyes settled on Agnes again and narrowed.

"Her keen has been blocked then?"

"Perhaps. However, a blocked keen would not stop me being able to read her mind." Savita flicked her gaze to Kent. "Something else is preventing me from using my power on her."

"Agnes?" Kent said delicately, though that hint of venom still laced the word.

She shook her head. "I don't know what she's talking—" She gasped as Kent lunged forward and slammed her against the wall.

Savita smirked. "Men like him make such easy puppets. I almost don't have to use my magic on them."

"What are you doing?" Agnes struggled, but Kent held her firm, his features strangely blank.

"Now, where is the charm that is blocking me?"

Kent shifted his grip, so he had her pinned with one hand. The other he ran along the side of her neck before hooking the thin twist of leather that held the charm from under the collar of her shirt. He tugged it, revealing the disc of robrillium, and then closed his fist around it and yanked.

The leather cord dug savagely into the back of her neck before it broke, and then Kent staggered backwards, turning a wrathful glare on Savita.

"How dare you."

"Oh please. I can't do it again now that you have that charm. Consider it a gift. It's not *your* mind I am interested in though."

Agnes backed away from her.

"Now, little tinkerer, you are going to sing for me. Where is Deana?"

Agnes shut her eyes and thought of everything except Deana. Pain sliced through her mind as Savita's dark gaze flashed across it. The image of Deana's face drifted to the surface, but Agnes pushed it back down. Her breath came in rapid pants as she struggled against the invisible webs that were roping through her mind and dragging up her deepest secrets. Deana, her father, Varlan. Savita paused on the memories Varlan had shown Agnes the day before. First the one of him handing Agnes the piece of heartstone and then the one of him brushing her hair behind her ear before he wiped her mind. Finally she pulled up the memory of last night, when he had pulled her into the shadows to hide from the very mage who was now tearing through her thoughts.

"Interesting," Savita whispered.

The image changed again but Agnes pushed back against Savita's hold as hard as she could, the scent of blood filling her senses.

"That is enough," Kent said. "I will not have you kill her while I still need her. Whatever personal vendetta you have can wait."

The pressure in Agnes' mind lessened and she opened her eyes, lifting her fingers to stem the flow of blood from her nose. The walls shifted, spinning and swooping away from her, and she fell to her knees as the floor seemed to buck beneath her feet.

"It would appear that Varlan has not been as loyal to either yourself or my father as he pretends. How he has kept it secret for so long is remarkable. But like so many before him, his heart has proven his undoing. I am certain he knows exactly where Father's keystone is and how to get you the heartstone you need." Savita's mouth curved into a predatory smile. "And we now have the incentive we need to ensure his cooperation."

Kent studied Agnes. "Well isn't that just perfect? But can you force her to use her magic or not?"

Savita's gaze darkened as it fell on Agnes again. "Child's play," she said with that same predatory grin, and Agnes' mind went blank.

When Agnes awoke, her head was pounding. She pressed her hands to it and forced her eyes to stay open. Her vision was blurred, and she squeezed her eyes shut before opening them again, hoping it would clear. She couldn't remember where she was, but it didn't look like her room. There were bars over the window and the only other furniture aside from the bed were a single table and chair. There was a jug and a cup on the table, and the moment they came into focus she realised just how dry her mouth and throat were.

She threw her legs over the side of the bed and staggered to them. Her hands shook, spilling water from the jug as she tried to pour some into the cup. She gulped that first cup of water down so fast it splashed inside her stomach and made her feel queasy. Gripping the edge of the table, she studied the dark sky out the window while she waited for the feeling to pass.

How had she gotten here and why did her entire body ache like she had been beaten within an inch of her life? She rubbed her hands over her face and fell into the chair before pouring a second cup of water.

She remembered walking Deana back from Nari's but from there everything was hazy except for a coal-dark stare that kept flashing across her mind whenever she shut her eyes—Savita. She dug into her shirt looking for the charm she had made to block mind magic, but it was gone, and the bruise-like pain at the back of her neck told her it had been taken by force.

If Savita had read her mind, then that meant she knew exactly where to find Deana and she would also know the plan Agnes had been forming to sabotage Kent's war machine. Was that why she had been thrown in here? This had to be one of the cells in the crow's nest given she could see the cloud-dotted sky through the bars on the window. But Savita would now also know that Varlan had plans to double-cross both Kent and Idir. The thought of Varlan triggered something in the back of her mind. '... *we now have the incentive we need to ensure his cooperation.*' What incentive had Savita been implying? As the thought stirred, so did another piece of the puzzle—the way Savita had paused over the memory of Varlan brushing Agnes' hair behind her ear. It had been an intimate gesture and his gaze had been full of admiration when he did it. But that admiration had been tarnished by something ... regret.

She pressed her hand over her mouth. She was the incentive Savita had been talking about. That is why Varlan had insisted on her wearing the magic-blocking charm. She had thought he just didn't want Kent to know he was working behind his back, but it was more than that. Varlan hadn't wanted Savita to read Agnes' mind because it would give her a tool with which to manipulate him. Just how many memories had Varlan taken from her? And how tangled was this web Kent and Idir were weaving?

The door opened, scattering her thoughts, and a guard walked in carrying a tray of food and a bundle that looked like clothes. He paused when his gaze fell on her sitting at the table.

"Thank the Bright you woke up. I wasn't sure you would." He sat the tray in front of her and brushed his sandy hair from his face. His eyes were a soft hazel and the smattering of freckles across his nose made him look younger than she suspected he actually was.

She eyed the food on the tray. It smelled wonderful, and she was starving.

"There's a change of clothes as well," he said as he placed the bundle on the foot of the bed.

Agnes studied him. There was something about the way he kept glancing at the door. "I recognise your face, but I don't think I know your name."

"Wes," he said.

The name didn't ring any bells. She glanced at the thin slices of meat and vegetables on the plate again.

"You should eat, while it's still warm." He reached for the jug, but she caught his hand. "I'll just refill it for you," he said, tilting his head towards the puddle that was soaking into the top of the table from her earlier efforts to fill her cup.

She released his fingers.

"I'll be back soon." He gave her a nod and left.

When the lock clicked shut, Agnes turned back to her meal. They hadn't provided any cutlery, of course. She picked at the food. It tasted as fantastic as it smelled but her stomach was still rolling too much for her to really enjoy it.

After eating half, she wiped her hands and moved to the bundle of clothes. It was heavier than it should have been, and when she unwrapped it, she found her satchel hidden within. She hugged it against her chest and threw a look at the door. Who was that guard?

"Agnes?" Wes' voice called as the lock scraped.

She thrust the satchel under the bed, nudging it farther out of sight with her toe as he peeked around the edge of the door.

"I hope they fit okay," he said with a nod to the clothes, a small smile plying one corner of his mouth as he placed the jug down. "Do you want me to leave this?" he asked, pointing to the tray.

"No, thank you."

He picked the tray up, and she opened her mouth to ask him about the satchel but closed it again as he shot a look towards the door and shook his head. He mouthed the word 'later' and left again.

CHAPTER SEVENTEEN

VARLAN

It was early. Too early. The magical lighting that lit the interior of Armada was still a subtle blue glow, despite the nearness of dawn. If Varlan hadn't wanted to catch Gethyn before he left his berth, he would still be wrapped up in bed. Instead, he was stalking through the bowels of the city, wondering if he should just wipe his hands of everything and head back to Osmar. But that would mean leaving Agnes and Deana vulnerable to Kent and Idir's whims, and whilst the Varlan from five years ago might not have had qualms about that, he was no longer that version of himself. The one that was only concerned with his own best interests.

He paused outside Gethyn's door. The old man was conniving, and that past Varlan wouldn't have trusted him, but Kent had killed Gethyn's brother, Olen. Not that anyone knew the truth of that, but the rumour alone was enough to stoke Gethyn's thirst for vengeance. And that made him a potential ally—at least until that vengeance was met.

The door opened as he lifted his hand to knock.

"What do you want?" Gethyn grunted and stepped back to let him enter.

"I want you to stop playing the game you're playing with Kent."

A shrewd glint entered Gethyn's eyes and he folded his arms over his chest. "My game is no different from yours."

Except Varlan wasn't trying to drag Agnes into danger. He was trying to get her out of it. He couldn't get her off Armada until she finished the commission for Kent. She was convinced that she couldn't control her keen once it had been activated, and he wasn't about to argue with her about that. With her broken keen-sense and the way Olen, then later Kent, had groomed her, she had become a slave to it. She could learn to control it if she was given time, but that was simply something they didn't have. "Agnes told you what she's building for Kent, so I don't see why you are still insisting on your clandestine meetings."

Gethyn rubbed his finger along the grove of his chin and then moved to the cupboard in the corner of his small kitchen. He pulled a stack of paper out and tossed it onto the table between them. "That keen of hers is uncanny. I've only heard of one other mage who had a keen like it, right down to the colour of his mage light."

"Are you referring to the mage who built the source ships?" Varlan asked as he flicked through the papers. Agnes' looping script edged the careful sketches of a leviathan-like machine. She had also drawn intricate schematics of individual parts and a list of possible materials. But it wasn't like her usual work—it was just snatches of her brilliance, and there was no way to see where all of this would come together to make the machine Kent had commissioned. When he glanced up again, Gethyn nodded.

"What Kent is asking Agnes to create is nothing compared to what she is truly capable of. It's a test. Even you should be able to see that."

Varlan had known Kent was testing the true extent of Agnes' power from the moment he realised what he was forcing her to build. But he'd also realised that once she was done with this machine, Kent wouldn't let her go. Especially once she proved she could make a true golem without the need for an intimate knowledge of runic magic. What was next though? He fanned the papers out again, hoping to see a clue he had missed before.

Gethyn let out a low sound. "Ah, yes. I've got that mind of yours working now, haven't I? The question we need to ask is, what does Kent want and is it in line with what Idir has been planning? Or is Kent foolish enough to double-cross Idir and take the treasure for himself?"

Varlan studied Gethyn as he traced his fingers along his lip. "Exactly how much do you know about Idir's plans?"

"I know what he told Olen and how that simple conversation led to my brother turning up half eaten in the underbelly with a knife still sticking out of his ribs. So, I know that he intends to raise Dumura and in doing so damn us all." He gave Varlan a calculating smirk. "So do you think Kent is having Agnes build a war machine to aid Idir or double-cross him, and if the rumours about Dumura are true, do you believe he would stop at only one machine?"

"He couldn't create that many though. A heartstone suitable to power just one golem of this magnitude is hard enough to find."

"True, but he only needs one stone, albeit a very special one. But just one, and if he finds it then he won't have Agnes build an army of machines—she will build him a hive."

A hive? An army of golems connected to each other. Drones under the control of—"Agnes," he whispered. "He'll use her soul to power the main machine."

"You're smarter than I gave you credit for. But we're not going to let that happen, are we?"

Varlan would die before he'd let Kent turn Agnes into some kind of queen bee for his golem army. "What do we need to do?"

"You need to keep your head down. Kent already suspects you

are up to something, even if he doesn't believe you would betray him outright. And Savita is whispering sweet nothings in his ear, influencing his judgement. We need to get that necromancer free and off Armada. The island girl too. They are both pieces of the puzzle. I just need to figure out if Kent is planning on double-crossing Idir or if he is actually working with him."

"We need to find Elijah," Varlan said. "If I can locate the heartstone before Kent does, I can destroy it."

Gethyn shook his head. "A stone of that kind is rare indeed, but I doubt that there would be only one in existence."

Then he would have Elijah draw a map to every such stone in existence and destroy them all. "Elijah is still an important piece of both Idir and Kent's plans. If we rescue him from wherever they have him then it will buy us time to figure out how to stop them." And he'd never convince Agnes to leave Armada until she knew her father was safe.

"I doubt he is still on Armada, but if he is then I imagine he is being kept somewhere well-guarded."

Varlan rubbed a hand over his face. He should have taken Agnes away from Armada a week ago, before Kent had a chance to trigger her magic. He'd had no idea what Kent was planning at the time, and he couldn't have imagined this. It didn't make sense; unless Idir or perhaps Savita had planted the seed inside his mind, but then what was their ultimate plan? If Idir managed to raise Dumura and wake Grandmother Ocean, then he wouldn't need an army of war machines. Were they a backup plan or a distraction? He blew out a breath and stood.

"Things are much simpler when you only have yourself to worry about," Gethyn said, his mouth pulling bitterly at the corner as he lifted a hand towards the door.

This conversation was over. Which was probably a good thing as it wasn't getting Varlan anywhere. He stood and left, heading to the dungeons. He had a suspicion that if anyone knew where Elijah might be it would be one of the guards down there. He'd already asked Wes, but Kent kept him up in the crow's nest and he knew very little about what went on downstairs.

As his feet hit the bottom step, he flicked a glance at the guard on duty. The man's black hair was pulled into a long tail that coiled forward over his shoulder. The right side of his face was marred by a net of burn scars, the ear completely missing. As his blue eyes fell on Varlan, they narrowed, and he let the chair he had been rocking on fall forward onto its front legs with a thud. Byron. Why the fuck did it have to be Byron? Not only was he a colossal arsehole, but he was a warden, which would make it difficult for Varlan to use his magic to get the answers he wanted. If he was careful, though, he might be able to sneak into the man's mind and implant a compulsion.

"What are you doing down here?" Byron asked as he stood to his full height and puffed his chest out. It might have been intimidating if he wasn't almost a head shorter than Varlan.

"Kent is concerned about Elijah's disappearance, so we're questioning everyone to see if they know anything that might help us locate him." Might as well try it without magic first.

Byron squinted at him. "Kent knows exactly where Elijah is."

Fuck. Okay, magic it was. He licked his lips and laid his keen very gently against Byron's mind. When the warden didn't respond, Varlan pressed a little harder.

Byron's eyes widened. "What the fuck are you playing at?" His suppression built, but Varlan was faster.

He pushed into the warden's mind. Byron fought back, his suppression trying to push against Varlan's keen, but Varlan just increased the pressure of his magic and sifted through the other man's thoughts. It wasn't a pleasant experience. Byron was one of those people who seemed to relish making others suffer. He moved past the memories of Byron beating prisoners and other people who refused to give Kent what he wanted. Then an image of Agnes drifted to the surface. It was night and she was sneaking into one of the corridors leading down to the abandoned berths. Byron had followed her, thoughts of cornering her in a dark alley consuming him. Varlan bit the inside of his cheek and pushed past the memory. He couldn't allow himself to be distracted.

"Do you know where Elijah is?" he asked softly.

Byron struggled against him, but an image lifted to the surface of his mind: Savita standing beside Byron, her hands wrapped around the bars of a cell as she stared in at a bound Elijah. So, he was down here.

"Take me to his cell," Varlan ordered.

Byron's body jerked as he fought the compulsion, and Varlan nearly lost his grip. He tightened it again and pressed the compulsion down harder, the beginnings of a headache nagging at his forehead.

The warden turned on his heel and marched along the line of cells until he reached the one that contained Elijah.

"Open the cell and free him," Varlan said, nearly losing his grip again as footsteps coming down the stairs reached him. He had to be quicker.

Byron struggled against him, but he unlocked the cell and then Elijah's shackles.

"Good. Now. Kent asked for Elijah to be sent up to the crow's nest. A guard came down to retrieve him—one of the newer ones." He brought up the image of one of the newer guards and sculpted a quick memory around it. It might not stick longer than a few days, but it would be long enough. When he pressed his fingertips to the centre of Byron's forehead, the warden's eyes slid shut and he swooned sideways.

Varlan rested him against the wall outside the cell and then helped Elijah to his feet. He didn't look good. They'd obviously given him a thorough beating. "Can you walk?"

"Barely. But they're not going to let you just saunter through the city with me in tow."

"I know." He flicked a look at the chute they used to dispose of the prisoners who couldn't hold up to Kent's questioning. "Think you can survive that drop?"

Elijah shrugged. "I'd rather risk it than go back into that cell." He hobbled over to the chute, and Varlan helped him onto the edge of it.

"Byron?" a voice called as footsteps started down the hall. "Don't tell me you're roughing up Elijah again."

"Go," Varlan hissed and gave Elijah a nudge. He turned just as the other guard came into sight and dropped a compulsion on him before he could react. "I wasn't here. You came looking for Byron and found him passed out. Probably drinking on the job again." He didn't lift his magic from the guard until he had climbed over the lip of the chute and was falling.

"Shadow's teeth, Byron, not again. You've got a fucking problem." The guard's voice followed Varlan down the chute before he landed in the rough pile of old bones and refuse at the bottom.

Elijah pulled him to his feet. "Agnes?" he asked, his russet eyes swimming with worry.

"She's fine for now. Come on. Nari should have a look at you then we need to get you to the Queen. Once Kent figures out you've escaped, he's going to tear the city apart looking for you."

"I'm going to have to start charging more," Nari said with a chuckle as she waved them inside her berth.

Varlan helped Elijah to a chair. The cartographer looked worse than he had in the dungeons. They had had to climb out of the pit and then sneak through the underbelly until they reached the closest corridor to Nari's. It hadn't been an easy task. He'd almost lost Elijah a few times when the tide washing in covered the rocks. They both now sported a collection of scrapes and cuts.

Nari sniffed in their direction. "And what exactly have the pair of you been up to? You smell like you crawled out of the pit."

"Because we did," Varlan said.

"Well, Agnes will be happy you're free at least," she said to Elijah as she scrunched her nose up. "Though I recommend a good wash before either of you go to see her."

Varlan leant against the bench, his hand brushing a jar there and knocking it onto its side. The dark shards within rattled against each other, releasing a thin coil of magic. He lifted the vial and tilted it to inspect the shards. They looked like some kind of shell.

"I wouldn't touch that if I were you," Nari said over her shoulder as she inspected Elijah's injuries.

Varlan placed the jar down and folded his arms.

Nari's keen built in a warm swell and a thin, green mist twisted over Elijah. He gave a hiss of pain and shifted in his seat.

"Oh, stop being a baby. It's not that bad. I spent most of the morning pulling shards of enchanted shell out of Deana's skin and she barely complained."

"You've seen Deana today?" Varlan asked.

Nari nodded. "Agnes and Gendry brought her in just after dawn. The shards in that jar were embedded in her hand. She said it was a message from a shrouded one, but I'm not convinced." Seemingly satisfied with Elijah, she turned her full attention to Varlan and a wave of heat rushed from his toes to the top of his skull. The small cuts and scrapes itched as they healed.

"What do we owe you?" Elijah asked as he stood, looking much steadier on his feet.

"Nothing. This time," Nari waved the question away. "Just tell that daughter of yours to be careful. She's in way over her head with Kent."

"Aren't we all?" Elijah muttered. Then louder he said, "Thank you, Nari. I'll keep an eye on Agnes, but you know how stubborn she is."

Nari chuckled, "Just like her mother." She let out a sigh as her mood seemed to sober. "Well, off with the pair of you then."

Elijah headed for the door, but Nari caught Varlan's arm. "Get them off this city as soon as you can. Whatever Kent and Idir are playing with is going to destroy us all." She released him and picked up the jar of black shards.

Outside, Elijah gave him a quizzical look but said nothing as they headed in the direction of the docks where the Queen was berthed.

Gendry came down the gangplank to meet them when they reached the dock. He clapped Elijah on the back and then waved him onto the ship.

"Any word?" Varlan asked once Elijah was out of sight.

Gendry shook his head. "Nothing. It's like the whole outpost has gone dark."

"Fuck." Varlan rubbed his hand over his face. "This getting dangerous, Gen. You need to get Deana somewhere Idir can't find her. Agnes, too. We might have to resort to clamping a pair of shackles on her to block her keen like you suggested. She'll hate us for it, but if it will stop Kent from abusing her magic further ..."

"Wren's right, though. It's not like bind-shackles are an easy thing to come by out here in the isles. And the shrouded ones already found Deana."

"I heard. What happened?"

"I'm not entirely sure. It was early, and no one was up, but we all heard Deana scream, and there was a shrouded one on the deck. At least, that is what I think it was. I've never seen one before. It was trying to give her this black shell. Wren said the magic emanating from it was like nothing she's ever felt. The second Deana touched it though, it shattered, and the pieces seemed to burrow under her skin, then she lost consciousness. I helped Agnes get her to Nari."

"Nari said it was some kind of message. Do you know what kind? Did Deana say?"

Gendry scratched the underside of his chin. "If it was a message, I think it was proverbial."

"You mean that whoever sent that shrouded one wanted to show Deana that they could reach her wherever she was?"

"Exactly."

Varlan folded his arms and studied the horizon. "I'll be back tonight. We need to free Bran, then get our arses away from here. If both Deana and Agnes are out of reach it will completely disrupt whatever it is that Idir and Kent are planning."

"We can't hide them away forever."

"We won't have to. We just need to get them out of the way while we figure out how to deal with Kent and Idir."

"Murder is an option, you know?" Gendry said with a half-arsed grin.

"We could take out Kent, but we won't get close enough to Idir and I am certain that Idir is the one pulling all the strings. Kent is just a convenient tool. If he outlives his usefulness, I doubt Idir would hesitate to kill him."

"Do you think Kent knows that? Is that why he's got Agnes building this war machine?"

"I don't know. That may be the case, but it also might be just another part of Idir's plan." He met Gendry's eye and drew a breath. "I spoke to Gethyn this morning."

"You have been busy. What did that old bastard have to say?"

"He thinks that this war machine is a test. That once Kent sees she can create a true golem, he's going to force her to create an entire army of them."

"Shadow's teeth. But surely there aren't enough heartstones for that."

Varlan shook his head. "That's what I said, but then Gethyn pointed out that Kent doesn't need multiple heartstones. He only needs one extremely powerful stone and the soul of a specific mage."

Confusion furrowed Gendry's brow then his eyes widened. "You think he means to use Agnes' soul?"

Varlan nodded. "Agnes or maybe Deana. But Idir has other plans for Deana, so I am guessing Agnes, and Gethyn seemed to think so, too."

"Shit," Gendry whispered.

"So, you see my dilemma."

Gendry flicked a look towards the Queen as though searching for someone—Wren, most likely. Aside from Varlan and Wes, Gendry was the only other soul who knew about him and Agnes. He'd considered stripping the knowledge from Gendry's mind, but he trusted Gendry—not only with his life, but his secrets. And that particular secret was just as valuable as his life. It was also comforting to know that someone else knew the truth. It made it real, and not some fantasy that existed only in Varlan's memory.

"I'll have a quiet chat with Wren. The Queen will be ready to leave as soon as you give the word." Gendry gave his shoulder a squeeze. "But be careful, and don't underestimate Kent. I'll see you tonight." He let go of Varlan's shoulder and headed up the gangplank.

Varlan blew out a breath and turned towards the city. He

needed to find Wes before his shift started. If they had any chance of breaking Bran out of the crow's nest, tonight was it.

CHAPTER EIGHTEEN

DEANA

The afternoon was starting to drift into evening and Agnes hadn't returned from the crow's nest. Deana pushed her meal around her plate. Her appetite had fled sometime around midafternoon. The shrouded one's visit still bothered her; the message of the shell floated in shadowy scenes across her mind that gave her a headache whenever she tried to focus on them. And despite Nari's healing, her fingers still ached as though shards of shell remained trapped under her skin.

"You should eat something," Dara said, resting her hand on Deana's arm.

Deana turned and gave her a small smile before placing her fork down. "I'll be alright. I'm not hungry."

Pippa made a noise, drawing Deana's attention to her, but she just dipped her head and shared a look with Kiki. Something seemed to pass between them, and then Kiki met Deana's eye and gave her a warm grin.

"I wonder where Agnes has gotten to," Elijah said. "It's not like her to miss a meal." He had been in the hold most of the day working on a map, his song permeating the air around him. It was soft but far-reaching and spoke of a curious desire to discover.

"I'm sure she'll be along shortly," Wren said, but she cast a long look down the dock that suggested she wasn't certain. "Varlan will be here soon. Maybe she's with him. Or if she's gotten caught up with her work for Kent, he will know."

But Agnes wasn't with Varlan when he came stalking along the dock a short while later. He hurried up the gangplank and dropped onto the deck. His warm gaze moved over them, the corner of his mouth tightening as he took in each face in turn.

"Agnes isn't with you?" Elijah asked, standing.

Varlan completely stilled and his song gave a little swoop that spoke of panic. "No, I haven't seen her all day."

"Should we go look for her?" Deana asked as she stood beside Elijah.

"There's no point. We know exactly where she is," Pippa said.

Kiki nodded. "Kent must have figured out she was planning on sabotaging his war machine. She's probably in the cell next to Bran."

"How would he have figured it out, though?" Wren asked. "She had that charm to block mind magic on her, didn't she?" She glanced at Varlan, and he gave a quick nod. "So Savita wouldn't have been able to pick the knowledge from her mind."

"It is a mistake to underestimate Savita," Deana said.

"Everyone just remain calm. We don't know for sure that Kent has Agnes," Gendry said, his voice steady as he lifted a hand. "She might have gotten caught up on some other business. We should send someone to check—" His eyes narrowed as they landed on something on the dock.

Deana turned to investigate.

A blond guard was hurrying towards the Queen. He skipped up the gangplank and fell into position next to Varlan.

"We have a problem," he said before anyone else could speak.

"Kent threw Agnes into one of the crow's nest cells."

Varlan's hands tightened into fists. His face remained neutral as though he was trying not to show his emotions, but Deana could hear the anxiety sharpening his song.

"That's fine. We can just rescue her when we rescue Bran," Kiki said, but the guard shot her a look.

"Kent knows Elijah is missing, and whilst he can't pin that on you"—he flicked a look at Varlan—"he suspects it; but more than that, he *knows*."

"Knows what?" the twins asked together.

Varlan met the guard's eye and gave a tiny shake of his head.

"He's doubled the guard on the crow's nest. There is no way you are breaking anyone out of there tonight," the guard said.

"Are there any secret ways into the crow's nest?" Gendry asked.

"Not unless you climb up the side of the city," the guard answered. "But it's treacherous. One wrongly placed foot or hand and you'll be falling to your death."

Deana studied the glass-like surface of the ocean, the voices of the others drifting into the background as the song of the waves rolled over her shoulders and crashed against her mind. "What if we use the ocean?" she asked as she turned back to face them.

"What do you mean, use the ocean? The crow's nest is too high to reach by boat," Varlan said.

"I know, but ..." She drew a long breath then opened her palm to indicate the ocean beside the ship. Her song built and she let it out, pulling the waves up into a pillar of water. She then leapt over the side rail and the water caught her, supporting her weight as she lifted her hand until she was standing a good metre above the side of the ship. It took a great deal of effort to keep the water steady, and as she grew short of breath, she lowered herself back to the deck. "We can climb up, and if someone falls, I can catch them."

"It still won't do you any good," the guard said. "The crow's nest is crawling with Kent's men. Even if you managed to get Bran out, you won't reach Agnes. Kent will do everything in his power to keep her."

"We should leave her there then," Elijah said softly.

"You can't—"

"I know how it sounds," Elijah cut off Varlan's protest. "And I want nothing more than to keep her safe. But despite holding her prisoner, Kent won't harm her—at least not until she completes his war machine. She's too rare a mage for him to do anything rash. If we liberate Bran, however, that will delay his plans. Necromancers are not common on Armada."

"It's too easy for something to go wrong though. What if he finds another necromancer and a suitable heartstone?" Varlan said as he paced across the deck.

"He could certainly find another necromancer, but it is unlikely he would find the heartstone. The kind he needs won't just fall into his lap. Unfortunately, we will have to go and find it because Agnes will be a slave to Kent's war machine until she completes it. But by freeing Bran and taking on the hunt for the heartstone ourselves, we will buy time to figure out how to get Agnes away from Kent. And we will have something to bargain with."

"I still think we should try to free them both tonight," Varlan said.

"It's too risky," the guard said. "If Kent manages to capture you, he'll kill you. He knows you've been scheming against him and that Agnes has been meeting with Gethyn."

"How? If Gethyn double-crossed her—"

"Savita plucked the information right out of her mind."

"But she was wearing a magic-blocking charm, wasn't she?" Wren asked.

"Savita took it from her," the guard said. "Look, whatever we're doing, we need to do it now and then get off Armada."

"No, Wes, you're to stay out of this; if we are seriously considering leaving Agnes behind, I need you to keep an eye on her," Varlan said. "Get back up to the crow's nest. I don't want to give Kent any reason to suspect you."

"Gendry, I need you to get a message to Nari. We're going to need her, but make sure she knows that if she comes with us, we won't be back on Armada for a while." He turned to the captain. "Wren, do you think you can summon a storm for us?" He asked.

She nodded.

"Good, that should provide a little cover. Deana, you and the twins are coming with me."

"What do you want me to do?" Elijah asked.

"Stay here and keep your head down. We'll need this ship ready to depart at a moment's notice, so you can help Rufus and the others."

Elijah looked like he might have been going to argue, but instead he gave a nod.

"Right. Our focus is getting Bran out, but if we see an opening to rescue Agnes as well, we are taking it."

Night was starting to fall by the time Deana, the twins, and Varlan snuck along the underbelly. The building storm brushed against her song—the turbulence beneath the waves set her on edge as thunder rolled sending a deep vibration from her toes to her fingertips. Lightning flashed and the wind picked up, whipping the loose strands of her hair into a frenzy.

Varlan slowed as they reached a section at the very back of the underbelly. Here the rocks were not completely overshadowed by the tall walls of the city, but a thin slice expanded out into the ocean. Even though Deana couldn't see beneath the dark surface, she could hear the reef there. The swirl of water through the coral and anemones had a different song to the calm shallows or the fathomless deep.

"Ready?" Varlan asked, and the twins nodded. "Deana?"

She gave a nod of her own.

"Alright, Wes should be back up there by now. He was going to secure a rope to one of the pillars near Bran's cell," Varlan said.

The twins shared one of those looks. "You know if you and Deana want to go after Agnes, we can get Bran," Kiki said. "We're more than capable of a little rescue mission."

Varlan shook his head. "Elijah is right. She's safe enough with Kent for now. It's too risky to try and go after both of them at once, and the others are expecting us to follow the current plan. Nothing ruins a job faster than one member of the group deviating from what everyone else is expecting."

"Let's get a move on then," Pippa said as she edged along the slick rocks towards a thick rope that was hanging a good five or six feet above them. "I'm going to need a boost." She turned and batted her eyelashes at Varlan.

He bent and made a net with his hands. Pippa placed her toes neatly onto his fingers and as she vaulted upwards, he gave her an extra boost. She caught the rope, her feet dangling above them as she let out a grunt and used the rope to pull herself up the wall. Once she disappeared over the top rail, it was Kiki's turn.

"Come on, Deana," Varlan said as Kiki finally disappeared over the rail. The wind had picked up considerably and fat drops of rain had started to fall. They stung with cold as they smashed against the skin of her face and hands.

She eyed the rope and then Varlan.

"You'll be fine, I promise. Just hang on tight and don't look down." His song brushed against hers and she flinched. It wasn't like when Idir entered her mind. It was as though he was trying to bolster her courage rather than read her thoughts, but the instinct to protect herself was strong.

She drew a deep breath and placed a hand on his shoulder to steady herself as she stepped onto his cupped fingers.

Varlan's hands dipped, causing her to wobble. He gave her a moment to steady herself before he started counting, "One, two—"

"Three." They said together, and Varlan pushed his hands upwards as Deana leapt.

She caught the rope but it slid painfully through her fingers as she tried to grip it, her own body, the wind, and rain all fighting against her. A few inches from the bottom of the rope she finally managed to tighten her grip and her descent stopped with a savage jerk as her arms took her full weight. For an instant it felt like her fingers would release their hold in protest, but she squeezed her eyes shut and gripped tighter, the rope slowly twisting her around in the air. With a deep breath, she heaved herself upwards until she could plant her feet firmly against the rain-slick wall of the city. Her shoulders still ached from the sudden stop, but she pushed the feeling down and focused on climbing.

Keep moving forward. Don't look down. A heavy gust of wind buffeted against her, and her grip slipped. She plummeted several feet downwards before she caught herself again. Knees and hands shaking, she pressed her teeth into her lip as she started upwards once more.

Finally, she reached the top and grabbed Kiki's outstretched hand. Both twins hauled her onto the wide catwalk and ushered her into the shadows of a corner to wait for Varlan. Time seemed to slow as they waited in the dark, trying to hear over the sounds of the storm if any guards were coming. Despite Wes' warning about the increase in guard numbers, the section of the crow's nest they were in was strangely quiet.

"Bran is in the second room," Varlan whispered as he climbed silently onto the catwalk beside them. "Pippa, you watch this hall and be ready to unleash some mayhem in case we need a distraction. Kiki, get your picks out and get to work on that door. Once you have Bran free, the three of you head back to the Queen without delay."

Pippa nodded. "And if things don't go to plan?"

"If it all goes to shit and we need to get out fast, or your way back to the rope is blocked, the main set of stairs is down that way. It will put you out on the north side of the market. From there, get your arses to the Queen as fast as you can."

"Understood," Kiki said as she pulled out a set of thin, metal lockpicks. "You take care of my girl, Dee. If anything happens to her ..."

Deana blinked at Kiki's use of her nickname. It still felt weird to have someone other than her family call her that.

"I'll take care of her. Now get to work," Varlan said and nudged Kiki towards the door he had indicated Bran was locked behind.

"What do you want me to do?" Deana still wasn't sure why Varlan had included her in this little rescue mission, especially now that it seemed he believed the twins could handle it on their own.

"I need you to lure Savita away from Kent so he and I can have a little chat."

He wanted her to intentionally get Savita's attention? She squeezed her hands to stop them shaking.

"Hey." He placed a light hand on her shoulder. "Deana, look at me."

She met his gaze, and his song brushed lightly against hers. She stiffened, but he didn't invade her mind. Instead, that steady bolstering of her resolve smoothed over her again, like he was damping the edges of her fear.

"You can do this. I wouldn't ask you to if I didn't believe that."

Honesty was not something she expected to find in Varlan's eyes. While she barely knew him, she'd heard enough from the crew members of the Queen to suggest he was a thief who held his own self-preservation above all else. But while she'd observed his calculating side, he seemed to genuinely care about others. And he certainly had a softness about him when he interacted with Agnes.

She nodded. "Alright."

He gave her shoulder a squeeze. "Go around this corner and then along the corridor to the big double doors. That's where Savita will probably be. Get her attention and then make a run for it. Head straight down to the market. Gendry should be waiting for you there—he'll help you throw her off."

"And if I can't escape her and make it to the market?"

"You'll be fine." He gave her a nudge towards the corner.

Deana swallowed as she strode along the corridor. Where were all the guards? This seemed too easy, like Kent was expecting something.

As she neared the double doors, they opened.

Savita was standing in the middle of the threshold as though waiting for her. "Hello, Deana," she said with a feline grin, stepping aside to reveal the room behind her.

Bran was tied to a chair in the centre of the space and beside him was an older man Deana recognised as the ink seller.

"Why don't you and your friends join us for a little chat?" Savita looked at something over Deana's shoulder.

Deana glanced back. A group of guards were dragging a struggling Pippa and Kiki toward her. Behind them Varlan was walking with his hands lifted, Wes' sword pressed to the centre of his back.

"Well, come on. You know how much Father hates being kept waiting."

CHAPTER NINETEEN

BRAN

The days were already starting to meld into one. Was it his third or fourth day being confined to this room? He'd never been very good at sitting still and waiting. To keep himself distracted, he tried to focus on perfecting the portal magic. It was getting easier, and he could now make a portal big enough for a large dog to fit through. The larger portals weren't as stable as Nea's, the edges rough and flickering, ready to snap shut without notice. But he had mastered the smaller ones to the point where he could summon one big enough to toss an apple through and leave it open for a few good minutes. The biggest he could make without losing stability was just big enough for a modest-sized cat to pass through, but he couldn't hold it open for nearly as long.

He had thought about using a portal to contact Nea, but this mess he was in wasn't hers to deal with. And, if he were honest with himself, as easy as it would be to get her to save his backside, he wanted to see what he could achieve without her help. He wasn't a child anymore; he couldn't just run to Nea or Niall whenever he got himself into a scrape. They had their own lives to deal with. Though they would berate him for it later—if he managed to live through this. And if he didn't survive, Nea would probably intercept his spirit as it crossed the Between just to give him a lecture about his stupidity and stubbornness. A chuckle escaped him and he rubbed a hand over his face.

Maybe he should let her know what was happening but insist he had it under control—she'd see straight through it, of course, and then she'd send Garret like she had before. Or maybe she would come herself, and he couldn't let her do that.

The door opened, scattering his thoughts, and he sat up. It was a guard he remembered from the dungeon. Bran didn't know his name, but it would be impossible to forget a face like his. The scars that spanned his right cheek and temple culminated in a puckered mess of skin where his ear should have been.

"On your feet," he grunted, and the numbness of his suppression passed over Bran.

It was a waste of effort; Bran couldn't do anything with his keen even if he wanted to. Necromancers couldn't really use their magic against the living. Except Nea, but she wasn't a normal necromancer. Of course, if Bran had access to a disembodied spirit, he could probably jam it inside the guard's body. But not only did the thought sicken him, it would take too long and there was a distinct lack of disembodied spirits just floating around.

Bran slowly dropped his feet over the side of the bed but made no further move to get up. "Has an appropriate heartstone fallen into Kent's lap or has he decided he doesn't need me after all and I am free to go?"

The warden strode across the room and grabbed his arm before hauling him to his feet only to take a faltering step back when he seemed to realise how much taller than him Bran was. "You keep your mouth shut and get a move on." He shunted Bran towards the door.

"Oh, you're just the escort and it's not in the job description to answer questions?"

That earned him a shove between his shoulder blades which nearly sent him falling, but he managed to steady himself after a few staggering steps.

"I said shut your mouth."

Bran bit his lip to stave off his retort and continued along the hallway.

The guards outside the central room stepped back to let them through the double doors. One of them eyed the warden with a curl of his lip but said nothing.

Inside the room, Kent lounged on his throne-like chair and Savita stood behind the small table which had been cleared of the papers from before to make room for a large black mirror. Sea creatures and coral had been carved into the ornate frame that encircled the fathomless glass. It was more grandiose than the ones Bran had encountered before, and even though the warden's suppression was preventing him from feeling the magic that clung to its fathomless surface, he knew exactly what it was. A spirit-glass.

"Sit," the guard ordered as he shunted Bran towards the chair in the middle of the space in front of Kent.

"Well, isn't this a nice little gathering?" Bran said as he lowered himself into the chair.

"Shut—"

"Byron," Kent warned, and the guard lowered his hand.

The warden grabbed Bran's arms and tied them behind the back of the chair.

"Is this really necessary?" Bran asked, raising an eyebrow as he met Kent's eye. "I have been compliant so far. What makes you think that will change now?"

"It is not *your* obedience that concerns me," Kent said and waved Byron away.

Byron muttered something under his breath and marched over to stand by the door, his arms folded across his chest and his scowl firmly planted on Bran. He was trouble, that one. Likely he was the type of warden who enjoyed abusing his power and got some sort of sick satisfaction from lording it over mages.

"He'll need his keen to activate the mirror," Savita said as she sauntered over and stopped just in front of Bran.

"That's inadvisable," Byron said.

Savita gave a simpering laugh in the warden's direction. "Oh, please. Don't tell me you are afraid of one little soul-singer? His powers can't harm you or anyone else in this room and even if they could, he doesn't stand a chance against my mind magic. Isn't that right?" She directed the question at Bran as she stroked a finger down his cheek.

He tilted his head away from her. "You caught me unaware before. It won't happen again."

Her smile didn't fade. If anything, it deepened until it was almost menacing before her obsidian gaze flicked to Byron again. "Drop your suppression, warden."

"I don't take orders from you."

"Byron," Kent cautioned again, his tone edged with steel. "Savita is a guest here and you will treat her with the respect she is due. Lest you want to become one of her father's little *pets*."

Byron let out a grumble and his suppression dropped. Bran was quick to pull up his mental walls, but Savita didn't seem interested in entering his mind just yet.

Instead, she gave the warden another of those wide, almost coy smiles and said, "Good boy."

The door opened, and a pair of guards came in dragging a man Bran didn't know.

"Ah, Gethyn, so nice of you to join us," Kent said as the guards, one of which was another warden, threw the man into the empty chair beside Bran. He looked like he had put up a decent fight. His lip was split, one of his eyes was almost swollen shut, and there were darkening bruises and small scrapes across his cheeks. His breathing seemed laboured, each outward breath whistling through the congealing blood that stained his nose.

"I found myself unable to ignore the invitation," the man said before he hawked and spat, the bloodstained spittle barely missing Savita's toes.

Her nose twitched and she took a step back as she flicked a look at Kent. "I don't know why you didn't just order them to kill him. It's not like he is of any real use to us."

"Gethyn is going to be very useful. Now, perhaps, it is time to contact your father."

Savita looked like she might argue but instead she gave a nod before turning back to Bran. "Activate the spirit-glass."

"I can't."

"You are a soul-singer are you not? Activate it or I will enter your mind and make you."

"You really have no idea how they work, do you?"

She blinked at him.

"They are touch-activated; I can't exactly touch it while I am tied up all the way over here. And you *are* aware that they are time limited. You can't just activate it and leave it open indefinitely. Not unless you want it to drain all your keen, or rather my keen since I would be the one using it. And frankly, even if I were inclined to activate it for you, I won't on principle."

"You are not irreplaceable. We can always find another soul-singer," Savita said.

"True, but we're not exactly common out here in the middle of the ocean, are we?"

Her dark gaze bore into him, and he kept his mental walls tight as her keen pressed over his scalp, leaving a wild itch in its wake.

"I might be persuaded to activate it for you if you said *please*. And, of course, you'd need to untie me." He was pushing his luck, but that little tremble of frustration that rolled across her features was satisfying.

"Untie him," Savita barked at the closest guard.

"Wait a moment," Kent said with a raised finger. "Who is in charge here?"

"You are, but you heard him. He cannot activate the glass unless he touches it, and Father is waiting. You know better than most how he gets when his patience has been tried."

The moment the words left Savita's mouth, a clap of thunder shook the crow's nest and a smile twitched at the corner of Kent's mouth. "It seems Idir will have to wait a little a longer. Our company will be here shortly."

Kent really needed to reconsider his definition of *shortly*. While they waited, Bran slowly worked at the rope around his wrists. Byron had been sloppy, and there was enough give that if he could twist his hand just right, he might be able to get it free. Feeling a warm throb of keen, he glanced sideways at Gethyn. The mage was staring at Byron with a distinct look of loathing. He was pulling so gently on the source that Bran wasn't surprised that Savita and the two wardens hadn't noticed.

Byron shifted and pulled at the neck of his armour, then rubbed a hand over his forehead as thunder rumbled again. "What are we waiting for?" he snapped.

"Patience, Byron. We must give our guests time to get into position," Kent said and then turned his gaze on Savita. "Why don't you go and see if our friends are on their way?"

She rolled her eyes but sauntered over and pulled the doors

open. Her posture instantly changed. "Hello, Deana." She moved just enough that Bran could see past her.

Deana stood in the middle of the double doors, fear widening her teal gaze as it flicked from Bran to Gethyn.

"Why don't you and your friends join us for a little chat?" Savita asked.

Deana tore her gaze away from the room to something outside in the hall.

"Well, come on. You know how much Father hates being kept waiting," Savita said as she grabbed hold of Deana's arm and pulled her into the room.

A group of guards followed, dragging Pippa and Kiki with them. Both twins looked like they had put up a good fight. One of the guards was sporting a set of angry scratches across his cheek, another had the beginnings of a black eye. Following them was Varlan, unrestrained, but with a sword pressed to his back. Bran recognised the guard behind him; Wes.

Kent stood and wandered over to Deana and Savita. He leant forward as though examining Deana and pulled something from under the collar of his shirt. The object caught the light in a flash of rose-gold. It looked like one of Niall's robrillium charms, but from this distance it was hard to tell.

"So nice to finally put a face to the name. Idir has told me so much about you and what your magic is capable of." He shot a look at Byron. "Lock her up in the room with Agnes."

Savita's grip on Deana tightened as Byron stepped towards them. "Father will want to see her; you can lock her up after. I suggest you release Bran and get him to activate the spirit-glass—we have kept Father waiting long enough."

"Do I need to remind you that this is my city and neither you nor your father are in charge here?" Kent said.

"Do I need to remind you what will happen if you try to double-cross Father again?" Savita said, pulling Deana behind her. "You promised Father as soon as we located Deana you would deliver her to him. You're lucky he is letting you keep Agnes."

A soft-fingered keen brushed the back of Bran's neck seconds before Varlan's voice entered his mind. *Bran, you need to be ready to make a run for it. Get yourself down to the Queen.*

Sure, as soon as I get this rope off and fight my way through all these guards. You have a plan, right?

I did, but this wasn't part of it. You were supposed to be in your cell. We were supposed to—

Bran's mind went silent as Varlan's words were cut off. He scanned the group and his eyes fell on the warden who had brought Gethyn in. The man's suppression was completely focused on the mind mage. Varlan was probably lucky that neither Savita nor Kent had noticed he was using his keen. They were still arguing over what to do with Deana.

Savita had let go of Deana, and she had backed up to the window, her fingers gripping the front of her shirt and her sea foam eyes wide as they flicked over each person in the room. What was she doing?

Pippa gave a minute nod when Deana's gaze met hers and then Deana slammed her elbow into the window behind her. She let out a yelp of pain and gripped her elbow as a web-like fissure appeared in the glass and both Savita and Kent whirled to face her.

A surge of power built as Deana grabbed hold of the source.

"Stop her!" Savita yelled at Byron.

But a wall of flame erupted in front of the warden and he was forced backwards.

Water slammed against the fractured glass, smashing it inward and sending shards flying towards Kent and Savita. The wave hit the spirit-glass, and Savita dove forward, catching it before it hit the floor.

She let out a growl and turned her rage-filled gaze on Deana.

Bran fought against the ropes as water pooled around his feet.

"Here, let me," Gethyn said, and he grabbed hold of the rope, heat brushing Bran's palms as the scent of burning reached him before the rope fell away.

"Thanks."

Gethyn gave him a quick nod then raced for the door.

Pippa and Kiki were surrounded by a group of guards. Fire danced around Pippa's hands and Kiki had hers lifted, two elegant snakes of water standing between her and the men. As one moved closer, she snapped her wrist and the snake lashed forward, forcing the man to retreat again.

Another approached and the second snake lunged, but it collapsed to the floor as one of the wardens threw his suppression over both women.

After locating the warden responsible for the suppression, Bran charged and tackled him. They hit the floor hard, rolling several feet before the warden managed to free himself from Bran's grip and get up. He grabbed the front of Bran's shirt and lifted him as his fist slammed into Bran's jaw.

Dazed and tasting blood, Bran grabbed at the warden's wrists and drove his thumbs into the tendons along their undersides. The warden grunted but didn't release him. Bran kicked his legs, trying to get purchase on the floor as he pressed his thumbs down harder. His foot caught the warden's ankle, and the man staggered, his grip loosening enough that Bran was able to twist free. He dodged away from the warden and stumbled into the wall, scanning the room to find his friends.

Several of Kent's guards were down. Varlan was nowhere in sight and neither was Savita. Pippa and Kiki were backing towards the door, but he couldn't see Deana anywhere.

A scream of pain sounded, and he turned.

Byron had Deana on her knees, his fist tangled tightly in her hair. He slapped her as she clawed at his fingers. They were in front of the shattered window through which the storm raged above a churning ocean.

The warden Bran had been fighting made a lunge for him, but he dodged, twisting at the last second and grabbing the man by the back of the neck. He slammed his head into the wall then charged towards Byron, pausing only to grab one of the overturned chairs.

He hoisted the chair by the back and smashed it against Bryon's side. The warden let go of Deana with a snarl and took Bran by the throat, forcing him against the wall by the smashed window.

"Run, Deana," Bran croaked as his throat constricted under the pressure of Byron's palms. But as Deana stood, her eyes darkened from their bright teal to a deep navy blue and the ocean outside the window roared as the wild surge of her keen stole Bran's breath more effectively than Byron's hands.

Byron's suppression stuttered, but whatever power Deana was drawing on was too much for the warden. He let go of Bran and moved as though he was going to grab Deana again, but a heavy shudder rocked the city and all the windows along the side of the room shattered as a wall of water slammed into them. Bran gripped the window frame in an effort to keep his feet as knee-deep seawater complete with ocean life swirled around him.

Deana lifted her hands and the water rose, forming a wall around her and Bran; brightly coloured reef fish drifted between them and the blurred forms of Kent and his men. Hands grabbed Bran from behind and hauled him out the window.

He twisted away from his assailant and lifted his fist ready to defend himself only to drop it as Varlan's face came into focus. "What about Deana?" Bran yelled over the roar of the ocean and the wail of the storm.

"I'll get her." Varlan vaulted through the window and emerged again pulling Deana along behind him. She flicked her hands, and the wall of water formed a seal over the windows, preventing Kent and his men from following her.

"Alright, how do we get out of here?" Bran asked.

"Deana?" Varlan turned his gaze on her, his voice laced with concern.

Her eyes were flashing between teal and navy, her body trembling. She was pulling too much power; she'd exhaust her keen if she didn't stop.

"Jump," she said in a rasp as she rushed to the side of the city and launched herself out into the open air.

CHAPTER TWENTY

VARLAN

"You heard her," Varlan yelled above the storm as he gripped the balustrade and vaulted over the side of the city.

Wind whipped against him, freezing his soaked clothes as he plummeted towards the churning ocean. Deana's keen pulled hard against him, and the waves lifted. He just managed to suck in a breath before he plunged into the rising swell. Watery hands grabbed hold of him and dragged him back towards the city before a surge lifted him above the dock and dropped him next to a waterlogged Bran.

Deana landed neatly on her feet beside them. She took two steps then fell to her knees and expelled a heavy breath.

"We have to get to the ship," Varlan said as he stood. An ache tore against his side, and he pressed his fingers to the wound there. When he lifted them again, they were tinged with scarlet.

Deana staggered to her feet beside them. She opened her mouth as though she would say something before pressing her fingers over it and swooning sideways. Bran caught her before she hit the ground.

"I'll be alright once the world stops spinning," she muttered as she slumped against the necromancer.

"You've exhausted your keen. You need to rest," Bran said as he slid an arm under her legs and lifted her.

"I can walk," she said in a breathless voice before her eyes fluttered shut and her body went limp.

"We need to get her to the Queen. Hopefully, Nari will be there," Varlan said as he started towards the ship.

"What about Agnes? We're not going to leave her with Kent, are we? You know he's forcing her to build that golem."

"We have to leave her for now," Varlan replied without stopping.

"But—"

"We had to choose which of you to rescue and we chose *you*," he said as he turned back to face the necromancer. "Rescuing you is the smartest course of action at this time, but only if we get you and Deana away from Kent and Idir." He rubbed his hands over his head and continued toward the Queen.

The deck of the ship was a hive of activity. Wren barked orders as the crew rushed about trying to prepare to leave in the storm— which would be suicide for any other ship. But the Queen wasn't a normal ship and Wren wasn't a normal captain.

Bran dropped onto the deck beside him, Deana still hanging limply in his arms.

"Get her down in the hold and then hurry back up here. Wren is going to need all available hands. She can't hold that storm much longer," Varlan said then pressed a hand over the aching wound at his side and crossed to Wren. "Where's Gendry?"

She pointed upward.

Despite his bulk, Gendry moved gracefully through the rigging.

"Has everyone else returned?"

"The twins haven't."

"Get this ship moving. I'll go find them." As he started away, she caught his arm.

"You'll never catch us in this storm. We can defend the ship if Kent's men come, but not for long." She let go of his arm and turned back to her crew.

He rushed to the stairs that led into the hold and nearly collided with Bran, who was re-emerging. "The twins haven't returned," Varlan said.

"You don't think Kent got them?"

"They're resourceful and I doubt they went down without a fight, but we have to find them ... for Wren's sake."

A warm touch of keen rolled over the back of Varlan's neck and the wound at his side turned from a dull ache into a nagging itch as the sides of the cut pulled together. He flicked a look over Bran's shoulder to Nari, who inclined her head and then disappeared into the hold.

"Do you know where they might have gone?" Bran asked.

Varlan shook his head. "We'll try the abandoned berths first. I am hoping that Wes managed to use the chaos to get them out and they are just hunkered down somewhere."

"You're sure you can trust Wes?" Bran asked.

Varlan gave a snort in response, then said, "More than I would trust myself were our roles reversed."

They hurried along the gangplank and to the edge of the dock where they could climb down into the underbelly. Varlan kept his head low as they wove their way across the slick rocks and between the support pylons of the city. Down here, the magic that held the city together thrummed through his body, almost setting his teeth on edge.

"Why was saving me instead of Agnes the best option?" Bran asked.

"Because without you to provide a soul to power the golem then it's nothing more than a useless hunk of metal."

"But if you rescued Agnes then she wouldn't be forced to build it in the first place."

Varlan rubbed a hand over his face. "She would still be plagued by the compulsion to build it because that is the way her magic has been trained to work. When Olen first discovered her ability, he used her to construct multiple improvements to Armada. Then when Kent killed him and took his place, he didn't stop grooming Agnes' power. If anything, he increased Olen's efforts. Now Agnes is a slave to it; once her keen has been activated, she can't fight it. Given time, she could take back control, but we don't have that luxury, so she is safer where she is for now."

"But—"

"Bran." Varlan growled his name, and the necromancer's snow-white brows flicked towards his hairline. "Just drop it. We need to focus on finding the twins."

Bran pressed his lips together and gave a stiff nod.

When they reached the hatch that led up to the abandoned berths, Varlan turned back to Bran. "Look, I'm not happy about it either. I would have rescued you both if we could. But Wes will keep an eye on Agnes and if it gets too dangerous, he will do what he can to get her out."

"Does Kent know about Wes' association with you?"

Varlan shook his head. "As far as Kent knows, Wes and I can't stand each other."

"What about Savita? Couldn't she just pluck the information from Wes' mind?"

He chuckled at the question. "I'd certainly like to see her try. Wes' mind is like a steel trap, even when he lets you in."

Bran nodded slowly. "There's history between you and Agnes, isn't there?"

The question caught Varlan off guard, and he bit the inside of his cheek. "She did a job for me a few years ago and I've known Elijah for a long time, but we never really had much to do with each other. Elijah tried to keep her away from his ... associates as much as he could. He didn't want her to be caught up in the sort of life he had led before he came here."

"I meant—"

"I know what you meant. As far as Kent knew, Agnes and I shared nothing more than a general acquaintance. Elijah and Agnes don't know the full extent of our relationship either. When the job I asked Agnes to do was complete, I wiped the mind of everyone who knew the truth except Wes. Gendry is the only other soul I told. But I can assume that since he knows, Wren knows too, because the pair of them might as well share a single mind. Neither of them would ever reveal the truth though."

"You wiped Agnes' mind? I certainly hope it was with her consent."

Varlan let out a long breath. "I wouldn't have done it if it wasn't. But we can talk about this later—we are running out of time to find the twins."

As they climbed up into the darkened berths and the sound of arguing reached them. They raced towards the raised voices and rounded a corner to find Wes with one of the twins slung over his shoulder. She was gripping a doorframe and thrashing against his hold as she called him every insult under the sun. Kiki would never curse so colourfully—Pippa then. Wes' suppression was a smooth bubble around them and were it not, he would probably be little more than a charred corpse given the savage ire radiating from Pippa.

"Put her down, Wes," Varlan said as they approached.

Wes frowned but set her on her feet.

The moment the warden let her go, Pippa made a dash along the corridor leading back towards the market. Wes grabbed her arm, and she let out a snarl as she was pulled up short. "Let me go! I have to go back for her!"

"You can't help her; you'll just be thrown in the cell beside her," Wes said gently.

Her blue eyes locked with Varlan's; they had a ferocity to them that her sister's could never possess; Pippa had a temperament to match her fire magic. "Kent has Kiki. I'm not returning to the ship without her."

"You have to, Pip. Wes is right. If you go rushing in there, you'll just end up captured too."

"But Kent has no reason not to hurt her. She's of no use to him and he'll need someone to punish for you taking Bran."

"Kent knows that you and Kiki are members of Wren's crew. He won't harm her if he thinks he can use her to bargain with Wren."

"What for? She has nothing he wants." Pippa's temper was calming but it was quickly sliding into despair.

"Wren doesn't, but I do. Wes, you know what needs to be done."

The warden nodded and then frowned. "Are you sure?"

"Yes, we can use this to our advantage. There's no way I will give him the real keystone, but I'll figure something out."

Wes gave a slow nod then took a few steps towards the stairs that led to the market. "HEY!" he shouted.

"Go." Varlan urged Bran and Pippa back towards the underbelly. "Don't stop until you're on the Queen."

"But—"

"I promise she'll be fine, Pip, but we have to go now."

Footsteps echoed along the corridor.

"Come on, Pippa." Bran took hold of her hand and dragged her away.

After a few steps, she glanced back over her shoulder at Varlan, fire burning in her eyes before she and Bran took off at a run.

"They're down here! Hurry!" Wes yelled. "You need to get out of here," he hissed through his teeth at Varlan.

"Take care of them both and be careful. If anything—"

"I *know*. Just get out of here."

"I will in a moment." A shadow appeared at the end of the corridor and Varlan lunged forward, slamming Wes against the wall. "Sorry," he hissed through his teeth. Then louder, he said, "Tell Kent I know exactly where the keystone is, and I am willing to trade it for both of them. But if he harms so much as a single hair on either of their heads, I will smash the fucking thing into a thousand pieces." He hauled Wes away from the wall and shoved him towards the guard who was running towards them.

Wes stumbled and fell, pulling the guard down with him. But he shot Varlan a quick nod before yelling, "Get off! He's getting away."

Varlan returned the nod and ran.

"Where's Kiki?" Wren asked as they reached the Queen.

"Kent has her," Varlan said.

Wren's face fell, and Gendry engulfed Pippa in a tight hug. "We'll get her back, lass," he said as he rubbed circles across Pippa's shoulders.

"We need to weigh anchor and get out of here," Varlan said.

Wren pressed her lips together and nodded. "Rufus."

"We can't—"

"We have to. None of us like it, but if we stay any longer, we'll all end up in Kent's cells or worse. We need to regroup and try and figure out exactly what Kent and Idir are up to. We'll come back and get Agnes and Kiki once we know what we are dealing with and have a proper plan," Varlan said, and the old boatswain's mouth twisted.

"Varlan is right," Gendry said over the top of Pippa's head. "Set a course for Weeper's Cove."

"We're taking on ghosts now, are we?" Rufus muttered as he strode away to bark orders at the rest of the crew.

Gendry guided Pippa to the hold and left her with Nari as Wren's keen stirred and wind caught the Queen's sails. The ship shuddered forward, rolling in a way that turned Varlan's stomach as it cut through the turbulent water created by Wren's earlier storm.

"We're doing the right thing, aren't we?" Bran asked softly.

Varlan licked his lip then nodded. "I don't know about right verses wrong, but we're taking the only course available to us at the moment that won't end with us all in Kent's prison. Or dead."

CHAPTER TWENTY-ONE

Thunder shook the entire crow's nest, leaving a buzzing sensation in Agnes' ears and a tremble in the tips of her fingers. She drew a deep breath and studied the objects laid out on the bed. A spare journal, the mahogany quill Gethyn had given her, a few pots of ink, and her tool roll. There was also a small package wrapped in grey cloth that hadn't been in her satchel before Kent had taken her prisoner. The wrapping had left the ends of her fingers feeling numb like the cloth hiding the green gem the mechanical cat had been guarding.

The cat was an actual golem and not a mindless automaton like the other contraptions she had built over the years. But how had she managed it and who had supplied the soul to power it? Had there been a necromancer involved back then?

Perhaps more confusing was the history between her and Varlan. He'd taken her memories of that time, but had he done it to protect her or himself?

Another clap of thunder rattled the walls as the wind began to howl. Agnes pushed the mysterious parcel, her tool roll, and all but one pot of ink into the satchel, and then hid it under the bed again. She settled herself at the small table and opened the pot of ink before testing the nib of the quill against the pad of her thumb and opening the journal. She needed to get as much as she could remember about Kent's war golem on paper. The way her magic worked meant she could only recall flashes of memory. Almost like the lightning that illuminated the edges of the furniture in the room and sent shadows dancing across the walls.

She started with a sketch. Thick plates of metal—she wasn't sure which type yet. Wood would make more sense given Kent wanted it to be able to move through the water, and wood was certainly more buoyant than metal. Magic could circumvent many laws of the natural world, but it still had limitations. Of course, some of the weight could be negated if she could include a ballast system that would stand up to the undulating movements of the serpentine body. A rush of pins and needles started at her fingertips, and she licked her lips. She couldn't afford to slip into the trance now. With a deep breath, she placed her pen down and pressed the heels of her palms to her forehead.

"Come on, Agnes. You can fight it," she whispered to herself as she squeezed her eyes shut, a roll of nausea turning her stomach and bringing a bitter taste to the back of her tongue.

Slowly, the prickle in her fingers died down and she felt her control returning. She picked up the pen again. Her magic needed another focus, one that would tire it out a little and allow her to think about Kent's golem without being swept into the trance.

The cat had been ruined when the shrouded ones ransacked the berth and took her father. If the heartstone still held power, she could fix the cat easily enough. But maybe she could make it better. She traced the tip of her tongue along her lips and flipped the journal over to work in the back of it. The moment her pen nib touched the page, pins and needles ran up her arm and settled in the back of her skull. She could make the cat a proper guardian; a golem that no one would mess with. Claws, fangs, and a larger, sleeker body—all she needed was a bigger heartstone to power it.

As her pen moved across the page, sketching out a panther made of metal, her mind started to go blank, the trance racing towards her like a wave ready to crush her against the shore.

Varlan had said she didn't need to be a slave to it—if they had more time, he could teach her how to control it. Could she control it and still get the full benefit of her magic? Her father wasn't a slave to his keen the way she was hers, was he? Maybe Varlan was right.

She stopped the movement of her pen and pushed back against the compulsion to let the trance take over. Slowly, she let it come forward, smoothing over her shoulders and into her mind rather than charging in and taking full control. The world peeled away, and she found herself standing in an empty room. The walls were a soft, almost glowing white. Her pen was still clutched in her fingers. Ink dripped from the nib and splashed against the floor.

"Where am I?"

A scrape behind her caught her attention and she spun around. The panther she had been imagining was sitting watching her, small flickers of bronze light glowing in its empty eye sockets. Beside the panther was a woman with starlight-coloured hair and silver eyes. The pale gold gown clinging to her body glistened as she moved and a slit opened in the skirt to reveal the dark amber, eight-pointed star tattooed on one of her shapely thighs.

"Who are you?"

The woman's face broke into an indulgent smile. The warmth radiating from her was almost unbearable. Her mouth moved as though she was speaking but no words came out, then the floor dropped from beneath Agnes, sending a swooping sensation through her stomach.

Agnes lifted her head from the tabletop. She was in her room in the crow's nest. Sounds of fighting were coming from farther along the hall, muffled by distance and the roar of the storm that threw torrents of rain against the windows. She glanced at her journal. Several pages were covered in notes and sketches of the panther, but there was also a small, eight-pointed star in the corner of one of the pages. It seemed to glisten with golden magic that faded as Agnes pressed her finger to it.

She hadn't stopped the trance from taking her, but she had never experienced it like that before. Normally, once her mind went blank, she would wake up, sometimes hours later with no memory of what had happened. It had almost felt like she had been in control, at least for a few brief moments.

The roar of the storm intensified for a heartbeat then the crow's nest shuddered. An arc of water slammed across the window leaving a gritty layer of sand and seaweed in its wake. Someone shouted and the sounds of booted feet pounding along the hall reached her. She grabbed her journal and stuffed it under the bed beside her satchel then perched herself on the edge of the table as the door opened.

The man who appeared in the doorway was sopping wet, his dark hair plastered to his forehead and his top lip set into a heavy scowl. One side of his face was covered by a burn scar that culminated in a web of twisted and puckered skin where his ear should have been. Byron. She fought the urge to shrink against the nearest wall and tilted her chin defiantly as she met his gaze.

"She's still here," Byron growled over his shoulder and stepped back to reveal Kent.

Agnes had never seen Kent look so angry. Like Byron, he was completely saturated. There was a fresh cut across the corner of his brow from which a rivulet of pink-tinged water traced a path over his cheek before dripping from the edge of his chin. An almost sinister grin curved the corner of his mouth, and he turned to Byron. "You can leave us."

"What if they come back for her?"

"They won't. Varlan is not a fool. He'll go to ground for now, but when he does regroup and return, we will be more than ready for him." He waved Byron away then stepped into the room and closed the door. "Now, Agnes, this is your final chance to do things the easy way. If you show even the slightest sign of defiance, I will have Savita take over your mind and turn it inside out, until you are as mindless as that mechanical cat of yours."

Something must have shown on her face because his smile widened.

"Oh yes, I know all about that and now you are going to tell me where you took the keystone it was guarding."

"I don't—"

"Don't lie to me, Agnes. I would hate to lose your beautiful mind to Savita's lust for brutality."

She swallowed. "Deana has it and she's on the Azure Queen."

"Now that wasn't so hard, was it?" He took several steps towards her until he was standing almost too close for comfort.

She fought the urge to retreat. Kent wasn't one to throw around empty threats and she didn't want to give him any reason to make good on his threat to let Savita have full control of her mind.

"See, we *can* be friends." He took hold of one of her braids and gently thumbed the length of it. "And I would certainly prefer it if we were."

Agnes didn't move, and after a few moments, Kent dropped her hair and left. She released a heavy breath and slid off her perch on the edge of the table to retrieve her journal. The altercation with Kent had left a sour taste at the edges of her tongue and a quiver in her fingertips that had nothing to do with her keen.

Settling into the chair, she opened her journal to the page with the eight-pointed star in the corner. She traced her fingertip over the lines of the mark. The glow had completely faded but did the page still radiate with magic? Without keen-sense, there was no way to tell.

She drummed her fingers on the table and took up her pen. Somehow, she had managed to control part of the trance, to reach that white room with the woman. Could she do that again? And if she could, did that mean she could learn to control it completely? If so, she would no longer be a slave to the magic and maybe she could learn how to destroy the compulsion entirely. If Agnes was the one in control and not the magic, then Kent wouldn't be able to exploit her keen and his war machine would never become a reality. But if Agnes refused to build the machine, he'd just have Savita force her to do it anyway—and she had no way to fight against Savita's keen. They had already made that clear.

A tremor ran through her, and her throat tightened as her eyes grew hot. It was hopeless. Even if she could learn to control it, she would have no choice but to do Kent's bidding and anyone else's who came after him. As long as she had her keen, tyrants would find a way to exploit it, to force her to be a slave to it. A tear rolled an itchy path down her cheek and dripped from her chin, smudging the ink on the page. She blotted the stain with the edge of her sleeve, then snapped the journal shut and shoved it back in the hiding place with her satchel before tossing herself onto the bed. As the storm raging outside the city started to die, she released the heavy sob that had been holding back the rest of her tears and let the internal storm take her.

The sharp cry of sea birds roused Agnes. After a few blinks, her gritty vision cleared enough to make out the banded shadows on the wall. She sat slowly and rubbed her eyes before letting her head fall back against the wall. When she had finally fallen asleep, her dreams had been chaotic in a way that left a heavy fog on her mind and an anxious tightness to her limbs.

"Good morning, Agnes."

Her neck protested as her head snapped in the direction of the voice.

Byron was sitting with his heels propped up on the small table, his fingers tented, and a smug smile on his face that set her stomach rolling.

"I hope you slept well; Kent has a big day planned for you."

"How long have you been there?" She tried to keep the tremor from her voice; the thought that he could just let himself in whenever he pleased terrified her.

He knew it, too, judging by the way the look in his eyes darkened and the corner of his mouth shifted. "Did you know you talk in your sleep? I wonder what secrets I could gather for Kent if I sat here all night."

She swallowed and pressed her spine harder against the wall. "Does he know you're in here?"

His smile dropped for a moment before pulling back into place.

That would be a 'no' then. Maybe that was something she could use to her advantage later, but would Kent care enough to do anything about it?

The sound of a key in the lock drew both of their attention right before someone rapped their knuckles against the wood and called, "Agnes?"

Wes, warning her he was coming in like he usually did—giving her time to ensure she was dressed, or her things were away out of sight in case he was not alone.

Byron let out a low curse and pushed himself to his feet.

As Wes entered, his hazel gaze landed on Byron and narrowed. "What are you doing in here? Typically, one guards from outside the room."

"Kent wanted her up and ready. I'm just making sure she isn't dragging her feet."

Wes set the tray he was carrying on the table and turned face to Byron. "Get out," he growled in a tone Agnes hadn't thought he was capable of.

Byron clenched his fists and stood taller.

Wes tilted his chin and half turned as he gestured at the hallway. "Out."

For a moment, Byron looked like he might have been going to take Wes on, but instead he muttered something to himself and marched towards the door.

"Oh, and Byron," Wes said, his voice still a deathly low growl. "If I catch you in here again, it's not Kent you'll have to worry about."

As Byron reached the door, he paused and threw a look over his shoulder. Agnes didn't know anyone who could make Byron back down the way Wes had done. It was so unexpected, too. With his fair hair, freckles, and soft eyes he seemed the opposite of intimidating. But with the dark look he was serving Byron and his shoulders squared in a way that made his presence seem to fill the entire room, he was frightening.

Once Byron had left, Wes' posture softened, and he turned a sheepish smile to Agnes. "Are you alright? He didn't do anything to you, did he?"

She shook her head.

"Good. If he ever does ..."

He didn't finish the sentence, but his meaning was clear.

"Thank you. Why, though? You barely know me, and if Byron tells Kent—"

"He won't. He was supposed to be on guard duty *outside* the door. If Kent found out Byron had been in here with you—the

215

crabs would be feasting on his entrails before his heart stopped beating." He cracked his knuckles and then indicated the tray. "You should have something to eat. Byron was right about Kent wanting to see you first thing this morning."

Agnes didn't feel like eating after the night she'd had. Something had shifted in the back of her mind when the woman appeared during her trance. Like a piece of a puzzle was clicking into place. But that feeling had brought with it a bitter sadness that settled on her chest like a heavy stone. "I'm not hungry," she said as she scooted to the edge of the bed and let her feet hit the cool floor.

Wes frowned. "Agnes—"

"Don't," she said almost too quickly, but his tone was one her father often used with her when she was being stubborn. "I want to know why you keep risking yourself for me. I'm sure it is not under Kent's orders."

A strange half-smile curved the left side of his mouth. "Because I like you and don't want to see you get hurt."

"You barely know me."

That brought a confusing wistfulness to his gaze. "I know you far better than you realise." The words were barely a whisper and he seemed to shake himself before meeting her eye again. "Just try to eat something. I'll be back in a little while to take you to Kent."

As he left, Agnes edged towards the tray. She lifted the cloth covering the plate to reveal a few pieces of fruit, a hunk of bread dotted with what looked like seeds and dried fruit, and a small pot of butter. Butter was a luxury here on Armada, fruit too, though they got that more regularly depending on the season. She gave the bread a tentative sniff; earthy spices tickled her nose and reminded her of the time her father had taken her to Osmar. She smeared some butter across it and took a bite. The creamy saltiness of the butter highlighted the spicy sweetness of the bread and ignited her hunger.

By the time Wes' knock sounded his return, she'd cleared the plate and pulled on a change of clothes. They weren't her own, so the fit was off but at least they were clean. She finished braiding her hair and looked up just as he opened the door. His gaze flicked to the plate, and he gave her a tiny nod.

"Kent is waiting."

He stepped back and waved her out into the hallway then placed a hand between her shoulders, his fingers flexing and guiding her forward with a slight pressure.

They didn't go to the central chamber. Instead, Wes took her down the main stairs and across the market. His hand never left her back, and when they passed Byron standing guard at the end of a hall, his fingers flexed again as he stared daggers at the other warden.

Agnes could feel Byron's gaze boring into her as they continued along the corridor into a part of the city that Agnes had rarely been in. This level held the dungeon.

Kent wasn't going to toss her into one of these cells, was he?

But Wes passed the stairs that led into the dungeon and stopped at a door at the other end of the catwalk. He nodded to the guard on duty, who nodded back and stepped out of their way.

Savita and Kent were both inside the room. Savita's dark gaze narrowed as it rolled over Agnes and settled on Wes. Did she know Wes wasn't as loyal to Kent as he claimed to be? Did she know that he'd brought Agnes' things to her and had been watching out for her?

"Thank you, Westly. You may leave us," Kent said and waved him toward the door.

Wes dipped his head in Kent's direction as his fingers dropped from Agnes' spine, and she felt suddenly exposed and vulnerable. She licked her lip as the door clicked shut and Kent's attention fell on her.

"We'll skip the pleasantries today." He gestured with an open palm at a collection of metal plates on the long table that stood between them.

"There is nothing more I can do until we have a heartstone and a necromancer to bind a soul to it," Agnes said carefully.

One of Kent's brows arched, and he fingered the robrillium charm he had taken from her. The one that had protected her from Savita's mind magic. "Remember our little talk from last night," he cautioned. "The necromancer's disappearance is but a minor delay, and as we speak, I have men chasing a lead on a heartstone. It seems if you apply the right sort of pressure people will happily give up their secrets. But even if my men come back empty handed, we still have so much work to do. You haven't told me what material you need to build the golem yet so I thought I would present you with some options." He waved his hand in a fluid motion towards the pieces of metal laid out before her.

She edged towards the table, fighting the urge to glance in Savita's direction, and ran her fingers over each thin plate before shaking her head. "We'll need robrillium," she offered at last. "A lot of it and ..." She moved back to one of the pieces and rested her palm on it. Her magic didn't seem to be responding.

"Stop stalling," Savita said.

Agnes rolled her shoulders. "I'm not stalling. I'm exhausted, and my magic isn't—" She bit down on the words as a sweetness came to the edges of her tongue. She clenched and released her hands as the tingle erupted in her fingers. It wasn't the usual hot-cold prickles; it was a wild heat that made her hands feel unbearably tight. The sweetness on her tongue intensified and she was thrust into the trance. The white room flashed in front of her as the heat flooding her veins intensified. When her body grew too heavy for her legs to hold, a cool hand touched her brow, plunging her into darkness.

CHAPTER TWENTY-TWO

ᗞEANA

Cool water lapped against her skin and swirled through her hair as she floated with her eyes closed. A breeze rolled over her, chilling the parts of her that were exposed, and she opened her eyes. Above her was a wide expanse of midnight blue sky dotted with stars and a thin slice of moon. Flocks of starlight-coloured birds wheeled across that banner of night and smooth scales brushed against her fingers.

Flipping upright, she let her toes dig into the silken sand beneath her. The water lapped against her hips as she studied the glowing fish that swirled around her legs. She cast her gaze along the pale curve that marked the shore. It was so pure a white it hurt to look at it. A song she hadn't noticed before coiled through her—it was fathomless and alluring—threating to drag her down into the deep.

She started towards the beach and a woman appeared. Her dark skin was adorned with smears of white pigment, and she held a twisted driftwood staff, the top of which appeared like a gnarled hand grasping at the sky. A bloodstained scrap of cloth hid her eyes and her tattered clothes were saturated, the water dripping from them turning the sand around her black. Her long hair was secured in dozens of tiny braids. The beads, bones, and shells hanging from them rattled against each other as she tilted her head as though regarding Deana.

Slowly, her full lips pulled back to reveal blackened teeth and she lifted the hand not holding the staff. "Come closer, little one." Her voice was layered; old, weathered tones brushing against melodic and youthful, as though she had not one voice but hundreds.

"Who are you?" Deana asked, not daring to take even the tiniest step closer to the woman.

"I have many, many names, but you know me as Grandmother Ocean."

Deana swallowed and reached for the charmed stone, but it was no longer hanging around her neck.

"You have no reason to fear me, little one. I gave you my blessing; I am not about to take it back." She tilted her head again as though listening to the breeze. "Yet, anyway."

"Where am I and why am I here?" The last thing Deana remembered was jumping from the crow's nest, the ocean rushing up to catch her, Bran, and Varlan as they fell.

Grandmother Ocean ran her tongue along her lip. It seemed vividly pink in contrast to her darkened teeth. "You are dreaming, little one, but you came here because I called you. And I called you because those who seek to exploit your power and take what they believe is their right have set in motion events which cannot be reversed."

"What events are—" A discordant note broke through the song and light fractured the dark sky above her. "Wait!" She reached for Grandmother Ocean as she faded from view, a roar of waves silencing every other sound as they crashed over Deana and stole her breath.

She bolted upright, her fingers wrapping around the comforting weight of the protection charm. The room rocked, the walls twisting away and then back again in a way that brought bile to her throat. A bucket was pressed onto her lap, and she gripped its sides as her stomach heaved.

Warm fingers touched a cool cloth to the back of her neck and then ran it along her brow as they brushed her hair behind her ear. She tilted her face enough to catch sight of Nari's pale blue gaze before she shut her eyes and drew a shaky breath.

Nari took the bucket from her and said, "here" as she pushed a fresh damp cloth into Deana's hands.

Deana pressed the cloth over her face and wiped her mouth as Nari's song thrummed warmly over her shoulders.

"Good," Nari said softly then held out a cup.

Deana took the cup and examined the liquid within before giving it a sniff.

"It's just water," the healer said with a hint of humour. "What did you see?"

"What did I see?"

"You were dreaming, though I get the sense that it wasn't a normal dream."

Deana rubbed her forehead and took a sip of the water while she tried to organise her thoughts. "I saw a woman ... She said she was Grandmother Ocean, but that's not possible—is it?"

Nari nodded. "It is quite possible. Did she speak to you?"

"Yes, but she didn't say much before the world started falling apart."

"I see." Nari nodded again and took the cloth and the cup from Deana before passing her a second cup. This one had only a small amount of dark liquid in the bottom that smelled like sour wine and fermenting flowers. "You'll feel better once you drink it. You used too much of your song. You're lucky Bran got you to me when he did, and I was able to stabilise you."

"Bran brought me to you? Am I still on Armada?" The room didn't look like Nari's berth, but it wasn't the hold of the Azure Queen either.

"No, we're farther south than that at the moment. We're heading for Weeper's Cove, but Wren wanted to stop and give the crew a chance to rest. You're in her quarters," Nari said, casting a look around the room. "She thought you'd be more comfortable here."

"How long—"

Nari lifted a hand, and Deana bit down on her question.

"Drink first."

Deana touched the cup to her lips. The liquid tasted much like it smelled and it burned a path right to her stomach. She coughed and rubbed the centre of her chest as both her own song and Nari's became deafening for a moment. After clearing her throat again, she asked, "How long was I asleep?"

"A full day. I thought I might lose you for the first few hours, but then I managed to get some of that restorative into you and your song stabilised again."

"Thank you for taking care of me. I can't pay you, but I will make—"

"I didn't take care of you because I wanted payment," Nari said.

"But—" Deana snapped her jaw shut at the look on Nari's face.

After a moment, the healer's features softened again. "I know you're not used to other people caring about you, but everyone on this ship does. They don't care about your connection to Grandmother Ocean and whether that makes you cursed or blessed. They don't care that you see the world differently, or act strangely. They just care about *you*—no strings attached. And that is the way it should be."

Deana's throat thickened and she dropped her gaze to her

fingers. "Kai ..."

"I know." Nari sat herself on the edge of the bed and placed a hand on Deana's knee. "I knew your brother. He was brave and kind and loved you more than anything else. After your parents died, he asked Nazali if he could take you to Armada. But she thought it would be better for you to stay on Lethata, where you would be close to the Guild of Singers."

"You knew Nazali?"

"She's my sister. The eldest, and she was always more ambitious than I ever was."

Did Nari know that her sister was dead? Should Deana tell her? Not that Deana knew all the details. Maybe Bran should have been the one. Not only had he been there when Nazali died, but he was a soul-singer. "Nari ... Nazali is ... she ..." She pressed her lips together and drew a tight breath. "Idir killed her."

Nari nodded slowly, no sign of shock or sorrow in her blue gaze. "I know."

"But you said she's your sister, as though she's still here."

A strange smile crossed Nari's features, and her eyes seemed to sparkle. "Death may have separated us, but she will always be my sister. I will always feel her presence in the cool breeze blowing off the ocean in the evenings. In the lament of the grieving, and the knowledge that death comes for us all in the end."

"I guess I never thought of it that way. Whenever I think of Kai, it's just this big, flat part of my song that feels like it will never be the same again."

"Because it won't. But death doesn't change the fact that he is your brother, nor does it mean you will never see him again. Death is but a transition to the next world." She gave Deana's knee a squeeze. "But perhaps we have lingered too long with thoughts of the departed. If you are feeling up to it, we should go out and see the crew. They are anxious to see you awake, some more than others." She gave a soft chuckle at that but didn't elaborate further. Instead, she pushed herself to her feet and collected a bundle of clothes from the shelf fixed to the wall. "Wren has donated a few of her things for you to wear—they should be a suitable fit. When you are ready, I will see you out on deck."

Deana studied the bundle of cloth in her lap. It looked like a pair of pants and a loose blouse with short sleeves that would only reach her elbow. There was also a tunic that had bronze buttons up the front and laces up the back. She'd seen a similar garment on Wren before—the laces pulled in at her waist, accentuating the curves of her body. And Wren had curves a plenty.

Deana slipped off the bed and gingerly pushed herself to her feet, but she found that she felt better than expected after several days of unconsciousness. Nari had also left a basin of water and a cloth. It wouldn't be as good as having a proper wash but at least she could freshen herself up. She stripped and then dipped the cloth into the frigid water. The cloth was rough against her skin, but it felt good, like she was sloughing off more than just a few days' worth of grime. Satisfied, she pulled the clothes on and settled the protection charm under the fabric of the shirt where it could sit warm against the centre of her chest.

She found a comb on the low table beside the basin. Her curls were an absolute mess, matted in places from her dip in the ocean. Carefully, she teased out the knots from the ends to the roots. Then she split it down the middle and braided each side as Agnes often wore hers. With a heavy breath to steady herself, she moved to the door and pushed her way out onto the deck.

It was almost too bright, and she had to squint at first as her eyes adjusted to the light. If she had to guess, she would say it was midafternoon. Most of the crew were spread out around the deck. Rufus was playing a game of dice with Gendry and Elijah, Wren was near them talking in hushed tones with Nari, and Bran and

Varlan were at the bow leaning on the rail and watching the horizon.

After a few moments, Bran let out a laugh at something Varlan said. It was a warm laugh, unguarded, the kind Deana had always wished for but had never been able to drop her guard long enough to enjoy.

Her attention shifted from Bran and Varlan to Dara, who was sitting with Pippa. Deana scanned the deck again with a frown. She couldn't see Kiki, nor could she hear her song. It was like she wasn't on the ship at all, but that couldn't be right. The twins went everywhere together.

"Deana, you're awake!" Dara said as her almost colourless gaze met Deana's.

The crew all turned to face her, and she shrank against the door, giving them a tiny wave.

Gendry was the first to reach her. He engulfed her in a hug that smelled of saltwater and spice. "You had us worried."

She sucked in a sharp breath and tried not to tense at his sudden closeness.

"Give the girl some space, you great oaf," Wren shoved him out of the way. "The clothes fit well."

"Yes, thank you. You didn't have to lend them to me. I could have made do."

Wren made a *pfft* sound and brushed Deana's comment away. "We take care of everyone on this ship, so you'd better get used to it."

Deana sucked her lower lip between her teeth.

"Alright, you lot, give the girl some space. She's not used to this sort of attention," Wren waved everyone away and they went back to what they had been doing before, except Bran and Varlan who were standing just behind Wren.

Wren gave them a nod and returned to Nari's side.

"Thank you for getting me to Nari," Deana said.

"You needed help; no thanks necessary." Bran smiled.

Deana glanced Pippa's way again. "Where's Kiki? Is she—" She couldn't finish that question.

Bran sighed, and Varlan's lips tightened into a frown.

"She's alive, but Kent has her," Varlan said.

"Oh no." Deana covered her mouth with her hands. "Why didn't we go back for her?"

"The same reason we didn't go after Agnes," Varlan answered. "Until we are certain about what Kent and Idir are planning, we need to pick our battles and sometimes that means making ..."

Sacrifices. He didn't say the word, but Deana felt it reverberate through her, bringing the hot sting of tears to the edge of her eyes. It wasn't fair; Agnes and Kiki shouldn't have to suffer just because—

Salt spray washed over them as a wave broke against the side of the ship, sending them staggering.

"You need to calm down, Deana," Varlan said as Bran took hold of her shoulders, his midnight blue eyes meeting hers.

"Hey," he said softly as though he had done it a hundred times before. "It's okay. We're not going to abandon them."

Her heart was pounding against her ribs. The ocean smashed along the hull again. Varlan's song rose, but Bran lifted a hand in his direction, not taking his eyes off Deana's, and it died down.

"Breathe," Bran whispered. "In ..." he said, and he inhaled slowly then held his breath, lifting his hand and counting silently to four with his fingers. "And out." He held his breath again for the same count.

Deana closed her eyes and focused on Bran's voice as he repeated the instructions. His song was brushing against hers, calm and cool, as his fingers flexed on her shoulders. Her song slowly lost its turbulence and became the soothing lap of waves against a shore.

"That's it," he whispered then released her and took a step back. "It looks like we'll have to try and keep you calm. At least while we're out here in the middle of the ocean," he said with a half-hearted grin.

"I've never ... it's never reacted like that before."

"It may have something to do with the way you used your keen on Armada," Varlan said. He was rubbing his fingers along his chin as he studied her. "Perhaps you unlocked some hidden talent you weren't aware of. Regardless, Bran is right. You need to learn how to control your emotions, so the magic doesn't get the better of you."

Get control of her emotions? She had gotten good at concealing her feelings from others a long time ago, but inside she was always tense, always worried about what others thought, always trying to stay out of the way and not draw too much attention to herself because if she did—

"Breathe, Deana," Bran said in that soft voice again.

His eyes were a fathomless dark blue, but this close they seemed to have shards of azure trapped in them. A knot tightened in her stomach, and she took a step back from him, tearing her gaze away.

Varlan flicked a look between her and Bran and then gave her a small smile. "You'll get the hang of it. Just try not to capsize us in the meantime." He nodded to Bran and headed over to Gendry and Elijah.

"I think there is someone you should talk to," Bran said, and he fished a silver pendant out of his pocket. The magic clinging to the pendant was deep and stirred a chill along Deana's spine that brought goose bumps to the surface of her skin. It was shaped like a rose. She'd seen the large, fragrant blooms in Beldaren—Indira had loved them. A pang of guilt jolted through her. She'd been so caught up in her own troubles, she hadn't stopped to think about

Indi or Samir. Poor Samir had been dragged off by the shrouded ones, and what if Idir did the same to Indira?

The song that overlaid the world paused for several heartbeats, then a tearing sound went through it and an oval of violet light appeared in front of Bran.

"Bran!" a vaguely familiar voice called out, and Bran took hold of Deana's hand.

"Sorry, this isn't going to be pleasant." He tugged her into the oval of light before she could even think about planting her feet.

Inside the oval, the sound was deafening—so many songs brushing over her and drowning out her own. Her skin felt too tight, her head throbbed, and her stomach turned—then she was stumbling onto solid ground once more and Bran caught her, only letting her go once she had regained her balance.

There were several other people in the room with them. A tall, broad man with dark red hair and grey eyes. Two women, both with golden hair, but one was tall and slender with warm brown eyes and the other was a head shorter and all soft curves. Her eyes were a bright blue several shades lighter than Bran's. The fourth and final person in the room had dark grey hair the colour of storm clouds rolling in over the headlands and violet eyes that seemed to stare right through you. Her cheek bore a thick scar from just below her temple to the corner of her mouth. Henry's mother, Nea. In fact, she recognised all of them. The man was Nea's heart mate, Garret, and the two women she remembered having met briefly as well, though she couldn't quite remember their names.

"I didn't realise you would *all* be here," Bran said.

The world suddenly seemed to spin away from her, and she gripped her head. Almost immediately the taller blonde woman swept forward and guided her to a chair by the window. "Portals are an awful way to travel. I hope Bran warned you." Her song brushed over Deana's, soft and soothing, spreading warmth from her toes to the top of her head.

"Of course I did," Bran said.

"Are you alright? When we hadn't heard anything—"

"Nea was ready to come looking for you herself," the other blonde said, cutting Nea off. "The rest of us told her that wasn't going to happen, but you know how stubborn she is."

"I told you. I'm fine."

"Of course you did, my lovely. Because you're always fine even when you aren't," a cheerful voice said from the door, and Deana glanced over the healer's shoulder.

The voice belonged to a tall man with dark, messy hair and bright green eyes. He had a slightly askew grin that softened as his gaze met Deana's.

"Declan," Garret warned in a low voice as the other man opened his mouth to speak again.

There were too many people in the space. Deana reached for the stone at her chest and pressed herself into the chair. The healer's warm gaze swept over Deana's face, and she gave a nod before standing. "How about we go catch up with Zephyr in the garden?" she said as she grabbed the other blonde's hand and pulled her towards the door. "You too." She gave Declan's chest a gentle shove, and he rocked back a step.

"But—"

"No buts. Just get a move on."

Once they had left, Nea's otherworldly gaze found Deana again. "It's Deana, isn't it? You were here with Queen Amara and Princess Indira."

"Yes."

"Sorry about the others. They mean well, but they can be a bit overzealous at times."

Garret chuckled at that, and Bran muttered, "That's an

understatement."

"Would you like some tea?" Nea asked, settling back into her chair and resting her cup on the swell of her stomach.

"No, we can't stay too long. I didn't tell Wren we were leaving and after the events of the past few days, she'll be having kittens when she realises we are gone," Bran said.

One of Nea's stormy brows arched as the right corner of her mouth pulled in. "Why are you here then?"

"Deana needs your help."

Nea's song brushed over Deana. "With what exactly? Her keen feels fine and—"

"Emotional control. The ocean seems to respond to her the same way the source does to you, so I thought you would be the best person to help her."

"Has this always happened or is it a new development?" She placed her cup aside and leant forward, her violet eyes shining with curiosity.

"It's never happened before today. But I've never really—I wasn't allowed to—my song is too dangerous, so ..." She curled her shoulders in and pressed her spine against the back of the chair even harder. Nea's gaze softened before it moved to Garret, who was tracing his finger along the scar that split his top lip.

"Who stopped you from using your song? Your parents?" he asked.

Deana shook her head. Her parents had wanted her to embrace it, but then when they had died and it was just her and Kai—"The guild. But Idir in particular."

"Idir?" Garret's voice was a low growl.

"I can understand Idir's stance on it, given what we now know. But the guild usually embraces those who have been touched by Grandmother Ocean. It's a blessing, isn't it?" Nea's voice was laced with unexpected concern.

Deana blew out a breath, not sure how to answer.

"So they say," Bran said, startling her. "Their view on Deana seems different though, and she's the only mage I've encountered who can control the ocean. Even Kiki ..." He paused and rubbed a hand over his face as a deep note of guilt quivered through his song. "... can't do the things I've seen Deana do."

"Kiki is a water mage; Deana isn't. Her keen is ... like the ocean personified," Garret said.

"Of course, why didn't I think of that sooner?" Nea shot him a warm smile and leapt to her feet. The movement overbalanced her, and she teetered for a moment before catching herself. Both Garret and Bran took a step towards her, but she waved away their concern with an, "I'm fine," then she hurried to the shelf behind the desk and ran her finger along the books there. "Where is it?" she muttered.

Deana glanced at Bran, and he shrugged.

Nea pulled several books out and flipped through them before tossing them onto the desk behind her. "There you are," she said to the fifth book and collapsed into her chair to flip through it. "Yes, I thought so ... Where did I see that though?" She drummed her fingers on the table. "Varlan! Family heirloom, my arse."

"You know Varlan?" Deana asked.

"Yes, we crossed paths briefly a few years back. We were both stealing relics from a mutual acquaintance. Varlan was after this." She held the open book up.

One page was a dense wall of text but the other depicted a large sketch surrounded by several smaller ones. The main sketch was a green stone inside a filigree metal cage. A stone that Deana had held in her hand—one that called to her as strongly as the fathomless deep. The ink on the page was a dull emerald, but in reality the stone was an almost luminescent bright green.

"What does the stone do?" Deana asked in a whisper.

"It's a key of some kind, but there appears to be some debate as to what exactly it opens. However, if we take into account your song and the presence of shrouded ones, I would suggest that the key opens something to do with Grandmother Ocean. An old temple or a tomb, perhaps. My biggest question isn't what it opens, but did Varlan know what it was and if so, why did he want it?"

"He gave it to Agnes to hide," Bran said.

"Agnes?" Nea flicked a look in his direction.

"She's a mage from Armada, a creationist. And Varlan is helping us. He is concerned about what Idir and Kent are trying to do."

"And Kent is?" Garret asked.

"The one in charge of Armada. He's forcing Agnes to build him a war golem. That's why he captured me. He needs a necromancer to animate the golem once Agnes is finished building it."

Nea's eyes widened at that, and an apologetic look stole across Bran's face.

"You were captured. Why didn't you use the anchor? We could have—"

"I didn't have it on me when they grabbed me, and even if I had had it, I didn't want to drag you into this. I wouldn't even be here now if I didn't think that Deana needed your help."

Nea chewed her lower lip. "Bran, this is bigger than—"

"No," Bran said firmly as he made a chopping motion with his hand.

Nea's mouth tightened and she folded her arms as she locked eyes with him.

"I have it under control—okay, not under control exactly, but we're figuring it out. There is no need for you or Garret or anyone else here to involve yourselves in this—beyond helping Deana manage the more temperamental aspects of her keen." His tone was firm but gentle. It was the same way Kai would have spoken to Deana when they were younger. Were these people his family? They certainly seemed to act that way. Or perhaps they were not blood relations. Perhaps they were like Wren and the crew of the Queen.

"What I don't understand is why Idir came here seeking our help with Samir if he was just going to kidnap him anyway," Garret said.

Nea opened her mouth as though she was going to comment but then closed it with a frown.

"He came here looking for Nea specifically though, and he recognised straight away that she was Shadow-blooded. Shadow-kin he called her, remember? What if he needed someone who was Shadow-touched? But she wouldn't go with him, so he accepted me as a substitute because my keen has been tainted by Nea's. Maybe that made him think I was like Nea, so I was an adequate substitute."

"Why would Idir need a Shadow-kin though?" Deana asked, and they all stared at her.

"Samir can apparently transfer living souls from one body to another. It's not an ability he was born with. Idir told us Chief Soma wanted someone to help them figure out how to fix Samir's keen," Nea said with a glance in Bran's direction.

"I didn't see Samir perform a soul transfer. And honestly, I am not sure how effectively he could do it; his keen is unstable," he answered.

"Unstable?"

Bran nodded. "Apparently it has been that way since the shrouded ones attacked him."

"They were looking for me, but Samir got between us. So they changed his song to punish him, made it discordant," Deana said as she studied her fingers.

"Samir wasn't the target of the attack?" Garret asked.

Deana shook her head. "They came to take me to Grandmother Ocean. I belong to her."

Nea's head tilted, and her eyes narrowed. "What do you mean you belong to her?"

"She claimed me before I was born. I am hers, and she always takes what she is owed. Except when I met her, she said—"

"You met Grandmother Ocean?" Nea stood and pressed her hands on the desk as she leant forward.

"I think so. I was dreaming but she was there, and she told me that events had been set in motion that could not be reversed."

Nea and Garret shared a look.

"Wait a minute, this isn't going to turn into another Usurper situation, is it?" Bran asked, and Nea shook her head.

"The Arcanarium refers to the Faridean gods as the sleeping gods. They don't have the duality of the Bright Mother and the Shadow Man, but rather an entire family of gods all linked to Grandmother Ocean and her heart mate." Nea's violet gaze flicked to Deana, a question sparkling in its depths.

Was she looking for confirmation? Deana nodded. "Grandfather Moon. Even in her sleep, Grandmother Ocean follows him."

"There are no myths that support a Usurper-like figure being responsible for the slumber of the other gods. Rather it is said that Grandmother Ocean is the mother of them all and as such their powers are interconnected. Which is why when she fell into her sleep they too followed. The question is what events is she referring to?"

Garret made a sound, and Nea's attention snapped to him. "That does sound a bit like what happened with the Bright Mother. Are you sure they are not different names for the same divine being?"

Nea gave him a curious look, her lip rolling between her teeth. Her song thrummed deeply for a moment, and Deana shifted in her seat before glancing at Bran, who shrugged and mouthed,

"*They are always like this.*"

Then he turned to Nea, and said, "Well?"

She let out a huff and rubbed a hand through her hair. "I don't know."

"But you *always* know ... or at least you always have an opinion," Bran said, and Garret chuckled.

Nea's mouth tucked in at one corner. "I don't *always* know. I make calculated guesses and hope I am on the right track. But in this instance, I don't have enough information to do that. My understanding of the Faridean Gods and their stories is limited, and there is always a possibility that this has nothing to do with the gods at all."

"The shrouded ones belong to Grandmother Ocean and—" That uncanny violet gaze switched to Deana again, and her voice fled. She swallowed and said softly, "And Idir is one of them."

"Is he just a pawn then?"

Deana shook her head. "He's a shrouded one, but he's not like the others. His song is still human. It completely fooled my song until he attacked me and his true nature was revealed by—" She touched her fingers to the stone and then gave a nod and pulled it from under her shirt. "—this."

"May I?" Nea held out her hand.

Deana's fingers closed around the charm, but she lifted the leather cord from her neck. She studied the stone, thumbing the hole at its centre before she held it out to Bran then nodded towards Nea.

Bran examined the stone as he moved to Nea's desk. Several new notes ran through his song, and he glanced at Deana over his shoulder before dropping the charm into Nea's waiting palm.

Nea's song increased in volume as she brushed her fingers along the edge of the stone and closed her eyes. "Curious," she whispered before handing it back to Bran.

"What is it?" he asked as he returned it to Deana, his fingertips briefly touching hers and sending a quiver through her song.

"It's *like* a seer stone but it's not a seer stone and it's not of this realm. It's from the Between." She rubbed the tips of her fingers together. "Where did you get it?"

Deana studied the stone again. "Kai," she whispered and cleared her throat. "My brother. Idir said he sold his soul for divine protection. But I don't understand how or why. I thought it was to stop Grandmother Ocean from finding me, but it doesn't stop the shrouded ones—it only burns when they are near. And it didn't recognise Idir until he touched it. It's useless. I just hold on to it because it's all I have left of Kai." Her eyes felt hot; the realisation that the stone was worthless settled in her stomach and lifted a lump to the back of her throat.

"It's not useless. It does protect you, but I think you are dealing with two separate types of shrouded ones. I think perhaps Idir has figured out a way to either create his own shrouded ones or control those already in existence. Here," she directed at Bran and passed him the book that had the image of Varlan's stone. "It might help and ..." She moved to the bookcase and pulled another book from the shelf. "That one may as well, and you could ask Mateus what he knows about the Faridean gods. He is a good deal more knowledgeable than I in that regard and might be able to point you in the right direction."

"Just don't tell him Nea admitted that there's something in the known realms that he knows more about than her. We'll never hear the end of it if you do," Garret said with a grin.

"And what about helping Deana with her keen?"

A smile quirked the corner of Nea's mouth and she shot a look at Garret who nodded. "I think you're more than capable of helping her but, Deana, why don't you go down to the grove with Garret while I discuss a few more things with Bran?"

Deana looked from Garret to Bran.

Bran gave her a tiny nod.

"Alright." She stood.

"It won't take long," Garret said as he gestured towards the door.

His song was soft and thrumming as it brushed against hers, but it also had a playfully curious undertone and the soft notes of Nea's song over-layering it. She'd never encountered a mage quite like him before.

CHAPTER TWENTY-THREE

BRAN

"She'll be fine." Nea's voice drew his attention away from the door. "It's you I'm worried about."

"Me?" Bran placed the books she had given him on the corner of the desk and sat in the chair Deana had vacated.

"Your keen is changing. Have you not noticed?"

"My keen—oh ..." He rubbed a hand over his face. "I have been experimenting with a few things."

One iron-coloured brow flicked upwards, and the right corner of her mouth pulled in as she folded her arms.

"Nothing bad." He held his hands up to reassure her. "Just ... watch." He focused on the air in front of his palms. The source pulled over his fingers, tightening until it split with a small ripping sound and a perfect oval of purple light appeared. The portal shimmered between them, bigger than any he had managed to create before and more stable too. Still not big enough for a person to pass through though. He closed his fist and the portal snapped shut.

Nea blinked at him. "How?"

"I think your keen did more than taint mine. It's felt different since the oathing. I didn't want to tell you because I didn't want you to worry."

"Is that all you can do?" She leant forward slightly, her eyes glittering.

Of course, she was curious. Bran should have known that she would be. Nea had made it her life's work to understand the ways in which the individual keen of different mages worked and how that keen could become altered by outside forces.

"I haven't tested anything else. I'm not sure I want to know if I can do *all* the things you can—no offence."

She gave a snort that could have been a laugh. "None taken. But you know what I am going to say; it's the same thing Garret will be telling Deana about her song."

"It's not the same."

"It is exactly the same. If you'd rather take it up with Garret, or Harvey ... or Father. Does he know?"

Niall didn't know, or if he did, he hadn't let on. "I don't think he knows. I am sure he would have said something if he did. And yes, I know it's important to test it, but how do you even test something like that?"

"Warren and Nonna made me kill chickens for dinner or eradicate rats from the barn."

"That's ... I'm not actually surprised." He sat back and blew out a breath.

"Look, I understand your reservations. But you, more than most, know the dangers of a mage who doesn't understand the limitations of their keen. I'm not asking you to strip souls. I am just asking you explore those limitations, to understand how your new keen works so that it doesn't become a problem if you channel it accidentally. Especially given what you may be dealing with in the isles. Come on." She stood and headed out the door, gesturing over her shoulder for him to follow.

She led him out of the manor and across the vegetable garden to the pen of chickens in the far corner. "Alright, now give me your hand." She held her hand up, palm facing him.

He pressed his palm against hers, and her keen immediately flooded through him, sending a shiver of cold down his spine before it retreated again.

"Thankfully we don't need to cover the basics and can skip straight to the practical. You know everything has a lifeforce. All you need to do is use your keen to find the edge of that lifeforce and then sever the threads holding it to the body. It is almost exactly like destroying a reanimation only infinitely harder because that lifeforce is not an interloper you are driving out. It is not possessing the body—it owns it." As she spoke, she brushed her keen over the chickens who had come out in the hope that Nea and Bran had brought food.

He let his keen follow hers until he could feel the shroud of life over one of the chickens. She was right that it felt different to a reanimation, but he could also see the soft shimmer that marked the edges where the soul was tethered to the body.

"Good," Nea whispered. "Now sever them."

Sever them? How, exactly? With a reanimation he would just let his keen take hold of those threads and tear them. He licked his lip and grabbed the edge of the chicken's lifeforce then gave it a yank. The chicken let out a squark and took off in a flurry of flapping wings, stirring the others into a frenzy.

"I told you it was hard." There was a note of humour in her voice, and he glanced at her where she was leaning against the fence, her hand resting on the top of her stomach and her lip firmly between her teeth as though she were biting back a smile.

"What am I doing wrong?"

"You're overthinking it. Magic is a—"

"Feeling thing, not a thinking thing." He finished her sentence.

"I *know*." Niall had certainly drilled that into his mind growing up, but it was true. Magic was easier when you didn't overthink, which was why the source responded to the fluctuations in emotions of mages like Nea and Harvey ... and Deana. "Okay."

He shook himself off and let his keen focus on the chickens again. They had all moved to the far end of the pen and were watching Bran and Nea as though they knew exactly what was coming.

This time, when Bran felt the lifeforce of the chicken he didn't hesitate. He grabbed hold and tore it with a precise snap of his keen as though he were snapping the bird's neck. It dropped like a stone and the others darted away from it. Bran walked over and picked it up before turning to Nea.

She gave him a satisfied nod. "Chickens are easy. But now you know what that part of your keen feels like. I hope you never have to use it on another human."

He studied the dead chicken and met her gaze again. "Why?"

Her eyes widened and he shook his head.

"Sorry, not why do you hope that. Why did my keen change?"

"I don't know. You're not a brightling, and I am fairly certain you are not one of Ambrose's experiments. But we don't know where you came from, so maybe you were. That would explain some things. Your keen has always been stronger than a standard necromancer's, certainly too strong for you to be a resurgence of necromancy in a dormant bloodline." She ran her hand through her hair. "It could have been the nature of the oathbond, or it could be that a piece of my keen broke away and you are channelling that rather than your own keen. Though I doubt that is the case. It doesn't feel like it ... I just don't know ... There are too many variables."

Bran frowned at his feet. "Did Agatha see who left me at the lock-stone?"

Nea shook her head. "She may have, but you know how she and the rest of the ancestors are. You only get told what you need at the time."

He let out a huff. "Of course."

"I know that not knowing bothers you, but in the grand scheme of things it is just a tiny piece of who you are. And knowing where you *belong* is vastly more important than where you came from." She gave him a warm smile—an old Nea smile—the kind she wore before she had been changed by the horrors she had witnessed at Kalhanna.

"You're starting to sound like Nonna." He gave her a half-grin.

"It happens to us all in the end I guess." She shrugged and gave a small laugh then waved him towards the gate. "All that matters is you understand what your keen has become, and now that you have a feel for it you should be able to figure out your new limitations fairly quickly. Let's go drop the chicken off to Nonna and then see if Garret is finished helping Deana."

As Bran's bare toes sunk into the lush grass of the grove, he let out a sigh. The magic of the ancestors vibrated up his spine and set his hair on end. It seemed to sooth hurts he wasn't aware he had and recharge his keen. Nea released a soft sigh of her own and then wandered towards the hawthorn at the grove's centre. The spirit known as Agatha sat cross-legged at the foot of the tree, her cloud of white hair stirring as though shifting in a breeze and her dark blue eyes closed. Her mouth curved up at one side as they neared.

"Welcome home, little foundling. Such a strange companion you have brought with you," she said as she opened her eyes. "We would have preferred to be introduced to her in the normal fashion, but I understand you were under some duress when you arrived. The brightling has rectified your slip in propriety."

"You made Deana perform the rite?" Bran asked, not quite managing to keep the annoyance out of his tone.

"She took no offence at being asked to; she understands both the necessity and intricacies of ancestral veneration. And had you brought her here via the lock-stone, she would not have been permitted entry without performing the rite, which you well know. So, I suggest you unruffle those feathers."

"I'm sorry. It's been ..." He rubbed a hand over his face. "She's been through a lot."

Agatha nodded and her form shifted into the ancestor that looked like a sharper-faced version of Nea with emerald eyes. "And you have both barely scratched the surface of your trial."

"You know what we are facing then?"

The spirit chuckled and shifted again, into a tall, slender man with violet eyes and a granite-grey goatee. "Nice try, but it is not our place to tell you what we know."

Bran let out a long breath and folded his arms but said nothing.

Nea laid a hand on his shoulder. "Be nice, all of you. I am sure you found it frustrating when you were in his position."

"He knows how this works just as well as you do, little death-bringer."

Nea's mouth pulled into a tight line. "But I also know there are details you can share, so instead of being cryptic maybe just come out with it."

The spirit changed back into Agatha and folded her arms. "And where is the fun in that? Would you like to hear—"

"No stories," Nea said, and Agatha's nose scrunched. "Not today. Bran doesn't have time. He and Deana need to get back to the isles."

"Fine." Agatha settled her sapphire gaze back on Bran and the smile she gave him was almost motherly. "In the repository there is a carved, ebony chest. To open it you will need to find three drops of the sea and three of the sky. Mix them with the metal that silences mages and the shards of broken voices. Once you have the key, you may open the chest and claim your prize. But choose wisely. Only one item will aid you. The others, if removed from their seat, will aid your enemy."

"How is that not cryptic? And why is a chest that has something to do with what is going on in the isles in the Hartswood repository?" Bran asked.

Agatha shrugged. "Destiny is a strange and wild beast. Do not try to understand it. Just cling to its mane and hope it does not trample you beneath its hooves." She settled back onto the grass and shut her eyes. "I believe the brightling is done with your companion," she said as she faded from view.

Bran blew out a breath and turned to Nea, who shrugged. "We should retrieve the chest and get you on your way."

"What are you two up to?" Garret asked as he and Deana approached them from deeper in the grove.

"Looking for answers and finding more questions," Bran replied.

Nea patted his shoulder.

"Been there," Garret muttered.

"Feeling more in control?" Nea asked Deana.

"I think so."

"It will get easier with practice."

"That's what Garret said."

Nea nodded. "Come on. We need to get down to the repository and then send you back to the Queen before Wren goes into full panic mode."

"I've never seen the chest Agatha mentioned, have you?" Bran asked, and Nea shook her head.

"That doesn't mean it's not down there though. And honestly, I am a little jealous. Agatha just gave you a much bigger hint than she ever gave me." She nudged him towards the manor.

They headed straight down to the repository, and Nea placed her palm against the centre of the door, feeding a little of her magic into it. A lilac quiver ran over the wood, and it swung away from her palm to allow them access to the room. It didn't appear as large as other repositories, but the magic in the air spoke of hidden secrets and when you weren't looking the shelves would rearrange themselves.

"Alright, Bran, let the room know what we're looking for and let's see what happens." Nea took a step back towards the door and pulled Deana and Garret to stand with her.

"Okay." He looked towards the ceiling and said, "I am looking for an ebony carved chest, one that can only be opened with a key made of the sea and sky."

The shelves quivered. If you listened hard enough, it almost sounded like they were whispering amongst themselves. After a few moments, they rolled back, and a small table ambled forward. Sitting on it was a little, black chest with waves carved around the sides and an ornate robrillium keyhole in the very centre of the top.

Deana gave a sharp intake of breath, and Bran turned to her.

"I don't think we should take it."

"Agatha said it could help us."

"Its song is ..." Her eyes widened and she gripped the protection charm. "Can't any of you feel it?" She cast a questioning gaze at Nea and Garret before settling on Bran.

He let his keen run over the chest. The magic clinging to it was shifting and elusive. It felt like—

"The Between," Nea and Garret said together.

"I don't think you'll have any choice but to take it now that it has revealed itself," Nea added. "Relics like this one can be very persistent." She nodded and spun on her heel. "I'll be right back."

Bran glanced at Garret.

He was rubbing the scar that intersected his top lip as he studied the chest. "Did Agatha say what it contained?"

"Something that can help us, but also something that could help our enemies if we chose wrong. We can only take one item from the chest and must leave all the others. However, before we can open it, we need to make a new key."

"And how are we going to do that?" Deana asked.

"Agatha told me what we need. We just have to gather the ingredients ... and then figure out how to form them into a key."

"I still don't know." She closed her eyes and shook her head.

"Deana."

She opened her eyes again and met his gaze.

"If it bothers you that much, we can leave it."

Something strange passed across her features, but she shook it off. "No. If it can help then we should take it. But, it ..." She swallowed.

"Hey, it's alright. I'm scared too. Terrified actually, but that's what tells me we are on the right track." He lifted a hand towards her but didn't touch her.

She stared at his fingers in the air between them then brushed her fingertips against his as though she were about to weave them together.

"Alright," Nea said as she returned.

Deana's hand hastily dropped back to her side, and she turned to face Nea.

"Here. You have just enough connection to the Shadow now that it should work for you. It worked for Harvey, and he didn't have my keen melded with his." She held out a small dark metal knife with roses carved in the handle. Familiar cold magic moved over the blade like oil on water.

Bran's fingers closed around the hilt, and Nea took a step back. The magic clinging to the knife gave a tug that tightened behind Bran's navel, and the blade lengthened until he was holding a sturdy longsword.

"It changes to suit the wielder," Nea held out a leather sheath.

He focused on the blade, and it shortened back into a knife. He tucked it into the sheath and secured the belt around his hips. "Thank you."

She waved his thanks away then held out the small stack of books he had left in her study. "Are you ready to go back to the Queen?"

Bran nodded as he took the books from her.

"Be careful, both of you, and if you need anything at all you know where to find us." She gave Bran a tight hug and then squeezed Deana's arm as a portal sprung to life beside her, bringing with it a saltwater-scented breeze.

Bran handed the books to Deana then picked up the chest and gave her a nod. She licked her lip and drew a deep breath then stepped into the portal. He followed her, nearly dropping the chest as he staggered onto the deck of the Azure Queen.

CHAPTER TWENTY-FOUR

VARLAN

"You're sure they went through one of Nea's portals?" Wren asked as she paced past Varlan and Dara.

The girl nodded. "It was Nea's magic." She tilted her head as though listening to something. Her keen plucked gently at the edges of Varlan's, bringing with it a heavy drowsiness. After a few moments, she nodded again. "They won't be much longer."

"Why did they go in the first place?" Pippa asked. She was leaning against a crate, her arms folded over her chest and her shoulders hunched. The further from Armada they sailed the more listless she became, and the darker the circles beneath her eyes grew.

"Deana needed help that we were not equipped to provide," Dara answered in a tone that was far beyond her years.

"Who is Nea?" Nari asked as she moved to Pippa's side, and her keen drifted out in a soothing warmth.

"She's a necromancer from Beldaren," Varlan said.

Dara made a noise. "She's not *just* a necromancer. She's a child of the Shadow blood, one of the most powerful mages in all of Beldaren."

Nari's brow rose slightly. "A true Shadow-kin? Does Idir know she exists?"

"Yes. He went to Beldaren to ask for her help with Samir. As far as I knew, the Guild had sent him to find Nea, hoping that she could succeed where their own necromancers had failed, but he brought Bran back with him instead," Wren answered.

"Bran's song is different to other soul-singers, but I would never have guessed he was Shadow-kin." Nari worried her lip and shot a look along the deck. "If he is then that changes things."

"How so?" Wren stopped her pacing and turned to face the healer.

"If Idir was looking for a Shadow-kin then his aim is not just to raise the Isle of Splendour and take its spoils for himself. He intends to wake Grandmother Ocean to break a curse and seek retribution for an eon of damnation."

"What curse?"

"The one responsible for the sinking of Dumura to begin with. The one that damned an entire bloodline and stole the power of the gods, throwing them into their eternal slumber. I can scarcely believe it is real."

Varlan studied the horizon. Until now, he hadn't been sure he *truly* believed that Idir could raise the Isle of Splendour or that doing so would lead him to the resting place of Grandmother Ocean and the other gods. Sure, he'd taken the keystone as a precaution, and he trusted Kai's judgement of Idir and his motives. But some small part of him had still thought that perhaps the treasure was indeed literal treasure. The bounty of the gods, Kent had called it once. The promise of that bounty laid bare for the taking had certainly been enough to prompt Kent to build his war golem; what better way to strong-arm his way in and take his pick? But Idir had never seemed the type to be motivated by the lure of treasures untold; there had to be more to his plan. And why did the mention of the curse light a flicker of memory in the back of his mind? Dumura had been sunk over an eon ago, and stories had a tendency to shift and change with each retelling. He turned back to Nari.

"Do you know anything about the curse?"

"Only the stories my grandfather told Nazali and I when we were girls. But I remember something about the blood of the sea having to sacrifice the moon ... or maybe it was the other way around." She rubbed her forehead.

"Deana has to be the blood of the sea, right?" Dara mused. "But why do you think Idir wants a Shadow-kin? Does the story mention them?"

Nari shook her head. "Not specifically. But time has a way of distorting a story as the truth gets stretched further each time it is told. The concept of Shadow-kin came to isles from Osmar; what they call Shadow-blooded, our ancestors would have called moon blessed."

"Is Grandfather Moon another name for the Shadow Man?" Pippa asked.

"Perhaps they were once the same entity, but the gods can change almost as subtly as their stories. What was once a mere aspect of a much larger being can breakaway and become something else entirely. At least, that is what my grandfather used to say. Power is born from belief; veneration keeps it alive and guides its nature."

A prickling sensation rushed up Varlan's spine and made him shift his shoulders as the source seemed to pull in too tight around him. Dara took several steps to the right as a seam of light appeared behind where she had been standing. The light split open into a portal and Deana stumbled out, the books she was carrying thudding against the deck as she lifted her hands to press them over her ears and squeezed her eyes shut. Nari leapt forward and caught her arm, steadying her on her feet before guiding her over to lean against the side rail beside Pippa.

Bran stepped out of the portal, and it snapped shut. He looked steadier on his feet than Deana, but his face was several shades paler than normal. "Take this would you?" He passed the dark, wooden chest he was carrying to Varlan.

It was heavy, and the magic clinging to it was older than anything Varlan had ever encountered before. The robrillium keyhole set into the top of the box glinted in the afternoon light.

"What is that?" Wren asked.

"Apparently, if we can figure out how to open it, it will help us."

"Are you sure it can help?" Dara asked, eyeing the chest as though she believed it was full of snakes.

Bran licked his lip. "There is a chance it could kill us if we choose the wrong item from it ... but the Hartswood ancestors seemed to think it was worth the risk. They gave me a list of things we'll need to construct the key. The robrillium and drops of the sea are going to be easy, the drops of sky and shards of broken voices though—"

"You're sure drops of sky doesn't just mean rainwater?" Pippa asked.

Bran's cheek concaved as though he were biting it, and his brow rose. "You might be onto something there, Pip."

"It could be that simple; depends on the mage who cast the original enchantment I guess," Nari said as she gathered the books Deana had dropped.

"Stow it away in the hold. We have more pressing issues to deal with," Wren said.

Varlan handed the chest back to Bran, and he disappeared into the hold with it.

"Right. We should reach Weeper's Cove soon; someone will need to go with Gendry to pay the tithe, so the locals don't bother us. It will be all hands on deck to get us in there, but don't blindly trust everything you see and hear as we pass through the headland. The source around the island is prickly and I know most of you know what that means."

"Should we risk it?" Deana asked, her voice soft.

"If it were any other crew on any other ship I would say no, but the Queen can handle it."

"I don't think she was questioning the Queen's capabilities, or those of the crew," Nari said.

"As long as we keep to ourselves and pay the tithe then we will be fine. Weeper's Cove is the safest place in the isles for us at the moment."

Weeper's Cove could only be reached by a narrow pass between two cliffs. If the Azure Queen were a larger ship, there was no way she would fit along the pass. As it was, there were moments when the cliffs pressed in close enough that Varlan held his breath, waiting for the telltale scrape of rocks tearing open the ship's hull. But the Queen was not an ordinary ship, and her crew was one of the best, and it wasn't long before they emerged into a shallow cove. A small collection of huts cluttered the land just beyond the beach and behind them a larger building adorned with strings of faded banners. Flags for the dead.

The source flickered around them, fragile and shifting. It whispered across the back of Varlan's neck.

"The voices are so loud here," Dara said weakly as she covered her ears and glanced at Deana beside her.

Deana was staring blankly at the beach, her keen surging around her like a rising tide.

"They'll calm down once Gendry goes and pays the tithe," Wren placed a delicate hand on Deana's arm, and the girl nearly jolted out of her skin. "Try not to listen to them. I know it's harder for you Faridean mages." The captain then turned her attention to Varlan. "Would you mind going with Gendry?"

Varlan gave her a nod and headed over to where Gendry and Bran were getting into the rowboat. "Wren asked me to go with you," he said as he climbed in.

"Of course she did. Doesn't want to admit she's too scared to face a few ghosts herself," Gendry chuckled before giving Rufus a nod.

"Wren is frightened of ghosts? I didn't think she was scared of anything," Bran said.

"Everyone has something that scares them. Some people are just good at hiding it," Gendry said as the boat hit the water and he unhooked it before taking up the oars.

"Did you ask Nea where to find a heartstone?" Varlan asked Bran as their boat cut a path towards the shore.

"No, I didn't think to. I was more worried about getting Deana the help she needed."

Varlan bit down on his lip. He couldn't blame Bran for putting Deana's needs first. They needed her to be in full control of her keen—if she lost control for even a moment the consequences could be catastrophic. "It's fine. Elijah is working on a map anyway."

The boat entered the shallows and Varlan climbed out to hold it steady for the others. They dragged it onto the sand and Gendry led them along the beach. On closer inspection, many of the huts were little more than ruins. A few people milled around, hardly paying them any heed as they passed. Shadows stirred at the edges of Varlan's vision, and the ticklish brush of phantom fingers against his skin made him roll his shoulders.

Bran's keen was a cold prickle up his spine. "There are so many spirits here," he whispered, most likely to himself. "Not all of them human," he added.

Gendry chuckled. "Best to ignore them until we've paid the tithe."

He led them to the biggest building. A large dish sat on a pedestal at the top of the stairs. There were scorch marks in the base of it and runes carved around the edges. Gendry took a bottle of something from his satchel, he then pulled a sea snail shell and a handful of coins from his pocket. He dropped the coins and shell into the basin then poured the amber-coloured liquid from the bottle over them. Whiskey of some kind, judging by the smell. He took the knife from his belt and used it to prick the end of his finger before he squeezed several drops of blood into the basin. With a satisfied nod, he passed the knife to Bran and indicated he and Varlan do the same.

As the third drop of Varlan's blood met the rest, the source pulled, tightening the air, and the runes around the edges of the basin lit up. They grew so bright that Varlan had to shield his eyes. Then with a final flash and a puff of smoke the basin was empty. A shockwave of light and sound radiated over the ruined town and across the bay. As the wave passed, the world seemed to shift. The ghosts faded and the huts all appeared new as a thriving community was revealed in their place.

A woman stepped out of the double doors behind the offering bowl. She had dark skin mottled with patches as pale as milk. One of her eyes was a deep brown and the other almost silver. Her hair was as white as Bran's and held in thin, tight braids. Some of the braids were wrapped in coloured thread and others were adorned with beads and shells. She tilted her head from one side to the other as she regarded them, her keen swelling out. Her magic was strange and twisting—one moment it was the sharp chill of necromancy, the next it was the deep warmth of healing magic.

But it was more than that—it was like she held a hundred different keens within her skin.

"The ancestors accept your tithe; the Azure Queen and her crew are welcome in these waters." Her gaze shifted from Gendry to Bran and her lips quirked as her keen swirled back to cold-fingered necromancy. "Curious," she whispered.

"Are you a brightling?" Bran asked as though he couldn't hold it in anymore.

"What I am or am not does not concern you. I am the guardian of this place and that is all you need to know ..." She tilted her head the way Dara often did, as though listening to something only she could hear. "For now at least."

CHAPTER TWENTY-FIVE

DEANA

From the deck of the Azure Queen, the village of Weeper's Cove looked like a rabble of half-burned houses and scuttled boats. Shapes moved through the wreckage. Some appeared human, others were harder for her mind to comprehend. Despite their haunting nature, the ghostly shadows were not as unnerving as the song of the cove. It twisted around her, the cold whisper of death and the deep throbbing of unfathomable sorrow, settling an unsteadiness in her knees. Something had happened here—something dark that stained the earth and air.

Beside her, Dara was whispering under her breath, her hands pressed over her ears as her song grew heavy. Deana glanced over her shoulder, searching for Wren, Pippa, or one of the other crew members who might know how to help the girl. Finding no one, she drew a deep breath and slid her arm along the girl's shoulders, folding her against her chest like she would Indi. "It's okay. They are just echoes," she whispered as she stroked the back of Dara's head.

The girl burrowed closer, clinging to the front of Deana's shirt as a shudder ran through her body.

Focusing on Dara's discomfort helped Deana find her centre, and her own song calmed from a crashing roar to a gentle, rolling swell. She focused on breathing the way Bran had shown her. *In ... hold ... out ... hold.* Each to the count of four, and she circled through the process another two times before a chime rang through the song of the cove and it changed as the ruins crumbled away to reveal a small, busy village.

Dara pulled back from Deana's embrace and gave her a glassy-eyed smile. "Thank you," she whispered before throwing her arms around Deana's waist and giving her a tight squeeze. "They said such awful things, and I saw ..." She pulled back and cast an almost panicked stare along the shoreline before shaking her head. "It's not important. They were just trying to scare me."

Warmth flooded over Deana as the soft notes of Nari's song brushed against hers. A jolt of energy ran up her spine, scattering the lingering melancholy that had settled there.

Dara rolled her shoulders before turning her pale gaze to the healer. "That is much better. Thank you, Nari," she said then skipped away to Wren and Rufus.

"Thank you," Deana said as she turned to Nari.

The healer gave her a nod. "The song of this place is ... heavy. I don't think we should linger here."

"Gendry seems to think it is safe."

"I don't doubt his judgement, but to linger here longer than necessary will put us at risk of losing part of ourselves to the beings that inhabit the isle."

Deana reached for the protection stone as she scanned the shoreline once more. The huts that had replaced the ruins seemed inviting in the warming afternoon light, but Nari's warning was settling heavy in her gut. The air had a shifting character that plied at the wispy hairs around her face and set a prickling sensation crawling across her shoulders. It reminded her of the grove at

Hartswood.

"Ready, Dee?" Pippa's voice sent a jolt through her. "Sorry, I didn't mean to startle you. Wren is ready to move to the island."

Deana followed the line of Pippa's arm as she indicated the boat where Wren, Dara, Nari, and Elijah were waiting. "What about the rest of the crew?"

"The others will be staying behind with Rufus for now. Come on." Pippa turned and waved for Deana to follow her.

They climbed into the boat, and Wren gave Deana's shoulder a pat as she settled onto the seat beside her. "They put me on edge too. That feeling will calm down once they get bored with studying you," she said.

"Who ..."

"The spirits," Dara answered, throwing her arms around herself as a shudder went through her small frame. "Stop that! It tickles," she said, glaring at the empty air behind her.

Wren cleared her throat and gave Rufus a wave. The pulley creaked, and the boat gave a jolt before moving smoothly downward. Once the belly of the boat met the water, Wren and Pippa stood and unhooked the ropes. Elijah took up the oars and guided them across the shallows.

As they neared the beach, a glimmer at the corner of Deana's eye caught her attention. A school of brightfish were swirling along beside their boat, but amongst the rainbow-coloured school there was one pearly white fish with long fins that seemed to glow. It twisted through the others, exposing its black belly before darting back towards the deeper water. Deana was still staring after the fish when the boat scraped onto the sand nearly unseating her.

"Are you alright?" Bran asked.

She turned and blinked at him before flicking her attention to the others. Wren and Dara were already out of the boat, Pippa too

—she was helping Nari and Elijah gather the bags they all brought with them. Deana looked back at Bran, and he gave her a small smile.

"This place is strange. It reminds me of Hartswood."

He nodded. "The barrier is definitely thinner than normal here. Thin enough for the magic of the Between to leach through."

Deana fingered the protection charm through the material of her shirt. "Do you think it's safe?"

He nodded again. "The spirits here are curious, but I don't sense anything malicious."

"Nari said we shouldn't—"

"What's the holdup, you two?" Gendry cut Deana off as he joined them. He gave Deana one of those wide grins that split his dark beard and deepened the edges of the scar that bisected his face.

"Deana just needed a minute; this place takes a little bit to get used to," Bran said.

Gendry waved the explanation away and held a hand out. "Come on, lass. I know the ghosts can be a little overzealous at first, but nothing here will harm you."

She studied his fingers before taking his hand and using it to steady herself as she stepped from the boat onto the firm sand. "Thank you," she said as she released him and took a step back.

He just gave her another grin and clapped Bran on the shoulder nudging him towards the village where a group of people were watching them.

When they reached the gathered villagers, an alluring song settled over Deana. It twisted and shifted, the melody changing almost so fast she couldn't follow it. An eerie wailing undertone joined the song but then it shifted again as the group parted and a woman stepped forward. Her skin was several shades darker than Deana's own and broken with patches almost as white as Bran's hair. The sharp eyes that met Deana's were mismatched; one a deep brown, the other a pure silver. Her mouth twitched as she studied Deana before it smoothed into a small smile. That smile grew warmer as her attention moved to Dara.

"Welcome to Weeper's Cove, I am Vatura," she said. "What an intriguing group of souls you have brought with you this time." Her mismatched gaze flicked to Gendry.

Bran shifted beside Deana, his arm brushing hers as his song danced in cool fingers down her spine. His head was turned away from the woman, eyes focused on the bay where a dark shape was moving through the water. The shadow breached the surface; a head of green hair, death-pallid skin studded with coral—

Her chest tightened; the smooth surface of the shallows broke into white-crested peaks as her song twisted out of her control. A light pressure against her hand drew her attention away from the cove. Bran's fingers were wrapped around hers; he gave a gentle squeeze as his song slid over her again, soothing the edges of her own.

"It's alright. It's gone," he whispered.

Someone beside them cleared his throat loudly and a sudden gusting breeze chilled Deana's fingertips as Bran dropped her hand.

"What happened?" Varlan asked as he studied the pair of them.

"There was a shrouded one in the bay," Bran answered.

"The damned cannot enter this place." The contempt in the woman's voice drew Deana's gaze back to her. The rest of their group and the villagers had dispersed, but she stood watching them, her face blank as her ever-changing song swirled around her. Her attention moved to the water and her mouth softened. Deana wouldn't call it a smile though. "There is so much fear tangled in your song; you see monsters where there are none ..." She inhaled slowly, her eyes sliding shut as she tilted her head this way and that for a moment. "You lack faith in your own abilities ... No. That's not quite it, is it? You believe that you yourself are one of those monsters or perhaps it is that you could become one. That the grandmother will claw her way from the depths and stake her claim on you."

As the woman spoke, the world closed in around them until it felt like she and Deana were the only beings in existence.

"It is not an inaccurate fear. There *is* some chance that you could become one of the damned. However, it is no greater a possibility than any of us possess." She tilted her head again and her mouth pulled into an almost menacing smile as she opened her eyes. "The question you need to find the answer to is what will you do when you are confronted with the choice of what it is you *want* to become?" She took a step back and the sounds of the world around them were almost deafening as they rushed in to fill the silent void.

Deana hadn't realised how close the woman had gotten to her or how far away they had moved from Bran and Varlan. She swallowed and let her gaze drop to her feet.

"Conquer that fear, that lack of trust in yourself, and you will find you have the power to move oceans." She turned and walked back toward the village, her steps seeming to glide over the sand in a way that left barely any trace.

"What did she say to you?" Bran asked as he and Varlan reached Deana once more.

She looked from his concerned face to Varlan, who was watching the woman as she moved through the village; the look in his eyes suggested he didn't trust her.

"She told me I need to conquer my fear, that it's holding me back."

"We could have told you that," Varlan said with a grunt as he turned to Deana. "You are both certain you saw a shrouded one?"

he asked, keeping his voice low and glancing about as though making sure no one was listening.

Deana nodded.

"It certainly felt like one," Bran said. "But given the nature of the source here and the thinness of the barrier, it could have been something else masquerading as one." He frowned and shook his head. "No, I am certain it was some kind of wraith. They feel completely different to regular reanimations and spirits."

"A wraith? Not a shrouded one?" Varlan asked.

Bran made a noise low in his throat and shook his head. "I believe that shrouded ones are a *type* of wraith, but without getting close enough to do a thorough examination ..." He shrugged. "Whatever that was in the bay, though, certainly looked and felt like a shrouded one."

"I couldn't hear its song," Deana said softly, and they both turned to her. "I was standing right beside Bran. If he could feel the shrouded one, I should have been able to hear it. But ..." The song of the shrouded ones was one of deep sorrow and chilling dread she would gladly never hear again. But the thought that they could be lingering close and she wouldn't know it until it was too late sent a twisting sensation through her stomach.

"Can you hear Bran and myself when you are not trying to?"

She placed her hands over her ears. "I hear everyone ... all the time. It's like this rushing, pounding vibration that permeates my entire being. Every so often a song will be louder, and I can choose to single one out. But, yes, I can hear you both now."

Bran's song was deep and twisting. It brushed against the edges of her own, leaving a chill at the tips of her fingers. Varlan's was softer and more alluring; it smoothed along her song, testing its defences as though trying to find the weak point to burrow in.

"Your keen-sense is still functioning fine then." Varlan frowned and scanned the bay before turning his gaze to the village. "I don't trust this place and I don't think you should be on your own while we're here, Deana."

Bran nodded. "I still can't feel anything untoward hiding amongst the spirits, but maybe Varlan is right, especially after the events of the last few weeks."

"There you are." Pippa came stalking over the sand towards them. "Elijah and Gendry are looking for you," she said as she pointed to Bran and Varlan. "Come on, Dee. I'll show where we are sleeping."

Deana looked over her shoulder at the bay as Pippa led her into the village. There was still a dark shape at the mouth of the cove. It was too far away to tell what it was, but the way it moved through the water sent a finger of dread creeping across the nape of her neck.

There was an eerie stillness to the air that left a hollow feeling in Deana's chest and a restless twitch in her legs. She sat up and studied the sleeping forms of Dara and Pippa curled together across from her. If either of them could feel it too, it wasn't enough to disturb their slumber.

She lay back and stared at the ceiling of the hut. It was probably nothing—just the result of sleeping in a new place, especially this place where Bran said the barrier between realms was thinner. She drew a deep breath to try to dispel the feeling, then closed her eyes and rolled onto her side.

Just go back to sleep. Her fingers found the smooth edge of her protection charm.

But sleep continued to prove elusive.

A soft melody twisted through the night and coiled around her with almost ghostly fingers. She pressed her eyes closed tighter and gripped the stone. It wasn't the song of the shrouded ones, but it held a similar quality and made the scars where Nari had removed the shards of shell from her hand ache. She rubbed her thumb across the centre of her palm and then circled it outwards to alleviate the pain.

"Deana," a voice called from just outside the hut, and she sat up again. It had sounded like Samir, but that was impossible; he had been taken by Idir's shrouded ones.

"Please, Dee, I know you're there," the voice said so loud that Deana was surprised neither Pippa nor Dara stirred.

"I know you're scared, but they just want to help because ... because Idir hurt them too." The words were soft, but it sounded like he was just on the other side of the door.

She studied the still sleeping forms of Pippa and Dara. What if it was really Samir? And what did he mean Idir had hurt the shrouded ones too?

Her knees shook as she stood and crossed the room to the door. She slipped out into the night, her fingers gripping the protection charm. There was no sign of Samir, so she closed her eyes and *listened*. A hundred different songs plied the air around her as ghostly fingers played with loose coils of her hair and smoothed over the skin of her arms. The owners of those phantom hands whispered too soft for her to make out any words, but it felt almost like they were nudging her towards the beach.

What was she thinking following someone who may or may not be Samir out into the night? She rocked back toward the hut she had just left.

"You should trust your instincts more," Vatura said as she stepped from the shadows.

"My instincts are telling me to go back to bed."

Vatura tapped her fingers against her staff as she studied Deana, her ever-changing song twisting across Deana's own. "You know

264

you are lying to yourself. You have let your fear control every aspect of your life for so long that you now believe its voice is your own. Fear is not a bad thing when it does its job correctly, but if we give it full reign it has the ability to crush the life from us from the inside out."

Deana swallowed, and Vatura cocked her head as though listening to the night.

"The king of the damned is not the only one hunting you and the more you unlock your powers, the easier it will be for them to find you. Already you can hear their song ... feel the pull of the deep ... but what will you do?" She stepped back and lifted her hand in an open-palmed gesture towards the beach.

The ocean was calling to Deana, its song coiling around her legs like whitewash before dragging against her ankles and setting a distinct pull behind her navel. She took a faltering step, and the corner of Vatura's mouth ticked; another step and the tick grew into a satisfied smile.

Before she knew it, she had reached the edge of the last hut, the pale expanse of sand glittering softly in the moonlight stretched out before her. A shadow stood towards the far end of the beach; he had his back to her, but she was certain it was Samir. The sand shifted under her feet as she started forward again; the night became still and eerily silent. That should have been warning enough, but when she reached him, she touched his shoulder and a wave of nausea rolled through her as a sharp note cut through the silence.

He turned. Glowing pink coral studded the length of his arm, the once warm brown skin ashen with patches of necrosis.

Deana's song twisted out of her control as she took a step back and covered her mouth with her hands to stop the scream that was building in her throat. Cold water rushed over her ankles and splashed up her calves.

Samir opened his mouth to speak but the only sound that came out was a soul-rending wail.

Violet magic flashed like lightning, shrouding Samir. He disappeared in a puff of black smoke, silver scales littering the ground where he had been standing.

"Are you alright?" Bran skidded to a stop on the wet sand beside her.

Her voice had fled, her breath coming in ragged pants as she tried to rein her song in. Water swelled around their feet, surging past Deana's thighs as it rushed into the nearby huts.

"Focus on my voice." Bran's tone was soft but somehow it cut through the turbulence of her mind. "It wasn't really Samir. It was a spectre pretending to be him to feed off your fear, but you're safe. Just breathe."

Bran's song was brushing against the edges of her own; the undulating pattern of cold, soul magic and the deep thrum of the fathoms was surprisingly soothing. She drew a long, halting breath and let it out. The third breath was smoother, and the water around their legs began to recede.

"That's it. Easy does it," Bran whispered as he let out a breath of his own. He reached out a hand but didn't touch her, just let it hover in the air between them. His eyes searched hers before he turned to look at something over his shoulder.

Pippa, Wren, Dara, Varlan, and Gendry were all standing at the edge of the village in various states of undress and with hair tousled from sleep. Wren started forward. She was wearing what looked like one of Gendry's shirts and nothing else. Deana rocked back a step, and Wren stopped and turned to the others. She said something that Deana couldn't hear then waved them away before moving towards Bran and Deana again.

"What happened?" she asked as she reached them.

"It was a spirit just taking advantage of an easy meal," Bran said and raked a hand through the wild tangle of his hair. The dark crescent tattooed on the inside of his wrist stood out against his pale skin. In her panic, she hadn't noticed he was shirtless. His pants, sitting low on his hips, were completely drenched from his thighs to his feet, which were bare. He looked as though he had just rolled out of bed.

"Are you alright, Deana?" Wren asked, drawing Deana's attention away from Bran.

She nodded though she still felt fragile and shaky. "I think so. I'm sorry to drag everyone out of bed."

Wren waved the apology away. "Don't worry about that. As long as you are fine that is all that matters."

"But the water ..." She gestured at the dark line where her magic had caused the tide to rush into the middle of the village.

"You did no permanent damage. Come on now. You should try to get a few more hours of sleep." Wren tucked her hand into the crook of Deana's elbow and gave it a gentle squeeze.

"I don't want it to happen again."

"It won't," Bran said and gave her a small smile. "I'll make sure the rest of them leave you alone." He gestured at the air around them. "Though I think they probably got the message. The one that you encountered was bolder than they usually are."

"Thank you for banishing it and helping me calm my song again."

"You're welcome, but you don't need to thank me. I should have realised sooner that you'd be a beacon for them. They prefer those of us who have darkness and sorrow in our past." He lifted his hand towards the village. "Wren is right, though. You should try to get some sleep."

Wren gave Deana's elbow another squeeze and led her away. Deana glanced over her shoulder at Bran, but he had turned his back on them and was staring out over the bay.

What had he meant by darkness and sorrow? Was that part of what had tainted his song?

CHAPTER TWENTY-SIX

BRAN

Vatura arrived once Deana and Wren had gone. She didn't speak, just stood beside him and studied the water lapping gently against the shore.

"You're lucky that spirit didn't harm Deana," he said after a while.

"I would never have allowed it to progress further than it did. I was simply curious. After all, it has been an eon since I encountered a mage of her ilk."

"She's not a toy—none of us are."

Vatura's mismatched eyes met his and a smile curved across her mouth. "So protective, *little foundling*, but you know as well as I that her mettle must be tested if she is going to have any hope of surviving the trials she was born to face. None of us can escape our destiny. We can only do that which is in our power to ensure we are ready to meet it head on."

The use of Agatha's pet name for him sent a jolt through Bran. He studied Vatura carefully. There was something about her that reminded him of the Hartswood elders, but as far as his keen-sense could tell she wasn't a spirit like them.

"Are you any closer to figuring it out? The answer to the question that has plagued you all your life? It is no coincidence that the king of the damned brought you here now, that your soul was shackled to the one you call the Shadow. You are as much a puppet of destiny as Deana is." She dug the butt of her staff into the wet sand, tracing the arch of the crescent moon. "Will you be able to look destiny in the eye and hold your ground?"

When Bran didn't respond, her smile deepened before she turned away from him and walked back towards the village, leaving him alone with his thoughts once more.

He released a long breath and raked his fingers through his hair before following her. There was no way he'd be getting any more sleep but there were few hours of night left.

When he entered the hut he was sharing with Varlan and Elijah, both men were sitting up, two steaming mugs of tea on the table between them.

"You look like you could use a cup," Varlan said and busied himself making it as Bran marched over and grabbed a dry change of clothes out of his pack.

By the time Bran was pulling his shirt over his head, Varlan was holding out a mug from which the sweet, smoky aroma of Faridean black was rising.

"Thanks," he said before taking a tentative sip.

"Is Deana going to be alright? When you tore out of here like the Shadow himself was on your heels, we didn't know what to think," Elijah said as he leant back in his chair.

Bran studied the liquid in his cup. "She'll be fine, but we shouldn't linger here. I know Gendry said Idir can't reach us on this island, but with the thinness of the barrier here we are risking more incidents like tonight and next time we might not be so lucky."

Elijah nodded slowly and then stood and retrieved a roll of

parchment which he smoothed across the table. "I agree we need to keep moving. This was just a stop to gather ourselves before we go after the heartstone, but there's one big problem."

A playful flurry of magic danced along Bran's spine as a creamy yellow mage light burst to life beside the cartographer. The orb of light danced low, illuminating the sketched lines that were clustered over the surface of the paper. It didn't look like any map Bran had ever encountered before.

"It looks like you're losing your edge," Varlan said dryly as he took hold of the map and tilted it to examine one corner.

Elijah grunted and snatched the map away. He ran his fingers over the page before thrusting it back towards Varlan. "This is the tenth time I've tried to draw the bloody thing."

"Does that mean that there aren't any suitable heartstones to be found? How will Agnes deliver a functioning golem without one?" Varlan stood and paced a few strides across the room before turning and marching back.

"No, it means that something magical in nature is interfering with my keen ... or hiding the stones."

"Stones? Plural?" Bran asked.

Elijah nodded. "I can feel three ... I think. But when I start drawing the map—" He gave the parchment a shove, crumping the edge of it.

"Three?" Varlan rubbed his hands over his face.

"There could be more," Elijah replied.

"If you can locate three, why can't you draw the map? Surely if they were shielded by magic, you wouldn't be able to locate them at all," Bran said.

Elijah shrugged. "I haven't the foggiest idea. I've never encountered something like this before."

Bran traced his finger over some of the lines. Elijah's magic stirred across the page leaving a prickle at the very tips of his fingers. He rubbed them together and tilted the map into the light. "What is this mark here?" he asked as he held the map out to Elijah.

The cartographer scrunched his nose up. "Nothing important. Just a symbol that keeps coming to me, but it only ever comes half formed."

Varlan pressed against Bran's side as he leant closer to examine the map again. "There's another here but it's slightly different," he said as he pointed to the second mark on the parchment.

"It's just gibberish. It happens sometimes when I am in the trance."

"I don't think it's gibberish ..." Bran folded the map so two of the strange symbols joined. "What if you combine them all?"

"It can't hurt to try, I guess. But I still don't see how it will make much difference." Elijah grabbed a piece of parchment and a pen. He made a few quick sketches of ways the marks could fit together and then held it out to show them. "See? It is not—"

"Mintura," Varlan said, cutting the cartographer short. "More specifically, the shrine of Moalana."

"And how in the known realms do you know that?" Elijah asked.

"That is Moalana's symbol," Varlan said, pointing to one of the sketches. "It could be directing us to her shrine."

"Moalana?" Bran asked.

"She's one of the sleeping gods. The goddess of women and children, I believe," Elijah answered. "It doesn't make any sense that there would be a heartstone at her shrine, let alone one powerful enough to animate a war machine."

"It's definitely her symbol though, and you said yourself that something magical was preventing your keen from working properly when it came to locating the heartstones." Varlan rubbed his finger along his chin. "Though have you tested it on anything else? Is it just the heartstones you can't find or is there a bigger issue with your magic?"

"It's just the heartstones." Elijah crossed his arms. "Regardless, Mintura is a sacred place. We can't just go waltzing in and digging up its secrets."

"I would never dream of desecrating a seat of the divine for personal gain. We will carefully search for the stone and should we find it, exhume it with the utmost respect," Varlan said, the corners of his mouth quirking in a smile. "I have no intention of bringing the wrath of the gods down upon myself; life is hard enough without throwing an immortal curse into the mix."

"Mintura?" Gendry asked as he pulled the platter of fruit in the centre of the table towards himself.

"That's the only island I know that has a dedicated shrine to Moalana," Varlan said, studying the liquid in his cup as though it might hold all the answers to their current problems.

"And Elijah is certain there is a heartstone there?"

"No, I am not, but it's the best lead we have—unless someone can decipher this," Elijah said as he tossed a beaten-up journal on the table between Bran and Varlan.

Bran picked it up and flipped through. A steady, throbbing keen clung to the pages. It reminded him of Garret's grandmother Camille's magic. If he had to guess, he'd say Kai had been an earth mage of some kind. Most of the journal was filled with the standard sort of entries you'd expect in a personal journal. Occasionally the entries would be split with a letter addressed to either Leilani or Deana, but the second half of the book was filled with what could only be called gibberish.

"Is that Kai's journal?" Varlan asked, placing his cup down and holding his hand out.

Bran passed him the book, and he flipped through it as Bran had done, his frown deepening as he reached the back pages.

"I thought you might know what sort of code he's used," Elijah said to the mind mage.

Varlan shook his head. "It's not a code I recognise, at first glance at least."

"Let me see it," Gendry said, and Varlan handed him the journal.

Gendry flipped through it and scratched his beard then nodded.

"You understand it?" Elijah asked.

"The gibberish at the end? Bright no, but I agree with his judgement of Idir's motives."

"Where does he mention that?" Elijah reached across the table and plucked the journal out of Gendry's hand.

"Third entry, right in the middle of that letter to Leilani."

"Did you ask Deana about the journal?" Bran asked Elijah.

"She didn't know it existed before I showed her."

"Even if she wasn't aware of the journal, surely she would know her brother better than anyone and might be able to provide some insight," Bran said.

"He kept that part of his life secret from those back on Lethata, especially Deana," Varlan said, taking up his tea again. "Still, Bran might be right about showing her the journal. You never know what sort of memories something like that can stir."

"Can't hurt. Now"—Gendry picked up a piece of bright yellow melon and popped it in his mouth. He chewed it thoughtfully before settling his dark eyes on Varlan—"you do realise that Splade's Watch is between us and Mintura."

"I am aware."

"And Splade's Watch is?" Bran asked.

"A ruined fort clinging to the remains of an island destroyed by a crazed mage who thought he could tame the power of a volcano.

A group of degenerates that Kent had forbidden from Armada were camped there until recently," Varlan replied.

"I'd bet the Queen that Idir has taken it over," Gendry said. "It's the perfect bolt hole. The carcass of the island is essentially a labyrinth of tunnels and caverns. And they say the mage's tower survived the explosion, though it is beneath at least a hundred feet of water. Still, if it is intact, who knows what secrets are lingering down there for the taking. It could be where Idir got his idea to raise Dumura for all we know."

"How would he even get—he's a shrouded one ... Right, never mind," Elijah said.

"No, he's wanted to raise Dumura for years; Splade's Watch only went silent in the last few weeks," Varlan said. "We'll just have to be careful. Elijah, could you draw us a map to avoid the island? One that keeps us out of Idir's reach, if he is there, but doesn't add too much time to the journey to Mintura?"

Elijah's keen gave a little flicker against the edge of Bran's keen-sense.

"Should be easy enough. It will take a few hours though."

"Right, well go and get started." Varlan shifted his attention from Elijah to Gendry. "We should get the Queen ready to depart."

Gendry picked up another slice of melon as he watched Elijah leave the room. He studied the fruit before meeting Varlan's gaze. "You know better than to go rushing off without a proper plan. Mintura's not going anywhere, and you've barely given yourself a chance to rest since we left Armada."

"I have a plan. Get to Mintura, find the heartstone, and then get back to Armada and—"

"Rush in like a bloody fool and get yourself and half the Queen's crew killed," Gendry interrupted Varlan calmly. "I know why you're in a rush, but you've got to keep your head."

Varlan's mouth pressed into a thin line.

"Just make a plan. A decent one. That's all I am asking. Even if we leave today, it will take us a while to reach Mintura. Then we've got to retrieve the heartstone—if that is indeed what Elijah's magic is leading us to—and then get back to Armada."

"What about trading the keystone for Agnes and Kiki? Is that still on the table?" Bran asked.

"We'd need to find a substitute keystone. I wouldn't want to risk the real thing falling into Kent's hands. But it might work."

"Then maybe we should get Elijah to draw a map to a substitute keystone instead of going after this heartstone. Gendry is right about Mintura not going anywhere."

"I tried that already, but he said that his magic couldn't find anything suitable." He pulled a crumpled piece of parchment from his pocket and tossed it to Bran.

Bran unrolled it. The marks on the pages were similar to the ones Elijah had drawn on the map for the heartstone. "Did you notice that these marks look a lot like the ones we deciphered last night?"

"What?" Varlan held his hand out, and Bran passed the parchment back to him.

"You're right."

"What if the reason Elijah couldn't lock in on a heartstone is because his magic was still trying to find the keystone?"

Varlan blinked at him and then turned and strode to the door. "Go round up Wren and the others. I'll meet you at the beach."

When Varlan left, Gendry shook his head. "I guess we'd better get a move on before Varlan decides to commandeer the Queen and leave us all stranded here."

CHAPTER TWENTY-SEVEN

AGNES

"You're her father. How could you let someone do that to her?" Varlan's voice carried down the hall, and she edged forward, the floor rolling under each step like the deck of a ship on rough water.

"I didn't have a choice!" her father replied in a tone she didn't hear him use very often. "Idir threatened to kill her if I didn't let him—"

"Idir needs her. He would never have killed her ... How long ago was it done?"

"When she was just a girl, before her keen had even fully formed."

Agnes had moved close enough that she could see both her father and Varlan through the doorway. Varlan was leaning heavily on the table and her father was standing across from him with his arms folded.

Varlan let out a tired sigh. "That's why she has no keen-sense." He pushed off the table and turned his back on Elijah as he rubbed his hands over his head. "He blocked it and in doing so made her a slave to her own keen."

"I did what I had to do to keep her safe."

"Safe?" He spun back around to face her father. "You let him take away her free will. All someone has to do is give her the right trigger and her own magic will ride her to her death."

"It didn't seem to bother you when you were exploiting her keen and risking her life by dragging her into your mess."

Varlan clenched his fists, his cheek bulging like he was pressing his tongue into it. "I would never have asked for her help if I thought delivering what I needed would harm her."

Her father's shoulders softened, and he leant against the bench. "You love her." His voice was soft; the words were a realisation, not a question.

Agnes pressed herself into the shadows as Varlan's gaze swept towards the hallway. "It doesn't matter how I feel. She won't know me as more than one of your occasional cartography clients come morning."

"Why leave then?"

"Because Idir has his hooks in Kent, and I can't let either of them even suspect that I have involved Agnes in this. They can't know what I had her build or that her safety means more to me than my own. Or that I will hunt to the ends of this world to find a way to undo what Idir did to her." He had slowly moved towards her father as he spoke. "That is why I must leave and why I need to alter your memories." He held a chair out, and her father slid into it.

"I'm sorry," her father said, but Agnes couldn't tell if he was apologising for Varlan having to take his memories or for what he'd let Idir do to her.

"I know," Varlan whispered and placed his fingertips against her father's temples.

The room tilted and everything went black as she was jolted

into a heavy body. Her limbs refused to respond; her eyes fluttered but would not open more than a slit that let in a sharp red-hued light. The bed pressed against her back so hard that she couldn't draw a deep enough breath. She thrashed within her own mind, silently begging her arms and legs to respond, but they refused to obey her commands. Fighting whatever this was wasn't working, so she stopped, and the heaviness of sleep started to roll over her once more.

The bed dipped as though someone had sat on the edge of it and a cool cloth was pressed to her forehead.

"Agnes?" a worried voice burrowed into the edges of her mind as fingers brushed along her brow.

"Agnes." There was an almost panicked edge to the voice as it said her name a second time. "Please ... please wake up."

But she wasn't asleep. She was stuck in a body that wasn't responding and she was tired—so very tired. The second she gave in to that urge to sleep, her body jolted awake, and she sat up.

Wes was sitting on the edge of her bed. He let out a relieved sigh and pressed a cup into her shaking hands. "Thank the Bright. I thought Savita had exhausted your keen to the point we would lose you."

She took a hesitant sip as she studied the room around her. Already the details of her dream were scattering, but two things stood out; Idir had tampered with her keen when she was very young, which was why she had no control over it now, and Varlan loved her. The first made her furious; the second she could barely wrap her head around. She passed the cup back to Wes and pressed her face into her hands.

"I have to tell Kent you're awake," Wes said as he stood.

"Please wait."

He reached over and gave her shoulder a squeeze. "I have to. He said the moment you wake, and I must keep up the appearance of complete loyalty."

"I don't want to be alone right now—I can't be." Her body felt like it was coming apart at the seams and she hugged her arms tightly around herself.

"I'll be right back; he just wants to know you're awake and that Savita hasn't done any permanent damage." He squeezed her shoulder again and placed the cup on the chair beside the bed. There was a plate with a small chunk of bread and a handful of dried fruit next to the cup. "You should try to eat something. I promise I will come straight back." He headed towards the door.

"You know the truth, don't you? About Varlan and I?"

Wes paused and turned back to her. "Varlan is my oldest friend. I would never betray his trust."

"I'm not asking you to. I just ... everything is ..."

He gave her a soft smile. "We are all playing a very dangerous game. If Kent finds out that the only person in this world who has my true loyalty is Varlan, he won't hesitate to have Savita force all my secrets from my mind and then kill me. And Kent is not fond of giving those who betray him a quick death; it will be slow and beyond brutal. But at the end of the day, it is not Kent that any of us need to worry about—it's Idir." With that he slipped out the door.

She swallowed and pulled her knees to her chest as the walls seemed to dip towards her.

True to his word, Wes returned quickly but he wasn't alone. Both Kent and Savita were with him.

Kent's shoulders were stiff, and his mouth a tight line. His gaze did a sweep over Agnes before he turned to Savita. "You were lucky this time," he growled.

"It got results, didn't it?" she said, barley sparing Agnes a glance.

Kent grabbed her by the throat and slammed her against the wall beside the door. "She's no good to me if you break her."

Savita's lip curled. "I knew what I was doing," she rasped as her fingers gripped Kent's.

"Do not overstep again or I won't hesitate to tear this pretty throat out and toss your still-twitching body in the pit." He let her go, and she slid down the wall. "Do we have an understanding?"

She licked her lip as her eyes locked with his. "If you think—"

"Do we have an understanding!" he roared.

"Yes," Savita answered.

"Good. Now get out." He gestured with an open palm towards the door. "You too, Westly."

Wes didn't spare Agnes a glance as he dipped his head in a nod to Kent and ushered Savita from the room.

As Kent turned to Agnes, his entire posture softened. "I am terribly sorry for the harm that Savita's enthusiasm for our project caused." He lowered himself to the edge of the bed.

Agnes shifted to try and place a buffer of space between them. "If she continues to force my magic to take over, she will kill me," she said. "As it is, she exhausted my keen to the point that it will take several days, or more, to repair itself."

"Westly told me as much. It is a delay I cannot really afford, but had she completely damaged your keen, or worse killed you, then I would have more than a frustrating delay to contend with. So"—he patted her knee—"rest up. I will send a healer to you in the morning to see if we can't speed up the process a little."

He stood and headed for the door, pausing to turn to her as he reached it. "Sweet dreams, Agnes."

Her dreams were not sweet. They were twisted and dark, the sensation of being trapped pervading every second until she managed to burst free and wake with a gasp, clammy sweat sticking her hair to the back of her neck. By the time morning finally came, her hands were shaking so badly she could barely hold the cup of water Wes had left for her.

She ran her tongue along her chapped lips as she leant her head against the wall and shielded her eyes from the light coming in the window.

"Agnes?" Wes called through the door before the lock clicked and he entered. He frowned when his soft, hazel gaze settled on her. "Did you get any sleep at all?"

She shook her head. "It certainly doesn't feel like I did."

That pulled a small smile from him, and he set down the tray he was carrying before lifting a hand towards the still open door. A man entered the room. He had the sharp features and light brown skin of an Osmarian. There was something about his eyes that was vaguely familiar though she couldn't recall having met him before.

"This is Luca. He's a healer," Wes said as he closed the door and leant against the wall beside it. "Kent wants to make sure Savita didn't do any lasting damage."

Luca walked slowly towards her and lifted his hands. "May I?"

She chewed her lip but nodded.

Heat rippled through her body like a fever only to disappear moments later. Luca's mouth twisted left then right before he turned to Wes with a sigh. "Aside from general exhaustion, there appears to be no physical damage. I can fix the exhaustion easily enough with my magic, however, it would be better for her to rest and let her body rebuild its reserves on its own. If I heal her while she is in this state, it would only be a temporary solution and the exhaustion is likely to catch up with her again."

"And that will cause further delays in Kent's plan?" Wes asked.

"If the exhaustion is not given time to heal on its own, then when it returns it will be far worse. It may even result in the loss of her keen entirely."

"Kent's not going to like waiting."

Luca folded his arms and his eyes narrowed as he turned from Agnes to Wes. "If he wishes to continue exploiting Agnes' keen then he is going to have to wait."

"I'll go let Kent know." Wes left.

Luca moved to the tray and the smell of something bitter filled the air before he returned to her bedside with a cup. "It's a restorative tea. It will help your body to heal itself, but it will also make you drowsy and help you sleep," he said as he offered the cup to her.

"I don't want to sleep."

His lips tightened briefly. If she hadn't been studying his face, she probably wouldn't have noticed the shift. "Sleep will help you heal faster."

She took the cup and examined the murky, green liquid before giving it a tentative sip. It tasted like dirt and bitter water, with a sweet edge.

"Drink it all," Luca prompted.

She swallowed the rest of the tonic in one gulp. Her stomach rolled and her mouth watered as a lump lifted into the back of her throat and she heaved. Thankfully, nothing came up except a grating cough.

Luca handed her a mug of water.

"You could have warned me about the taste," she rasped before taking the mug from him and drinking half its contents in one go.

The corner of his mouth quirked but he rubbed the smile away with the side of his index finger. "Now I suggest you try to get some sleep." He held his hand out for the mug, and she quickly finished the rest of the water before passing it to him.

"Why didn't you just heal me like Kent would have wanted?" she asked as he walked back to the tray and placed the cup and mug on it.

"As I already told Wes, it is better to let your body heal itself in this instance," he answered with his back to her.

"You can just heal me each time my keen is exhausted though. Why endanger yourself by getting on Kent's bad side?"

He let out a huff and turned. "It is in our best interests to delay Kent's plans. In fact, I believe a more permanent delay is order." The corner of his mouth twisted, and something flashed behind his eyes.

Agnes' attention dropped to the cup that had held the restorative. "Did you?"

"Poison you?" He gave an indignant grunt. "*Technically,* no."

"Technically?" A strange numbness was shifting through her body.

"The difference between a medicine and poison is often just the dosage."

Her vision started to blur and she blinked rapidly, trying to clear it as her tongue felt suddenly thick and her body slumped onto the pillow. The door opened and a shadow entered. A muffled voice asked Luca a question, and the sharp tone that followed his answer made it clear they weren't happy with what he had done.

Footsteps thumped towards the bed then cool fingers brushed across her forehead and a featureless face ringed by a halo of golden hair hovered directly in front of hers for a moment.

"Don't fight it, Agnes. It's going to be alright; I promise," the face said as Agnes' eyelids finally grew too heavy, and she was plunged into a silent black void.

CHAPTER TWENTY-EIGHT

#

Mintura wasn't Varlan's least favourite place in the known realms, but it was right up there on the list of places he would be happy never to set foot on again. It was nothing against the island itself. It was gorgeous with its ornate pavilions scattered through the jungle and its glittering main city. The air from the moment you reached the docks was thick with the scents of devotional offering flowers and incense. The heady, imported-from-Osmar kind of incense that made him feel like he was always on the edge of sneezing.

Of course, the longer he stayed on the island the more chance there was that he would run into his mother. She was the head custodian, leader of the mages and monks responsible for taking care of the island and its shrines. The chances of bumping into her out here on the street away from the central pavilion were slim but not non-existent. So he kept an eye out, ready to duck out of sight if he caught even a small glimpse of her. He didn't have time to be getting caught up in her business, and she would certainly try to stop him if she found out why he was on the island in the first place.

As they walked along the main street of the town, Dara danced ahead of them, rushing from one stall to another and exclaiming about the different offerings the pilgrims to the isle could purchase and the assortment of sweets available. A breeze stirred the hairs on the back of Varlan's neck as it rattled the wooden chimes hanging at a nearby stall selling petition papers and a rainbow of coloured ribbons.

"So where is the shrine of Moalana?" Bran asked as he fell into step beside him.

"Not too far out of town. We will need to wait for nightfall when the petitioners leave and the custodians close it to the general public."

"And you're certain we'll find what we are looking for there?"

Varlan nodded. "I know Elijah couldn't pinpoint it and he's still not sure if it is a heartstone or a keystone, but Moalana's symbol was coming up on his maps for some reason."

They continued on in silence until they reached the bathhouse and tavern.

"Alright," Wren said, clapping her hands together as she stopped them all. "Rufus and Pippa, you're on resupply duty. Nari, do you mind keeping an eye on Dara?"

Rufus and Pippa nodded and disappeared as Nari said, "Not at all, as long as she doesn't mind a trip to the bathhouse. These old bones could use a good soak."

"Do you think they have those little soaps carved to look like different flowers?" Dara asked, tugging Nari towards the tavern door.

"Deana." Wren looked past Varlan and Bran to where Deana was standing with Gendry. "I am going to make the most of having access to a hot spring. You are welcome to join me unless there is something you would prefer doing."

The haunted look Deana had been wearing since they left

Weeper's Cove had finally shifted, but she still didn't seem completely at ease—almost like she was waiting for something to pounce from the shadows. After everything that had happened, Varlan wasn't surprised.

"I'll come with you," she said in answer to Wren's question.

The captain gave her a nod then rounded on the rest of them. "Right. You four stay out of trouble ... at least until tonight."

"You don't have to worry about me, Wren. I think you and Nari have the right idea," Elijah said before he headed into the bathhouse.

"We're always on our best behaviour, lass," Gendry said.

Wren just stared at him until he broke eye contact with her and scratched his fingers through his beard.

"I'll see you back at the Queen tonight. And remember—in and out ... and no mayhem."

"But the mayhem is the best part," Gendry said with a wide grin.

"You can save it all for Kent and Idir." She kissed him on the cheek. "Come on, Deana. We'd better get inside before Dara steals all the best soaps."

"Well. Any ideas how to kill half a day?" Bran asked, as Wren and Deana headed for the bathhouse.

"A proper bath does sound good," Gendry said, his attention following Wren as she disappeared. "Wait up, my love!" He jogged after her.

"Shall we?" Bran asked, and Varlan shrugged. There was less chance of running into his mother in the bathhouse than just wandering the market.

By the time night fell, everyone except Bran, Gendry, and Varlan had returned to the Queen. The three men crept along the edge of the path that led from the main centre of town out to the shrine of Moalana. The jungle was silent, almost too silent, as though it knew what they were about to do.

It wasn't long before the jungle thinned, and they entered the garden around the pavilion on which the shrine sat. The source here was like a swirling current. It rolled around Varlan, raising the hairs on his arms and sending a chill quivering down his spine. In Weeper's Cove, the source was thick and prickly and there was an underlying sense of sorrow and dread. This was the opposite—the hopes and appeals of millennia of petitioners giving life to something that could awaken and crush them in an instant, if the old stories were to be believed.

As they neared the pavilion, the statue of Moalana came into view. Her serene face turned down to gaze upon the faithful who would kneel at her feet and implore her to aid them.

"Where do you think we should start?" Gendry asked as he gazed up at the statue.

"If I had to guess, I would say beneath the statue," Varlan answered.

Bran circled the statue slowly before joining them once more. "I can't see anything that looks like it might be a door or a lever." His keen swelled in a cold rush and then receded again.

"Can you feel the stone?" Varlan asked, letting his own keen drift out to inspect the area around the statue.

Bran shook his head. "I didn't expect to. It's not like the stone would just be sitting out where anyone could take it. That is never how these things work."

Varlan let out a laugh at the necromancer's dry tone. "No. In my experience, it is quite the opposite."

Gendry pressed his hands against the plinth on which the statue was standing and gave it a push. He strained for a few moments then gave up and stood back, brushing his hands together. "I thought it might have been a brute force thing." He shrugged.

"Is it ever a brute force thing?" Bran asked, a hint of humour in his tone.

"One day it will be," Gendry replied with a grin.

Varlan stepped back and studied the pavilion. Maybe the statue wasn't the answer, but then what was? The tiles that covered the floor were a simple grey stone, the occasional tile slightly darker than the others, but there was no real pattern to the placement of the darker stones. At four points around the very edge of the pavilion was a larger square made up of smaller mosaic tiles that formed the symbol of Moalana. On closer inspection, these mosaics were aligned with each of the cardinal directions.

He crouched to study the mosaic at the east point, tracing his fingers over the lines of the symbol; magic stirred under his skin. He pressed his palm flat over the centre of the relief and pushed. Nothing happened. Placing his palm down again, he fed a little of his keen into the tiles. Again, nothing seemed to happen.

"What did you just do?" Bran asked.

Varlan turned. Both Bran and Gendry were standing in the centre of the pavilion, their heads tilted back as they studied the ceiling. He followed their line of sight. The roof was covered in tiny swirls of glittering magic. They twisted about, forming, unforming, and then reforming the lines of what looked like a map.

He ran to the north mosaic and fed it a bit of his keen. The glittering magic changed. It still looked like a map but some of the lines were different, as though it might be a separate part of the same map.

Bran's keen gave a cold pull and the lines changed again. Varlan turned to find him standing by the west compass point.

"What if we activate them at the same time?" They asked together.

Varlan crouched and glanced Bran's way again. "On three?"

The necromancer nodded. "One."

"Two."

"Three." They said together, and Varlan let his magic bleed into the tile under his palm.

"Stars above!" Gendry exclaimed.

Varlan examined the ceiling. Parts of the map were clearer, but it still twisted in and out of focus. "We need two more mages," he said. "And Elijah."

"I'll go back to the Queen and get them," Gendry took off much faster than you'd expect someone with his bulk to move.

"What do you think it's a map of?" Bran asked.

"If the heartstone isn't here, it may be a map to that or it might lead to something else entirely."

Bran nodded slowly. "Do you really think this will work?"

"With a mage for each compass point and—"

"No, I mean this plan to trick Kent and get Agnes and Kiki back. If there is a keystone here and not a heartstone, and we take it to Kent, what's to stop him from just taking it and killing the rest of us? He has numbers on his side."

Varlan sucked in a breath and rubbed his fingers across his forehead. "I'd like to say that that isn't Kent's style, but I don't know any more. However, even if he does *try* to take the stone and kill us all just so he can keep Agnes, I like to think that I can still outwit him."

"There's a lot riding on you outwitting him though, and I've seen the lengths that people will go to, not only to claim power but to keep it." There was a bitterness to his tone that Varlan hadn't heard before.

He had just assumed Bran was easygoing and nothing really got him down, but he'd been on the sidelines of a world-ending cataclysm, one Varlan had very briefly brushed against when he met Nea on Quel'sapar. "I can't promise Kent is any different, but he's not the smartest. He generally relies on others to come up with the plan and he just sweeps in at the end and claims all the glory—son of a bitch! Why didn't I see that before?"

"What?"

"Kent and this golem plan ... It never made sense. But I figured Kent was just looking for a way to protect himself from Idir, should he decide their working relationship was no longer viable. But the subtle change in attitude, the sudden shift towards blind cruelty. Kent has always been an arsehole who likes to lord it over others, but he was never cruel for the sake of being cruel. Idir can be though. Fuck!" He paced across the centre of the pavilion. Why hadn't he noticed sooner—Idir had been playing them all the entire time.

Kent he could have dealt with easy enough, but if he wasn't the one pulling the strings, if Idir was ... But how? Savita. No, Kent had taken Agnes' blocking charm, so his mind should not be able to be influenced as long as he had it. And he still had it, didn't he?

"Are you alright, Varlan?" Bran asked.

"None of us are. Idir has been ten steps ahead this entire time. Kent was just a distraction."

"What do you mean?"

He raked his fingers over his head as he met Bran's dark blue gaze. "I mean, Idir has been playing us all. The golem might have started as Kent's plan, but I don't think so. I think it was Idir all along. He's the one who took away Agnes' keen-sense when she was younger, and he's the one who has been pulling the strings the entire time."

"Wait, Agnes doesn't have keen-sense?"

"No, it's been completely blocked. I tried to fix it once, but whatever Idir did seems to have damaged it in such a way that it is beyond my ability to repair. I believe that her lack of keen-sense is what makes her a slave to her magic."

Bran's cheek bulged as though he was pressing his tongue into it, but whatever he was thinking, he said nothing. He just started pacing towards the statue, tilting his head back to study the goddess as though she might hold the answers they sought.

The map above them had faded, and Varlan rested his spine against one of the support pillars and turned his senses to the night around them. He couldn't hear any sign of Gendry's return, but the odd rustle of nocturnal creatures reached him along with the crash of waves against the shore farther away. You'd never notice it during the day when this shrine was a bustle of activity, but here in the silence of night it was a steady whoosh almost like an inward and outward breath.

When he was younger, before he'd run off to find adventure, he'd come out here at night and lay against the tiles of the pavilion, his eyes closed as he listened to the world around him breathe. Things had been easier then, before his blood started to yearn for something more, as though something other than himself was dragging him out into the wider world.

"How young was she when Idir tampered with her keen-sense?" Bran suddenly asked, scattering the memories.

"Elijah said it was before her keen had fully formed."

Bran swore under his breath. "The damage is probably permanent then." He glanced down at his feet and then his head snapped up again. "Wait a minute. If she was that young, how did Idir know how her keen would work? Creationists are almost a complete unknown until their keen matures."

Varlan rubbed his fingers along his brow. "I ..." It was a damn good question. How *had* Idir known that Agnes's keen would develop into something he could exploit? Did he tamper with her keen-sense just in case she developed the *right* kind of powers? No. Idir was far too calculating for that. He had to have known that Agnes would be useful in the future. "I honestly don't know. But you're right. If she was any other kind of mage, it would be easy enough to see how her powers might develop at that early an age. But creationists are an anomaly. Unless it wasn't just her keen-sense he tampered with."

Bran's mouth tightened and he seemed paler than normal for a moment. "The mess in Beldaren was caused by a mage trying to play god and create his own breed of super mage," he said. "But I doubt he had anything to do with Idir. And to get the results he wanted, he had to conduct a series of inhumane and perverted experiments on keen-touched children and expectant mothers."

"I don't think Idir would have gone to similar lengths. But I wouldn't put it past him to figure out how to make sure Agnes' magic developed in a way that worked in his favour."

Bran rubbed his hands over his face and opened his mouth to speak but closed it again as the sounds of footsteps reached them.

They both slipped into the shadows behind the pillars and waited.

"It's just us," Gendry said.

He was flanked by Deana and Pippa on one side and Elijah on the other.

"What do you need us to do?" Elijah asked.

"Deana and Pippa, we need one of you at each of those mosaics," Varlan said, pointing to west and south points. "Elijah, did you bring your sketching tools?"

The cartographer patted the satchel at his side. "Never go anywhere without them."

"Good. Be ready to take down the map that appears on the ceiling. I am not sure how long you will have once we activate it." Varlan walked to the north mosaic, and Bran took the east while Deana and Pippa moved into position. "Alright. You just need to feed a little of your magic into the centre of the mosaic." He crouched and placed his palm on the centre tile.

"Are you sure about this?" Deana asked. Her keen washed over his own as though she was using her keen-sense to study the pavilion.

Varlan nodded. "It will be alright." He resisted the urge to use his magic to calm her fear as he'd done in the past. "Are you ready?"

She drew a long breath and her keen washed over him again, but she nodded.

"Alright ... One, two, now."

Deana's magic surged out in a crashing wave. It twisted with the wild heat of Pippa's fire keen and the steady chill of Bran's necromancy. Varlan's own magic poured into the stone, coiling around the others', and the map flared to life above them so bright it lit up the entire pavilion and the surrounding garden.

Elijah made a small sound and his playful keen flickered as he hastily scrawled across a page in his journal.

The map started to fade, the lines at the edges coiling back over themselves and dissipating like smoke on the breeze. Elijah's pen moved faster, and he let out a curse as his keen shifted from that playful flicker to a hot, stabbing sensation. Then the map above flared brighter again for a moment before blinking out of existence and plunging them all into darkness.

Varlan placed his palm on the floor again. The subtle prickle at the ends of his fingers was gone and when he tried to feed his magic into the tiles again, nothing happened. "Did you manage to get it all down?" he asked Elijah as he summoned a mage light, the soft pink glow barely reaching to the edges of the pavilion.

"I got enough of it that my keen can do the rest, but it may take a while."

Varlan nodded slowly.

"There was no heartstone here, only this map?" Deana asked.

"So it seems, lass," Gendry replied.

"Then what is that?" Pippa was standing by the statue where a small panel had opened to reveal a dark cavity with something glistening inside it.

Both Varlan and Bran edged closer. Varlan's mage light swooped forward and illuminated the object in the alcove. It looked a lot like the keystone to Grandmother Ocean's tomb, but where that one had been broken and then welded back together with robrillium, this one was flawless. It was also inanimate. Any magic it might have once held was long dead. Varlan gingerly reached forward.

"Don't touch it!" Deana yelled.

But her warning had come too late. As Varlan lifted the stone, the tile on which it sat make a soft click as the mechanism beneath it activated.

CHAPTER TWENTY-NINE

BRAN

A grating sound filled the air and the floor at the centre of the pavilion slid open to reveal a dark pit. Bran edged forward and summoned a mage light. The violet orb bobbed low over the floor and reflected off what looked like a smooth dome of metal at the bottom of the hole.

"Any guesses what they might be?" Gendry asked.

Bran let his keen-sense roll over the dome. It was magical in origin—the thin webs of source clinging to its surface were enough to tell him that.

"I think we should leave," Deana said, her eyes locked onto the metal dome as she backed towards the edge of the pavilion.

"I agree with Deana." Elijah stuffed his sketching things back into his satchel and took a handful of steps away from the pit.

The source clinging to the dome stirred and rust-coloured runes burned to life across the metal in a pattern like the plates on a tortoise shell. The ground shuddered and the dome lifted itself up on four stout legs. Dust rained down on the bottom of the pit as a massive reptilian head with a snapping beak emerged from inside the shell.

"That's the mother of all tortoises," Gendry said.

"I think it's a golem," Bran said.

The golem started making a weird spluttering noise and when the splutter stopped it was followed by a click. Seconds later, a jet of flame erupted from its mouth, tearing straight towards Bran.

He dove out of the way as Pippa's keen flared in a hot rush down his spine and she leapt in front of where he had been standing, her hands outstretched as the flame splashed against the air in front of her before dissipating.

If it was a golem, then it had to be powered by a heartstone. Perhaps he could sever the threads binding the soul to the stone and powering it. He let his keen out, the brittle chill a stark contrast to Pippa's fire magic. Shimmers of violet light roved over the tortoise, but there was no sign of a heartstone at all.

"It's not a golem. At least not like any I've encountered before," he said to the others.

The tortoise let loose another jet of flame, forcing Gendry and Deana to dive for cover as it started to haul itself out of the pit. The roof of the pavilion groaned in protest as massive cracks webbed their way across the tiled floor.

"What do you mean it's not a golem—it certainly looks like one," Elijah said as he dodged the snapping beak and landed beside Pippa.

"I mean, it's not powered by a soul. Not one housed inside its own body anyway," Bran answered, diving away again as the tortoise rounded on him.

"Elijah, catch," Varlan yelled and then threw the stone he had removed from the alcove to him.

The cartographer caught it and slipped it into his bag.

"If it's not powered by a soul, how to we stop it?" Gendry asked.

"We can't fight it—we have to run," Deana said, her keen a wild surge around her.

"We can't run, lass. If it follows us, it will tear the city apart. We have to figure out how to destroy it."

"When one of Agnes' gadgets gets out of control, usually the only way to stop it is to smash it with a large book," Elijah said.

Bran studied the ceiling above them as it groaned again. "Do you think that would be heavy enough to crush it?"

It was Varlan's turn to dodge as the tortoise lurched towards him, its beaked maw sheering through the pillar he had been standing in front of. "Doubtful," he said. "But I don't know what else we could try."

Wild heat rushed up Bran's spine again as Pippa diverted another jet of flame from the tortoise.

The fire wasn't magical in origin, which meant it must have had some kind of fuel source. If they could somehow ignite that fuel source, the machine might melt from the inside out.

"Do you think you could overheat that thing, Pip?" Bran asked.

"Good thinking," Varlan said.

"If you're thinking I can melt it ... I doubt I can make fire hot enough. But if I time it right, I might be able to ignite the tank holding the flammable oil it keeps spitting. Though if I do it is likely to explode," Pippa said.

"Exploding it'll work." Bran, Varlan, and Gendry said together.

"Can you ignite it and run at the same time, Pip?" Varlan asked.

She shook her head.

"What about shielding us from the blast?"

"I won't be able to shield all of us. I suggest either making a run for it or putting something nice and solid between you and the tortoise."

"You heard her—get down," Varlan said and waved them after him as he ran towards the jungle.

The tortoise lurched to give chase, leaving Pippa alone at the foot of the statue.

"Hey, get back here!" she called after it.

Bran skidded to a stop and grabbed a stone then ran back towards the pavilion and pelted it at the tortoise. The rock bounced off the top of its head and it shuddered around to face him. A gurgle sounded deep at its core then the spluttering sound that preceded the jet of flame. But the flame didn't come. Instead, there was a roar and a groan. Bran raced past Pippa, grabbing her as he dove behind the statue. He pushed her against the plinth, shielding her with his body as he covered his ears to try and block the echoing boom.

Debris rained down on him and Pippa. A piece of hot metal sliced a path across his shoulder and thudded into the ground several paces away. Pippa let out a gasp of pain and burrowed closer to the statue as a crack formed up the plinth and the goddess started to tilt away from her base. Bran ignored the pain in his shoulder as he dragged Pippa to her feet and ran towards the trees.

Behind them, the entire pavilion collapsed in on itself, chunks of molten metal and smouldering wood, littering the gardens.

"Are you alright, Pip?" Bran asked.

Blood was trickling from a nasty gash in her cheek and small whispers of smoke were rising from parts of her clothes.

She patted herself down and gave him a nod. "How about you?"

"I'll live. That was amazing by the way."

"I know!" Her eyes glistened as she grinned. It was the most animated he had seen her since they had left Armada. "I've never blown anything up before. I can't wait to do it again!"

He laughed then pulled her behind him as someone stepped out of the shadows beside them.

"We need to get back to the Queen," Varlan said, and Bran relaxed.

"I don't think just wandering through the centre of town is a good idea though. They had to have heard that explosion."

The words had barely left Bran's mouth when a group of custodians and townspeople came running from the path that led back to the city. They all stopped and stared at the destroyed temple, some of them dropping to their knees.

Slowly, a murmur of whispers started. It grew louder and louder. "What happened?", "Who could have done this?"

The whispers all stopped as a tall woman with a dark braid that reached to her waist moved through the middle of them. She didn't stop until she reached the very front of the group.

"We really need to go now. That is the head custodian," Varlan whispered urgently and grabbed the back of Bran's shirt, tugging him towards the city.

"I know you are there," the woman said as her sharp gaze scanned the trees.

Bran fought the urge to freeze as a smooth-fingered keen caressed the back of his neck.

"Move it," Varlan hissed, waving Pippa ahead of himself.

Bran shook off the compulsion that had started to settle at the edges of his mind and took off at a run after Pippa.

They didn't slow their pace until they reached the edge of town where they slipped into the shadows of a building to watch the town guards and custodians who were mobilising to look for them.

"Do you think the others made it back?" Pippa asked.

"Hopefully," Varlan said. "This way." He waved for them to follow as he ducked low and darted across the open alley to the next building.

After several near misses, they finally emerged onto the dock. But there was a line of guards between them and the gangplank that led to the Queen. "By order of the head custodian, you are to disembark your vessel and present yourselves to the grand pavilion for questioning," one of the guards said as he approached the ship.

"We would like a moment to consider your request," Gendry yelled back to the guard. The gangplank banged onto the dock and the familiar surge of Deana's keen rolled over Bran as the ocean rose in a curtain that forced the advancing guards back.

"What now?" Pippa hissed as they dove into the shadows behind a stack of crates.

Bran eyed the water below them. "Wren wouldn't leave without us, would she?"

Pippa shook her head. "She'll try to buy us time to get to the ship, but how?"

"What if we swam around the other side?" Bran asked.

Varlan nodded. "It's worth a try. Let's go."

They kept their heads low as they hurried to a ladder leading off the side of the dock. The water at the bottom was colder than Bran was expecting but he dove forward, taking long, wide strokes beneath the surface.

Pippa rounded the back of the ship and surged towards the middle where she treaded water. Her keen sparked and an orange mage light zoomed up over the side rail of the ship. It reappeared, hovering just above where they were before she sent it flying back onto the deck again.

Rufus appeared above. He leant forward and squinted at them.

"Throw down the ladder—this water is freezing," Pippa hissed.

"Look out, Rufus," Deana said as her keen surged again and the water beneath them lifted, carrying them up until they were level with the side rail and able to pull themselves onto the deck.

"You're lucky. Captain was about ready to leave without you," Rufus said.

"Those thugs are threatening to dry dock my ship. Everyone to your posts," Wren said as her keen sparked, the static charging the air and making Bran's hair stand on end. Moments later, wind caught the sails and the crew members of the Queen scurried into action.

Once the coastline of Mintura disappeared over the horizon, the crew seemed to let out a collective breath. The static prickle of Wren's storm magic dissipated and the magical wind that had filled their sails dropped away.

Nari had healed both Bran's shoulder and Pippa's cheek and was now farther down the ship with Dara and Elijah.

Varlan joined Bran at the bow. He rolled the dead keystone around in his hands before passing it to Bran.

"Do we have a plan yet?" Bran asked as he examined the stone. It was a dull smoky green and any magic it may have held was long gone.

"I haven't had much time to think of one, but how does don't get killed or caught sound?"

Bran let out a huff of a laugh. "It's a good plan, I guess. Are you really considering giving this stone to Kent? Surely even he will be able to tell it's useless?"

"Safer to give him a dead keystone than an active one. We just need to figure out a way to make it look functional. If we can do that, we can get Agnes and Kiki back and be well out of Idir and Kent's reach before either of them realises they have been duped."

"What about Agnes' magic? Won't the compulsion to create the golem still be a problem?"

Varlan stared out at the horizon. "We'll cross that bridge when we get to it. But if we can find a pair of bind-shackles ... or if we— no, I'd rather not resort to that."

"If we what? Wait, you're not suggesting dosing her with mage bane, are you?"

"As an absolute last resort." He rubbed his hands over his face.

Bran's distaste must have been clear because Varlan quickly added, "I'd never do it without her consent."

"Without keen-sense, the effects of the mage bane would be extremely unpredictable."

"I know that, which is why I said as a last resort," Varlan snapped.

"Sorry," Bran said and turned his attention to the stone in his hand.

"It's fine. I shouldn't have suggested it. Even as a last resort, I doubt I would ask her to take that risk. I just ..." He shook his head and lent on the side rail of the ship. "Bright damn that undead son of a bitch and his thirst for revenge. I should have never involved Agnes in this mess."

"Idir involved her in it long before you did though."

Varlan let out a huff that sounded like a bitter laugh. "That he did."

"Have you tried feeding this thing some magic?" Bran asked, holding up the stone.

"Might be worth a try." Varlan seemed to shake the melancholy that had settled on him away. "Would you like to do the honours?"

"Are you asking me to save your own skin in case something goes wrong?"

"Maybe a little." Varlan grinned.

Bran laughed and shook his head as he let his keen build. He focused on the stone and let his magic rove over it in a lilac glow. Nothing happened.

"Well, it was worth a try," Varlan said.

"Maybe it's not the right sort of magic," Bran offered the stone to Varlan.

He repeated the same process as Bran, but the stone remained inanimate.

"What are you doing?" Pippa asked as she and Deana wandered over to join them.

"We thought if we fed the stone some magic it might wake up enough to fool Kent into thinking it's the keystone," Varlan passed the stone to Pippa.

"I don't see how feeding it a little magic will fix it," Pippa said, but her keen built in a warm rush and a flicker of flame danced over the stone's surface. "Wait, did you see that?" She held the stone up to the light.

The sunlight hit the stone at just the right angle to reveal a murky shape at the stone's centre and throw a scattering of emerald-coloured reflections across the deck at their feet.

Deana gasped and curled her hand against the centre of her chest as her keen built in a rolling swell. Teal magic flickered in the air around the stone, and it started to glow brighter, the dark shape at its core shifting to life.

"That's not a keystone," Deana whispered.

She was right. Now that the stone was feeding off her keen, Bran could feel the shifting magic of the Between. But more than that, he could feel the soul trapped in the confines of the stone. "I don't understand," he whispered.

"What is it?" Pippa asked as she lowered the stone, and Deana's keen calmed again.

"I think ..." Deana glanced at Bran as though seeking confirmation for what she was about to say next. "That stone is not a keystone or a heartstone ... It's a prison."

Bran nodded. "It doesn't feel like a heartstone, but there is definitely a soul trapped inside and whoever it is, they are not happy to be awake."

CHAPTER THIRTY

Agnes stood in the middle of Kent's throne room. Two of the windows on the ocean side had been hastily patched and there was a gritty layer of sand around the edges of the floor.

Luca hovered around her, his features blank as though he was schooling them. They shifted into an irate frown as he turned back to Kent.

"Well?" Kent leant forward in his chair, his eyes narrowing as they settled on the healer.

"No change. I fear Savita may have damaged her keen more than I thought," Luca said as he flicked a gaze to the woman in question.

She was standing to the side of the room, dressed in an emerald outfit that hugged her body and left a swathe of her smooth, dark skin showing at her waist. Her ebony hair was pulled up into a ponytail so high and tight it made Agnes' eyes water just looking at it.

"Do you believe the damage is permanent?" Kent asked.

Luca turned back to Agnes and made a show of examining her again. "It is hard to say. I have done all I can to hasten her healing, but a mage's keen is a delicate and intricate—"

"I can fix it." Savita took a step towards Agnes, and Kent's gaze immediately snapped to her. "Don't look at me like that. I will not make the same mistake twice and the healer is here to supervise. Besides, she is useless without her keen, so what do we have to lose?"

Kent's nostrils flared as he let out a breath and lifted a hand to indicate Agnes. "Fine, see if there is something Luca has missed. But be careful. You know what awaits you should you damage her more than you already have."

Savita moved to stand in front of Agnes, her ink dark stare locking with Agnes' own as her hands lifted towards Agnes' face.

"Don't you dare touch me," Agnes said as she took a step back.

"Agnes," Kent warned.

"I was just trying to make the process more comfortable for you but have it your way." Savita's lip curled, and Agnes' stomach flipped.

Pins and needles flashed up the backs of her arms and the room started to spin away from her as a sharp ache throbbed behind her eyes. She gripped her head and fell to a heap on the floor, her skin becoming so hot that it felt like it was peeling away from her bones.

"That's enough," Kent said, and the sensation dulled.

Agnes lifted her head. The room around her was blurring in and out of focus and the inside of her mouth was bone dry. Her stomach heaved, and a cold sweat broke out across the back of her neck as she lost her breakfast on the floor.

"Luca?" There seemed to be an edge of concern to Kent's tone.

"She'll be alright. It is just a passing reaction." Luca's fingers were warm on the back of her neck as he applied just enough pressure to tell her to keep her head down. "Deep breaths, Agnes. The nausea will pass."

"Well, Savita, what did you learn?" Kent asked.

"Something is preventing her keen from rousing, as though her connection to the source has been blocked."

"Blocked, how?"

"I am not certain. Given time, I am sure I can circumvent the blockage and get her keen functioning again."

"That is inadvisable," Luca said. "Forcing her keen when her body is not ready for it will kill her."

"She only needs to live long enough to complete the project," Savita said coldly. "Or perhaps you should seek the opinion of another healer if Luca is too squeamish to do what must be done to get results."

Luca's fingers tensed on the back of her neck. "If you kill Agnes to complete this project then you are wasting a valuable resource."

A series of heavy footfalls sounded before Kent's booted feet appeared in front of her. "Luca makes a valid point." He must have waved Luca away because the healer's hand left her neck and he moved into her peripheral.

Kent's long fingers touched her chin and lifted her face. The light stung her eyes, but she fought the urge to squint. "Luca has three days to get your keen functioning again. Should he fail, I will split his gut open and throw him into the pit. Then I will let Savita do whatever it takes to finish the work you started. So, if this *blockage* is your way of rebelling against me then I suggest you wake up and realise that it is a futile endeavour. I own you now and you will obey me." He let her go and stepped away. "You have three days, Luca. Do not disappoint me."

Luca grabbed her arms and hauled her to her feet before guiding her across the room to the door.

Hours later, Agnes was leaning against the wall of her room, her forehead pressed to one of the bars over the window. Her body was heavy and numb, almost like it wasn't her body at all, but that she was just a parasite puppeteering the husk of its host. Whether it was a symptom of her exhaustion, or the bittersweet tonic Luca had been slipping her, she couldn't tell.

"Agnes?"

She lifted her head at the sound of Wes' voice and turned to face him, keeping her back pressed to the wall to maintain her balance.

He let out a long sigh as he studied her face. "Kent wants to see you down in the workshop."

"I can't use my magic."

"He knows. He's hoping that seeing the machine will hasten your ... recovery." He pulled a small vial from his pocket.

"What's that?"

"Mother's balm. It will counteract the mage bane just enough that you can convince him your magic is returning." He held it out. The liquid within was crimson and seemed to shimmer with a golden sheen.

"Do you trust Luca?"

He studied the vial in his hand and then nodded. "I'm not fond of his method and I know he can be abrasive, but he has your best interests at heart."

She bit down on her lip as angry tears stung the corners of her eyes. "Keeping me drugged and cut off from my magic is in my best interests?"

"Under normal circumstances, I'd never agree to it. But he's buying us time. If you could control your keen, things might be different."

"What does it matter if Kent has a war machine? Is stopping him worth destroying me? Because that is what is happening, and it makes you no better than him for allowing it."

He had the decency to look chastened before taking a step

closer and pushing the vial towards her. "It's complicated, but trust me, Agnes, Kent won't stop at one machine. And if I am completely honest with you ... I am not even certain that it is Kent inside that body anymore."

She opened her hand, and he pressed the vial into her palm then closed her fingers around it.

"Just a few more days and then we'll run."

The door banged open, and Wes took a step closer, his hand closing around her arm.

"What's taking so long?"

Agnes peeked around Wes' shoulder and met Byron's cold stare; his lip curled, lifting the scarred side of his face into a grotesque mask.

"We're coming. I was just making sure Agnes knows exactly what is expected of her." It was frightening the speed at which Wes could go from warm concern to cold indifference.

Byron studied them and then thrust his chin towards the door. "Get a move on."

Wes ran the tip of his tongue along the seam of his lips before turning to face Byron. "I suggest you remember your place before I am forced to put you back in it," he said in that soft, deadly tone before he reached out and grabbed Agnes' arm again. He pulled her in front of him and guided her towards the door.

She stumbled, and his grip tightened.

"Sorry," he whispered as he leant in close and steadied her on feet. "Drink that vial now," he urged before he stepped away and nudged her towards the door again.

She glanced over her shoulder, but Wes' bulk completely blocked Byron from view. The vial felt warm in her hand. She trusted Wes, didn't she? This was her last chance. She pulled the cork and downed the liquid in one go. It was sweet and slightly minty and seemed to tingle all the way down to her toes. As she passed the empty vial back to Wes she felt the flicker of something at the very edge of her senses and a warm relief flooded through her.

"Enough dawdling," Wes said and gave her a gentle push along the hall.

Byron shadowed them all the way into the space Kent had set aside for her to work in. When they entered the room, she rocked back a step, her hand covering her mouth. The walls were covered in her sketches—some of them neat and precise and others rough, as though they had been completed by a child trying to emulate her work. She moved as quickly as her unsteady legs would carry her to the closest wall and inspected the notes there.

"So nice to have you join us once more, Agnes. I hope this is a sign that we can continue with our *contract*," Kent said. He was standing in the middle of the room behind the large table. The pieces of metal that had sat there last time had been removed and in their place was a small, metal sculpture of a serpent-like creature.

As Agnes neared the table, the sculpture twitched to life and Kent's grin deepened as he watched it slither across the table. It didn't stop when it reached the edge and Agnes held her hand out, catching it. It coiled around her wrist and turned its head towards Kent, the small orbs of bronze light in the place of its eyes glittering.

"Well now, that's a pleasing sight." He looked at something over her shoulder. "Byron, if you would deliver Agnes' reward to her room."

"My reward?" Agnes studied the serpent coiled around her arm.

"An incentive for you to continue cooperating. Wes." He indicated the door at the far end of the room.

Wes' hand pressed between Agnes' shoulder blades, and he guided her towards the door in question. When they reached it, he stepped around her and opened it slowly. A breeze rushed into the room, fluttering the notes pinned to the walls and bringing the scent of saltwater. Outside the door was a set of stairs that led to the underbelly, but as Agnes got to the bottom step she stopped and tilted her head back to take in the massive form in front of her. It looked identical to the serpent still coiled around her arm. Except that the smaller automaton was made from a sleek, dark metal studded with rose-gold robrillium and the full-sized version was a conglomeration of different metals, etchings of robrillium covering its sleek, twisting—but still unfinished—form.

"Magnificent, isn't it?" Kent purred as his hands fell on her shoulders.

"It's ..." Her voice fled as the prickle of magic started to arc across her fingertips. She could see all the areas it needed improvement, could tell the difference between something her magic had created wilfully and something that it had created under duress. The golem was a monstrosity, one her magic was urging her to fix. She bit down hard on her lip, the sting driving the creeping sensations of the imminent trance away.

"You may take her back to her room. Ensure she has access to her writing implements," Kent said.

Wes drew her away from the unfinished golem and back into the gloom of the workshop. He paused by a shelf in the corner and collected her old journal and a stack of papers then led her to her room.

The serpent still coiled around her wrist was a comforting weight against her skin. Had Kent intentionally let her take it, or had he forgotten about it in his euphoria at realising that her magic wasn't completely lost?

"What's going on here?" Wes' voice cut through her thoughts. He was standing in the door to her room. Byron had Kiki pinned to the far wall, her chestnut hair roped through his fingers as he pressed her cheek against the wood panelling and hissed something in her ear.

"You wouldn't be saying that if I had my keen. But it's hard to talk while you're drowning," she growled back at him.

Byron's hand pulled away as though he would slap her, but Wes lunged forward and caught it. He twisted Byron's wrist backwards sharply, and Kiki let out a yelp of pain as Byron's other hand tore through her hair. She dropped to the floor and darted towards Agnes as Wes slammed Byron against the wall where he had pinned Kiki moments before.

"Listen here, you perverted fuck. You keep your Bright damned hands to yourself, or I will cut them off myself. Is that clear?"

Byron thrashed as though trying to twist away, but Wes only pushed him harder against the wall.

"Is that clear?" Wes growled in that tone that was full of ice and steel.

"Crystal," Byron grunted, and Wes gave him one last shove into the wall before shunting him towards the door. "One of these days you're going to slip up and your little loyalty act is going to shatter, and when that happens, I'm going to be first in line to take you down."

Wes tilted his chin towards the door. "Get out of my sight."

Once Byron had left, Wes moved and closed the door. He rested his head against it for a few seconds then turned to Agnes and Kiki.

"Are you alright?" he asked Kiki softly.

"I'll live," she said, her tone strained as though she was trying to put on a brave face.

Agnes studied her. Her cheeks were hollow and the dark circles under her eyes suggested she hadn't been sleeping well. Her hair was a wild tangle where Byron had pulled it and her normally golden skin was covered in a motley of bruises and scrapes in various stages of healing.

Wes took a step towards Kiki and cleared his throat. "Kiki—"

"No, don't!" She lifted both her hands in front of her, cutting Wes off. "I am barely holding myself together and I can't deal with your concern right now, Wes. So just don't. I'll be fine."

"Alright. I'll be back later with Luca." He met Agnes' eye as he backed towards the door and then he was gone.

Kiki drew a halting breath and turned to Agnes then she let out a sob and collapsed against Agnes' side.

"Shush, it's going to be alright," Agnes said as she wrapped her arms around Kiki and rubbed circles on her back. She wished she could say it with more conviction, but she wasn't sure she actually believed it.

Kiki was curled tightly against Agnes' side. She had fallen asleep almost the moment they had climbed into bed after admitting that she had barely slept because she wasn't used to sleeping alone. She seemed content enough, but it had taken some time before she stopped startling awake every time Agnes shifted her position.

Agnes wished she could sleep the way Kiki was now, but her body had become feverish, a clammy sweat breaking out across her chest and the back of her neck. The tightness at her temples threatened to bloom into a headache at any moment, but it had been that way for at least an hour while she watched the dark shadows lighten as dawn sent a thin bead of light across the ceiling. She shifted her weight, manoeuvring the pillow into place so Kiki could cuddle against it instead of her side. Kiki stirred just long enough to wrap her arms tight around the pillow and then burrow farther under the blanket.

With a sigh, Agnes let her feet meet floor and retrieved her satchel from under the bed. She then moved to the table where her mechanical serpent was lying in a tight coil, the glittering spots of bronze light in the place of eyes the only sign that it was active. She stroked her index finger along the smooth coils and studied the small pile of papers next to the serpent. Her notes about the war machine. She summoned a mage light to get a better look at the notes; it flickered in the air beside her then abruptly extinguished itself. Setting her hands on the table, she tried again. The light bloomed to life, but the effort of holding it steady caused black spots to dance across her vision.

"Come on. You can do it." She pulled all the power she could. Her fingertips started to tingle, and the serpent stood up on its coils. Its head swayed as though it was watching her.

The light spun back to life and hovered steadily in the air beside Agnes as she collapsed into her chair. It shouldn't have been that hard. Was it the aftereffects of the tonic Luca had been giving her? Was the damage to her keen permanent?

She rubbed her hands over her face and fished her old journal out from underneath the pile of notes. Thumbing through the pages she paused when she came to entries that held the earlier schematics of the golem. Judging by the details in the notes, Savita forcing her magic had had an adverse effect on translating the plans. The full-sized golem should look much like the tiny serpent —sleek and smooth. But it had looked like it hadn't been created by her magic at all but rather a bunch of blacksmiths trying to make sense of her diagrams.

She shifted the golem notes aside and pulled her newer journal from her bag. Her tool roll was still tucked neatly in the satchel along with several pens and a pot of ink. As she dug for the ink, her fingers brushed over a cloth-covered lump. She freed the parcel from where she had wedged it in the bottom of the bag. The grey cloth left her fingers numb and the mage light flickered beside her but didn't go out. Licking her lip, she unwrapped the package, slowly letting the objects contained within balance on her open palm.

Six shards of purple stone each glittering with a strange luminescence from within. She'd seen a piece of this stone, held it and worked it into the power source for her cat golem. But *was* this the same stone or just one extremely like it? A quick examination told her that some of the pieces would fit together like parts of a puzzle. Could a broken heartstone be mended? And if it could, would it still be functional?

The dull throb at her temples sharpened as the prickle of her magic started at her fingertips. She rubbed them together and wrapped the shards of heartstone back in the grey cloth before tucking them away. Her hands had started to shake, and the clammy fever had shifted up to her cheeks and across her forehead. The mage light blinked out of existence again and the room felt unsteady.

She pressed the heels of her palms to her eyes as the door lock clicked. After shoving everything back into her bag, she dove for the bed and threw it under and out of sight. But she'd moved too quickly, and the room spun away from her. She barely got her hands out in front of her as the floor slammed against them.

Kiki sat up with a gasp, a wild terror in her gaze as it found Agnes then darted towards the open door.

"My apologies," Luca said as he swept into the room with his tray of tonics, a pale green mage light bobbing beside him.

Agnes gripped the edge of the bed and hauled herself back to her feet. The room did that swooping thing again and she flopped sideways, swallowing the lump that had become lodged in her throat.

"I told Wes this would happen," Luca said neatly. His fingers touched Agnes' brow and relief washed through her in a warm throb.

"What's wrong with me?" she asked as she opened her eyes.

"It's an aftereffect of the Mother's balm purging the mage bane from your system." He moved to Kiki and touched a hand lightly on her shoulder.

She flinched but didn't pull away completely, and very slowly the bruises and scrapes faded.

"Now." He rubbed his hands together as he moved back to his tray. "Kiki." He lifted a vial and twisted it in the light. Agnes recognised the crimson liquid it contained. "This will not be pleasant. I have doubled the usual dose, which means it will clear the mage bane from your system faster, but the side effects will be stronger."

"Will it make me sick like Agnes?" Kiki asked as she drew her knees to her chest.

"It may, but every mage handles it differently. I am hoping that you burn through the worst of the side effects before we make our break to get off this Bright forsaken city," he said as he unstoppered the vial.

"Get off this city? You mean we're going to escape? What about Kent's commission and my magic?" Agnes asked.

"I don't see how that will be a problem without Savita to control your keen with her mind magic. Kent certainly can't finish the golem without you."

He didn't know the truth then. Did Wes not trust him enough to tell him?

"Now, the sooner you have this the better," he said to Kiki and held the vial out to her.

"You're just going to give me my magic back? Doesn't that go against Kent's orders?" Kiki said as she eyed the vial.

"Have I given you any indication that I care one ounce about Kent's orders?"

"Yes. When you force fed me mage bane while his guards held me down."

Kiki had a good point. But as far as Agnes knew, Luca was like Wes. Maybe not as friendly; his bedside manner could certainly use some work, but he wasn't loyal to Kent. She wasn't sure who he was loyal to, but as long as it wasn't Kent or Idir she didn't think it mattered at the moment.

"You have me there ... but I am sure that you can understand that there are times we must do things we don't agree with in order to keep up appearances. Now please take this tonic before Byron gets here to escort Agnes down to the workshop."

"Byron? Why not Wes?" Agnes asked.

"Because Wes must do whatever he can to keep up his façade of loyalty to Kent." He stretched his arm out until the vial was nearly resting against Kiki's knee. "You don't have to trust me, but I am sure you'd like to have your connection to the source back. I am told that it is a special kind of torture for a mage to be cut off from their magic for any great length of time."

Kiki eyed the vial and drew a deep breath before she gingerly reached out and wrapped her fingers around it. She gave it a tentative sniff, then squeezed her eyes shut and threw it back. "Oh, I was expecting it to taste worse than that." She licked her lips and exchanged the empty vial for the cup of water Luca was now holding out to her.

The door slammed open, and Kiki nearly jolted right out of her skin. Water splashed from the cup onto the bed and Luca's head snapped around so fast Agnes was sure he must have pulled something in his neck.

"Good morning," Byron said, a smile that could only be described as malicious snagging the corners of his mouth.

"Was that completely necessary?" Luca asked, taking the cup from Kiki and placing it back on the tray.

Byron's smile twisted into a smirk. "Got to keep them on their toes." His gaze landed on Agnes. "Up you get. Kent is expecting you."

Agnes glanced at Kiki.

"She stays here. If you're a good girl, Kent will let you keep her." He started towards Agnes, but she jumped to her feet and grabbed her boots as she sighed away from his reaching hand.

"Byron," Luca said sternly, and the guard's attention shifted to him. "Agnes' keen is still in an extremely delicate state and stress is detrimental even to a stable keen, so I suggest you refrain from terrorising her, lest you cause the blockage to return."

"It wouldn't be a problem if *you* could do your job right," Byron all but growled.

Agnes slipped her boots on and gathered her papers from the table. "I'm ready." She didn't like the idea of going anywhere alone with Byron, but he was less likely to do anything to her if Kent was waiting for them.

"Get a move on then." He reached for her arm, and she snapped it away from him as she took a twisting step out of his reach.

"Don't touch me."

Byron's top lip curled, but Luca cleared his throat, and instead of reaching for Agnes again the warden merely indicated the door with an open palm. "Have it your way."

Agnes followed the corridors leading towards the workshop with her head held high despite the crawling sensation that Byron's stare caused. As she entered the lower levels, the crawling intensified and the hairs on the back of her neck prickled in warning seconds before she was grabbed from behind and pushed against the wall.

Byron's breath ghosted across the back of her neck. "I know Kent is waiting, so I'll keep this short. One of these days I'll get you truly alone. And with no uppity healers or self-righteous arseholes around to save you, I'll *touch* you however I Bright damned please. You understand?"

Agnes was saved from answering as a door opened at the end of the hall and Byron promptly released her before taking several steps back.

"Quit dawdling. Kent is waiting," Byron barked as he shoved her along the hallway. As they passed the open door, the old woman the berth belonged to watched them, her eyes narrowing as they flicked from Agnes' face to Byron behind her.

"Get back inside," Byron growled, but the woman didn't budge. Instead, her mouth shifted into a grim smile.

Agnes turned her attention away from the old woman and kept moving towards the stairs that led to the workshop, quickening her pace to get there faster.

"Good morning, Agnes," Kent said as she entered the workshop.

Savita was in the room, but so was a woman with stone-grey hair and the sharp features of an Osmarian. The sides of her head were shaved in a similar fashion to Varlan's, the centre left long and secured in a braid that reached to her waist. Her eyes were a light golden brown and as they did a sweep from the top of Agnes' head to her feet, an appraising smile worked across her mouth. "She certainly is something special, isn't she?"

"Agnes, I would like you to meet Jada, my new necromancer."

Her magic stirred at the mention of necromancy, and she swallowed as a sharp pain shot across her temples.

"Now, are you going to cooperate or will you need Savita's *assistance*?"

Agnes moved to the table in the centre of the room and laid her hands against the smooth surface. "I'll cooperate."

A deep smile slid across Kent's mouth. "Good girl. I knew you'd come to your senses eventually."

CHAPTER THIRTY-ONE

VARLAN

"We don't have the numbers for a full-on assault, and we probably want to keep the Queen ready to depart. I suggest we take a smaller boat with just a couple of us and sneak in. I need to find Wes and let him know we are ready to get Agnes and Kiki out. Once Wes is caught up on the plan and everyone is in position, I will confront Kent one on one to propose swapping the keystone for Agnes and Kiki." Varlan held up the green stone they had retrieved from the shrine of Moalana. The dark mass inside swirled and the magic radiating from the stone throbbed against his palm. "While I have Kent distracted, Bran and Gendry will meet up with Wes and Luca to break the girls out of their cells."

"Who is Luca?" Bran asked.

"A healer. He's a prickly pain in the arse but he's on our side."

"What about the rest of us?" Wren asked as she leant on a crate.

"I still don't think we should risk Kent getting his hands on that stone. If he manages to release whatever is in there—" Deana said, eyeing the stone as though it were a rabid dog.

"It will be fine. It is impossible to release the spirit—"

"Improbable," Bran said in an automatic tone and then chuckled.

"Sorry. You are correct that a specific set of conditions would need to be met to release the spirit. And Kent is certainly not equipped to meet them."

"But Idir could be." Deana hugged her arms around herself and met Bran's eye before flicking her attention to Varlan.

"I imagine Idir would be capable of releasing the spirit, but he's not going to get the chance. I've done this sort of thing plenty of times before. I promise I won't let anyone get their hands on the stone."

She chewed her bottom lip and turned her gaze away from his.

"In answer to your question, Wren, the rest of you need to stay on the ship to be ready to run at a moment's notice. I know I can't stop you from coming, Pippa," he said as the woman in question took a step forward. "But everyone else is better off here, especially you, Deana. If everything goes south, then don't worry about us. Just get away from Armada as fast as you can."

Wren's mouth twisted and her keen gave a little jolt. "You expect me to leave members of my family to suffer at the hands of a tyrant and his undead overlord?"

"I did fear it would be asking too much."

"I am not happy with it," the captain started, but Gendry settled a hand on her shoulder.

"We'll be fine, lass. We can be in and out before Kent has a chance to rally his men. It would be far more dangerous for the entire crew to charge in on the attack."

Wren reached up and took hold of the sides of Gendry's beard. She pulled his head down so his face was level with hers and looked him square in the eye. "If you mess this up and get yourself killed ..."

"I know, lass." He cupped the back of her head and pressed a kiss to the centre of her forehead. "I won't make any promises that I don't know I can keep, but I will try my hardest to bring those girls back safely and not get myself killed in the process."

"Fine." Wren pressed a kiss to Gendry's lips, and he looped his arms around her waist, lifting her off her feet.

Varlan cleared his throat. "We're still trying to plan a rescue mission here."

Gendry chuckled and placed Wren back on the ground before turning his attention to Varlan and the others.

"Right, so, Pippa, you will go with Bran and Gendry. But no matter what happens, you need to keep a cool a head."

"You know, I—"

"Promise me, Pip. Because if you see something that sets you off, you could blow the entire mission and we won't get another chance. Your life and Kiki's are not the only ones at stake here."

The air around him warmed as fire flashed in Pippa's eyes. "I will keep a level head but if that bastard has done anything to Kiki, then—"

"*Pip.*"

"Fine. I promise I won't do anything rash."

He wasn't sure it was a promise she could keep but it was likely the best he would get. "Alright, we—"

"I-want-to-come-too," Deana said in a rushed whisper as though scared of admitting it out loud.

"What was that?"

She swallowed as he turned to her. "I ..." Her keen gave a little surge, but it calmed again as she drew a breath. "I want to come too," she said firmly as her teal gaze met his.

"It's too dangerous," Bran said. "If Savita or Kent catch you, they will take you straight to Idir."

"I am willing to take that risk and my magic might be useful; we would never have escaped Kent last time without it."

"As useful as your keen might prove, Deana, I have to agree with Bran on this one. You are a key piece of Idir's plan. If he was to get his hands on you—"

"I think it should be up to Deana to decide," Pippa said, cutting Varlan off. "The lot of you can posture about protecting her all you want, but at the end of the day she could use her magic to hand all your arses to you without breaking a sweat." She slid an arm around Deana's shoulders.

Deana tensed but didn't pull away. "Please let me come. I want to help."

"You can help by staying safely out of Idir's reach," Bran said, but his tone suggested he knew he was fighting a battle he wouldn't win.

Varlan studied Deana's face and then Pippa's, and he let out a long breath. "Alright. But no one else is coming and if everything goes to shit, you get your arses back to this ship and put as much distance between you and Armada as you can."

"Yes, sir," Pippa said, giving him a mock salute.

"Thank you," Deana said.

"Go get ready. We should reach the waters around Armada by midafternoon." He glanced at Wren for confirmation, and she nodded.

Everyone left except Bran, who leant against the side rail and folded his arms.

"I don't like it either, but Pippa is right. It should be up to Deana," Varlan said.

"I know. I'm just annoyed you didn't argue harder."

"Well, you can keep an eye on her. You and Deana can go after Agnes while Pippa and Gendry get Kiki. We won't know where Kent is keeping either of them until I meet up with Wes and it is possible they are being kept in separate parts of the city."

"Do you honestly think this will work?"

"I wish I could say yes, but I don't know. I underestimated Kent last time and I am just hoping I am not about to do it again."

As the hulking outline of Armada appeared on the horizon, it looked different to before. A dark extension had been added to the far end. Gendry stood beside Varlan, spyglass lifted as he studied the addition.

"Do you want the good news?" Gendry asked.

"It's the golem," Varlan said.

Gendry nodded. "It doesn't look active though and it seems to be tethered to the city. Take a look." He handed the spyglass to Varlan.

The dark shape focused into a serpentine form. Gendry was right it did appear to be tethered to the side of the city by large chains, possibly to prevent it from sinking.

There was something off about the golem. Agnes' magic usually created objects that were sleek and precise but even from this distance it was clear this construct was, for lack of a better word, rough. It was a crude representation of what she was actually capable of. Was it unfinished? Or had something happened in the creation process that affected Agnes' abilities?

"We need to get a closer look at that thing, and I have to find Wes before tonight." Varlan passed the spyglass back to Gendry.

Gendry nodded and then slipped his fingers into his mouth and let out an ear-piercing whistle. Wren, Pippa, Deana, and Bran all hurried over.

"Is that what I think it is?" Bran asked as he indicated the dark shape pressed against the city.

"Yes, but it doesn't look complete, and it's definitely not activated," Varlan answered. "We should get ourselves over to the city and find somewhere to lie low until nightfall."

"If we bring the Queen in close—"

"No, Wren. You need to keep the Queen back until nightfall.

Then bring her close enough to reach for a hasty escape but don't dock her."

Wren grunted, "I'm not an amateur."

"No, but I am worried that bleeding heart of yours won't let you leave the rest of us if you need to. The important thing is getting Agnes and Deana beyond Kent and Idir's reach."

Wren opened her mouth as though she would object, and Varlan held up his hand to stop her.

"I know, but if we don't make it back to the ship, we'll make our way back to Weeper's Cove however we can."

"Why Weeper's Cove?" Deana asked, her eyes shining with something akin to fear.

"Because it's the one place in the isles that Idir can't step foot," Gendry answered. "Once we have had a chance to regroup, we'll assess our other options."

Deana didn't look comfortable with the idea, but she didn't object further.

"And how long are we to wait around with the spooks at Weeper's Cove? What if you get captured or killed? Do we just stay there indefinitely?" Wren asked.

Gendry met Varlan's eyes and scratched his fingers through his beard.

"I'd say wait a few weeks and then head for New Brenna," Bran said. "Go straight to Leith and get him to send word to Hartswood. As much as I'd rather not drag Nea into this mess, she is your best hope of figuring it out. Worst case scenario, I am sure Leith will grant you sanctuary."

"That would work," Gendry said, and Varlan nodded in agreeance.

"Why not just head straight for Beldaren then?" Pippa asked.

"Because we'd rather not take this fight to them unless we absolutely have to," Gendry answered.

"Alright, so is everyone on board with the plan? Pippa, once you have Kiki—"

"Get back to the Queen. We've been over it a dozen times now."

"Twice, Pip. Not a dozen." He laughed, then turned to Deana. "You too, Deana. If things look like they aren't going in our favour, just get back here to Wren and the others. Don't take unnecessary risks."

They both nodded, and Pippa said, "We get it. You're starting to be a worse mother hen than Wren." She grinned.

"Get in the boat, Pip," Varlan said with a grin of his own. It was good to see her in a lighter mood.

With Deana using a small thread of her magic to propel the boat through the water, they slid into the underbelly in no time. Keeping their heads low, they navigated their way up to the abandoned berths where Agnes had been meeting with Gethyn. Once they were settled, Varlan crept out into the city. He needed to find Wes or maybe Luca then get himself back down to the berth to await nightfall.

He stayed in the lower levels and worked his way carefully around to what would be considered the poor quarter if Armada was a typical city like Dalthera or New Brenna. He edged along the corridor and knocked on a door about halfway along. Meryl, the old woman who opened the door, grinned widely and hurried him inside.

She reached up and gripped his cheeks as she studied him then shook her head and slapped his arm. "Took you long enough. Tea?"

"I know you won't let me leave without having a cup, so why not."

"Bertie!" she yelled as she moved to make the tea.

A small, dark-haired boy emerged from deeper in the berth. He blinked at Varlan then turned his attention to his grandmother.

Behind the boy was Gethyn. He looked like he'd seen better days. The bruises on his face were fading but he still sported a badly healing split lip and a limp.

"I thought you'd be dead," Varlan said by way of greeting.

"Those bastards certainly tried. I'd be happier to see you if you had Nari in tow. That prick Luca refuses to come down from on high to help us bottom dwellers."

Meryl clucked her tongue at the ink seller and then turned to the boy. "Off you go, and make sure the guards don't see you." She waved him towards the door. "Luca has his hands full keeping up appearances for Kent. He can't just waltz down here to patch up every ungrateful, old grump," she said as she placed a cup on the table in front of Gethyn and then handed one to Varlan.

"Is there anything I need to know before Wes gets here?" he asked as he cradled the cup in his hands, the warmth soaking into his fingers.

"Not anything that you couldn't guess yourself. Kent's time is coming to an end. His abuse of both Agnes and Elijah are the last in a long list of violations." She sat at the table with Gethyn and traced her finger around the rim of her cup.

"Are you implying that there might be a movement in place to overthrow him?"

Meryl circled the edge of her cup with her fingertip again. "I am saying there is a seething discontent here in the lower berths, a discontent that could be taken advantage of."

"So, if something were to happen tonight, could your people provide a distraction? Knowing that they would be putting themselves in harm's way by evoking Kent's wrath?"

She made a *pfft* sound as she blew on her tea. "You forget that most of us are not vulnerable village folk with little more sense than sheep. Some of us were fighters, thieves, and pirates. And those who were not, well, you know better than most how this life tempers a person."

He took a sip of his tea, the smoky, sweet notes of the Faridean black bringing an immediate sense of calm to his mind. "And if Kent were out of the picture, then who would step in and fill the void?"

Gethyn cleared his throat.

The ink seller wouldn't be Varlan's first choice, but then again there were few people who would be. Not that it mattered, really. Varlan wasn't here to help them overthrow Kent. He was here to rescue Agnes and Kiki and then put as much distance between him and Armada as possible.

"Well, perhaps we can kill two birds with one well-timed stone. I have business with Kent tonight and if your people could cause a distraction that would lure the bulk of his guards away from the crow's nest, I'd be in your debt."

The door opened and Varlan flinched, ready to duck out of sight, but it was just Bertie returning with Wes in tow.

"We don't have long; I have to get back upstairs before the shift change," Wes said as he gave Meryl and Gethyn a quick nod.

"Where is Kent keeping Kiki and Agnes?" Varlan asked

"The crow's nest. They are sharing a cell up there. But Agnes is currently down in the workshop. Kent will move her back up to the crow's nest in an hour or two."

Varlan rubbed his fingers along his lower lip. "It would be easier to get her while she is away from the crow's nest. But the Queen won't be in position until after dark and if we make a move to rescue Agnes, Kent is likely to punish Kiki."

"Luca can get Kiki out. But without access to the ship, the lot of you would be sitting ducks ... Can you signal Wren to move in sooner?"

"There's no way to get word back to her and we can't change the plan now. We'll just have to wait until dark and break both of them out of the crow's nest. Can you let Luca know to be ready? The plan is to rescue Kiki and Agnes and then return to the Queen. Wren will be ready to leave once Agnes and Deana are back on board, regardless of where the rest of us are."

"You brought Deana here?" Wes rocked back a step. "Are you out of your fucking mind?"

"I know it's a huge risk. But she wanted to come, and her keen might prove useful."

Wes shook his head. "You've just added a level of complication that the plan didn't need."

"It's done now. There's no sense arguing about it. I need to return to others and let them know what's going on, then I need to sneak up to Kent's quarters and wait for him. Meryl's people are going to give us a distraction down here to hopefully pull some of the guards away from the crow's nest."

"Wait, you should know he found another necromancer. One who is working with him freely."

"Does this necromancer have a heartstone?"

Wes shook his head. "No, but I just thought you should know, she has convinced Kent that if Agnes can finish the shell of the golem, they won't need her to activate it. And she's close. If Luca hadn't given her the mage bane, she'd be done by now."

"He did what?" Varlan fought the urge to yell and instead his voice came out in an enraged whisper.

"He only did it to buy us time, but Agnes isn't recovering the way she should. I don't know if it's because Savita has been forcing her to use her magic to the point of exhaustion or a reaction to mage bane itself. But he kept the dose low—just enough to cut off her magic and not a drop more."

Varlan's cup shattered against the far wall, sending tea and shards of porcelain flying. He drew a strained breath and raked his fingers over his skull. "Sorry, Meryl," he said as he moved to clean up the mess.

"Leave it. Bertie will clean it."

The boy who had ducked below the edge of the table emerged and hurried to take over from Varlan.

"You were supposed to keep her safe," Varlan said as he turned back to Wes.

"I did what I could, but Savita was going to kill her. I could see it every time she forced Agnes to use her keen. The mage bane gave us a reprieve and we used that time to work out an escape plan. Luca has stopped dosing Kiki as well—he only did that under Kent's orders," he added the last as Varlan's fists clenched. "And her keen is nearly back to normal. We were going to wait until Agnes finished the machine and make a run for it."

"How close is the golem to being finished?" His voice was still tighter than he would have liked, and he drew another breath. The messy construction now made complete sense; it wasn't completely Agnes' work. A good bulk of it had been constructed by Savita through the lens of Agnes' keen. That had warped the magic and created an inept monstrosity.

"Close. She may even finish it today."

Would her keen be satisfied if the shell were complete even if it wasn't animated? If this necromancer had convinced Kent that she could animate the golem without Agnes' assistance, then maybe that was a loophole? Regardless of what happened tonight, he had to get Agnes away from Savita. They could worry about getting Agnes' keen under control once they had some semblance of safety.

"Is Kent in the workshop with Agnes?"

"Yes."

"Who else is down there? Savita?"

Wes nodded. "And Jada, the new necromancer, and Byron." His lip curled over the warden's name.

"Excellent. I'll check back in with Gendry and the others then to get up to Kent's quarters before he returns."

"I don't know how you'll manage to reach the crow's nest unseen without climbing."

"If Kent, Byron, and Savita are currently preoccupied, you should be able to get me up there." He turned to Meryl and Gethyn, who had been watching their exchange. "I'll send Gendry and Deana to you. They will help you get everyone into position for the distraction." It would be safer for Deana to stay down on the lower levels where she could get back to the Queen faster. And there was also a chance they could use her presence to lure Savita away from the crow's nest. The more disruption they could seed in Kent's inner circle, the better.

Meryl inclined her head. "We will be ready. Don't you worry."

Hours later, as evening was starting to darken the windows of Kent's quarters, everyone was in position. Gendry and Deana had joined Meryl and Gethyn and were waiting for the signal to initiate the rioting in the lower levels. Bran and Pippa were hiding out in the market, ready to burst into action when Luca came down the stairs with Kiki after the fighting started. Pippa would have preferred waiting up here with Varlan, but it had been hard enough to sneak him in on his own.

Hopefully Kent wouldn't take too much longer because the restless energy Varlan had been feeling all day was starting to get the better of him. He paced across the room and rolled the stone from Moalana's shrine back and forth between his hands. He turned when he reached the window that overlooked the golem, and the door opened. But it wasn't Kent who entered. It was a woman Varlan had never seen before. Her stone-grey hair was a dead giveaway, but so was the cloud of cold that seemed to radiate from her. Kent's new necromancer. Her eyes widened as she studied Varlan, but then her attention was completely absorbed by the stone in his hands.

"Where in the realms did you find such a precious thing?" Her crooning tone was at odds with her sharp features as she took a step towards him, her hand reaching towards the stone.

"Oh, Savita, stop pouting. Just because the golem is finished, doesn't mean Agnes—" Kent had followed the woman into the room, his gaze on Savita behind him as he spoke to her over his shoulder. But he cut himself off the moment he turned and saw Varlan. "Hello, old *friend*. I hope you're not too disappointed to learn that you're too late." As the words left Kent's mouth, the city shuddered beneath them under the assault of a wave that sent spray slamming against the windows.

"Don't tell me you were stupid enough to bring Deana back here," Savita said, a triumphant smile sliding across her lips.

"You had best go and find her, lest you disappoint your father by letting her slip through your fingers again," Kent said, and Savita rushed from the room. "I see you've met Jada." He indicated the necromancer who was still fixated on the stone.

"He has brought the most intriguing prize with him," the woman said, pointing to the stone.

"Is that what I think it is?" Kent asked.

"Maybe. How open are you to doing a trade?"

Kent let out a snort of laughter. "A trade? You are slipping, Varlan. You must realise that you are in no position to bargain. No, I think I will simply take that stone and if you let me do so without a fight, I will let you walk away for old time's sake. Should you decide to make things difficult, however ... Well then, I would like to say it was a pleasure knowing you."

A guard came bursting into the room. "There's rioting in the market. Byron has gone to make sure Agnes is secure." He snapped his mouth shut when he saw Varlan.

"Get it under control," Kent growled, his attention flicking towards the guard.

Varlan used that moment to strike. He lunged forward and grabbed Jada, throwing her into Kent and then barging past the guard and out into the corridor. He slammed the door behind him and used the key Wes had given him to secure the lock. It wouldn't hold Kent for long, but it would be enough to buy him time.

A stream of guards were running for the stairs, and Varlan rushed through the middle of them as he spotted Luca arguing with Byron. Byron slammed the healer against the wall and raced around the corner.

"I'm fine," Luca said as Varlan reached him. "He's going after Agnes and Kiki. They're going to need your help."

A scream sounded, the familiarity of it turning the blood in his veins to ice. He left Luca and took off in the direction Byron had disappeared, praying to the Bright that he wasn't too late.

CHAPTER THIRTY-TWO

AGNES

It had taken several days to fix the issues Savita had caused in the construction of the golem, but Agnes' magic had finally completed the repairs. Now she took a step back, the grogginess of the trance making her knees wobble.

Kent steadied her and bent to meet her eyes. "Well?"

"It's done. There is nothing more my magic can do until we have a heartstone."

There was something in the smile he gave her that turned her stomach and brought a quiver to her hands, but she clenched her fists and tilted her head back to study the golem. The last light of the sun was glinting off its metallic form. It was still a crude representation of what her magic was truly capable of, but once animated it would be completely functional. She moved to gather her things.

"Well done, Agnes. Byron, if you could escort her back to her room," Kent said.

Agnes swallowed as she tucked her journal and notes into a neat pile. Byron hadn't touched her since the day he had slammed her against the wall and threatened her, but his lurid stares made her skin crawl. And the knowledge of what he had done to Kiki ignited both a deep rage that he had gotten away with such a vile act and a wild fear that it was only a matter of time before he did it to her.

"Let's go," Byron said, and she flinched as he reached out and gave her shoulder a small push.

"Please remember to be gentle with her," Kent said, and Byron's hand dropped away from her.

She sucked in a relieved breath and kept herself several steps ahead of him as he escorted her all the way to the crow's nest. They passed Wes on the stairs, and the look he gave Byron should have melted him on the spot. Instead, Byron cleared his throat and stepped closer to Agnes, making her speed up. When they reached her cell, Luca was inside with Kiki. His tray of tonics was on the table, and Kiki was cradling a cup of tea. Most of her injuries had healed, the physical ones anyway, and the colour had returned to her cheeks.

When her blue gaze landed on Byron behind Agnes, she shrunk against the wall behind the bed and her hands began to shake.

"Evening, Agnes," Luca said and offered her a cup from his tray. It was a restorative tea he had been giving her for the last few days to keep the symptoms from the mage bane under control; without it she was plagued by savage headaches and nausea. Tonight's offering shimmered with a swirl of gold as though he had included Mother's balm in the mix. The smooth minty taste confirmed it.

"I don't believe lurking in doorways is part of your job description, Byron, and your presence is bothering my patients," Luca said in that dry tone of his.

Byron's lip curled but he left the room. The slamming door made Kiki nearly jump out of her skin.

"Right," Luca said as he glared at the door. "We are breaking you out tonight. Varlan has several of his people in position in the city. As soon as they give the signal, we are getting out of here."

"How though? The only way out of the crow's nest is via the main stairs," Kiki said.

"There is one other way."

"Agnes is in no state to be climbing down the side of the city."

"That is not the way I was referring to. There is a hidden chute, impossible to climb but perfect for a hasty retreat. I am not certain even Kent knows of it, but Gethyn told me how to find it. I am to take you to it and get you down to the docks. We may need to swim out to the Queen ... I trust you both know how to swim?"

"Of course, I know how to swim," Kiki said, and Agnes nodded. Swimming was a compulsory skill when you lived on a city floating in the middle of the ocean.

"Good, now. As soon as we get the signal, I will return. Make sure you are ready." He gathered his tray and then left them alone.

Agnes pulled her satchel out from its hiding place under the bed and stuffed the notes she had brought up from the workshop into it. She was too nervous to sit. The knowledge that Varlan and the others were somewhere in the bowls of the city, waiting for the moment to rescue them was a massive relief. But there was still so much that could go wrong and if they failed, Kent was likely to punish her and Kiki. Would he throw Kiki down into the dungeon where Byron could reach her again? Would he be mad enough to toss Agnes down there too? She stopped pacing and drew a deep breath.

"It's going to be alright," Kiki said. "They wouldn't rush in without a sound plan."

"That's what you all thought last time though and look how that ended up."

Kiki bit back a gasp and blinked rapidly as though forcing back tears.

"Shit, Kiki. I'm sorry. I didn't mean ..."

"I know ... It's okay. But we have to believe that this time it's going to be different." Her voice was thick, and she didn't quite meet Agnes' eye.

Agnes nodded. "I'll try."

A short while later, water splashed against the window and a shudder rolled through the city.

"That was Deana's magic," Kiki said, and she glanced towards the door as shouting started in the hall.

The door opened, and Luca hurried in. "Alright, run to the east end of this corridor. There is a panel on the wall that will open—you have to press the top right corner. It will reveal a sloping tunnel. Just slide to the bottom and then get yourselves to the Queen. The rest of us will join you there. Hurry." He left the door wide open as he ran in the opposite direction from where he had told them to go.

"Come on. We'd better hurry." Kiki pulled her out onto the catwalk, and they ran to the corner. "Which panel do you think it is?" Kiki asked as she studied the wall in front of them.

"Try the one on the very corner, and I'll try this one," Agnes said as she pressed the top right corner of the panel in front of her.

Something slammed into her from the side.

"Oh, no you don't." Byron had her pinned to the ground, one hand tangled in her hair as his knees pressed down on either side of her. He shoved her against the ground before hauling her to her feet by her hair.

Kiki let out a snarl and lunged for Byron. He let go of Agnes, shoving her out of the way as Kiki tackled him.

Agnes staggered backwards, her hip colliding with the rail that ringed the catwalk as a wave of nausea took her. The world tilted and she slipped over the rail, catching it at the last moment. The ocean churned far beneath her. She tried to grip the rail tighter, but it was slick under her fingers. "Kiki," she rasped as wild panic stole her voice and she scrambled to pull herself back up.

She sucked in a sharp breath and let it out in a scream. "KIKI!"

The other woman appeared at the rail, her normally golden skin pale as she gripped Agnes' hand. "I've got you—just hold on." She tried to haul Agnes up. Her fingers slipped, and the bottom dropped out of Agnes' stomach as she fell.

A warm hand caught her wrist and with a grating yell, its owner hoisted her upwards and over the rail. She fell against him and burrowed her face against his chest. There was something eerily calming about the scent of his shirt, and she tightened her grip, not game to open her eyes in case this was just an image conjured by her terrified mind and she was still plummeting to her death.

"You're alright. I've got you."

She recognised Varlan's voice, despite the oddly fragile quality it had taken on.

"But we have to keep moving." He released his grip on her and pulled away.

Agnes finally opened her eyes. Varlan was between her and the rail she had fallen over. Luca and Kiki were a short distance away beside the now open hatch.

"Where's Byron?" she asked, noting the splatter of blood on the floor. A quick look told her it didn't belong to any of the other three.

"Ran off with his tail between his legs, but not before Kiki managed to break his nose and half drown him with his own blood," Luca said. Was that a note of pride in his voice?

"You!" Kent rounded the far corner, his rage zeroing in on Varlan.

"Move it!" Varlan's hand shook as he nudged Agnes towards the opening in the wall as Luca and Kiki ducked inside.

The floor of the passage was a steep downward slope and Agnes' body picked up speed as she slid on her backside around the sharp corners. The passage spat them out in the corridor that led to the abandoned berths. She stumbled out of the way seconds before Varlan emerged behind her.

"Keep running. Don't stop until you reach the Queen. I have to go help the others."

Kiki and Luca didn't need telling twice. They took off towards the corridor that would lead them to the docks.

"Thank you for saving me," Agnes said as she met Varlan's gaze.

He gave her a small smile. "Just get to the Queen."

She nodded and turned to leave.

"Agnes, wait." He caught her arm and pulled her against him, one hand cupping the back of her head as he pressed his lips to her crown. Her initial instinct was to freeze. She liked Varlan well enough, but the gesture was so intimate—the way the fingers of one hand twisted in her hair and the other spanned across her lower back. His breathing deepened as though he was a man dying of thirst and trying desperately to drink her in. But as strange as the intimacy was, it also felt *right*. Like they had stood in this position a thousand times before. So she leant into him, her hands gripping the sides of his shirt as her knees shook. She was certain that if he hadn't arrived at the crow's nest when he did, her body would be washing up in the underbelly at that very moment.

"I'm sorry I left you behind," he whispered against her hair before releasing her and taking a step back then shaking off whatever feeling had seemed to overcome him. "Be careful. Savita is down here somewhere," he said as he gave her a little push in the direction the others had run before disappearing towards the market.

Agnes' head was swimming as she chased Kiki and Luca along the darkened corridors and catwalks. A pale blue light bobbed ahead of them, casting reaching shadows back as the sounds of fighting echoed from the market.

Finally, they pounded out onto the docks. The Queen was anchored a short distance away, a swirling mass of dark clouds in the sky above her. There was a boat tethered to the side of the dock, but no sign of oars. Luca had been right about the need to swim.

"Kiki!" Pippa yelled as she came running towards them with Gendry and Deana in tow.

Kiki lunged forward and collided with her sister as she pulled her into a crushing hug.

"Less rejoicing, more escaping," Luca said as he nudged them towards the water. "The others?" he asked Gendry.

"On their way, but Varlan told us not to wait. As soon as Agnes and Deana are on the Queen we are to leave."

Luca nodded. "Let's get a move on then."

"Everyone in the boat," Deana said as the healer moved to dive into the water.

"There are no oars," Luca said.

"We won't need them."

Gendry held the boat steady while Deana and the others climbed in. Deana closed her eyes and the water beneath them bubbled to life before the boat surged towards the Queen as though propelled by a team of invisible oarsmen.

Rufus was waiting for them with a rope ladder. He hauled each of them over the side rail of the Queen then Nari hurried forward to check them all over. Dara clung to Kiki's side and dragged her towards the hold once Nari was satisfied with her.

"Agnes!" Her father swamped her in a hug that smelled of ink and black tea. It was the same hug he used to give her when nightmares woke her in the middle of the night, and she felt the hot prick of tears at the corner of her eyes. "Thank the Bright you are okay," he said as he pulled back and studied her face.

Wren came forward and gave Agnes' arm a squeeze. "Where are Bran and Varlan?" she asked Gendry.

"We lost them in the thick of it, but you know what has to be done."

"You're seriously going to leave them behind?" Agnes scanned the dock for any sign of them.

"We have to, lass. Varlan was clear that once you and Deana were on board we were to depart."

"But Kent will kill them."

"They wouldn't want us to stay and risk Kent getting his hands on you or Deana."

"But—"

"We promised we would leave them no matter what," Deana said, though she looked about as happy about the idea as Agnes felt.

"Don't worry. Varlan is used to squeezing out of situations that seem impossible to escape. I am sure they will be fine," Wren said, and she turned to Rufus. "Weigh anchor. I'm about to release the storm."

"Wait, look!" Luca was leaning over the side of the ship and pointing to something in the water at the edge of the city. Lightning from Wren's storm flashed, and the object was illuminated for a few seconds. It was a small boat with three waterlogged forms inside. The water was too rough for them to make any real progress and each rising wave threatened to capsize them.

"Deana, can you control that boat the way you did ours?" Agnes asked.

"I didn't control the boat—I controlled the ocean, but I can try." She settled her hands on the side rail of the Queen and turned her focus onto the boat. The water seemed to still for several heartbeats and then a massive wave curled under the small vessel. It tilted forward but didn't capsize, instead it rolled towards the side of the Queen. "I can't hold it," Deana said through her teeth as her eyes flashed a dark navy blue.

The three men in the boat dove into the water a second before it was smashed to splinters against the hull of the Queen. Bran's head broke the surface first, easy to spot with that tangle of white hair. He swam to the side of the ship and started up the ladder as Varlan emerged. He twisted in the water as though looking for something then dove under again.

Time seemed to drag until Varlan finally broke the surface again with Wes held tightly under his arm.

"Get another rope!" Gendry yelled.

"Here." Pippa pushed a massive coil of rope into Gendry's hands, and he hastily tied off one end as he flicked the other out to Varlan.

"Pull!" Gendry yelled, and Luca and Elijah joined him in hauling the men up. Once they reached the top, however, it was only Wes secured to the rope, his side bloodied and his breathing shallow. A green thread of magic twisted over his skin as Luca knelt beside him and checked him over.

Where was Varlan? Agnes rushed back to the side rail and studied the churning water, her search becoming more and more frantic.

"Looking for something?" Varlan asked, and she spun around. He was sopping wet and leaning heavily on Bran. His shirt was covered in blood, but it was hard to tell if it was Wes' or his own.

She released the breath she had been holding and pointed to his shirt. "How much of that is yours?"

He looked down and tilted his head. "It's mostly Wes' and a little of Byron's. The cracked rib, though, that's all me," he said with a groan, and Nari appeared beside him.

She touched her fingers to his side, and he let out a relieved breath of his own.

"Alright, hold on to something because things are about to get dicey," Wren said as the cloud above released an echoing boom and the ship pulled forward as her sails filled with wind.

They stopped to regroup at a small island halfway between Armada and Weeper's Cove. Gendry had wanted to race all the way to the cove, but Wren said they needed to stop sooner to give the mages a chance to catch their breath. Agnes didn't mind. She wasn't too fond of the idea of an island full of ghosts, especially not since Deana told her what had happened the last time they were there.

As the sounds of the others stirring reached her, she crawled out of the tent she had been sharing with Deana. Deana had left a while ago to walk along the beach. Agnes had offered to go with her, but she'd said she would rather be alone as it gave her time to centre her thoughts. Truth be told, after the small amount of sleep Agnes had gotten in the last few weeks, she was happy for the chance to sleep in.

"Morning, Agnes," Bran said brightly as she reached the small campfire beside which Gendry was overseeing what looked like a cauldron full of porridge. "Deana not with you?"

"No, she went for a walk earlier. She said she wanted to be alone, so I didn't press her."

He frowned and turned his attention to the beach. Agnes followed his line of sight but there was no sign of Deana.

"Did anyone hear that strange music this morning?" Dara asked as she came wandering from the tent she had shared with Nari and the twins, her hair still a tangle from sleep.

"I didn't hear anything," Agnes said, but Bran had moved to the beach. He bent to pick up something and then turned back to Agnes as a look of dread stole across his features.

"What's wrong?" Agnes asked as she and Dara hurried to him. Clutched in his fingers was a smooth stone with a hole through the centre.

"It's broken," Dara said softly. "Deana wouldn't have left it. Even if it's magic died, she could never cast it aside."

"Its magic is not dead though," Bran said.

"What is it?" Agnes asked.

"Deana's protection charm. The one her brother gave her," Bran said as he ran his fingers along the leather cord that was laced through the hole in the centre of the stone. He lingered on the split ends. The break was far too clean to have been torn—it had to have been cut.

Bran closed his eyes, and the hairs on the back of Agnes' neck prickled. After a while, he opened his eyes again and looked up at the others who were approaching them. Varlan, Wes, Wren, and the twins. Farther back by the fire, Luca, Nari, and Agnes' father were sitting with Gendry and the rest of the Queen's crew.

"Bran?" Dara asked, her fingers touching his arm. "What did the re-enactment show you?"

"Samir was here, and he led Deana into a trap."

CHAPTER THIRTY-THREE

DEANA

The camp was silent as Deana slipped out of the tent she was sharing with Agnes and wandered towards the beach. It had been such a turbulent few weeks that she was grateful for the moment's respite. Their fight was far from over, however; they all agreed on that. Idir still had to be stopped, but rescuing Agnes and Kiki from Kent had been a win—one they needed to celebrate.

She found a spot halfway along the beach under the dipping fronds of a large tree and sat, digging her toes into the sand as she rested her chin on her knees and settled her gaze on the horizon.

"I'm sorry I haven't stopped to talk to you lately. Things are changing almost too fast for me to keep up with ... I'm changing." She chewed her lip and hugged her knees tighter. "It started on Mintura, and I'm scared, Kai. The more I use my song, the more it changes me. It's not a bad change, really. I know I am still me, but I'm not the same girl you gave up everything to protect. I'm tired of hiding, of running when things get too much to bear."

"You don't have to keep running, Dee."

She leapt to her feet and spun to face the boy who had spoken. The last time she had seen him, it had been a spirit wearing his face at Weeper's Cove. But her song told her this was the real Samir. His arm was dotted with coral, as the spirit's had been, but instead of reaching all the way to his shoulder, the afflicted skin stopped just below his elbow.

"What are you doing here?" she asked, taking a step back towards the camp.

"The others heard your song and came to find you. They need you, Dee. You're the only one who can help them. And they can help you. Please don't fight them. They don't want to hurt you."

The morning stilled as an oppressive silence settled over her. She backed towards the camp, only to slam into something solid after she had taken half a dozen steps.

Large, heavy hands grabbed her from behind. She twisted and thrashed, but the grip that held her was vise-tight. The silence around her had stolen her voice along with her song, so she couldn't call for help, couldn't use her magic to fight back. She struggled until she managed to free one hand and reach for the protection charm.

"You won't be needing that," a woman said, and the leather chord that held the stone pulled tight against the back of Deana's neck as a blade flashed in the early morning light.

The stone dropped to the sand with a thud as Deana was hoisted over her assailant's shoulder. The silence shifted for a moment. She drew a deep breath, ready to scream, but a tightness closed around her throat again, and she could barely manage a raspy squeak. The tightness shifted and her limbs grew heavy as a deep nausea overtook her and the world spun.

"Don't fight it," the woman's voice said as she stepped into view. She looked Beldaren, with creamy skin and golden hair that hung forward over one shoulder. One side of her head was hairless, the skin adorned with a deep green and purple coral. Her eyes were the same dark blue as Bran's, but there was a deep sadness swimming in their depths as though she had known nothing but pain and sorrow.

Deana tried to speak but that tightness closed around her throat again.

A small hand gently touched her arm, and she tilted her head until she met Samir's gaze.

"Just go to sleep, Dee. It'll be okay. I promise."

Just go to sleep? As though she wasn't being dragged away by complete strangers, one of which was certainly a shrouded one. But her body did feel heavy, and her eyes were burning enough to water. Maybe if she shut them for a moment the world would stop spinning.

Strange music drifted along the edge of her consciousness, and she got the distinct feeling she was floating. A breeze made the loose strands of her hair tickle her face and gentle fins brushed against the backs of her legs. She opened her eyes. A midnight blue dome stretched above her; a cloud of silver birds undulated across the sky as though chasing a swarm of gnats. Standing slowly, she dug her toes into the white sand beneath her, the pearlescent fish swirling around her legs twisted to show their black underbellies before darting away.

She had been in this dreamscape before. Last time, Grandmother Ocean had been standing on the shore waiting for her. Water splashed as she spun around to scan the shoreline. Grandmother Ocean was nowhere in sight, but two children were sitting on the sand sculpting something. She walked slowly towards them, their voices carrying on the gentle breeze.

"I can't wait to show Mama and Papa the new feathers I found," the young girl said. "Do you think they will be home soon?"

The boy, who was in the middle of his teenage years, nodded slowly. "Nazali said they should be home with the next tide."

Deana flinched as they both turned to study the ocean behind her, but they seemed to stare straight through her. Heaviness settled in her core as she realised that those cheerfully expectant faces would soon be drawn in a deep sorrow. Their parents wouldn't return with the next tide or any that followed.

Her dripping clothes left a trail of dark spots on the pristine sand as she edged closer and reached out her fingers to brush the boy's cheek. The moment her skin touched his, both he and the younger version of herself collapsed into a pile of glittering silver scales.

"You returned," the layered voice of Grandmother Ocean said from behind her.

She reached for the protection charm, but her fingers only found bare skin.

"I told you before that you would not need that trinket." There was something like humour in her voice this time.

Deana turned to face the goddess. The smears of pigment that had covered her dark skin last time were gone and her clothes were pristine, instead of the water-soaked rags from before. The cloth that hid her eyes was the bright blue green of a parrot's wing and the gnarled fingers at the top of her driftwood staff were closed in an intricate fist of knotted wood.

"Come, child. There is something I must show you before we are disturbed again." She held out one hand. A swirling, golden tattoo marked the centre of her palm. It sent a gentle thrumming note through the air that made the hair on Deana's arms prickle. "I promise all will be well if you place your trust in me."

Deana lifted her fingers towards the outstretched hand but curled them back at the last second.

Grandmother Ocean's mouth softened at one corner, and she

gave a slow nod. "Not yet then ... but soon." She retracted her hand and turned to face the jungle that edged the beach. "Follow." She rolled her fingers towards the trees, and they moved aside to reveal a twisting path. "It's not as far as it looks."

With a slow nod of her own, Deana followed Grandmother Ocean into the trees. She paused as they shifted behind her, blocking the way back to the beach, but started forward again when the goddess cleared her throat and waved her onward.

It's just a dream. Your dream. You are in control. She told herself as they continued along the path.

They turned a corner and the trees opened out again to reveal a sun-soaked cliff of white-streaked red stone. The dark sky had been replaced with splashes of pink, orange, lilac, and gold in a mockery of a sunset. The slices of white stone glittered as the light from the descending sun hit them.

Grandmother Ocean walked right to the very edge of the cliff and stopped. She tilted her head as though looking back over her shoulder at Deana. "You're almost there. Just a few more steps."

Deana licked her lip and crossed the distance to join the goddess at the precipice. The churning ocean below tossed about a ship, roughly the size of the Azure Queen. Shadows in the form of people scurried across the deck in a frantic effort to save their vessel as a monster wave capsised it. Her hands grew slick as she leant forward, praying the boat would right itself.

The song of the dreamscape changed. A sombre roll of low chords that spoke of despair and regret settled over Deana's shoulders as the ocean drew all the way back to the horizon. The departure of the waves left a vast expanse of wet sand with the carcass of the wrecked ship sitting in the middle of it. Bodies littered the sand in a ring around the wreck, and cargo had been strewn as far as the eye could see.

Deana was no longer on the cliff but standing amid the carnage.

The song of the dreamscape was drowned out by the silence of death. A pained gasp caught her attention, and she ran around the bulk of the ship. Hope that she may be able to help swelled in her chest only to be replaced with a dread-filled sorrow. Her father lay on the sand, his chest rising and falling rapidly, his fingers gripping the chunk of wood that protruded from his gut. He twisted his head as though looking for something, his warm brown gaze widening. She followed the line of his sight. Her mother was a short distance away. A man had her by the throat, the coral-studded skin of his arm catching the light.

"No!" Deana screamed at the same time her father did, but neither of them could prevent what was about to happen.

The man dropped her mother's limp body and turned. Idir. He stalked slowly across the sand and crouched to inspect her father's wound. Her father thrashed, trying to move away. But Idir caught his jaw and made a tutting sound, his song stretching out around them, thickening the air with its dangerous allure.

"Did you honestly believe you could hide the truth from *me*?"

"She's—" Her father's words were cut off by a bubbling cough that splattered the front of Idir's shirt with blood.

Idir made a shushing noise low in his throat, the muscles of his face pulling grotesquely around the coral that studded his skin as a wicked smile crossed his mouth. "I know how precious she is, and I promise I will take *good* care of her."

Her father's body started to shake, but his eyes bore into Idir's with a grim determination.

A jolt ran through Deana and the scene started to crumble as shards of light sliced through it. Her body grew heavy, and her knees thudded against the wet sand, her fingers digging small furrows as she tried to push herself back up. But the harder she fought to hold on to the dream, the faster it twisted away from her and the heavier her body grew.

She awoke with a gasp.

The room around her was lit by the soft, golden glow of candlelight and smelled of dust and stale herbs. Voices carried from elsewhere in the building in a low rumble that she couldn't decipher. The images of the dream lingered when she closed her eyes. Idir had killed her parents. That knowledge brought a savage rage to her core. It was a foreign feeling that had started as a bitter seed as she watched him kill her mother. When Idir had gloated as he watched her father die it had blossomed into a sharp flower that left a prickling of hot tears behind her eyes and an edgy restlessness in her fingers.

"Dee?" Samir's voice caught her attention, and she scanned the room looking for him.

He was sitting by the small window, a plate of food resting on his lap, his eyes wide as they studied her.

"You're finally awake. Astrid and Rami will want to know." He placed the plate on the table and started for the door.

"Samir, wait."

He paused halfway to the door and looked over his shoulder at her.

"Can they be trusted? The woman is—"

"Her name is Astrid. And yes, they can be trusted. They saved me from Idir's shrouded ones." He approached the edge of the bed.

Some of the colour had returned to his cheeks and the dark circles that had been present under his eyes since the night Kai died were gone. Her gaze drifted down to the coral-studded skin of his arm. The leather cuff he always wore was still around his wrist and the coral seemed to originate from beneath it before spreading up his forearm to his elbow.

"Did they do that to you?"

His gaze dropped to the afflicted wrist, and he shook his head. "No, that was Idir's shrouded ones. They planted the seed the

351

night when Kai—" His cheek concaved like he was biting the inside of it. "Astrid is nothing like those shrouded ones. She has been showing me how to control it."

"Control it? Samir, it will consume you." She pushed herself to the edge of the bed and let her feet hit the floor with a heavy thud. "Slowly and painfully until all that is left is an empty husk."

Samir was shaking his head almost violently now. "No, Dee, you don't understand. It's not always a curse. The shrouded ones, the original shrouded ones, they are nothing like the ones that Idir commands. They've been looking for you. They need your help to save their brothers and sisters."

She rubbed her fingers through her hair, wincing as they tugged through several knots. "Samir, if they can be trusted, why didn't they just ask for my help instead of kidnapping me? My—" A jolt ran through her; she had been about to say friends. She hadn't ever said that word before and truly meant it.

"Please, don't judge them until you at least speak with Astrid. I'll go get her." He started for the door again.

"How?" The question stopped him as he pulled the door open and turned to face her once more.

"How what?"

"How did they save you from Idir?"

He blinked at her, a frown furrowing his brow. "Why is that important?"

"Because they could be working for Idir and just pretending—"

"They're not! I know you don't trust anyone. People haven't exactly been nice to you, so you've got a good reason. But you know what it's like to be *different*. Astrid is like you; she speaks to Grandmother Ocean ... and she hates Idir. Just talk to her and Rami. I promise they won't hurt you." The look in his eyes was completely sincere and the chilling echo of his song was steady.

Deana gave a small nod. "Alright, I'll talk to them."

A smile lit his face. "I'll be right back."

After Samir left, Deana moved to the window and looked out. The drop outside told her she was on the second floor of the building. A wide patch of white sand dotted with grasses and saltbush stretched from the base of the building to the edge of a tangled jungle. It was hard to tell where exactly she was, but they couldn't have taken her too far. Was she still on the same small isle as the Azure Queen's camp? They hadn't seen any signs of inhabitation.

"You'll at least hear me out before you run, won't you?" a melodic voice asked from behind her.

"I wasn't ..." she said as she turned, her words trailing off as she took in the woman leaning against the doorframe. She was tall, at least half a head taller than Deana, her slim form poised with an almost liquid grace as though ready to leap into action on a moment's notice. The golden hair that covered one side of her head was braided neatly and hung forward over her shoulder. Around the purple and green coral that adorned the other side of her skull, the skin glistened as though covered by a layer of scales. She cocked her head as she studied Deana in return, her song twisting across Deana's like the pull of a riptide. The melancholy that usually accompanied the song of the shrouded ones was not present. Was this woman truly a shrouded one or something else entirely?

"I see your brother in the line of your mouth. He was a good man."

"My brother? You knew Kai?"

"Who do you think gave him that protection stone?"

"I never—he didn't—what do you want with me?"

"Straight to the point. That's admirable." She pushed away from the door and sauntered into the room. "Sit." She gestured to the chair as she perched herself on the edge of the bed. "I am guessing that Samir already told you, but I am Astrid."

Deana lowered herself into the chair. "Deana. But you already knew that."

The smile that touched Astrid's lips didn't quite meet her eyes. "Indeed. I have known of you—been waiting for you for several centuries."

"Centuries? But you're ... That can't be true?"

"My kind do not age as yours do. It is our punishment for daring to seek that which was never meant for mortal hands. Idir has never been content to live out his share of the sentence in silent acceptance. Instead, he has searched from one end of the realm to the other in an effort to find a cure. At best, he has found a temporary reprieve from the external symptoms. But that reprieve has alienated him from his brethren and comes at too high a cost. We learned an eon ago that it is foolish to covet the power of the gods, and nothing is worth evoking their wrath—not even a cure for this curse."

"Idir is like you? But your song is so different from the other shrouded ones ... You look different too."

"Idir's drones, those you call shrouded ones, are a perverted reflection of my kind. They are souls shackled to an eternity of torment, serving only to feed Idir's power and keep his own affliction at bay."

Deana worried her lip between her teeth. "Why have you waited for me for so long?"

"You can lead us home, so we may atone for our impertinence."

"And where is home?"

"Dumura. All you need to do is bring it back into the light." She lifted her hand in a graceful open-palmed gesture towards the ceiling.

Deana stood and paced to the window, gripping the sill so hard her knuckles paled. "I can't."

"There is a difference between can't and won't. You *can*. Deep down inside, your song knows the truth, but you do not want to accept it." Astrid's song washed over Deana, bringing a twist to her stomach and a bitterness to her throat. Moments later, her fingers landed on Deana's shoulder and spun her around.

They were nose to nose; this close, Astrid's eyes were not only the same colour as Bran's—right down to the shards of azure that ringed her pupils, but they were the same shape. Her song swooped away again, and the line of her mouth softened. "But given time I can change your mind. Help you understand the destiny that has been placed upon your shoulders and show you the possibilities that helping us will open to you."

Deana leant back, trying to put distance between them. But Astrid's fingers were cruelly tight on her shoulder, and the windowsill pressed hard against her lower back. She shook her head.

"Grandmother Ocean gave you the greatest of her gifts. Why are you so afraid of it?" Astrid threw her hands in the air as she released Deana and took a step back. "It's Idir's doing, isn't it? He wanted you meek and afraid—malleable. You are just a piece on the gameboard to him. Just like the metal-singer. He reached her first and tainted her song, making her useless to us."

"Metal-singer? Do you mean Agnes?"

"That is her name."

"Idir did something to her? When?"

"Years ago, at least two decades. We found her but he had beaten us to her, ruined her so we couldn't use her against him. We can't fix what he did to her song, but we can fix you. And when we do Idir will never know what hit him." There was a fire in her eyes now and twist of something deep ran through her song.

Deana swallowed and examined the drop out the window from the corner of her eye. A hulking shadow of a man was out there now. He lifted his head. Putrid, yellow-green light shone in the empty sockets where his eyes should have been. His wide jaw was set into a smile that bordered on a grimace as he rested his hand on the hilt of the wicked-looking sword at his side. She turned back to Astrid.

"You have yet to officially meet Rami. Don't worry. He's not nearly as monstrous as he looks. At least, he won't be, as long as you remain cooperative and don't do anything foolish. Like trying to run."

TO BE CONTINUED ...

THANK YOU FOR READING
A SONG OF SORROW

I hope you enjoyed the first book in the *Isles of Bright and Shadow* trilogy. I would love it if you left me a review either at your favourite online store or on Goodreads.

Follow the link below for news about upcoming releases and future projects:

GLOSSARY

Bind-shackles: Bands of robrillium that prevent a mage from using their keen by blocking their connection to the source. Each pair is struck with its own key. If this key is lost, that pair can only be unlocked by a warden's keen.

Brightling: Extremely rare keen-folk who have the ability to absorb and use the keen of others or turn a mage's own keen against them, even though they seem to have no keen of their own.

Brightfish: A type of fish found primarily in the Faridean Isles, they moult at the beginning of their mating season and the colour of their new scales is said to be prophetic in nature.

Corruption: A type of possession / magical disease that primarily affects mages. The afflicted become increasingly violent as they slowly lose control of their minds and their keen. There have been no cases of corruption since the defeat of the Usurper.

Creationist: A type of mage who doesn't manipulate an element but can alter a certain type of matter. Elijah is a creationist whose talent is related to ink and parchment, specifically the realm of cartography, and Agnes' affinity is metal.

Dream-singer: A Faridean mage who has the ability to control the dreams of others. They are extremely rare, and Dara is the only known dream-singer currently in existence.

Heart mate: The Faridean term for soul mates.

Heartstone: A magical crystal in which a necromancer can trap a soul to be used to animate a golem.

Keen: The soul essence of an individual or the 'flavour' of their magic. Interchangeable with the word magic, however, *keen* generally refers to the feeling of the life force of an individual and how that part of them interacts with the source as a whole. Magic is more so the direct effect they have on the world through channelling the source.

Keen-folk: A general term that covers all types of magic-users, not just mages and wardens, but seers and other gifted.

Keen-less: Those without magic.

Keen-sense: The ability to sense magic. Something all keen-folk innately have but also something that certain keen-less can possess (though this is rare).

Keen-touched: Sometimes interchangeable with keen-folk but generally used to refer to those keen-folk who are not mages or wardens. Seers and those gifted with 'low-magic' i.e. savants and prodigies who cannot control the source but have uncanny abilities regardless.

Keystone: A special stone used to unlock magical locks or open trans-dimensional portals.

Lock-stone: A trans-dimensional construct that can be used as an anchor for magic. The lock-stone outside Hartswood solidifies the wards around the estate and protects it.

Mage: Keen-folk who have complete control of the source in one element E.g. weather (storm mages), fire, earth, water, healing, mind, death and the spirit world (necromancers) etc. There are certain nuances among the generic types of mages. For example: Sophia is a water mage, but she is particularly skilled with frost and ice magic. Declan is a storm mage who has an affinity for lightning, something not all weather mages are comfortable with.

Mind-singer: The Faridean term for a mind mage.

Oathing: A kind of soul marriage between two mages. The bond dissolves after death. Often used for shorter-term pacts between individuals.

Oathbond: (sometimes called an oath ward) Refers to the connection created by an oathing.

Oathmark: The physical representation of the Oathbond often appears like a kind of tattoo.

Reanimation: Undead given 'life' by a necromancer. They are created by forcing a spirit, whether once human or not, into a corpse. They are generally mindless puppets controlled by the necromancer who resurrected them.

Robrillium: The enchanted metal used to create bind-shackles. It ranges in colour from light-pinkish gold through to a deep rose gold.

Silencer: The Faridean term for warden.

Singer: Because Faridean mages most often experience magic as sound they refer to their mages as singers.

Shadow-kin: What the Farideans call those who possess the blood of the Shadow.

Shadow-touched: Those that have been somehow touched or tainted by the Shadow. They could be divine-blooded or cursed. Those who are possessed or corrupted are sometimes also referred to as Shadow-touched.

Shrouded ones: Undead merfolk-like creatures who are said to be the handmaidens of Grandmother Ocean. They are rumoured to be able to infect people through the magical coral that adorns their skin.

Song: Instead of calling the magic / life force of their mages keen, Faridean mages refer to it as the song of the mage. In some cases, song seems to be another term for what Beldaren and Osmarian mages will call the source, though Faridean mages do still refer to the source.

Source ship: A rare magical ship. There were only a dozen ships ever created though many of them have been lost over time.

Soul-singer: The Faridean term for necromancer or spirit mage.

Spirit anchor: A relic that contains a small piece of a mage's keen.

Spirit-glass: Enchanted mirrors, usually made of obsidian or black glass, through which necromancers use to communicate. They can become corrupted and slowly steal the life force of those using them; functioning ones are rare as a result of this.

The barrier: The veil between realms as seen by necromancers. It can appear in a range of different ways depending on the individual interacting with it. E.g. Nea's barrier is a hedge of pale-pink and grey roses, and Nonna's is a bramble of blackberries.

The Between: A magical spirit realm that the souls of the dead are believed to pass through on their way to the grove of the ancestors.

The Source: The fabric of the universe from where keen-touched get their powers.

Warden: Keen-folk who can suppress the keen or connection to the source in other keen-folk. Theorised to be a type of mage even though they don't channel the source. Originally called ward mages.

ABOUT THE AUTHOR

C. E. Page writes emotionally rich, character driven tales of magic and adventure, primarily in the adult epic fantasy genre. Her stories feature demigods and other divinely assisted misfits who would prefer it if megalomaniac fools would stop trying to destroy the known realms in their search for power.

She lives on the east coast of Australia with her partner Evan, their two children, and one of the world's quirkiest dogs. An avid reader and gamer, she loves devouring a good story in whatever form it takes.

You can find out more about her and her upcoming works at: www.cepageauthor.com

ALSO BY C. E. PAGE

SOVEREIGNS OF BRIGHT AND SHADOW

Nea has spent the three years since the purge at Kalhanna on the run. Convinced that if she keeps running then the dark fate that awaits her will spare those she loves—But fate has other ideas.

Corruption is a disease with no cure that ends with a rapid descent into madness and violence. And until now it only targeted mages. But an infected warden has shown up challenging everything Margot thought she knew. To understand this recent development, she needs someone who knows possession ... She needs Nea and lucky for Margot, her warden friend Garret has been ordered to track the rogue necromancer down.

From the moment Garret finds Nea he is dragged into a deadly game of dark secrets and brutal machinations. A game that spans not only centuries, but the barrier between the known realms. After a revelation that will change the lives of mages and wardens forever, he must learn to trust not only himself but the enigmatic necromancer whose fate has become irrevocably tied to his own.

Can they find a cure before it's too late, or will they be swept away by powers beyond any of their control?

THE STORY BEGINS IN

DEATHBORN